Timbuktu Frequency Five

Pieter Cook

MALI

TIMBUKTU

NIGER RIVER

MOPTI

SIBY ☀ BAMAKO

SAKORO
BOUGOUNI

Dutch Domes LLC

www.dutch-domes.com

ISBN: 979-8-9881980-0-0

Dedicated to Abigail and Amélie.
May building a better future be adventure enough.

COVER DESIGN

Beth Sankey created the cover based on an image of Timbuktu by René-Auguste Caillié—the first recorded European to return from the ancient city. He was a French explorer who reached Timbuktu disguised as an Arab to prevent being killed, the unfortunate fate of his predecessors. His strategy worked, but it took him a full year to travel from the coast of modern Guinea to Timbuktu due to an illness. His exit route was up through Morocco.

A prize was given to him upon his safe return to France where he settled down and started a family, only to die of tuberculosis at age 38. I am grateful to have experienced a much easier journey and hope to make it past the age of our intrepid explorer.

ACKNOWLEDGMENTS

Creating almost any novel is a team effort and this one is no exception. I never would have been able to get to this point without help and support from my friends and family. Various readers provided critical feedback needed to get through the initial rewriting stages. A special thanks to Mike DeWit, Jeffrey Brown, David Heiser, Scotty Hilberg and Chris Peoples for their detailed and insightful commentary.

My editor, Willem Wordragen, played an essential role in polishing the final manuscript. Joni M. Fisher also provided valuable editorial feedback along with sound publishing advice. Drew Philp encouraged me to cut out some boring details and focus on the story. Betsy Cook helped with proofreading. Beth Sankey designed a beautiful cover. I learned a lot from all of you!

Phase One: Ionization

Ionization   *noun*   / ˌaɪənəˈzeɪʃən /
The process atoms go through in order to gain or lose electrons.
Transforming from a gas into a plasma.

November 2004

Souleymane Samaké could not stop staring at the ragged t-shirt in front of him. It was as if the unmoving boy who wore it did not even exist. The tattered, outlined form printed on it almost glowed the longer he looked. Not quite a horse or a cow, but an imaginary beast with a long face and two giant humps on its back. *Could it really be a living thing?*

The trance was broken by yet another member of the village offering blessings and squeezing onto the dirt floor of the cramped mud-hut. An unnatural silence permeated throughout, awkwardly binding the mourners together.

The only sound that entered Souleymane's awareness, nearly drowned out by the constant village chatter outside the walls of their enclosure, was the harsh scraping of two shovels digging through densely packed, red earth. *My father's hole. It must be nearly finished by now.* The bundle of rags tightly wrapped around the body outside was and wasn't his father.

Souleymane's parents fled from their birthplace in Western Mali many years ago. They feared for their lives. They wanted a good place to start a family. Spirits in the village of their ancestors had turned against them. Guinea worm ravaged the population. These parasites lurked in the water and were liable to deliver an excruciatingly painful death to their hosts. Up to one meter, they grew inside blood vessels like tapeworms within intestines. In contrast to tapeworms, they could be clearly seen and painfully felt traveling up and down arms and legs.

Short of mutilation, the only way to get rid of these faceless beasts was to allow them to chew through the skin, usually around the ankles, and slither out, one bloody segment at a time, searching for water to lay their eggs in. The living nightmare of watching friends and relatives succumb to such gruesome attacks was too much to bear.

Over half the children could not leave their homes, disabled by pain, fever, and vomiting. Unthinkably, crops were left unharvested. Souleymane's parents gathered all they could and walked twenty

1

kilometers to a place where an occasional bus could be found. They traveled as far south as their money would allow, two hours beyond the sprawling capital city of Bamako, before they were forced to stop and find a village chief who was willing to let them settle down and farm a small piece of land.

Immediately after the funeral, Souleymane Samaké realized he needed to pack his own dusty bag just like his parents had all those years ago. He could not bear to spend another night in the village of Sakoro. It was the place where he had been born, learned to walk, learned to hunt, learned to farm, learned all the old stories and traditions from the men who talked around fires at night; he had even fallen in love. In spite of this, the feeling of home that he saw in the eyes of his friends and neighbors had never been reflected back from his own.

Souleymane was a rarity in the country of Mali. He had no brothers or sisters. Everyone else in the village had big families. Some of the wealthier men even had more than one wife. Souleymane grew up alone, with only his father. His mother died during childbirth; tiny Souleymane came into the world healthy and strong even though his delivery was different from what the midwives were used to.

After the cord was cut she still seemed to be in labor. They expected a huge baby to come out of that enormous stomach, not the tiny, screaming infant which was hastily wrapped in worn cloth.

The custom was to name babies after they had been alive and breathing for a full week. Despite the best efforts of several kind women from the village, Souleymane's sister, who was born as his mother gasped her last breath, never got a name.

As an immigrant, Souleymane's dad was too poor to marry for a second time. Souleymane ended up doing most of the women's work around the house. He learned to clean and cook. He had to work three times harder than any of the other boys.

The dusty bag was made of fraying plastic fibers designed to mimic burlap. Several grains of corn poked out of the dirt on the bottom which Souleymane Samaké vigorously shook out before piling a few of his father's tools, a change of clothes, and several handfuls of unshelled peanuts inside.

He swung the bag over his shoulder and closed the twisted wooden door of the mud hut behind him for the last time. He gave it a stronger push than usual, knowing that the slight shower of dirt it would release from the thatched roof would not be his to sweep up.

The funeral party had left the area around the hut in a rather untidy state. His father would have demanded that it be cleaned before bedtime. The fact that he could now do as he pleased began to settle in. As he walked away, his shoulders straightened out and a slight bounce lifted his steps.

A grin of freedom almost crossed his wide face, but he checked it before it could appear. Smiling on the night of a funeral could never bring good fortune. He suddenly realized, contrary to the kind words of those who had offered their condolences, that he would not miss his father; he would miss what his father could have been.

August 2009

Nothing but dunes undulated before them. Two companions took part in a collective sigh of relief as the final rays of sunshine flickered out, mercifully allowing the Saharan landscape to cool off. They sat down on a humble mound of sand clinging to a small bush crowning its top. The arid wasteland stretched far beyond their field of view. Behind them, the ancient city of Timbuktu held its ground: a stronghold protecting all of humanity from the hostile desert.

Mostly the pair sat in silence. Kano's thoughts turned to Johanna, wishing she could share this incredible moment in space and time with him.

As the sky darkened, they heard shuffling footsteps approaching and instinctively shifted toward what little cover the lonely vegetation had to offer. Kano and Jerry looked at each other inquisitively as the wandering figures slowly passed by, not seeming to notice them at all.

Covered from head to toe, four women walked out of earshot as Kano asked in a low voice, "Where are they going?! There is nothing out there but sand!"

"I haven't a clue, but it gives me a strange vibe. I think it is time to head back to the hotel, mate." Jerry stood and dusted off his pants.

"Fine by me."

As they turned their backs to the desert, one of the women fished a cell phone out of her gently flowing robe and spoke several simple syllables which would bend and break the course of lives.

November 2004

As the distance from the village grew, Souleymane felt more alone than ever. Although he walked in this direction regularly, the path looked much different at night. He figured the waking sun would be erasing stars from the sky by the time he got close to the bustling city of Bougouni. The last time he had been there was so long ago that he was small enough to ride behind his father on the back of a bicycle.

Sleep would have been most welcome, but a newfound fear of snakes prevented him from napping in the bush. A snake had killed his father.

Even though his teenage body was hardened by summers bent over corn fields and endless hours of cooking and cleaning, it was still dependent upon the unshakable routine of getting a good night of sleep. His calloused feet ached. Stars remained bright in the sky. Darkness rendered the path unrecognizable. A distant glow from the city kept him from getting lost. *How much farther could it be?*

Eventually, Souleymane emerged onto a shockingly smooth plane of asphalt, leaving the thin, winding donkey trails behind. His right ear, which had always stuck out farther than the left, picked up a fiercely low thundering noise in the distance. He slowly stepped off the pavement and seconds later was temporarily blinded by a set of harsh lights marking the front end of a huge truck. The speed and ferocity of its passing nearly sucked the air out of Souleymane's lungs. He was used to seeing the little van which came to bring people to the village market every week, full of hand-painted color and much taller than it should have been due to the mountain of overstuffed sacks and noisy goats strapped to the top. Rarely had he seen trucks this big, and never in the dark.

He gathered up his courage and kept walking toward the city, staying off the unfamiliar blacktop. He preferred the feel of gravel poking through his worn sandals to the unnaturally smooth pavement.

It wasn't long before huge billboards darkly materialized in front of him. They were big enough to function as a roof and would work much better than those expensive pieces of metal which made so much noise in the rain. *Why would anyone put such valuable materials out to rot along the side of the road?*

Souleymane knew the city was close, but no buildings were yet in sight. He couldn't stop his eyelids from drooping as his neck became rubbery, allowing his head to drift down before being jerked back up into place. Edging in and out of sleep, he faithfully put one foot in front of the other. The occasional vehicle passed, startling him back into full consciousness.

After he slowly grew accustomed to cars and trucks, perfectly square and smooth buildings began to appear. He wondered how they had been made. Then he saw a huge structure, built out of something other than earth with long, stick-like pieces poking out of the top, spewing smoke into the early dawn sky. They were even taller than the eight-hundred-year-old cotton tree looming over his village like a twisted old man scolding young children. He shuddered at the memory of the chief giving him a beating underneath that giant tree for accidentally killing one of the young chickens he had been playing with.

A fork in the road greeted Souleymane with a choice. One of many he would soon need to make, although none of them really seemed to be choices. He stayed on the gravel because crossing the all-too-flat blacktop didn't appeal to his semi-conscious mind.

Awareness grew with the light in the east. Buildings took the place of vegetation, giving him more to observe.

The city slept. At this time, in his village of Sakoro, women would already be preparing breakfast and pounding grain in giant, cracked mortars carved from the trunks of trees. Chickens would scamper and dash underfoot, some of them chased by children with distended bellies. Souleymane did not hear familiar noises in this strangely quiet city called Bougouni, so he listened for something new.

He was looking for a place filled with people. Work must be everywhere here. Mysterious buildings, shops, and places to eat; so many possibilities. He had brought with him all the money remaining in the house, barely enough to survive in the city for a week.

Bougouni spread before him with a splendor that shamed the mud huts lining his village streets. Gates made from iron, concrete walls decadently covered in paint, metal roofs undulating like ripples in water. It was powerfully beautiful in the softly growing light.

He wondered how these people could afford to build such things. *Did the corn grow so much better here?* Freshly rising orange sunlight flickered between two buildings and entered his peripheral vision. In that moment, he made a promise to live in such a magnificent house someday.

Sunlight beckoned him. For his whole life he had avoided the great fire in the sky, but today he felt the urge to follow it. He tried to keep the burning glow in view as it poked in and out of spaces between houses, briefly disappearing behind mango and palm trees. It led him over a short bridge and into a large clearing. His ears perked up at the sounds of voices and men working.

Souleymane turned the corner and stopped in his dusty tracks. He suddenly faced more vehicles than he had seen in the entirety of his young life, a few of them still arriving but most were parked. There were mopeds, motorcycles, cars, big vans like the one that came to Sakoro, and two gigantic buses.

Gas and metal mixed to fill the air. People unlocked doors and opened up boarded windows. Colorfully bold pictures painted on the sides of their stands gave clues as to what they were selling. One rendering of a baguette with eggs drew him in like a homing beacon. Without restraint, he bounded toward the solution to his most pressing problem.

August 2009

Kano and Jerry lost their way back to the hotel. Everything looked different without the burning sunlight. Relief swept over them as a dim streetlight revealed a familiar store selling prayer mats. Suddenly, a bright set of headlights turned and sped straight toward their position. The driver flicked on an additional rack of lights above his head as he slid to an uncontrolled stop in front of the two Westerners.

The sudden brilliance temporarily blinded the pair like a flash grenade. Jerry said, "Let's go," and pulled Kano into a nearby alley too narrow for the heavy SUV. Behind them doors slammed and voices shouted.

An unsteady flashlight beam threw shadows further into the alley as they ran. The pursuers, experts at running through sand, quickly closed the gap. Gunshots shattered the air. Sand in front of Kano exploded as if a snake in hiding had burst out.

Jerry went down first, rough hands smothering his shouts into the powdery ground until he became silent and his body relaxed. Kano couldn't register Jerry's words. He was captured in the same manner, although he managed to land an elbow straight into the nose of his tackler, breaking it with a satisfying crunch. His efforts were rewarded with a blow to the back of his head which turned the darkness of the desert night into a blinding flash of light, followed by pure black.

November 2004

The man was busy organizing long baguettes, crates of eggs, and a few vegetables. Souleymane interrupted his work to ask, after the formal greeting, with eyes much bigger than normal, if he could have something to eat. They spoke in Bambara, the dominant regional language.

The man replied, "Have you got any money?"

"Yes, of course," answered Souleymane proudly.

"Then what do you want?"

"What do you have?" asked Souleymane wisely; he didn't want to order something that would make him look foolish because they only ate it in villages.

"I make a good egg sandwich," came the muffled reply as the man stooped to pick a knife up from the gritty floor.

Souleymane peered over the counter on his tiptoes to see if anything else had fallen. "How much is it?"

"Depends how many eggs you want."

"Three eggs." Souleymane wanted to celebrate his freedom with a gluttonous amount of breakfast.

"Then it will be seventy for you, my friend." Although he said seventy, Souleymane knew to fish 350 CFA out of his money pouch, the coins clinking together in protest. The number a person says out loud needs to be multiplied by five to get to the actual amount.

"I have it," came the over-confident reply. Souleymane did not feel confident. He could eat rather luxuriously for a whole day in his village for that sum. Guilt crept in for what his father would have called wasting money. He pushed it away like the rising sun which had overcome darkness that very morning, filling himself instead with what he knew to be, deep down, false pride in setting out alone. He firmly resolved to celebrate this moment in spite of his doubts.

The Sandwich Maker finished his preparations and lit the ravenous burner which rose directly out of the top of a dented and scratched propane cylinder. He precariously placed a thin, once-round pan above the hissing blue flame. The misshapen skillet was so deformed that it must have been used as a cockroach killer nearly as much as an egg cooker. Next came the palm oil. It was kept inside a smudged and murky water bottle that had long since lost its label. A few splashes of viscous, yellowish liquid sunk into the metal depression. He cracked three eggs which sizzled, spattered and jumped in a hopeless escape attempt.

The mouthwatering smell of eggs popping in oil made Souleymane's stomach rumble fiercely as he stared at crusty, white bread with huge eyes. The worn and cracked hands of the Sandwich Maker deftly sliced a chunk of baguette down the middle in one fluid motion as if he had been a warrior in another life. He pried the flaking bread open with calloused, unwashed fingers and slopped on two spoonfuls of mayonnaise from a nearly empty jar which had been mostly sheltered from direct sunlight for the past week.

Souleymane could barely restrain himself. The eggs were hardened and crispy, sloppily dumped, dripping with oil, into the waiting baguette. Bits of grit protested as the egg and mayonnaise sandwich slid across the narrow countertop to Souleymane, who surrendered precious coins. The exchange was made, and he bit into the all-too-hot grease bomb with wide eyes and a burning tongue.

As if by magic, the sandwich disappeared. Even the Sandwich Maker, who had spent decades making food for hungry travelers, was surprised by how fast Souleymane had eaten it. His narrow face wrinkled into the slightest of smiles. The boy sat in stunned contentment for a few moments while the man worked with grunts and clangs. Souleymane looked up and asked with admiration, "Sir, this was the best sandwich I have ever eaten. Can you teach me to make such a thing?"

In that moment, the Sandwich Maker realized he was seeing himself thirty years ago. He paused in silence, holding a spatula in his left hand while carefully studying the curious face of the young boy before him who had surely just come in from one of the surrounding villages. He gave a response that he wished he could have heard back then: "This is a one-man operation, but perhaps there is something you can do. Do you see those people over there sitting and waiting for buses? Go and clean up their trash and sweep the ground. You may use my broom, but if you don't bring it back to me by the end of the day you will get a beating. If someone asks what you are doing, tell them I sent you to clean up."

The boy bowed his head and said, "Thank you, Sir. May God shower blessings upon you for your kindness." He took the broom and headed toward the benches resting under a crooked lean-to which sheltered open ticket booths protected by thick metal bars: a jail designed to keep people out.

All day Souleymane cleaned and swept, the smell of diesel fumes filling his nostrils as dust and smoke turned his hair from black to brown. When he needed a break from the blisteringly direct sun, he returned to the frowning Sandwich Maker, where the food was getting cheaper. He brought back the broom after a dinner which was almost free and then continued to pick up garbage as night fell. Not a single word was said to him by anyone from the bus companies.

After the last bags were unloaded and the drivers departed in search of a cool bed, Souleymane claimed a bench, barely noticing painful lumps of steel pressing into his back. He fell asleep listening to the scurrying noises surrounding him that competed for his cleaning duties. Cockroaches and rats had taken the night shift.

This was the first time he truly slept in almost three days. His father's slow, agonizing death had kept him awake and busy the night before his escape into the city. He could have slept twice as long, but the noise began before dawn.

A crash of metal on metal abruptly popped his eyes open. He was drawn to the yellow glow of a flashlight and found a mechanic working under the hood of one of the smaller buses. It was the stubby sort of vehicle Souleymane had seen before in his village. He went up to the man, greeted him formally, and asked what he was working on.

"Hole in the radiator," the mechanic barked, clearly not too happy about having to talk before the sun came up. Or maybe the broken radiator upset him.

Souleymane scuffed his toe in the dirt. "What does that mean?"

"It means they have to stop this pile of junk every twenty minutes to put more water in." Another burst of cracking from the hammer.

"How do you fix it?"

"I'm putting on a patch. Might last a week if they are lucky."

"How do you make it last longer?"

"Need to use the welder."

Souleymane leaned in to see the patch. "What is a welder?"

"It's fire that's hot enough to melt the patch to the other metal. I gotta finish this before the boss gets here. Get lost, kid."

Souleymane wandered off, waiting for the Sandwich Maker, as the city around him slowly came back to life. Sounds of roosters greeted the fresh, pre-dawn air. Soon that relative peace would be overtaken by the excitement of noisy engines and poorly combusted fossil fuels. He couldn't imagine a place he would rather be.

August 2009

Kano Griffin awoke, completely disoriented, inside a concrete box. The air smelled like stale dust and his tongue was completely dry and cracked open. He forced himself to focus and take in his surroundings.

Walls, floor and ceiling were all the same shade of gritty, unpainted grey. This implied new construction. Under him was an old blanket which served as a mattress. On the other side of the room, about three meters away, sat a bucket that he knew would be his toilet. He felt the first twinge of panic as the realization came that he was now a prisoner.

The ceiling was so high. Kano got the dizzying sensation that he had fallen into a pit. Instead of a light overhead, he saw a small camera. A tiny slit at the top of one wall brought in a few rays of daylight along with an occasional breath of fresh air.

The door was the only thing which struck Kano as being out of place. It was not in the shape of a rectangle, nor was it made of thick metal. The intricately carved and painted wood rose to a pointed arch and showed signs of aging as if it had been crafted for the palace of a long-forgotten Sultan.

As he rose to examine the door his head exploded into shards of pain. Steadying himself with one hand against warm concrete for a few moments, the throbbing agony began to fade. As his vision cleared, Kano noticed a circular panel in the center of the door, just below eye-level, that was slightly loose. He poked and prodded until he realized the panel could slide toward him and rotate down on a telescoping pin.

It revealed a porthole to the world beyond his cell. His intriguing discovery unveiled nothing but a smooth, white wall extending farther than his limited perspective in either direction.

Before long, footfalls emanated down the hall. The slow, shuffling steps set butterflies alight in Kano's stomach. After what seemed to be an eternity, two rather contradictory figures entered his narrow field of view.

The first person approaching the unusual door was an old man wearing a piercing indigo robe which glimmered iridescently, with the exception of a detailed patch of embroidery around the collar. He stepped forward slowly with the help of a sleek, ebony cane. The man's bright white beard matched the shade of his crisp turban perfectly, surrounding his brown, wrinkled face in a brilliantly clean halo. His eyes locked onto the porthole and seemed to burn with the same indigo as the robe he wore.

Escorting him was a young man wearing an immaculate but simple white robe and a matching kufi cap clinging tightly to his skull. His contrasting ebony skin held Kano's eye because this was the first black person Kano had seen in Timbuktu; everyone else had brown skin and narrower faces. The young man gripped a well-worn Kalashnikov firmly, walked with purpose, and seemed to have a swollen nose.

After a muted electronic beep, the door swung in without a sound. Kano struggled to make sense of the opposing worlds strangely coming together before him. The dark figure dressed in white clenched the assault rifle with one hand, eyes never leaving his prisoner. In his other hand was a chair he gently set in the corner. Without a word he exited the room to stand guard outside the doorway, with nothing but the barrel of his gun remaining visible. Kano got the impression he would follow the indigo man into the Lake of Fire.

The aging gentleman eased himself into the chair and beckoned Kano to sit on the floor in front of him. Kano hesitated, knowing he should feel fear, but somehow felt calm. After appraising the Westerner in silence for well over a minute, the indigo man took out a white pipe made of tusk or bone, carefully packed in tobacco, and lit it with a match. A few puffs later, he spoke to Kano with an archaic tone, like a ninety year old recording. A burnished British accent articulated his perfect grammar. "It has been some time since I have been made to speak in English. I hope you will forgive my less than perfect skill. Let us start simply. What is your name?"

A thousand harsh retorts jumped through his mind, but he managed to answer the simple question and put his burning indignation on hold as an unexpected mix of respect and curiosity toward the enigma in front of him arose.

"Kano Griffin," he muttered.

"Very good. I trust they did not hurt you last night?"

"Depends on your definition of *hurt*," grumbled Kano.

"You will need to speak a bit louder, young one. My ears are not what they once were."

"I am fine," said Kano curtly.

His wrinkled eyes narrowed slightly before responding. "That pleases me. Your needs will be met here although your desires will be left wanting. This is good for your troubled soul. I believe a measure of time spent alone is the only way for you to move forward."

After waiting through several drawn-out puffs, Kano asked, "Who are you? Why am I here?"

"Such powerful questions. The answers are complex and will take time, but I intend for you to receive them." A haze filled the room as acrid tobacco smoke spread its tentacles throughout the space.

"Can you start me out with the simple truth?" The tone was laced in cynicism.

"No truth worth being spoken aloud is simple. I will try to satisfy your need for answers to demonstrate that I never tell a lie. I am known as The Scholar and was recruited by an organization in my more impressionable days. Although there is much we do not agree on, our relationship is one of what you might say is rather…what is the word…*symbiotic*." He drew out the vowels for emphasis. "We have a similar need of capital, something our lands do not offer up freely. You have been taken for the funds we can extract from your presence, but I believe the full reason goes far beyond that. The coming weeks will serve to either cleanse or corrupt and then we will know more."

Kano silently gazed into the ground as the gravity of his situation descended. After sending one last puff of smoke on a slow course toward the slit on top of the wall, The Scholar gracefully used his cane to stand and said, "Enough for today. I shall return when you are ready so that we can talk more. The boy will attend to your needs."

As if on cue, the young man entered the room, effortlessly collected the heavy, wooden chair, and set down a chunk of bread on a chipped plate next to a cup of instant coffee. Kano wondered who had prepared and delivered it. The ancient door silently sealed shut behind the unlikely pair, leaving Kano alone and in silence. He devoured the puffy, pita-like loaf complete with millions of tiny grains of sand which scoured his teeth. A fear slowly began to settle in his stomach that the abrasive walls surrounding him would soon begin a similar scouring of his mind.

November 2004

For the next few days, Souleymane would roll off his twisted, metal bench before dawn, buy food from the Sandwich Maker, and start a conversation with anyone trying to fix a vehicle. His responsibility to keep the sitting area spotless was taken quite seriously, but nobody asked him what he was doing there. Until the fat man dropped his pen.

Souleymane was sitting with the Sandwich Maker at the time, halfway finished with his favorite egg and mayonnaise baguette. Out of the corner of his eye, he saw the dust settle behind a boxy, grey Mercedes. He turned his full attention toward the unbelievably shiny car. The driver hauled himself up and out of the door. He was amazingly fat; a sign of great success. The whole vehicle rocked back and forth a few times, protesting the end of its short journey.

As the front door snapped shut, the man took two steps toward the rear of the car, allowing a fine layer of dust to coat his highly polished shoes in the process. He bent down to lift a black briefcase from the back seat. As it bumped against his hip, a silver pen bounced out, skittering across hard-packed dirt. The man closed the car door and sauntered toward his office without noticing.

Souleymane abandoned his precious food and ran toward the car, the Sandwich Maker looking on with a smile. He swiped up the pen and cleaned it off with the inside of his ragged t-shirt. By the time the fat man disappeared into the dark ticket office, Souleymane had almost caught up to him. He hesitated before entering, but then boldly followed the man to his desk.

"What do you think you are doing in here?" The booming accusation startled the boy.

"So...so sorry to bother you Sir, but you dropped your pen," replied Souleymane with his eyes glued to the tiled floor, as social convention demanded. He held out the shiny silver writing utensil in the direction of the man who seemed to be the same size as the desk he sat behind.

"Oh, I see." His tone softened. "Tell me, what is it that you are doing at my bus station? I have seen you sweeping around the benches."

"I am looking for work. I am good at cleaning, and I want to learn how to be good at other things too." He indicated toward the direction from which he came while keeping his eyes down and continued, "The Sandwich Maker told me to keep the space near the benches clean."

"Ahhh, my old friend Mariko." He tapped the pen on his desk a few times in thought. "Very well. First, I will see how good you really are at cleaning. Boys tend to spread the mess around instead of actually removing it. Take the bucket and rag from the toilet and clean the floor of this office. Then you can clean the toilet. You will find water next to the toilet; just turn the tap on the wall."

"Right away, Sir," came Souleymane's over-enthusiastic reply. He stood up taller and lifted his chin slightly. It seemed strange he could get water by turning something. *Who pumped the water? How did it come out of the ground?*

When he found the bucket and turned the tap, he was astounded by the amount of water gushing out. He was accustomed to waiting for a trickle from a hand pump that happened to be right next to his father's house. Nobody else really used the oddly clear pump water. Nearby wells had cloudy water, brought up with a rope and bucket, and the flavor was much better.

Souleymane was certainly a boy of his word. Filthy, uneven tiles were scrubbed until they glimmered in the dim light. He focused on his work, never making eye contact with others in the office. A shredding sense of guilt and regret about abandoning his sandwich crept in. Wasting food was an unthinkable sin.

After completing the first task, he moved on to the toilet. Earlier, he had noticed something strange, but couldn't figure out what it was. The toilet looked like the type he was used to, a small hole in the ground, except it wasn't much of a hole. It stopped after about the length of his hand. *How could this work? Where did the waste go?*

Upon closer inspection he discovered part of the answer: the hole did not stop, it continued into an angled blackness. *Why the angle? Did one need to push their own poo down with a stick? Was it a way to check for disease?*

A creak from one of the office chairs curtailed his curiosity and he meticulously poured the bucket of dirty water into the floor drain, making sure not to get the floor wet before its time. He refilled the bucket and scrubbed the floor and the inside of the toilet. After repeating the process, this time even more careful not to spill on the newly pristine floor, he filled the bucket for the third time and started on the walls and the door. Unable to keep the drips from sullying the floor, he quickly realized he should have done things in a different order.

Next to the door he saw a small cream-colored block sticking out of the lavishly tiled wall. It was made of plastic. While attempting to remove fingerprints with the rag, the top part shifted toward the wall producing a slight click. A second later there was a flickering noise from above and the quality of light in the room changed. It was suddenly brighter and bluer. Souleymane looked up in wonder to discover he had created light by touching the plastic box. He switched it on and off several times, thinking about how easy it would be to cook and clean at night if he could see this well.

Raised voices from the office startled him into redoubling his cleaning efforts. When he got to the wall behind the toilet, he paused to examine a large box clinging to the tiles. It had a chain dangling from it with a wooden handle at the end. Although he could not quite reach the top of the box to clean inside it, the handle and chain quickly became shinier as he moved the rag up and down the linked rings of metal, holding the wooden handle firmly.

Suddenly there was a whooshing sound and he felt tiny droplets of water spraying his feet. He jumped back with surprise and wonder as water flowed through the toilet hole like it did through the village dam after a thunderstorm. Understanding joyfully spread across his face. Sunshine after the rain. *The toilet cleans itself! But where does the water go? How did it get into the tank in the first place?*

He could hear the noise of water flowing, even though it was no longer going through the hole in the floor. After his shock wore off, he couldn't help but pull the little wooden handle again.

The toilet area had blown his young mind. Water for cleaning poured from the wall with the turn of a handle, waste could be flushed away with the pull of a chain, and he could see all of these wonders happening after the sun had set with the push of a tiny plastic lever. As he returned to the big desk, he promised himself to work hard enough so that he could one day have the privilege of using a toilet like this.

"Finally done, eh?" said the fat man from behind his oversized desk. "Sure took you long enough." He slowly twisted his thick neck around inspecting the floor. "I have never seen such a clean floor in this place. Good thing I won't be paying you by the hour."

Souleymane kept his eyes on the floor as his back straightened with pride. He looked over his work and absorbed the compliment.

"I will work out a deal with Mariko to keep you fed. You will continue to sweep the benches and make sure this office stays clean. The key to that blue shed outside hangs here," he pointed to a skeleton key hanging from a small nail protruding from a crack in the dirty, cream-colored wall. "There you will find a broom and other cleaning supplies. Whenever one of my Banimonotie buses comes back—these are the ones with three blue stripes, lightest on top, darkest on the bottom—you will wait for all the people to come out and then clean the inside of the bus. We will be known as the cleanest bus line in Bougouni." His deep voice ended with a punch of pride.

"Thank you, sir, I will keep things very clean here." The boy nervously tried to remove a scuff with his cracked plastic sandals.

"I am sure..." He was interrupted by a blast from a horn which shook the walls. "Look at that, a bus has arrived from Sikasso. You must get to work as soon as everyone is off. Find the *parantigi*, the one who is unloading the baggage, and tell him you will be helping with his cleaning tasks. You must do this whenever a new bus comes in until you have informed everyone. You can tell them it is I, Mr. Traore, who has said so." The fat man dismissed the boy with a nod and resumed his paperwork.

Souleymane strode across the dirt driveway toward the shed and beamed at the sight of his new tools. He informed the *parantigi* of the change in task after a multitude of travelers had collected their bags. The outfits the passengers wore screamed color and boldness in a way which could only be echoed once or twice per year in the village—most notably for the feast of Ramadan.

Women had tall head wraps made from the same fabric as their tailored, full-length gowns. Men also wore a sort of gown with a masculine cut which draped down to their shins, exposing the bottoms of matching pants underneath. Most women and men flaunted an expensive fabric called *byzan*, a highly waxed material that shimmered in the sunshine like precious gems. It was a wonder they did not suffocate under all those waxed layers, packed into a hot bus without a single open window.

Souleymane hoped to be able to afford such clothing one day, but he did not worry about being too warm. It was the cold which scared him. Stories were told around the fires at night of pale, ghostly men who lived in places where ice fell from the sky. He never believed such nonsense. *How could anyone survive?*

It was said these people came from a devilish land. Perhaps it was ice which turned their skin an ugly shade of pinkish white, like that of the ostracized albinos. Souleymane shuddered at the thought of white skin and ice, grateful these things were nothing more than stories and nightmares.

If such a cold place really did exist, he would never visit it. He would love to travel on the big buses, though. *What would the countryside look like at such speeds? Would it all blur into a green and brown swath?* He had been on plenty of donkey carts, and nothing looked different, but once he rode on the back of a moped and the leaves next to the path streaked by. *A bus must go so much faster!*

August 2009

Kano spent the morning trying to find a way out of his prison. Blood was dripping from the side of his hand and his shoulder throbbed from attempting a parkour move he had once seen that looked easy at the time. The athlete used his momentum and the inside corner of a wall to launch himself up onto a roof that must have been about the same height as the small opening that looked barely wide enough to wriggle out of.

As he tore a piece of his t-shirt to use as a bandage, the idea of ripping up the blanket to create some sort of rope surfaced. He needed weight to send the end flying through the crack of daylight. Nothing in the room could serve as an anchor save the circular part of the door which telescoped toward him. *Maybe it could be broken off.*

Even if he managed to climb the wall, he wasn't sure if the slit was wide enough. There were no tools for chipping away concrete. His thinking shifted back to the old door. Obviously, there was more to it than aged wood. The electronic activation and the way it sealed shut seemed like it was designed to keep a deadly virus at bay. *Perhaps the electronic lock could be manipulated.*

Kano knew nothing about electronics. To make matters worse, if he got close, a pair of eyes were likely watching him through the camera embedded into the concrete ceiling. Kano thought back to all the tricks he had ever seen in a spy movie or read about in an action novel. Nothing applied to his current predicament. Hope drained away, mirroring the blood soaking into dirty fabric wrapped around his hand.

Eventually, he realized there were only two possibilities for him to leave this place alive. The first, and most likely, was something he had no control over. His parents would simply need to come up with the money to pay The Scholar. Even then, a lot could go wrong with the exchange, and it would take a long time.

The second possibility was one that he did have some control over. His captors were the only ones who could let him out. Perhaps if he could build a relationship with them, they would make a mistake. If he could just get his hands on that assault rifle…

Dilemmas and plans and expectations all whirled into one sinking feeling collecting in the pit of his stomach as Kano turned his desperate thoughts toward Johanna. He wondered how she would take the news. *When would she leave Mali?* As long as she was in the country, he felt a small measure of comfort even though despair spread uncontrollably.

What about Jerry? He knew his family didn't have much money. *What would The Scholar do when he figured that out?* Kano shuddered to think about it. *Was there a way to get Jerry out?* If he tried to help Jerry, he knew his own chances of escape would take a big hit.

Hopelessness crashed down on him and the battered bucket in the corner collected all that was left of his half-digested bread and fake coffee. The acidic whirlpool subsided. Kano shakily curled around the bucket, facing the corner and finding temporary escape into a tormented world of dreams.

December 2004

After several weeks of cleaning, one *parantigi,* assistant to the driver, fell ill. Mr. Traore called Souleymane into his office. "My friend Mariko, the Sandwich Maker, was right about you. I have never seen a boy clean with so much energy. Did your mother teach you to do this?"

Souleymane respectfully kept his eyes on the floor and responded quietly. "I never knew my mother. She died when I was born."

"So, who did the chores around your house? An aunt perhaps?"

"No, I have no family in Sakoro where I grew up. Some of the neighbors helped my father until I was old enough to do the work myself. That is how I learned to clean. I knew I could not bring my mother back, but I tried to fill her place so my father would not be so sad."

"Hmmmm," said Mr. Traore thoughtfully, "and where is your father now?"

"He died from a snake bite just before I came to Bougouni."

Mr. Traore stared at the boy for a moment in silence and then spoke with an authoritative air of confidence. "Very well. You have proven yourself so far. From now on, think of me as your father. Mariko, the Sandwich Maker, will be your uncle. A sad life it would be to have no family." He paused to let Souleymane absorb the proclamation with widening eyes. "One of my workers has fallen ill. You will take his place. You will ride the bus to Bamako and back. It is a short route. You will load and unload the baggage. You will *make sure* everyone who gets on the bus shows you a ticket. You will clean the bus after each ride. You will stand tall and grow into a strong man. You will make your new family proud."

Mr. Traore paused again as tears from the boy splashed across the clean tiles. "What are these tears, my son? Tears of anger? Of happiness? Tell me."

Souleymane stood in silence. He was overwhelmed with an emotion he could not identify. It was so strong he was unable to speak. He simply looked down in shame and shook with sobs.

All in the same moment he was mourning the mother he never knew, the loss of his childhood, and the death of his father. He was also celebrating the new life before him. His newfound family. His exciting career.

After staring down for what seemed like forever, joy somehow boiled up from the cauldron within and a smile crossed his face. He squeaked out a pathetic, "I am happy, Father."

Mr. Traore opened his generous mouth and laughed, the deep waves resonating throughout the entire space, wrapping Souleymane up like a warm blanket on a cold night. "So am I. Now go and gather your things. There is work to be done."

August 2009

The stifling concrete cell seemed to grow smaller and smaller. Hotter and hotter. Kano's body rebelled. He couldn't stop scratching patches of itching, prickly skin, causing it to open up into oozing sores. The bucket contained more food that had been rejected by his body than processed through it. He rapidly lost weight, even though a week could barely have passed. The physical strain of malnutrition conspired with torturous heat to accelerate the withering effects of solitary confinement.

His only place to retreat or escape was into his mind—a scary destination. He felt it unraveling. Paranoia setting in. Flashing back and forth from past to present so often that separating the two challenged him. Memories fused with his current circumstances, making him question what had actually happened to him in the past.

Joyful memories became unreal, as if he had dreamt them, a world so disconnected it ceased to have meaning. Painful memories became more intense. He relived each excruciating second over and over again. Those memories then twisted and warped to such a degree that he wondered if the damage could ever be undone.

Although he lay still to conserve energy, sleep would not come. His mind flashed uncontrollably from one event to the next, lighting up like a pinball machine. In the beginning, Kano could activate the flipper when the ball approached, preventing his thoughts from disappearing down a black hole. After some time, the flippers took on a life of their own as the flashing lights and sounds overwhelmed his fragmenting consciousness.

February 2005

After the first few months had passed, the excitement of Souleymane's newfound livelihood had all but worn off. The initial rides were thrilling. Landscapes rushed by with nearly incomprehensible speed. Responsibilities were stacked on top of him, just like the baggage which doubled the height of the smaller bus up ahead, currently slowing their progress.

Although his tasks made him feel top heavy and off-balance at first, he had mastered them in less than a week. Intense spurts of work and activity as the mad rush of passengers pushed onto and flowed out of the bus were followed by seemingly endless periods of nothingness; he simply had to wait for the bus to leave, or to arrive at its destination. Most of his day was spent sitting in silence—something he had rarely experienced in the village of Sakoro. It felt wrong.

He knew the boys he had grown up with would consider him to be quite well off. He had work and never had to eat alone. In spite of this privilege, he felt poor. All his attempts to discover more about the world around him were snubbed. The new things he saw were fascinating, but whenever he tried to learn about them, his questions were met with curiosity killing contempt.

He now spent more time in Bamako, the sprawling capital, than anywhere else. Its people were much less friendly. He was considered a nobody in the business, at the lowest rung in the ladder, and merely a boy. True connection and acceptance were what he longed for—he felt it with his new father and the Sandwich Maker—but he didn't see them enough.

Sometimes a person with ghostly white skin, a *Toubobou*, would get on the bus. Souleymane was shocked and afraid at first, but then became intrigued with who they were and where they came from. *Could the nightmarish stories of a frozen land be true?* Something in the way they walked and the look in their eye held him back from trying to make conversation. He was embarrassed about his lack of ability in French, so he wouldn't have gotten far even if he had started up some dialogue. It was the brown skinned people who really got his attention.

Brown skin was not a new sight. One family had lived on the edge of his village, and there were a few more in Bougouni; Bamako had a lot of them. He knew they came from the North. They could live for days in the desert heat with almost no food or water. Any person who could do that was truly remarkable. Surely, a pale *Toubobou* would not last more than a few hours.

After taking so many bus rides that he had memorized the details of every single village alongside the road, something new and unreal popped up. They were on the outskirts of Bamako and quickly gaining speed. The driver drifted into the oncoming lane to make space for a man riding on the back of an animal. From a distance, Souleymane saw it was something different. Much lighter in color than a donkey. It was also significantly bigger. Its long, curved neck brought its head to the same height as that of its rider. *It could eat mangoes out of a tree too high to reach without a pole!* As the bus sped by, he got a glimpse of a squashed face narrowing into silly looking lips. His mind flashed back to the day of his father's funeral, remembering the image of that very same creature on a t-shirt. With a shocked tone and wide-open eyes, he blurted out, "What is the name for that animal? I must know!"

The driver laughed and replied, "Well if you must know, the French call it a *Chameau.*"

"I want to see one up close," replied Souleymane with wonder in his voice. "Where can I find another?"

"You will have to go to the North for that." The driver took a sip out of his dirty, plastic cup. "Not many in Bamako. Stop asking so many questions and let me drive."

"Then I must travel North. I will ask my father the next time I am in Bougouni."

Souleymane was able to convince his father to get him onto a bus which ran between Bamako and Timbuktu, although they were saddened by the fact they would see even less of each other. His father's final words rolled around Souleymane's head like an off-balance tire, shaking his entire being.

"Far be it from me to stop a boy from exploring." The giant man probed his desk drawer with a fleshy hand. "Honor my good name while you find your *Chameau*. Bring back to me ever greater stories of adventure. May peace follow in your footsteps." He stood and held out a silver pen to the boy, the same one which brought them together. "Use this and think of me. Find someone who can teach you. Without reading and writing you will always be nothing." His deep voice seemed to resonate throughout the structure long after he had stopped speaking.

Souleymane took the pen gratefully and shuffled out of the office with eyes downturned in sadness. Uneasiness crept in at the thought that he would probably not see his father or his uncle again for months. It felt like he was leaving home for the second time. All of the worries he faced upon abandoning his village resurfaced and tore through his stomach, combining with the realization that his new family might be left in the past.

May peace follow in your footsteps. He could not stop wondering what his father meant. The words gave him an unfamiliar sense of foreboding. He reflected on them for some time while sitting in the front seat of the bus on its way back to the capital. Mud huts and scrubby bushes blurred his peripheral vision.

Why could peace not light my path...
What will guide me...
Where will my footsteps lead...
How could a great thing such as peace follow me...
I am nothing.

The rest of the journey blurred together into nothingness, and suddenly Souleymane saw Castel's Brewery on the right, a blight on the fabric of Islam, and realized Bamako had arrived. He mentally prepared to jump out of the bus, lift open the heavy doors underneath, and swiftly drag out all the baggage.

August 2009

Kano's mind shifted uncontrollably into the past. His present and future felt hopeless. There was nowhere else to go. The murky haze covering and distorting his memories felt a lot like pervasive smog infiltrating the Californian streets of his childhood.

He relived a memory from high school, unsure if it had actually happened that way, or if his present circumstances inserted a nightmarish quality where the events took a slight departure from reality.

In vivid detail, he saw houses, cars, stores and smog spreading endlessly throughout the Los Angeles basin. If one were to look more closely, the divide between Kano's community and the ubiquitous urban sprawl would reveal itself like a trembling fault-line threatening to split open and isolate good from evil once and for all. Much of Loma Linda's population consisted of strong and disciplined Seventh Day Adventists.

Their community ties seemed immovable: intertwined roots of an old-growth forest somehow thriving in the desert. Common vices like alcohol and tobacco were virtually non-existent. Convenience stores had a better supply of meat substitutes than beer or wine. Even the Post Office closed early on Fridays and waited to deliver its weekend mail until Sunday so nearly everyone could observe the Sabbath.

In the midst of pervasive air pollution and moral depravity, this cultural island produced statistically significant results. Loma Linda became one of the top three communities on Earth with regards to life expectancy.

This particular fact motivated Kano's parents to buy a house there. They didn't care to investigate what caused the abnormally long life spans, but the thought of something so irreversible as death getting in the way of lives destined for greatness was unconscionable.

If Loma Linda were an island within the basin, Kano Griffin, especially as an only child, lived on a much smaller island ruled by his parents. His father, Jack, was on the board of a Fortune 500 company and spoke with *his* father's Irish accent whenever he drank, which was often. The twisted, flattened nose served as a constant reminder of his two seasons as the starting center for UCLA's basketball team. His dominating physique had not diminished significantly over the years. Coupled with a fiery temper and a sharp mind, things generally went his way.

Kano's mother, Lina, could not have been more different. She was an exquisitely small Japanese woman who seemed to carefully calculate each word which left her thin lips, her face never revealing the slightest indication of what they might be. The meticulous foresight she employed had paved the way for her to become the Dean of Economics at the prestigious University of Southern California.

Jack and Lina were both away on business, so Kano invited fifteen or twenty classmates to hang out. Their task was to scratch the surface of a rather extensive alcohol collection. It boasted more than all the surrounding neighborhoods combined, but that wasn't saying much. None of their neighbors drank.

The climate-controlled cellar was stocked with over one thousand bottles of wine, so if a few went missing, nobody would be the wiser. Kano started by grabbing a bottle of Ghost Horse *Apparition* Cabernet, not because his parents had paid nearly thirteen hundred dollars for it, but because the bottle looked cool.

The deeply colored liquid sloshed languidly, one dissentious glug of protest at a time, into an ornate crystal punch bowl. Kano chopped up a few kiwis, added a quart of raspberry sherbet, and when nobody was looking, a generous amount of Bacardi 151.

A few hours earlier, he had skipped English class to go surfing. Epic waves. Even though he hated getting sunburned, the bottle of sunblock was left untouched on the kitchen counter all afternoon. The initial sting of redness burning into the back of his neck was already beginning to ache.

While juicing oranges picked from a tree in the backyard, he knocked the forgotten bottle of sunblock onto the floor. Paper towels had been reduced to nothing but a cardboard roll, so he grabbed the roll itself in a half-hearted attempt to remove the white lotion from oversized floor tiles. Blood rushed to his head as he bent down, sending prickles into the sunburn, so he left the cleanup job unfinished.

At the party, Kano's punch was a hit. Sugar masked nearly all of the 151 bite. The incredibly intense Ghost Horse *Apparition* Cabernet was lost in the mix as well. Within the first forty-five minutes, the group of high school seniors was smashed. Kano most of all. He had failed to take into account the sunburn effect.

After a few hours, people started to get hungry. Ashley, a girl Kano had his eyes on all evening, stumbled over and tried to be heard above the mixture of Dr. Dre's beats and the harsh articulations of Eminem. She wasn't making much headway because Kano's eyes kept wandering up and down her body in a way which made her wonder if he was even trying to listen. "So why did you have to quit the basketball team anyway? They really aren't that good now that you left."

Kano mumbled something incomprehensible.

She quickly changed tactics in her search for conversation and asked about food.

In response, he awkwardly pushed himself off the couch and pointed his body toward the kitchen. With one swirling step after another, he slowly waded through the highly compressed sound waves and randomly placed bodies. White kitchen tiles felt cold and foreign to his bare feet as if he had just crossed the border into winter. Three more steps to the enormous fridge. It was nearly within reach.

His right foot made contact with the oily smear of sunblock spreading across three-quarters of a tile. It was rendered invisible; the inversion of black ice on the exit ramp of a highway up in the mountains. The next body part to touch the frigid floor was his elbow, accentuated by a sharp crack. In quick succession followed the muted popping of his shoulder joint and the sickening thud of his skull.

Kano didn't feel a thing. It all happened so fast. He saw his body lying on top of a twisted arm and the corner of his mouth was leaking blood. It struck him as curiously odd that he was looking down upon himself from above. The contrast of the expanding pool of red on top of white tile reminded him of the strawberries and whipped cream he had planned on fetching for Ashley. *Or did I have other ideas for the whipped cream?*

As he thought of Ashley, he looked in her direction. His dazed consciousness tried to shake off its distracted line of thinking and take in the unexpected change in the adjacent room. Instead of twenty friends sprawled about the furniture, he saw more like forty-five or fifty people crammed into the living room. This confused him. It didn't really matter to Kano, but he puzzled over it nonetheless.

He stared at the people and noticed differences between them. Age struck him first. There was a wide range, all of the way up into the seventies. The only person older than seventy Kano had ever seen in this living-room was his Grandpa, and that was ten years earlier. After about twelve seconds of careful scrutiny, Kano realized he was looking at his Grandpa.

But that couldn't be. He had surrendered his wealth and died in a Northern California hippie commune five years ago. Kano remembered skipping his funeral because he had only seen his Grandpa twice. Both times ended with harsh words exchanged between the old man and his son. He asked himself with detached curiosity, "Why is Grandpa here?"

Kano realized some of the bodies had a distinct glow around them. The more he looked, the brighter they glowed. All the others drifted into shadow.

After a moment, he realized his friends were glowing. The rest seemed dull and pale, reminding him vaguely of those Holocaust victims they had seen in History class.

Kano also observed his friends weren't moving. It was as if they were frozen. He couldn't be sure, because they were in a lethargic state when he had set out for the kitchen, but they didn't even seem to be breathing.

The dull people did everything incredibly slowly. It looked like they were really, really cold but couldn't shiver. Whispers grew into a dissatisfied murmur, as if an unpopular speaker said something particularly unpleasant. Kano heard someone shout, "Why won't you listen to ME!" and realized it had come from his Grandpa.

Kano was absorbed by the growing crescendo. Suddenly, his attention was pulled in another direction as he saw a middle-aged, balding individual with furtive eyes slowly creeping in the direction of the lifeless body that was hiding on the opposite side of the kitchen island. The man had a cigar in one hand, a glass of whisky in the other, and was wearing a thin poker cap.

With his head down and eyes darting about beneath the brim, he approached the corpse-like figure on the cold floor. The red pool had ceased its growth. Kano's state of detachment was vaporized with a brutal sensation of horror as the man crouched down next to his faintly glowing body and pulled at a tuft of hair. As if unzipping a body bag, the intruder created a shaft of darkness opening from the top of the head down to Kano's abdomen. The nervous man checked one last time to make sure nobody else was watching, jumped inside, and the shaft closed behind him.

Suddenly Kano was coughing. Coughing. Coughing up blood. Spitting blood out onto the white tile, allowing the red pool to expand once again. He tried to prop himself up on his arm but screamed out in pain instead. Another cough and his airways became clear enough to breathe. He turned to his other side and pushed himself up off the ground. His good arm reached the black marble counter and pulled. His eyes rose above the perfectly level surface and saw a few friends moving toward him. They were coming to see what had happened.

Confusion rolled through Kano's mind. He saw blood on the floor. The dreamlike apparitions dissolved quickly as he shook them away. Ashley touched his forehead. In that instant, the image of a furtive poker player doing nearly the same thing rushed back like an ocean wave breaking violently on the shore, only to dissipate almost as quickly as it came. She asked if she should call 911. He heard himself slur, "No…just got into Michigan…Dad said he wouldn't fix it again."

Kano slowly stood, the room twisting and turning as his vision blurred. He felt a wave of nausea rising up from the deep. Quietly, he announced that the party was over, and they all had to go. The ones who had surrounded Kano moved toward the living-room to rustle the others up and off the couches. In a matter of five minutes the house cleared out, although Kano had the strange feeling not everyone had gone. In a state of inebriated shock, he worked his way toward his bed and made a mental note to see the doctor about his arm soon.

The next morning, digital numbers from the clock face burned their green glow into Kano Griffin's surfacing consciousness. He never woke up before his alarm, so concern quickly crept in. Pain shot up his arm and stabbed through his shoulder like a thousand misplaced acupuncture pins as he tried to roll over. He quickly realized he had to get to the hospital. Calculating the alcohol should have been mostly processed, he stood upright, wincing in pain.

Still wearing the same clothes as the night before, he slipped into a pair of flip-flops and clumsily grabbed the keys to his 2001 Honda Prelude with his left hand. Pain necessitated keeping the right arm as motionless as possible.

It was a challenge to duck down into the low bucket seats. Fortunately, shifting wouldn't be much of a problem. In order to change on the way to basketball practice he had developed creative driving skills. His left hand had no trouble working both the steering wheel and the gearbox. The aftermarket turbocharger sucked him snugly into his seat, hissing into action as the engine surged above 3000 RPM. It barely dropped below this mark until he squealed to a stop at the emergency room.

He told the doctors he had an accident on the long-board coming home the night before. They quickly administered Kano a strong analgesic and used a closed reduction technique to pop his dislocated shoulder back into its socket. In short order, a sling was fashioned, and Kano was told to wear it for a few days. They also said he needed to be careful in the future; shoulder dislocation is much more likely to happen a second time, and then surgery might be required.

The ER doctor could not prepare Kano for the discomfort he felt which went well beyond his shoulder. Creeping in the back of his mind, he sensed an unnatural whisper. It fed the irrational suspicion his injury would never fully heal. Something had gained access to his thoughts and feelings, influencing him from within.

The very same unnatural presence nudged his consciousness back into the present reality of his dim and gritty concrete pit. Pain throbbed just like it had all those years ago, and, once again, he felt as though his mind was not entirely his own. In opposition to the prickling heat, a cold shiver traveled up his spine as another whisper came to him: *the odds of escape are so low, you might as well fold.*

March 2005

Two weeks had already blurred into a new routine. The twenty-four-hour bus ride, stretching the limits of the most patient people in the world, still held Souleymane's attention captive. He counted eighty-seven *chameaux* on the side of the road thus far. Some were plodding slowly forward with bags strapped to their humped backs, led by what was in comparison a tiny man. Others carried riders sitting tall with their heads wrapped in cloth to fight the blazing sun.

Souleymane watched diligently for every change in the landscape each time the bus traveled north, leading him to a city of wonder. The bushes grew smaller and farther apart. Trees all but disappeared. Red earth gave way to tan sand in the same way black-skinned people were replaced with brown. The prominently wide facial features of the South narrowed and sharpened as if a harsher life starved joy from the body itself. Even clothing faded, sun and sand conspiring to deprive the people of color.

Every time Souleymane made the journey he felt as though he was slowly entering a different world. He practiced French whenever possible as none of the brown skinned people who so intrigued him could speak Bambara, his native tongue. He longed to learn more about their mysterious lives. He wanted more than anything to ride on the hump of a *chameau*.

One night in Timbuktu, long after the passengers had dispersed and dinner was winding down, Souleymane rinsed off his hands in the tin can and turned to the driver and the mechanic and said, "I am feeling a bit sick tonight. I must get some early rest."

"Suit yourself," they replied with a grin. "Better chances for us with the women if you are already asleep. They don't feel at ease when boys are around."

Souleymane rolled his eyes and left the table. After bathing and putting on clean clothes, he looked around to be sure his colleagues were nowhere to be seen. He slipped out of the compound and made his way toward the central square. Open, sandy space was dominated by a structure which looked as if it had been flown through outer space and abandoned there by aliens. Souleymane had seen unusual glass and steel construction in Bamako, but it felt completely out of place in this city made of sand.

An old man was standing with his back toward the spaceship staring vacantly at the mosque. Souleymane approached, using his best French. "Good evening, sir. What this strange building is for?"

The old man was especially hard to understand. Only a few teeth remained inside his head. French was clearly not a language he was accustomed to speaking. Nonetheless, Souleymane picked a few words out of his lengthy reply: "South Africa...library...old books...money."

Why would rich South Africans come all the way to the edge of the great desert where there was no money to be made? Souleymane felt there was a mystery hidden behind every ornately carved, sultanic door which bejeweled the streets of sand. Not one having to do with wealth, though. He had no idea why such a distant and prosperous country took interest in these mysteries. *Old books? What must they contain? How could I find out?*

Perhaps religious men of the community would know more. The wrinkled, sunken eyes before him came to life as the crackle of a megaphone stopped the old man mid-sentence. Tinny, overpowering sound poured into the square stemming forth from a singer's vocal cords. The song itself Souleymane knew well. He heard the call to prayer every day in the South. Somehow, the song was different here. The acoustics of sand were not the same as red dirt and green leaves. Glass and steel echoed each tone eerily.

The voice itself had an ethereal quality, a conduit for a higher power. In Sakoro, where he had grown up, the singers had much lower tones and were often confusing their notes. Perhaps this was why he had never, until now, been moved by the call to prayer.

The old man plodded with an aching slowness toward the silently opening door of the six-hundred-year-old mosque: a sandy, geometric porcupine bristling with staffs cut from ancient trees. A shaft of yellow light illuminated the bumps and curves of the sand directly in front of the door, delving more distant depressions left by feet of wandering souls into darkness as dusk fell. Souleymane was drawn to walk with the man. "The music beautiful here," he said, "may I pray with you?"

The man spoke his muffled words and Souleymane could only make out: "No...old...tradition...after."

Souleymane chose to follow him toward the open door, peek at the bare walls inside, and wait next to a peculiar bread oven. Its shape reminded him of a sticker on one of the bags he had unloaded from the bus that afternoon: a little green man with a conically rounded head. He had asked the passenger about it and got the strangest answer.

The man replied in French, "This is an alien, someone from another planet."

"What you mean," Souleymane asked incredulously. "What other planet?"

"Well, I don't know which one, perhaps Mars, but maybe he isn't even real."

"What is Mars?"

The man sighed and looked down. "I suppose you didn't go to school either. Sometimes I feel it is my duty to educate this entire country, even down to the boy who brings me my luggage. Mars is another planet similar to the one we are standing on now. Planets are like giant footballs floating through space. It is a different world entirely, but I don't think anything lives on it now. There are an uncountable number of planets out there and we have no idea what lives, or doesn't live on them. Perhaps a little person like this is out there somewhere wondering what we look like."

"How we find out? Will we visit them some day? Can we learn their…"

The man cut him off before Souleymane could say more. "Too many questions for a boy. I hope we will be able to visit them one day. We would need a spaceship, something like an airplane, but much more powerful. It would take a long time to get there. Speaking of a long time, this bus ride has soured my mood. I must be on my way."

"Thank you for your wisdom, Teacher," said Souleymane with eyes looking down to catch one last glimpse of the little green creature. The man's words wrenched on his imagination and although he found them nearly impossible to believe or to understand, deep down he felt their truth.

Perhaps the wise, old ladies in his village were wrong when explaining to him that the world was flat. It seemed flat. *How can I know for sure? If they were wrong about this, what else had they been wrong about?*

Souleymane settled into soft sand with his back leaning against the crumbling bread oven as weariness from another long bus journey set in. His thoughts drifted around distant planets and strange green men and then into the dimension of dreams.

Souleymane awoke with a start as an unusually colorful dream escaped from the grasp of his mind like a handful of powdery sand slipping through gaps between fingers. Bright magentas, neon greens, and midnight blues wafted away through the desert air. A tapping sensation on his shoulder continued, but before his eyes alighted on the nearby face, he noticed everything had grown darker and quieter. The mosque was a smudge in the night. Sounds of the city all but disappeared.

His eyes didn't have to wander up very far to see a child standing at his side. The boy was only a head higher than Souleymane in his slumped, seated position. He pulled lightly on Souleymane's shirt sleeve and repeated a few words in a whisper that Souleymane could not understand. Soon he did make out the French word *manger,* to eat, and quickly realized the small dinner he shared with his bus crew disappeared along with his colorful dream. After a slight rumble of approval from his stomach, he chose to follow the boy through the sandy streets of the sleeping city.

It didn't take long for the crisp, clear air to sharpen Souleymane's senses. He followed in silence, wondering where this angelic little boy had come from, why he wasn't asleep like everyone else, and who would offer a meal to a stranger so late at night. The whole situation felt other-worldly. Perhaps pieces of his dream still lingered more closely than he imagined.

After a ten-minute walk to the outskirts of Timbuktu, the boy took his hand and led him under an archway opening up into a rather ornate and dimly lit courtyard. Souleymane thought it strange the gates would not be closed so late at night. The only person who seemed to be awake, other than the young boy, sat before him now.

An old man with a long, white beard took a slow drag on a black pipe and held the smoke in for what felt like an eternity. Eventually, the man opened his mouth not to speak, but to let white tendrils escape, reminding Souleymane of the Bamako mists emanating from the Niger River early in the morning during the cold season. After completing a slow assessment of the young man in front of him, he spoke with a low, crackling tone, like a glowing campfire. Although Souleymane could understand nothing of what was said, he felt as though the desert itself spoke.

The small boy pulled up a chair and a table, beckoning Souleymane to sit, then quickly disappeared through a darkened opening. Souleymane and the old man sat in silence. Soon the boy returned carrying a coffee tin full of water for hand washing and a bowl of food, leftovers from what must have been an extravagant meal. He set them down and vanished into the darkness.

The old man motioned for Souleymane to begin. He observed the smallest details as the young man before him savored each handful of couscous and vegetables, then slowly separated greasy chicken from bone.

Souleymane ate his fill, washed his hands again, and settled into his chair. Several drawn-out puffs of smoke rose into the starry sky before the old man spoke again. His sandy voice had a slight echo, as if he were in several locations at once. Souleymane's eyes darted about as he concluded the shape of the small courtyard might have something to do with this unearthly effect.

Ancient lips moved as if in slow motion, but their articulate French told Souleymane he was speaking with a highly educated man. He could finally understand most of the words set before him. "I see you come from far away. Your customs are not like our customs. Allow me to introduce myself. My given name is Fahim, meaning clear-sighted one, but most people call me The Scholar. I am here to be your guide into the New World, eventually your father, should you so choose."

Souleymane was caught off-guard by this proposal. *Why would someone I just met offer to be my father?* He replied in his best French, "Oh wise one, two fathers have I already. First one dead, second in Bougouni. Second father give me job. I work on bus."

"I see," came a thoughtful reply, "then why are you searching? What are you looking for? A father and a job are enough for most young men."

"I don't know why I wander, oh wise one. First, I leave village. Then, I come North. I love long bus trip. Today I listen to beautiful prayer music from mosque. Not so beautiful in South."

"What is your name?"

"Souleymane."

"Your name means peaceful, but your spirit is not yet at peace. You are searching for brothers. You went into the city alone because the older men from the bus do not accept you. The village where you grew up has left you nothing but wisps of memory. Your second father grows dim. I can see it is time for a new family. A family of the greatest kind. One bonded with the divine ties of God Almighty. One with a vision of the New World. We are here to become a shining beacon of light into the darkness that surrounds us. This task is not without hard work. Your body has not been conditioned for it. Your mind lies dormant. Your soul thirsts. You will need to strengthen every part of your being."

Souleymane's heart beat faster as he struggled to take in the meaning of these words. "Oh, Wise One, what about job? I must work to eat. To live."

"Your new job is here. You will be given food and shelter. The real work will not begin until your training is complete."

"Who will take my place at bus? I need take care bags."

The Scholar waved a thin hand in the air. "A small trifle. One of my students will not complete his training. His body is strong but his mind is weak. He will return with you tomorrow. You will tell the bus driver that you have found a new job and that you have also found a suitable worker to take your place."

Souleymane's heart raced, and his mind froze up, as if someone had carefully placed a stick into the delicate gears that kept his thoughts turning. He sat in silence for several minutes as The Scholar patiently kept the embers in his pipe glowing brightly. This whole night seemed unreal; suddenly he had been offered a new way of life. The desert was calling. All at once, with the slowing of his hammering heartbeat, the occlusive stick cracked, and he knew he must answer the call.

August 2009

The withering conditions of the oven-like pit continued to warp Kano's consciousness. He found himself plunged deeply into another memory. There was no possible way his besieged mind could separate the reality of his past from the distortion caused by his current situation. Even the lines between awake and dreaming blurred into oblivion.

Oblique rays of light threading their way through the open slit above him brought his mind back to the first time he woke up in Rome. As soon as the early morning sun reached down to illuminate Kano's closed eyelids, they sprang open like the iris diaphragm housed within his single-lens reflex camera. He sat up slowly, getting his bearings. Jet lag was doing strange things to his mind. He was still on top of the bed wearing all his clothes and something smelled. It didn't take long to realize the unpleasant odor came from himself.

After a quick shower, Kano propped a pair of polarized lenses on top of his head, slung the heavy camera bag over his shoulder, stuffed his wallet into the pocket of his shorts, and grabbed his phone. As he was heading for the door he realized the phone probably wouldn't work here, and tossed it back into his bag.

He was determined to see everything Rome. Highlights from the guide book were committed to memory during the flight across the Atlantic. Kano decided to work his way up, starting with the smallest of ruins and ending with a whole new country. *The Vatican.* He was becoming a pleasure delayer, leaving behind the instant gratification that drove him during his early years at the University of Michigan.

He no longer enjoyed one night stands. They were far too easy. A long game of cat and mouse was more satisfying than its inevitable conclusion. When playing poker, he preferred to bleed his opponents dry instead of the efficient knockout in several rounds he had perfected during his freshman year.

No need to rush, Rome has been here for more than twenty-five centuries. I don't need to see everything in a day.

After meandering through narrow streets which spilled into noisy, repulsive thoroughfares or expansively grand piazzas for much of the morning, Kano snapped out of the mindset of a photographer. He knew it would take him hours to process the pictures he had already captured. The sun was too high to provide any interesting lighting and its intensity sapped his gusto for exploration. It was time for an espresso—*a real one*—and he anticipated the taste with pleasure.

When most people look for a place to eat in a new city, they rely mainly on visual cues. *How does it look? Comfortable? Friendly? Are there locals or tourists inside?*

Kano cut through what he saw as irrelevant details and focused almost entirely on what his nose reported to his brain. Nothing caught his attention at first. His eyes were not permitted to wander from side to side, which would surely lead to distraction.

After seven minutes of walking, Kano's focus unraveled. His pace slowed. Eyes broke free from their constraints and roamed about. He even stopped paying attention to the dizzying array of smells which entered his mind, ranging from fresh bread to moped exhaust to drying laundry. The street narrowed, removing the sun from the sky. Bright colors turned old and dirty. The strongest feeling of déjà vu surrounded him. Involuntarily, he made a sharp turn to face a rusting, green door on his right.

Six times Kano rapped on the door in a robotic fashion, as if he was programmed to do so. A small hole slid open and a voice muttered something in Italian, the syllables inconsequential. What triggered Kano's brain were the molecules of strong coffee which spilled through the slit before the man's voice could reach his ears. One word came into his mind and exited verbally without thought. "Espresso."

Kano found the exact smell his nose had been searching for. After a bit of muttering, the greenish door creaked open and he stepped into a chillingly damp hall. A short, balding man badly in need of a haircut led him toward the outdated kitchen where he prepared a shot of espresso with a blur of what was clearly muscle memory motion.

He handed the concentrated liquid over and gestured for Kano to go through the other door leading further into the house. The acrid smell of heavy tobacco curdled the pleasure of coffee as he entered a narrow hall. As his eyes adjusted to dim lighting, he thought there were wisps of smoke seeping around the outside of a closed door as if the room behind it was on fire.

He walked up to the spectrally blue surface and wanted to feel the wood for heat before placing his hand on the metal doorknob, as he was taught to do by the fireman who came to his elementary school many years before. Much to his surprise, his body did something entirely different. As if on autopilot, his knuckles reached out and rapped on the door five times in short succession.

Four crisp syllables of Italian reached his ears. Without hesitation, he grasped the handle fully, although a part of him half expected to feel searing pain. The door opened before him into a billowing cloud of smoke. His eyes instantly blurred. After the relatively fresh hallway air cleared the smoke, he took in a scene which put him instantly at ease.

A small voice in the back of his head constantly wondered what was leading him to this place, but once Kano saw the poker table before him he figured that on a subconscious level he had been searching for a card game. His small, critical voice wasn't appeased for long.

A man pointed his Godfather-like Cohiba straight at Kano and said something in a harsh tone of accusation. Kano was about to respond in English, but three strange syllables escaped from his mouth. He had no idea what they meant, but it worked like magic. Everyone around the table paused for exactly two seconds and then laughed at the same time. It was as if the real world had suddenly morphed into a movie set and Kano was playing a role he had practiced many times before.

One empty chair remained, and the man with the Cohiba motioned for Kano to sit in it. He spoke in a slight Italian accent, although his grammar was perfect. "I see you are an American. Please, tell us how you found this game."

"I could smell the coffee from the street," said Kano with a disarming smile. "This looks better than soaking up more history, so deal me in."

"Very well. It will give us a chance to practice our English like we did with the last American who used to play at this table. I don't think I ever saw him without that stupid little visor on his head," he grinned ruefully with the memory. "We haven't heard from him in years. He never used to miss a game. What part of America was he from?"

Across the rounded table, a man sporting a thin mustache and dark sunglasses spoke up. "California, I think."

"Yeah, Los Angeles," another one confirmed.

"I thought it was San Francisco," challenged a voice next to Kano with the harsh, monosyllabic tone of a coffee grinder.

"Doesn't matter," said the man with the biggest cigar. "He is long gone, and he was better at drinking than he was at playing cards. Let's see how much money we can take from our tourist. Grab him a cigar, Bruno."

Bruno scowled but did what was asked of him. He addressed Kano, "Whata er you, eighteen and you looka green arounda da gills from thisa smoke. I stole my firsta cigarette from da ol' man backa when I was eleven. Been goin' stronga since. Supposa nows a good a time as any to give it a goa."

He gently slid a finely rolled Montecristo cylinder out of the box and tapped it for luck. He cut the end, handed it ceremoniously across the table to Kano, and said with a sly smile, "Eeva yur gonna starta, start wit the besta. You donna need a pay me for it becausa I weena alla your cheeps."

Kano replied with a smirk, "I'll pay you back for the cigar, but with the chips I take from your pile."

The man with white hair sitting next to him lit up, and kept the flame on for Kano while piping in. "Most of us needa work for a living. Somaday your rich parents won't cover for ya."

Kano took a drag and then erupted into a cascade of coughing. Pain shot through his shoulder as he violently dipped his head below the raised rim of the table.

A chorus of laughter resounded. When Kano re-emerged from the shadows Bruno said, "Dona breathe it in, stupida. You gotta keepa dat smoke in your mouth. Hold it in for a while en try da blowa some nice smoke rings, like dis." He puffed out two rings swirling straight for Kano, diffusing into the haze about halfway across the table.

The game was Texas Hold'em, just like the online Party Poker he was so accustomed to. Each player was dealt two cards. Kano lifted the corners in front of him and saw a pair of Queens staring defiantly back. Bets were placed, cards on the river were flipped, and Kano knew the odds of his Queens with little effort. 71% was much higher than his standard 25% minimum, so he placed an aggressive bet, but with an oddly unfamiliar reservation. Cards were laid on the table and Bruno quickly gathered the pot with a glint in his eye. "Maybe you wonta need ta pay me back for that cigar after alla."

The next hand showed odds of 17% so Kano folded, although he felt something inside him pushing to continue. Kano never bluffed. His game was all about math. This time he saw it wouldn't have been a bluff—his ace high would have taken the pot.

When the third hand was dealt, Kano decided to pay more attention to the suggestions which floated into the back of his mind. Odds were at 48% and his newfound sensation agreed with the math, proving to be a winning combination.

After a few more hands, Kano didn't feel much of anything other than the tobacco going to his head. He was getting dizzy. It felt a lot like a good buzz from a few shots of Bacardi. His focus dwindled along with the pile of chips in front of him.

The cigar was down to the point where the air entering Kano's mouth nearly burned his lips. Bruno told him to give it up. The moment he crushed red ember into the curved glass bottom of the ash tray, his nagging headache exploded into what felt like a full-fledged hangover. Eyes burned, head throbbed, and stomach churned.

Kano never left a poker game early, but he found himself stumbling toward the toilets. He barely made it in time.

After rinsing off his face and mouth, he took a big drink of water, and winced his way back to the table. The guys chuckled as he returned and swiftly proceeded to deal out the next round.

Kano was too embarrassed to focus on the hand, but after folding he overcame the shame and pushed himself back into action. His mind was sluggish but the odds still surfaced. He was only at 28% but had a strong urge to bet. Kano still felt miserable and figured if he would go out now, he should do it with a statement. All in at 28%.

Bruno matched it, and Kano expected the worst. Cards were laid down, and Kano took the pot. The stack in front of him doubled and his energy returned. The clairvoyant input didn't stop. He calculated its strength into his odds. This changed his game significantly. After thirty more minutes he cleared the table. Bruno, being an honorable man, wouldn't accept any money for the cigar, as he gave its luck the credit for an unexpected comeback. Kano swore he would never smoke a Montecristo again.

The short, bald man put down his cigar with disappointment. "So you came for some history?" he asked in a gruff tone.

"Yeah," said Kano, "kind of an unplanned thing, this trip. Finished up with school but not ready for the suit yet."

The big man with the smoldering Cohiba spoke up, "That's when we all met, you know. Right after school. Wanted to see the world so we signed up to crew a boat. Bruno was the cook. Almost killed us a few times with food poisoning. Not sure if it was worse on the way down or on the way back up again." Everyone except for Bruno chuckled.

"Wish I finished the job backa then you olda dog. Woulda have saved us lotza trouble to be getting on withowta you," Bruno shot back.

"Anyway," butted in the man with the mustache as he brought his cigar up for another puff, "that is how we learned to speak English, although Bruno still thinks a strong accent makes a strong man."

"We all learned the delicate differences between the ladies of all different colors. Let me tell you about this dame I came across on the shores of Thailand..."

The banter and stories continued as Kano reflected on this singular game, feeling a greater need for fresh air as each minute passed. It was as though he had played here for years. Somehow he seemed to know what each person was thinking. Every tell held immediate meaning, so Kano knew when they were bluffing as surely as if he saw their cards.

Kano hadn't sat around a physical card table for a long time, preferring the pixelated versions, and never had he been to a game where the smoke was so thick. Maybe he could get used to it eventually. The experience, and the winnings, could be even richer at real tables than the digital manifestations which had so easily paid for this trip.

"All right boys, that does it for me. I think I have enough now to get a nice steak dinner every night for the rest of the week. If you want, I'll stop by again tomorrow and you can try to win your money back."

The voice behind the Cohiba emanated, "Do all Americans play cards like this? You remind me of our old friend. He always seemed to know whether I would fold or not before I knew myself, unless his buddy Jack Daniels got the better of him." He shifted his chair back with irritation. "We always said his love for Jack would cost more than a game of cards, but he never was one to listen to good advice."

As Kano jammed coins and rumpled bills into his pockets and stood up to leave, he said, "Jack Daniels might have gotten the better of your friend, but if you keep smoking like this, those Cubans will get the better of you!"

Bruno chuckled and said in a small voice, "Cubans arenta da problem. My Grandpa smoked at leasta cigar every day of his life an he is 97. It's my wifesa cooking dat will kill me!"

"That sounds a whole lot like Karma, friend." Kano backpedaled toward cleaner air.

The men laughed again at Bruno's expense and then reverted to Italian, presumably throwing insults around about each other's wives, as Kano made his exit. Once the blessed sunshine kissed his face, he felt as though he could breathe again. The reason wasn't only that the air had become exponentially cleaner every step he took away from that dark room of cards, but because something at the core of his being had been put on hold for his time inside that dingy, smoke-stained house. He couldn't quite put his finger on it, but it felt like a piece of his soul was now stretching its hands into the sky with a great big yawn as it awakened from a long slumber.

Even though Kano had just arrived in Rome, he felt the city was somehow too small for him. A desire to see the whole continent rose up and crystallized. While he knew his poker winnings would allow for a luxurious travel style, he also knew they could insulate him from truly experiencing the journey.

Not far from his hotel was an outdoor shop. He settled upon one of the most expensive backpacks they had, a German brand he hadn't heard of before. He filled it with things he would need for a nomadic lifestyle. A small tent, sleeping bag, inflatable mat, gas burner, solar charger, and a host of other items.

Once fully packed, he felt he could go anywhere, see anything. He decided to begin and end his journey in this incredible city to which all roads lead.

Determined to see every European capital, learn bits and pieces of many languages, and experience life without a home, he set out to spend time with people as different as he could imagine. Seeking out card games along the way would provide extra entertainment and, at a minimum, cover his costs. The additional challenge of making money *while* traveling added a layer of excitement.

Nearly a full year passed before his adventures brought him back to the very same hotel in Rome where it all began. A year of pictures and stories, of learning and exploring, of a strange battle which grew within himself to be ready for the day ahead, coupled against a nearly uncontrollable desire to drink himself under the table. The wine of France, English cider, Belgian beer, Russian vodka, it all seemed to pull him into small taverns and cafes with a force which somehow felt apart from himself and yet impossible to ignore.

The fight was won and lost many times over. Kano more than tripled his extensive financial reserves in exchange for a scarred liver, calloused feet, and a soul weary to the point of collapse.

A different sort of exhaustion permeated his body as his mind transitioned from reliving past experiences to the present pain of a full bladder. He limped over to the bucket. A lack of movement combined with sleeping on nothing more than a blanket transformed any sort of motion into an uncomfortable experience at best.

After relieving himself, his lips curled up in disgust. The acrid taste of cigar filled his mouth, as though he smoked a Montecristo the night before. Throughout the day it became so bad he even tried to erase it with powdery sand that tended to collect in the corners of his pit.

This made him thirsty, and a desire much stronger than any hunger he had ever felt overwhelmed his being. His body shook uncontrollably. He needed alcohol. Any kind of drink. Even the awful palm wine he had become accustomed to in the South of Mali. He banged his head into the wall incessantly until it bled. Until an unseen form came to deliver a scant meal through the opening in the door. He begged, shouted and cursed at it for a drink. All he heard in response was the slow retreat of sandaled feet.

March 2005

Souleymane awoke before the sun rose. The small boy shook his shoulder until he rolled over and yawned. He was led to the toilets and given leftover couscous for breakfast, which they ate together. Then the boy led Souleymane into The Scholar's study.

The sun was rising, filling the room with glorious, orange light. Its indirect rays illuminated a wall which held far more than the total number of books Souleymane had ever seen in his lifetime. His mouth opened slightly in wonder. *What a life it would be to know what was inside those books! What mysteries could be locked up, hidden within their pages?*

The Scholar interrupted his thoughts with a low, scratchy voice. "Good morning, Souleymane. I see you would like to explore my collection. Some day you shall." He motioned for Souleymane to sit before him. "First you have much to learn. I normally select boys younger than you, teaching them all they need to know by the time they are your age. And yet, I see in you a certain curiosity, a wisdom, a subtle quality most boys do not possess. I accept any gift Allah brings. I have tried to imbue others with the spark burning within you, but have found it to be something I cannot give."

The Scholar spoke slowly and paused for a moment, letting the young man process the complexity of the French language. As the orange light took on a yellowish intensity, he continued. "Your advanced age requires you to work twice as hard to find the place where the other boys are. You must master French and learn Arabic as well—in written and spoken word. Weapons training and physical endurance will be essential to your future missions. Above all, you must study and obey the Koran, maintaining peace with our Creator."

The Scholar turned and selected two well-worn books from the shelf. He placed them delicately in front of Souleymane and opened them simultaneously to the same page. The scent of old paper drifted up. "What do you see?"

Souleymane bent over for a careful look and responded in his best French. "I see one page with symbols like by side of road and most shops. Other is page with different symbols. It look more connected. I see before on buildings here in North." He glanced up eagerly to see how his teacher would respond.

"I see those things too. Learn to draw conclusions based on limited information. Complete your answers. What languages are they?"

He focused on the books for a moment. "Must be French and Arabic. What other languages would you show?"

"Well stated. Answering a question with a question. I see potential in you. These two books are yours to study from. Each a copy of the

Koran. I have opened them to my favorite page. Learn it first. Mehdi, the boy who has been helping you, will teach you the symbols and help you to understand the words. You will study morning, afternoon, and night. You will sleep for a full eight hours. Every moment you are awake will be filled with the training of your mind, body, and soul. Before we begin, the boy who is not meant for my household will accompany you to the bus station and offer his services to the driver in your place. I trust you will be able to find your own way back. That is all for now."

For the next few months, methodical routines permeated throughout Souleymane's being. He was lulled into a rhythm of the mind, like nothing he had experienced before. Life in the South consisted of physical labor and social interaction. He now realized this had been holding him back from a buried potential which would have remained undiscovered without help from the house of The Scholar.

He felt a pang of longing for his father in Bougouni, who could be sitting at his desk now, listening to rumbling buses come and go, wondering what had become of the boy who was so good at cleaning. Then he remembered those last words. *Find someone who can teach you. Without reading and writing you will always be nothing.*

Souleymane looked down at his books and felt pride swell within him as he realized he could now accomplish the task his father had set before him. In that moment, he decided the time had come to fully adopt The Scholar as his new father.

Every morning he rose before dawn; there was no longer a need for Mehdi to wake him. Guided by the light of a dented lantern's smooth flame, he studied the Koran for about an hour as the eastern sky brightened. Boys gathered for breakfast when the sun broke through the horizon. After the meal, half of the morning was filled with language practice, followed by combat and strength training until lunch.

The others were very talkative while they ate, a cultural habit Souleymane was unaccustomed to. He preferred to observe all that was happening, taking in every interaction with acute attention to social detail. He knew they were training for a mission, but the specifics were hard to imagine.

The Scholar regularly spoke of the coming New World and their sacred duty to illuminate its arrival. Souleymane failed to comprehend how it would work in practice. This was one of the few lingering questions he had kept from The Scholar.

After lunch, the rigid routine continued. Boys separated for individual study. Souleymane absorbed himself in French and Arabic. The Scholar gave him materials beyond the Koran to learn from. Souleymane painstakingly worked to understand each word in the tattered newspapers which were bestowed upon him. Every other day he would meet with The Scholar to discuss any parts he failed to find meaning in. The Scholar would carefully explain everything in terms of good and evil, offering practical solutions to many complex problems. Souleymane focused every cell of his being upon absorbing the words and wisdom of his new father during these intense sessions.

Before dinner was a grueling, one hour run through desert dunes. Then came a small bucket bath, food, and sparse conversation with the other boys. Finally, Souleymane spent the rest of the evening studying the Koran, forcing many words and passages into his long-term memory.

Whenever he grew weary, the words of The Scholar would surface to the top of his mind like an ancient rock exposed by strong winds removing the sand which sheltered it. He had said, "Israel's God rested, and told his people to do the same. Our God needs no rest. Neither do we. Our Sacred Purpose is to allow his light to shine brightly throughout the world. Only then will his people come to know their Sacred Purpose. Without us, they will continue to wander through life like sheep in the darkness. Some of them will even become wolves."

Souleymane meditated on these words as if they came from the Koran itself. They carried him past the temptation to slow down, to let his mind wander, and in his darkest moments, to quit.

Day after day, Souleymane grew more disciplined, more focused, and more committed to the vision of The Scholar. By the time he could converse, read, and write fluently in both French and Arabic, he had no idea how much time had passed.

While the other boys stayed together during their daily run into the desert, Souleymane pushed past them, gliding over the sand as if it had turned hard like the reddish-brown earth of his birthplace during the dry season. Every day he felt the same unstoppable drive to excel, stretching his mind and body to new limits. He had all but forgotten the shell of the boy he had once been.

September 2009

Kano tried with all his might to put her out of his thoughts. Unfortunately for him, his mind had taken on a life and will of its own. Every time he made use of the bucket in the corner, a bit more strength and control slipped away. Thoughts of her made him feel as though death had already come—the contrast between his time with her and his current circumstances so impossibly great.

He knew she was lost. Things could never go back to the way they were. And yet, his mind exquisitely tortured him with twisted recollections of their every encounter. It even pieced together scraps of what she had told him about her student life with his own experience in the Dutch city of Utrecht.

The limited information morphed into a film strip of the mind. Stopping, starting, jumping back and forth. He imagined what it had been like for her. And then, suddenly, the images would abruptly end with an unexpected shock, leaving him with nothing but fingernails digging deeply into his scalp, often drawing blood.

Uncontrolled, ambient light in Kano's pit dimmed as his powerful mind switched on another film to draw his attention away from the present. Sound flooded his consciousness as pervasively glorious medieval bells filled the city of Utrecht just as they had for the past six hundred years. The sound entered her open window along with every other corner, arch, and edifice of the historic architecture. It penetrated throughout, like warmth seeping into her body as she slips under steaming bath water during a cold and cloudy winter day.

Thankfully, winter had recently passed, and the morning sun shone brilliantly, drawing her to the sculpted lines of the one hundred and twelve meter Gothic tower housing the cast-iron origins of the harmonious peals of sound. The largest bell, *Salvator*, weighing eight tons and spanning more than two meters in diameter, could be heard for kilometers in every direction.

The lonely tower used to be connected to the rest of the Cathedral of Saint Martin. After climbing four hundred and sixty-five steps, she looked down into the heart of her own city and then beyond it towards the congestion leading up to Amsterdam, but couldn't quite make out the smoke of Rotterdam's endless refineries beyond the smoggy horizon. The view was tremendous. Flat and fertile farmland spread about in all directions. Much of what she saw had been stolen from the sea. She wondered if the sea might one day steal it back.

After enjoying the heightened perspective as time lost its meaning, she returned down spiraling steps and walked across a wide square to see the inside of the church. Its entrance reminded her of a museum, showing pictures and paintings of the cathedral's history.

A 'swirling storm' destroyed part of the nave back in the 1600s. Budget cuts necessitated a lack of flying buttresses during one stage of construction—the bit which no longer exists. It took nearly one hundred despondent years to clean up the rubble from the massively unstable structure. Johanna was surprised that the distance she had just walked, from the tower to the main entrance, used to be indoors.

She wondered what sort of collapses today's budget cuts would lead to while wandering through the rather drab interior. It didn't match the High Gothic outer layers. If only the stained glass had survived the war, the dramatic effect would have been much stronger.

As she exited through the towering doorway, bright sunshine blinded her for a moment. Kano saw every detail of what was happening. The ground trembled and shook. *Why didn't she notice? Why didn't she run?* The falling brick structure temporarily blocked out the sun, catching her attention a moment too late.

It was as if the heavy bells pulled the top down faster than the rest, violently filling the gap that used to be the nave with wreckage once again. Shock waves turned the solidly cobblestoned earth into what looked like a liquid, simultaneously shattering all the surrounding windows. Johanna became nothing but a small piece of the rubble.

Hollow reverberations from Kano's shouts went unheard beyond the coarse walls of the pit. His mind relentlessly dropped him back into another twisted fabrication. The research proposal was to be presented the next day and there was still plenty of work to be done.

She pushed herself upright in bed and her legs swung down, lining up perfectly with her slippers. After sliding into them, she stood up on her shiny, clutter-free laminate floor. The room was only twelve square meters, so she didn't need to take more than a step to slip into her pink bathrobe. A Christmas present from eight years ago.

She hadn't grown since she was fifteen. As a Dutch girl, she had always been the shortest in her class, although her natural beauty more than made up for the vertical challenge. Her features matched the ordered cleanliness of her room. Even upon waking up, the straight, blond hair scarcely needed attention. There was nothing puffy at all about her pale but perfectly proportioned face, set around deep, blue eyes.

A sigh came out as she unlocked the door and entered the chaos of the student house wrapping itself around her immaculate island. She gingerly stepped across the sticky hallway and opened the door of the bathroom. It was more like a small broom closet with a shower and toilet crammed together.

A tall person could hardly sit on the pot without knees banging into the door. Being short had its advantages. The walls were covered with stickers imitating Delft Blue tiles, but the subjects were not tulips or windmills. They showed Dutch boys and girls in traditional dress experimenting with various sexual positions.

After making it through another shower with shockingly abrupt variations in temperature thanks to the guys upstairs, she quickly dried off, wrapped the towel around her head, and slipped back into the pink robe, allowing fog to escape by opening the warped door.

She walked into an odor of decay when crossing the crooked threshold of the kitchen. A large pot with burnt rice on the bottom was trying to hide a stack of dirty plates, forks, and cups. It failed.

Cleaning up after someone else was simply not an option. Her studies demanded too much time and energy. Besides, she was principally against the notion. Her dishes were always immediately washed, dried, and placed back into their rightful positions within her tiny cabinet.

Just to get to a plate, she needed to remove three glasses. She did so, and kept one on the counter, filling it with barely chilled orange juice. The drafty window above the dying mini-fridge could provide enough of an assist in the winter, but in the warmer months, food tended to spoil rather quickly. She added an extra slice of overly soft cheese to her piece of bread. On the second sandwich she spread margarine and topped it with *hagelslag*, also known as chocolate sprinkles.

Johanna set the plate and glass on top of a wooden tray and took it carefully to her room. The door clicked shut and her tense body relaxed. It was as if her whole being had to hold its breath whenever she entered the house's common areas. When her meticulously maintained order returned, she could unwind.

Naturally, there was no room for a table and chairs. The desk, dresser, and bed left her with only a few square meters of uncovered flooring. She usually ate her meals on top of her precisely-made bed, afterward smoothing out all the wrinkles. She had trained herself never to drop a single crumb.

After swiftly cleaning up breakfast, she returned to her sanctuary, locking the door behind her. She made sure the blinds were completely shut and proceeded to slip out of her robe and into tight, black, synthetic pants. Kano stopped breathing and watched with intense desire, but couldn't quite make out her beautifully toned form in the dim light.

The sports bra interrupted his focus. It came down over her head, sliding itself into place like a climbing harness. It was followed by an indigo tank top which brought out even more depth of color in her ocean-like eyes.

The morning was warm enough that she didn't need a track jacket, so her matching shoes were forced to stand alone. The backpack, still packed from the day before, sidled over her prominent collar-bones, buckling across a flat stomach. Locking her door on the way out, she turned gingerly to the side and dropped down a narrow staircase with an angle steep enough to be a ladder. The racing bike awaited her in the hall. She only took it outside when the weather was good. After unlocking it, she pushed it out of the peeling door and swung a slender, athletic leg over its frame.

It would have taken most people twenty minutes of cycling to arrive at the University of Utrecht's main library. She did it in twelve. After wrapping one chain between the front spokes and another through the rear, both were slid inside the frame and attached to the semi-circular steel tube protruding from the concrete of an underground bike garage.

Keys in hand, she bounded up the steps two at a time. A gym membership was too expensive, so she had to find other ways to stay in prime condition. She knew the coming months in West Africa would demand it.

Her eyes were always drawn up as she entered the airy space, pronounced with wide staircases and black, Japanese flair. The modern structure housed numerous workspaces. Most of the computers were unoccupied on Sunday mornings. She ran up to the top of the staircase, getting the blood flowing before gluing herself to a chair for the morning. The view from above always gave her a jolt of motivation, even when it was early and she was the only one in the building.

She thought about what had to be done from her heightened vantage point. The research and most of the writing about land rights in Mali was finished, but she still needed to wrap up the final section and proofread the document. A presentation summarizing her proposal was also in the works. She let out an overwhelmed sigh.

Kano tried to warn her. He shouted and screamed. *Why couldn't she stop staring over the stupid railing and turn around?* Nobody would question her death. A stressed out student taking her own life was not a new story. The man in the hoodie approached softly from behind, grabbing her by the waist and pitching her over the edge like she was nothing more than a sack of potatoes. The scream scraped down his spine and he felt the sickening crunch which followed deep inside in his bones.

At the very last moment he caught a glimpse of the wicked man's face. It was as though he was looking into a mirror. He saw his own face glinting back at him from the shadows of the hoodie.

Ragged fingernails dug deeply into his skull. These waking nightmares had to stop or he would break completely. Perhaps he already had. This one was far more convincing than any of the previous hallucinations. He could still smell the stale recycled air preserving books and computers from the damp outdoors. Involuntary tremors produced drops of blood oozing toward his forehead. Finding control of his tattered mind was quickly becoming a lost hope.

Kano's soul shriveled even more than his emaciated body. He reached a level of despair and loneliness which he had never imagined possible. His precious mind, always a source of such strength and power, allowing him to look down upon and take advantage of nearly anyone he wished with ease, had crumbled and broken like a fortress made of sand.

That very night, he woke up thrashing through the throes of another nightmare. It felt as though a different sort of battle had taken place within. As his consciousness shifted from a desperate dreamworld to his forsaken pit, a presence disintegrated inside of him. He saw it flow into the space high above, out the thin slit just like a dark cloud of cigar smoke.

It brought back warped recollections of his Italian card game. Of his mysterious ability to read the minds of other poker players. Of his insatiable cravings for alcohol. Of the night he dislocated his shoulder. *Could it all be connected? No, it must be the corrosive effect of this place on my mind.* He comforted himself with the thought that he really was losing it, as that notion was easier to accept.

Kano quickly rose to his feet to see if any trace of the escaping wisp he had seen remained, but could detect nothing. He paced in small circles and felt lighter. He could stand straighter. The ever-present need for alcohol left him. His body didn't seem to hurt quite as much.

He also felt abandoned, somehow more alone and empty than before, but free. In stark contrast to what his confinement implied, he felt able to make his own decisions, to choose the direction of his life. After pacing his deprived muscles into a state of wobbly fatigue, he fell into a far more pleasant world of dreams with a subtle grin on his face, the kind usually associated with an insane asylum.

Phase Two: Recombination

Recombination *noun* / ˌriˌkambəˈneɪʃən /
*The rearrangement of genetic material by artificially
joining segments of DNA.
Transforming from a plasma into a gas.*

September 2009

The rasping voice of dehydration brought Kano out of his twisted slumber. He banged on the door and called for water as though his life depended on it. His perception of the world around him sharpened, augmented with extra sensitivity. After what seemed like an eternity, the water finally came. It tasted better than anything he had ever had before. He begged for more.

This time it was The Scholar who brought it. They had not met since their initial conversation weeks ago. The sound of English words quenched a thirst in his soul even more powerful than physical dehydration. It was as if, for the second time that morning, he had been released from some form of captivity even though the rigid walls confining him remained.

Kano barely registered the verbal meaning behind The Scholar's first few sentences. He basked in the tone and melody as if it were profound music played by one of the greatest orchestras on Earth. The last time The Scholar had visited, he addressed Kano in the same way a judge would inform a convicted felon of his fate. Before Kano tuned into the meaning of the actual words, he noticed the tone had changed to a professor lecturing a misguided student.

"....and as such I expect your family to take some time to gather the amount necessary to safeguard your release. It pleases me to see that your time alone has produced the necessary cleansing effect. While you remain with us, Souleymane and I will educate you in the ways of our world. Perhaps you will come to see we are not as different as you may imagine."

Kano's delight soured into slumped shoulders and a scowl as the implications of what he heard sank in. "And if I choose not to go along with your brainwashing?"

The slowly spoken reply echoed as if coming from a faraway place. "This is your right, although I do not see what else you plan to do with your time. I have read that many who experience extended periods of solitary confinement suffer from adverse and irreversible psychological effects. When I underwent a short time alone, comparable to your recent ordeal, it strengthened my connection with The Designer and enhanced my purpose on this Earth. I am providing you with a choice. You may submit your brain to continued deterioration from lack of stimulation, or you may reverse that trend by enriching your being through the study of Truth."

"And your Truth involves kidnapping, confinement, and extortion?"

The Scholar sighed ponderously. "Alas, I also have choices, and unlike the organization I partner with, I would never choose such tactics unless absolutely necessary. I do all that is in my power to assure the greater good is served. As they say, one must break eggs to make an omelet."

Kano responded with a tone of defiance, "I am the egg you choose to break. Why?"

"There is something in your eyes telling me you are not that egg." He paused to consider. "Based on what I have observed, I believe this has already been a spiritually healing experience for you. I also believe you will continue to grow during your time here. I know something profound happened last night. That is why we are speaking again."

Kano's mouth hung open for a few seconds. He tried to understand how The Scholar could have come to this conclusion, and realized everything was caught on camera. Whoever was watching the video would have witnessed strange behavior. "Last night? Last night I started having hallucinations." He smacked the side of his blood-stained head several times. "You said you read about solitary confinement. Hallucinations must be common. How can you think this is helping me?"

"If you actually believe what happened was a hallucination, I have misjudged you. I will assume your comment is either a product of your culture's growing denial of the spiritual realm or a blatant lie, something forbidden in my culture and punishable by exile in my household. I will never lie to you, although withholding certain truths may be necessary on occasion. Should that strong desire you exhibit for the English tongue continue, you must never again lie to me. Even though the choice to be here is not yours to make, it is you who will decide the quality of your captivity. This decision will determine the rest of your journey on this Earth. You have twenty-four hours to contemplate our conversation. We will speak again tomorrow morning."

Kano interrupted his exit. "Speaking of lies, where is Jerry?"

"I told you I would never lie to you. Jerry is a broken egg."

Kano's face turned white. "What does that mean?"

The Scholar spoke quietly and without emotion. "My disreputable allies demanded a hostage they could make an example of. They wanted to demonstrate their power in this region."

Kano turned his eyes to the floor and felt sick, unable to form a response as his captor walked out of the door. His mind did not stop turning for the rest of the day. He revisited every potential path to freedom. He visualized the situation from the perspective of each person he knew to be involved. By the time dinner came, a feeling of peace overwhelmed his being. He knew he only had one option: to follow along, at least superficially, with whatever propaganda he was forced to swallow.

By cooperating, at the very least, his mind would receive stimulation, and he might earn extra privileges. Any opportunity to be outside this cell could lead to a chance of escape. The mere thought of continuing with the torturous isolation experienced over the past three weeks was simply unbearable.

That night Kano tossed and turned, his sleep sabotaged by unrelenting dreams of helpless disaster. Dreams in which he was hunted but couldn't will his legs to move. Dreams of pavement rushing up to crush his body as he was thrown from high buildings after losing the fight. Dreams of car chases ending in the deafening roar of twisting metal and shattering glass.

Morning eventually came. A slight rush of air pushed toward Kano by the ancient door's noiseless motion roused him toward the waking world. The Scholar shuffled in and sat down on the chair Souleymane carefully positioned for him, resting quietly.

Kano sat up against the wall and with sarcasm laced into his tone said, "Good morning, *professor.*"

"Good morning. Today we shall begin with your training."

"Training? Who said I agreed?" Kano's eyes glared suspiciously.

"I believe you just did when you called me *professor,* although you may call me *The Scholar* as everyone else does. While I understand your hesitation to accept my role as your teacher, the sooner you release yourself from it the more effectively you will be able to use your time here among us." He motioned for his dark-skinned assistant to take away the bucket of filth.

"And what is it you want to train me to do? Will I be following his program," Kano nodded toward the young man, "and learn how to kidnap tourists? Or perhaps the intricacies of becoming a suicide bomber? A lesson in how to have my friends kill my hostages because I am too much of a coward to do it myself?" Kano's entire face quivered and turned red with rage.

The Scholar dismissed the emotions with a downward glance and a subtle shake of his head. "Your impressions of my household are misguided. Kidnappings are an unwelcome last resort. If a better option were available to me I would have taken it. We all must learn to make the best of the situations we find ourselves in."

"And how do you think Jerry is making the best of his situation? What about his friends and family? How are they making the best of it?"

He lifted his eyes and answered, "I hope and pray they are able to find peace with their Creator."

Kano leveled his gaze with fury. "Peace with their Creator!? What about you? How will you ever find peace knowing what you have done?"

"Alas, I cannot know what the future holds for me. But I do know my purpose in life. To fail to work toward that purpose means an eternity without peace. I am here to preserve and protect the powerful ideas and ways of living that have endured here for centuries. Ideas have more importance than any individual. Sacrifices and compromises must be reached. It is our way."

The bucket returned, dripping with clean water.

"What if it isn't our way?" Kano sat up straighter with his arms crossed and leaned away from the wall aggressively. "What if someone's life is more important than *your* obsolete ideas and backward way of living?"

The Scholar paused for a moment to consider. "It seems we will not reach common ground on this topic. Not yet anyway. You come from a culture where the individual is treated like a king, with rights and privileges unknown to us. I am, relative to the people of my city, a wealthy and powerful man. Yet, the well-being of my household comes before my own wishes and desires. It is my role to serve them."

Kano spoke to the floor with menace in his voice. "Fine, but what you did to Jerry is unforgivable."

"I do not ask for your forgiveness. I merely ask you to put what has happened behind and focus on what is to come." The Scholar continued to sit with one hand on his lap, the other resting on a staff, without moving.

Kano considered this and decided to play along, resolving to bring down this strangely educated terrorist after finding a way to escape. He brought his eyes up to face his captor and forced himself to shift into a submissive tone. "You said you were locked up before. How did you make the best of it?"

"I was not confined in the same way you are. As my ancestors before me, I have learned to avoid dangerous situations. Do not think our city is a stranger to foreign occupation."

"So you kidnapped me? To scare away the white people?" Kano rolled his eyes.

"The reasons why I am detaining you are not the purpose of my visit this morning. We are here to discuss your training. You will begin by studying the Arabic language. You can think of it as the Latin of Timbuktu. There aren't so many who speak it today, but it is the basis for much of the learning and history within these walls."

"Why would I want to learn about the history of this city?"

Souleymane shifted nervously on his feet, wishing he could understand what was being spoken about with such intensity.

"You are the one who must examine your own motivations. I will tell you this. I assume you are like so many other Americans who don't understand their place on this Earth. By learning about *our* origins and culture you will come to understand your own in a new way. This will lead you to your proper place. Is this not the reason why you are here?"

Kano actually thought about the question for a moment and realized he had never really understood his reasons for coming to Mali. "I came to this country for some adventure and exploration, not to be locked away in an oven-like pit while my family sells everything they have to get me out."

"And what is it within you that seeks adventure and exploration?"

Kano thought again for a moment and shrugged. "Boredom."

"Yes, a concept we are rather unfamiliar with here, even though so many of us cannot find work. You seem to be traveling the world with the hope your adventures will reveal something to you about yourself. Once you are confident your place has been found, boredom will be something of the past. Trust that my methods, in time, will bring you to your place."

Kano replied with an undertone of condescension. "And what would those methods be?"

"Routine and discipline are paramount in my household. You will rise with the sun and every day shall be filled with its light. Allow me to formally introduce you to Souleymane." At the mention of his name the slightly slumped, unsure shoulders straightened. The Scholar motioned for the patient figure to set down his gun and come in from the hall. "He will continue to care for you. He will take control of your growth. No minute will be wasted. Mental, physical, and spiritual aspects of your being will all be pushed to their limits. Solitude was the first step in your training. You have reached the threshold of peace. Now we can build."

Kano sighed with resignation.

"Once every week I will speak with you unless Souleymane suggests differently. Our conversations will become more frequent at a later point in your journey. Please remember that even as a prisoner you are a part of my household and this means that until your family attains the proper resources, you will abide in my protection and gain privileges as long as you follow our rules and customs."

Kano's ears perked up at the word *privileges,* his thoughts jumping toward the possibility of escape.

Once again, the slight movement of air caused by the ornate door swinging in woke the prisoner from another night of tremulous sleep. The young, black man in a white robe stared down with a look of bewilderment. After three weeks he still hadn't grown accustomed to the ghostly, tortured presence. White people usually came in big expensive vehicles and carried mountains of respect wherever they traveled. They were the closest thing to royalty he had witnessed in person. Standing over what he knew to be one of those noble *Toubobous* in such a lowly state did not make sense. It seemed wrong.

There was something odd about the emaciated, unearthly face which reminded him of the Chinese people who built the tall buildings and roads. It wasn't quite like the other white faces he had seen. He simply didn't know what to make of the wretched figure lying before him.

Kano interpreted the drawn-out stare as an invitation to speak, so he asked, "Souleymane, what is your last name?"

Souleymane held a tray of food, and, to Kano's dismay, nothing else. He cocked his head to the side and continued to stare.

"Your name? Don't you speak English?" More stares. Kano wondered how far away the AK-47 was. He had hoped to overpower him and retrieve the weapon to make an escape. He tried again. *"Français?"*

"Oui," replied the man with a low, rather guarded voice.

Kano spoke slowly to exchange names. *"Mon nom Kano Griffin. Votre nom?"*

"Souleymane Samaké," came the deep reply, followed by something Kano didn't understand.

"Ok, we got the names out of the way, but I don't much speak French...er...*Je parlay pas Français."*

Souleymane paused.

Kano took a moment to think. He knew almost no one in the North spoke Bambara, the language he had learned while living in the South, but the individual standing in front of him did not look like the locals. He gave it a shot. *"I bey Bamanankan men?"*

Souleymane's face lit up as if he had won the lottery. His native language, coming from a *Toubobou*, especially one who didn't speak French very well, must be a sign from Allah. He answered back with surprise in Bambara. "How do you know my mother tongue?"

Kano confidently replied in Bambara, although his grammar was far from perfect. "I was live in Siby for some time. Nice people they learn me how to speak."

Souleymane beamed. "Yes, yes! There are very good people in the South where I come from. I heard that Siby is a beautiful place from some of the travelers on my bus. Here in the North customs are different. There are still many good people, but they are not as friendly."

"So what brings you to here where they make you to carry that thing around?" Kano was trying to ask about the AK-47 Souleymane had left somewhere.

"It is simply the will of Allah. I am fortunate to be trained to wield my mind, body, and spirit in service to Him."

"Are you serve Allah or The Scholar?" Kano's eyes narrowed.

"It is one and the same. The Scholar serves Allah, so as I serve him, I also serve Allah." He gestured to the heavens.

"What if The Scholar makes wrong understand of Allah?"

"The Scholar understands more than I could ever hope to. He memorized much of the Koran and knows the world as one who has traveled in it for many years."

"But not it possible that he can wrong be?"

At this Souleymane became angry without really knowing why, and raised his voice, tilting the tray so the food almost spilled. "Should we speak, we will speak about other things. Nothing more about The Scholar. He is a great man and shall always be!" He emphasized this proclamation with a drawn out scowl.

Souleymane let the tray clatter onto the floor and turned his back toward Kano, a strong insult, sealing the door behind him as he stormed down the white hallway, unable to understand his emotional reaction.

News of their only child's capture had reached Kano's parents. It hit their unexpectedly tenuous lifestyle like a rocket launched into piled snow drifts clinging to the edge of a craggy mountain, releasing a beautiful but terrible torrent of energy and destruction, crushing everything and everyone in its path.

The marriage itself was the first thing to shatter as if it was a poorly built ski shack high up on the slope, disintegrating under the avalanche. Trees of friendships were torn and twisted like toothpicks; even the glamorous house they lived in bounced away, a huge boulder hurled by the advancing wall of snow.

The Scholar, through secretive channels which could never be traced back to him, demanded a sum of three million US dollars if they ever wanted to see their son alive again. The insurance they had purchased to cover their travels in Mexico should have provided the silver bullet, but the company balked at the amount, and a small army of lawyers had to fight for months to extract a clean million from the inexorable underwriters.

The Scholar's response to this paltry sum was a simple laugh. As he said from the start, this was not a negotiation. Subsequently, the house sale partnered with unending appeals to everyone from the government itself to friends and neighbors. They would squeeze all their contacts until nothing remained. Even the treasured wine collection was destined to be auctioned off.

This painful process was packed with fights, sleepless nights, snowballing bitterness, and countless smoldering bridges fueled more by perceived obligation than anything else. At the distant end of the turmoil they would still be short, eventually coming up with a final total just shy of 2.3 million.

The day Kano met with Souleymane in that first, fiery encounter, his diet changed. Souleymane reluctantly joined him, still stinging from the attack on The Scholar's authority. They ate a hot and rather delicious meal.

The cuisine was exotic to even Kano's well-traveled palate. After the tasteless slop he had grown accustomed to, the spices, texture, and substance were a fresh breeze invigorating his hot and stuffy cell.

Souleymane brought in a worn desk and chair reminiscent of a sixth grade classroom about one hundred years ago. It still had an ink well bored into the top and was much too small for Kano.

On top of the desk, a workbook created for native English speakers trying to learn Arabic waited to be unwrapped. Alongside the book sat a neatly placed notebook and two pencils. Out of the inkwell rose a tall candle and several matches. When Souleymane finished arranging everything to perfection, he looked at Kano and said in Bambara,

"Now we begin. I will tell you a few small things about Arabic. You may ask questions. This book has much to teach you."

Kano looked up at his captor with suspicion. "The Scholar he said you my routine make. What we do every day?"

"You must learn to rise with the sun, as The Scholar says. After bathing and before breakfast, our time is for prayer and meditation. After breakfast and before lunch you will sit at this desk and learn. After eating lunch together we will again take part in prayer and meditation. Then comes your physical training." A sly grin crept across his face. "This is something I am told white men cannot do. You will be hungry after, so we will have a large dinner and talk over the day. Then I will light the candle at your desk and you will study until it burns out. Prayer and meditation will return you to the world of dreams."

"I see. Seven or eight hours studying every day?"

"Yes. The Scholar expects you to know everything in the book when he meets with you next week. He will test you."

"What if I don't?"

Souleymane paused. "Our food will not be so tasty."

Kano raised an eyebrow. "You get trouble too?"

"Of course. As your teacher, I share your success and also your failure."

Kano allowed a shadow of a grin to creep across his face. "What is when I know book done early?"

Souleymane offered a condescending frown in response. "Your body will be very tired from our training; it will not let that happen."

"And if it does?"

"Perhaps you will be given extra training in prayer and meditation. The Scholar thinks this will be a weak place for you."

"Your reward?"

"I am a servant of The Scholar." Souleymane bowed his head with genuine respect. "My greatest reward is the success of my student."

After a short description of how to read Arabic, Souleymane left Kano alone for his first session of study. Kano's brain was tangled and slow after weeks of mind-warping solitude. He felt the same way his grumbling Chevy Tahoe must have when he forced it to start on one of those torturous, sub-zero mornings in Michigan. The engine would slowly turn over with a tired cringe. Fortunately, after a few minutes, the big V8 was running smoothly enough to pump a small measure of heat into the frigid cabin.

It took more than a few minutes before Kano could process the words smoothly and focus on their meaning. Unknown characters made it much more difficult to learn than the bits and pieces of European languages he had picked up during his travels.

Heat levels gradually increased until drops of sweat threatened to fall from his face onto the workbook below. By the time Souleymane returned for lunch, a stormy headache was building and his stomach rumbled as if to echo the sentiment.

Kano didn't have questions about the material, so they ate without speaking as was the custom in the South. After the last bits of a rather small but tasty chicken were finished, Souleymane announced in a deeply proud Bambara voice that it was nearly time to go outside into the blazing sunshine. He told Kano with a bright smile, "It will be harder than any white man can handle, so The Scholar said you will need to darken yourself. Can you really change the color of your skin like a chameleon?" He asked the question with great skepticism. Kano shrugged. His head was throbbing.

Souleymane continued, "After your time spent in prayer and meditation, we will begin by taking a walk. Do not think of running as you could never go farther or faster than me. Besides, you have no money, so where could you hide? White people are not very welcome here. This is not Siby."

"I no can run in sun anyway." Although Kano knew he would be waiting intently for any small opportunity for escape to present itself. He figured he could find his way back to the hotel where the pilots stayed, and hopefully they would be there to take him back to Bamako. His eyes gleamed with the hope of waking up from this nightmare.

After an hour of rest, his hopes rose as he followed Souleymane beyond the ornate door and into the white hallway where the ceiling was much lower than his cell. After passing several other doors, his much anticipated first breath of outside air in what felt like months hit his lungs with a touch of fire. Nothing but the desert rose to meet him. The compound was situated on the northern edge of Timbuktu. His exposed skin burned and every bit of fabric clung to his drenched body within ten minutes. The heat of the sand seemed to melt his shoes. Each step took extra effort. Ancient, powdery grains gave way under his diminished weight like quicksand. Running would be nearly impossible. His lungs would probably turn into raisins after a few short minutes. Hope shriveled.

Kano looked over at Souleymane who smiled widely in return. One or two drops of sweat barely formed on his brow. He appeared to be taking a walk in a park on a warm spring day.

Their hike lasted an hour. Monotonous sand dunes afforded nothing more than a glimpse of the city upon their return to the compound. Kano felt like the entire afternoon had passed. By the time he stumbled back into his cell he could barely see. The glaring sun scorched his eyes into a state dangerously close to blindness. Souleymane brought him a jug of water and he drank the whole thing before collapsing onto his dirty mat. He wasn't sure if it really was that hot outside or if the desperate weeks alone in the dark pit had taken more out of him than he had imagined. Perhaps a bit of both.

After offering a moment to recover, Souleymane said, "This was the beginning of your endurance training. We must also train you in strength. We begin simply, like this." Souleymane dropped down for some pushups. "You must join me."

Kano did, but after twenty seconds he collapsed onto the concrete. "Ten more! Up."

The workout continued with a dizzying relentlessness which hit every muscle in Kano's body like a hammer. Kano used to lift more than nearly anyone else at the gym, but this was a whole new level of exertion using nothing but the floor, the wall, and his own body weight.

By the time dinner filled the sweaty confines with its delicious aromas, Kano's shaking arm could barely lift the food to his mouth. Heavenly spices and flavors were almost entirely lost to his exhaustion. After the bowl was finished, Kano turned his prayer and meditation time into a nap. It was kept short as Souleymane quickly set up the desk with a candle which would burn for about three hours.

Kano took his place and struggled immensely to keep his aching eyelids open until it was time for bed. Twice, he nodded off but was awakened by a loud banging against his locked door. Clearly the camera was being monitored.

After the candle finally burned itself out, the hard floor felt feather-soft to Kano. Within seconds of lying down, he was out. The terrifying world of dreams was kept at bay; not a single color, shape or sound floated up into his deeply sleeping consciousness.

Kano went from one extreme to another. Three weeks of solitary confinement in a kiln-like pit had driven him beyond the blurred edges of sanity. Now his training with Souleymane pushed him over and above different sorts of limits. Any down time he had was meant to be used for prayer and meditation, but in truth, it was simply a recovery period. At least his brain and body were no longer fermenting into mush.

Hours became days and days turned into weeks as the routine sharpened his mind and hardened his body. The quality of their meals had not dropped. If anything, the food improved. Kano had never slept so well in his life, despite the fact he remained without a bed. The weather felt like it was cooling off. Nights had a certain chill which seemed to be missing before. Daily walks in and among the endlessly shifting dunes included a small amount of running.

The Scholar was impressed with his grasp of written Arabic. One morning, the venerable old man shuffled into Kano's cell for their weekly meeting and carefully sat in the chair Souleymane provided, giving silence a few moments to overtake the room.

He lit a pipe and Kano shuddered. The image of smoke drifting toward the open vent brought him back to the nightmarish vision he experienced not so long ago. Eventually, The Scholar began in his customarily slow, methodical tone. "I have seen your progress grow quickly. Clearly you are a capable student. I believe the time has come for you to apply your skills to the study of ancient texts I have waiting to be translated. You will work together with Souleymane. He will translate into Bambara while you translate into English."

"What are the texts about?"

"Some are simple accounts of historical events that have happened in my city. There are also many teachings containing wisdom of the ages."

"Why do you want them translated?"

He slowly blew more smoke into the room before speaking. "The people of the South are Animists at heart even though they pray in a mosque. The Western World has lost its soul, cruel though it once was. Timbuktu was a great center of learning for many years. The wisdom of this place is a light that can shine into the shadowy places of our Earth."

"I thought you wanted to wipe out those places, or rule them with Islamic law," Kano quickly replied in a harsh tone.

The Scholar took another drag and slowly released the smoke in three distinct puffs. "Once again, you have mistaken me for my allies. I am not Al Qaeda. I work with them out of necessity. While that uneducated organization and I both believe the corruption and evil rampant on this earth must end, I am able to separate a soul from its deeds. Al Qaeda chooses a journey of destruction while I choose to restore and resurrect ancient truths and wisdom. Surely their ruinous path will spread to my household unless they do not already see me as one of their own."

Kano paused for a moment, looking down while he considered the logic of this explanation. "But if you leave the door open for them, and help their cause, isn't that even worse?"

Souleymane stood nearby, knowing they spoke of something important as frustration mushroomed within him. He whispered a prayer to Allah that someday he would also command the English language.

"I believe you have a saying. Something about keeping your friends close and your enemies closer…"

"So what are they? Friends or enemies?"

The Scholar relaxed and spoke gracefully, gesturing with his long fingers for emphasis. "A bit of both, I suppose. The world is not the black and white place your culture has led you to believe. Because they pose a threat to all that I am, all that this city is, I must monitor their organization closely. The best way to do this is by becoming one of them. We do share some common beliefs."

Kano paused for another moment to think. "But won't you lose yourself? When do you stop being you and start being one of them?"

"Ahhh, the *us and them* view of the world. This has torn your country apart before. It will do so again. By the time your people realize there is no such thing it will be too late."

"Too late for what?"

The indigo eyes narrowed slightly. "We can discuss this another day. You are not yet ready. There remains work to be done."

"So why don't you translate these documents yourself? Your English is nearly perfect."

An understated sense of urgency entered his resonant, sandy voice. "You must understand my library contains over forty-five thousand crumbling manuscripts and it would take more years than remain in my lifetime to preserve and translate them properly. I know you will show them the respect and attention they deserve."

"I am sure if I don't Souleymane will put a bullet through my leg, so I suppose you have nothing to worry about."

He waved his pipe nonchalantly in the direction of the door. "Souleymane would never wish such a thing upon you, but of course he will act if given no choice. He tells me your training is going rather well and you are exceeding expectations. I trust you have been enjoying your meals. That is all for today. Souleymane will bring instructions for handling and translating the manuscripts."

In the beginning, translation was a slow, meticulous process. Kano frequently needed to look up words in his Arabic/English dictionary to achieve the most direct result possible. Souleymane carried in a second desk to work alongside his intensely focused pupil, using his best Bambara, although he did not have the luxury of a dictionary.

Souleymane's translations were less direct. They were an attempt to capture the meaning and reproduce it in the commonly spoken language. He wondered how much it really mattered; once he overheard pasty-skinned *Toubobous* on the bus discussing loudly in French the fact that three-quarters of his fellow Malians were illiterate. His focus shifted from Bambara, which was always finished quickly, to understanding the English Kano recorded. He would interrupt from time to time to ask questions about what was written.

Kano developed the habit of reading aloud his sentences so Souleymane could learn how the words were pronounced. Souleymane was surprised that even though the letters looked basically the same as

French, they could carry such a different sound. The Scholar spoke English well, therefore it must be an important language, so he worked even harder to understand it.

The days continued to blend together into weeks and months until a change in the weather finally gave Kano a point of reference. His nose bled and continued to do so off and on throughout the day. During their regular excursion into the dunes, the predictably endless landscape transformed. First, the horizon disappeared. Shortly after, a thickening haze filled the air until even the omnipresent sun failed to shine. Kano stopped abruptly to stare and asked Souleymane in English, "What is happening? Is this dangerous?"

They were developing the habit of speaking to each other in their native languages. It turned out to be the most efficient form of communication, and efficiency was important with such a brutal routine. Souleymane replied in Bambara, "During this time of year winds come from the North scraping up the smallest bits of desert and carrying them through the air. Sometimes it is so bad you cannot breathe without a cloth to filter the dust. It is said the effects reach across oceans."

"Does it have a name?" Kano dabbed at his nose.

"Of course, doesn't everything have a name? It is known as the *Harmattan*."

"Is that why my nose is bleeding?" He pinched it to stem the flow.

"I think so." Souleymane nodded in thought. "The dry air can even kill trees. Death that comes from the desert cannot be taken lightly."

Kano lifted an eyebrow. "You mean this kills people?"

"Sometimes, but there are many things from the desert that kill people. The desert is Death itself."

"Do you fear the desert?"

Souleymane coughed. "Yes. Any person who can think clear thoughts must fear the desert. Not only the heat but the way that heat dries up the very rains themselves, making way for even more heat." Souleymane lowered his voice as if someone might be listening in. "The people who cross over bring me the most concern. It is said, surviving such a journey requires a piece of the soul to be sacrificed. The part that remains is often twisted and without mercy." They turned their backs to the growing haze so the hike toward the compound could be completed before the mild sandstorm enveloped everything.

"How do people make it across?" Kano nervously picked up his pace.

"They have done it for thousands of years. In some ways trucks have made it easier. In other ways harder." He motioned to the bumpy buildings spreading before them in the distance. "This city has been sought after by wise men and conquering armies for many generations. The Scholar has told me this. His family protected manuscripts from every invasion and band of thieves that have come to claim them. Moroccans did terrible damage to what was a great city over four hundred years ago. The practice of learning evaporated, and the French allowed the remains to crumble away into what little is left today."

Kano allowed a bit of irritation to slip into his English, "But the French brought new things. Good things. Language. Government. Sanitation. Those still are here."

Souleymane stopped with his hands on his hips and bored into Kano with deeply brown eyes. "Who is to say they are good? They stripped my country of its dignity and all that remains is a government too weak to fully bring together the North and South. Most of the country takes care of itself like it always has and speaks little French."

"How did the French strip your dignity? Haven't Malians been living basically the same way for thousands of years? They are the happiest people I have ever met!"

Souleymane sighed and looked back to make sure the dust cloud was not building too quickly. "I will tell you a story of what happened in the village where I was born, Sakoro. I heard this story spoken by one of the Elders when I asked him about something I had found in the forest. The Scholar has shown me pictures of many things in the world, and one picture in particular reminds me of the thing I found in the forest. He called it something like 'Stonhegge' and said it was somewhere in England."

"You mean *Stonehenge*." Kano's curiosity was aroused.

"That was it. The Elder told me I had stumbled upon the ruins of a fortress his grandparents helped build for protection against the French. The walls were once so thick a horse could ride on top of them. Colonizers and their mercenaries could not capture slaves from the village because everyone would run inside the fort for protection. The people were kept safe by its walls for many, many years, although the French did not forget this insult to their authority. Long after the slave trade ended, they came with airplanes. They dropped bombs inside the walls killing many, many people. All because we would not give up our best men to them." Souleymane paused for effect; he was a natural storyteller. "Now the French pretend to be our friends, but such deep scars are never forgotten."

Kano was silent as they passed over a small dune. He had learned a lot about slaves in school, and how difficult their lives were in America, but he had never considered the place they came from. *They had families and homes. Some were even able to build a successful defense against slave traders.*

He felt dizzy. Perhaps from the dust filling the air, or perhaps because he felt his world slipping and shifting beneath him like desert sands. He realized he could never go back to life as it was before he left America, and a faint smile crept across his face as he realized this was probably a good thing.

His life had been defined by his pursuit of pleasure and a voracious need to exceed his peers in every possible way, which was rarely much of a challenge. He realized he lacked purpose and direction. It was time to set his own path, to accomplish something unique.

Those first words The Scholar had spoken to him resounded with truth. He had a purpose which went beyond that of a prisoner. It was here he would discover his future. Or at least be pointed in the right direction. This place would shape his character and resolve it into something which could impact the world.

The fear he would die as a prisoner completely left him, as if an unexpected thunderstorm had come to quench Californian wildfires fueled by voracious Santa Ana winds. In that moment, he gave up the constant vigilance it took to search for any opportunity for escape; he knew he would leave when the time was right.

Kano's whole being shifted out of a state of tension as though he had exited rush hour traffic on Los Angeles's 405 freeway and was now winding down a quiet, country road. He had no clue where it was taking him. That felt just fine.

Phase Three: Deposition

Deposition   *noun*   / ˌdɛpəˈzɪʃən /
The formation of a substance, layer by layer, over the course of time.
Transforming from a gas directly into a solid.

October 2009

Steam rose and twisted from heaped couscous in a particular manner which made Kano rather uneasy. He tried to break the intangible feeling with conversation. "Don't you ever get tired of eating the same stuff?"

Souleymane continued the habit of replying to Kano's English with Bambara. "Are you joking? This is the best food I have ever had in my life. We get vegetables *and* meat at every meal. There aren't even rocks in it. How could you possibly get tired of this?"

Kano released a knowing smile. "You can get tired of anything that happens too much. Even if you really like it at first."

After shaking his head in disbelief, Souleymane took another bite of fish. "I would never get tired of eating this way if it were possible to do so for the rest of my days."

He laughed. "That is only because you haven't had anything better. You can't even imagine what exists!"

Souleymane pondered this deeply and did not reply for several minutes. "Perhaps you are right." He eventually replied, his curiosity taking control. "Tell me about the best food you have eaten."

Kano thought about this while taking a deep drink of water. "I must say, the best meal I have ever had was right here in Mali, down in Bamako. Although, that may have been more about the company than the food." He felt a sinking sensation and tried to shift the focus of their conversation. "Memories have a funny way of altering themselves as time passes. You must understand, there is more to food than flavor, texture, and nutrition. It is about the feeling you have when you eat it. The sounds, light, and smells in the air. Creating memories that come flooding back later on."

Souleymane laughed out loud, covering his mouth to hold back any bits of food searching for an escape route. "How could you possibly think up such nonsense? We must be giving you too much free time. Your mind is warping with ridiculous ideas. Food is simply the fuel we need to get on with our lives. Now get on with your story. Tell me about the best food there is."

With a slight wariness in his voice, Kano continued. "Everyone has their own opinion of where the best food is, but I don't want to talk about that meal in Bamako. Let me tell you about two other meals instead."

As he told the story, he became immersed in memory, detaching himself from the present as his mind traveled back to Ann Arbor, Michigan. It was a warm spring evening in 2008. Kano turned right onto Main Street from Packard and immediately took another right, illegally parking his dirty, dark grey Tahoe next to a bank where he knew nobody would check after six.

Ryan sat in the passenger seat and two rather attractive young women were in the back. The group was going to the Chop House. Ryan had hit a home run, engineering-style, and they needed to celebrate. A generous signing bonus would take another dent. Most of it went toward a down payment on a 2006 Acura TSX. He loved that silver, precisely-built machine more than any other car, and promised to drive it until the rust got so bad he felt the same pain he imagined the car must feel.

Ryan's new job would be in Seattle, working for Boeing. The aerospace industry offered lucrative opportunities, but finding one stacking up to his new position was nearly impossible. He started out at 83k per year, plus benefits, and had the freedom to run his own research projects relating to the newly developing field of sustainability. The resources they were putting at his disposal would have made his professors jealous.

Kano, on the other hand, had a father who kept bugging him about opportunities in his company. Kano ignored these intrusions, saying he had other plans. In truth, he was clueless. Dinner at the Chop House was enough of a plan for now.

Wine did its work in helping to animate the conversation. The celebration pulsed with uncertainty and excitement about the future. By the time the main course arrived, Kano was ravenous. The medium-rare eleven ounce filet mignon disappeared before his eyes. He could have sliced it with a butter knife.

Garlic mashed potatoes, grilled asparagus with parmesan, and sautéed wild mushrooms did not last much longer. Delicious flavors and electric energy filled the air around their table, giving way to sublime creations from the pastry chef.

After penguin-like servers had done their part, the party of four descended into the Wine Cellar for another bottle. The late hour eventually sapped the crackling energy from the group. Kano was too drunk to drive home, but he did it anyway. He had already proven the Tahoe could go just about anywhere. Fortunately, no more mailboxes needed to be sacrificed on this particular evening.

He was in a solitary sort of mood. After dropping everyone off, he checked the balance in his student checking account. This was where he kept his poker money; a convenient way to buy things without his parent's knowledge. His cumulative pot had become rather massive after years of obsessively playing Party Poker, an online game. Then he turned on the TV.

The next afternoon, he woke up with a headache and vaguely remembered making yet another bad judgment call the night before. It all rushed back to him. He was flipping through channels when a pizza advertisement caught his attention. He had always wanted to visit Italy. Money was of little consequence. Final exams took place in two weeks. A job was waiting for him if he wanted it. No responsibilities or commitments. He had booked a ticket to Rome. This time, he decided to stick with his drunken logic and get on the plane.

The safety card inside the vinyl pouch Kano's knees pressed up against said he was riding in a Boeing 767. This made him wonder how Ryan's dream job was starting out. He didn't sleep well over the Atlantic.

After a long layover, the much smaller airplane taxied to a halt at Fiumicino Airport. Stale air filled with metallic sounds of over one hundred people simultaneously unclasping their seat belts. His baggage came through unscathed and soon he stood on the platform waiting for the next bus to whisk him toward Termini Station in the center of Rome.

As the doors hissed open, humid night air welcomed Kano like a warm kiss. People and noise surrounded him. He set forth into the Eternal City. Although he had been traveling all day, there was not a tired bone in his body. He wasn't hungry either, but his first mission was to get a slice of pizza—the kind that caught his attention on the TV screen two weeks before. He was determined to enjoy every bite.

It wasn't long before he came upon a promising pizzeria, picked a table, and sat down. The menu didn't offer slices, only whole pizzas. No matter, he thought, leftovers will be good for lunch tomorrow.

After far too much time spent waiting, the pizza was set before him, and he let out a small sigh of disappointment. The entire thing amounted to a couple of slices. It was way too thin. A big cracker with sauce and a few morsels scattered about on top. Strangely, it was not cut, and there was no pizza cutter to be seen. All he had been given was a fork and a knife, but he made do.

The subsequent explosion of flavor flipped his doubts upside-down. *How could such a meager presentation have so much hidden inside?* Even though the thin crust was scantily clad with cheese and toppings, it proved more than enough to satisfy his appetite. It embodied the very taste of freedom.

After paying the bill, he set out to find a place to sleep. Hotels were not in short supply, and he wasn't picky, so the choice was quickly made. He ran into a wave of tiredness thick as a marble wall, and collapsed onto the freshly made bed still wearing his clothes, entering a sleep so deep he didn't dream.

Kano drifted back toward the present, facing his captor. "As you can see, food can be far more delicious than what we eat every day. It is about more than food, though. The steak dinner was a celebration of finishing school, of a promising future. The pizza was all about freedom and living in a world that can exceed my expectations."

"I must know," Souleymane said with his eyes to the ground, "how much did that steak dinner cost?"

Kano laughed uncomfortably, "Oh I don't know, three or four hundred dollars? It was nothing compared to Ryan's signing bonus…"

After sadly shaking his head while making the calculation, he replied, "You know, the cost of your meal was enough to feed a whole family in my village of Sakoro, breakfast, lunch and dinner, for a complete year."

"I suppose you are right," came the thoughtful reply, "but then, who in your village could get a job at Boeing?"

"Nobody. This is a topic for another conversation, although I will say that you should know well enough why. It has little to do with the differences in human potential between this Ryan you speak of and somebody from my village." Souleymane gave his anger a moment to disperse throughout the cell before continuing. "And what about your special meal in Bamako? What was that about?"

Kano looked away and shifted uncomfortably. The animated color drained from his face. "Tonight is not the night for that, either. We have a routine that needs to be finished."

Souleymane allowed silence to fill the air and then lowered his voice and replied, "I believe tonight is indeed the night. Clearly you have something that must be discussed. This can replace a portion of our translation duties."

Kano swallowed uncomfortably and continued to sit in silence. He allowed his thoughts to wander back to that dinner not so long ago, although it felt like a different lifetime. With reluctance, he slowly and quietly related his experience to Souleymane with a feeling of longing, once again immersing himself in the flavors and emotions of that extraordinary night.

Café du Fleuve was a riot of oranges, pinks, yellows, and every bright and lively shade in between. The colors did their best to cover up the fact that the room looked like a cramped church nave with aisles on either side designed by opposing master builders. One aisle was set off by short, square poles holding up incredibly shallow arches. Thick, round columns supported unnecessarily wide beams on the other. The unbalanced look was accented by a mismatched tile floor which was, like all the tile floors Kano had seen in Mali, uneven and poorly finished.

The only acoustic dampener in the room apart from bright yellow and red tablecloths was an undersized knick-knack shelf clinging to the wall as if someone had cut it out of a tree using nothing but a hatchet. There was no mistaking they were dining in Africa.

Kano pulled out Johanna's chair with exaggerated motions, mocking the true gentleman. The conversation leading up to the main course was light and flirtatious, just like the wine they drank. By the time steaks were served, the world seemed to stand still.

Butter knives barely needed encouragement to cut through perfectly cooked tenderloin. Each bite came directly out of a culinary magazine. It melted in their mouths. Without the intention of doing so, Kano and Johanna both upheld the local custom of silence during the meal.

It wasn't long before the last delicious morsel disappeared and Kano broke the trance by asking incredulously, "Where did they get those steaks? Were they flown in from France?"

"Not a chance. The French would never part from such a thing of beauty."

"But I have seen the cows here. They look like refugees."

"You haven't seen all the cows here. Besides, in your country the food has plastic added to keep it from falling apart. You just aren't used to real food." She sipped on the last bit of wine with a grin.

"Oh, and you are going to tell me your country is any different?"

She pointed her knife at him menacingly. "At least we don't put corn syrup in everything. Read any label. The only sweetener you will find is sugar."

"Fair enough. But have you had a steak like that before?"

"Of course. But not in the Netherlands."

"Where then?"

"France."

"Figures. When was this?"

"Last year."

"What was the occasion?"

"Fifth anniversary trip." An awkward silence ensued.

"What anniversary?! I don't see a ring..." Kano asked with a rare show of worry in his eyes.

"Just my boyfriend. It had been five years since we met. Marriage isn't so popular with the Dutch. I mean, clearly it doesn't work out too well for you Americans."

Kano averted his gaze for a moment. "I suppose not. I didn't hear you say ex-boyfriend."

"Probably because I didn't."

His heart stopped for a moment. His voice softened as he managed to ask, "Why are you telling me this now?"

Johanna raised an eyebrow with surprise. "I assumed you knew. It is on my Facebook page."

"What makes you think I looked at your Facebook page?"

"I thought everyone did nowadays."

"You thought wrong. I have been staying away from technology since I got here."

"Noble of you. Still happy with your choice?" She drove her condescending tone home with a provocative grin.

Infuriated, but still able to rely on his poker face, Kano politely excused himself and headed toward the toilets. He stared into the oddly shaped mirror vacantly as his brain engaged the problem full on, instantly pushing away lingering effects of the wine. He had messed around with girls who had boyfriends before. The problem was, given the rate at which his heart was currently beating, he knew this wasn't just messing around.

Nearly six years was a long time to be with someone. On the other hand, she seemed to be enjoying the male attention in anything but a guarded fashion. Perhaps it was an American thing, but girls who are in love with their boyfriends can't stop talking about them. She hadn't mentioned this guy yet. His logic quickly concluded he had a shot. The way forward was to proceed delicately. He resolved simply to ignore this unwelcome revelation.

On the way back to the table he changed his mind, and for the first time in his countless adventures with women, he decided to take the Dutch approach: honest and direct. After his chair awkwardly screeched back into place, poker face in full force, he asked, "So, tell me about this guy. I don't even know his name. How does he feel about you being here?"

"I don't think he really notices I am gone. We aren't living together. Never have." Kano began to feel a tide of relief and allowed his face to relax under its influence. "In fact, he is five years older than me and lives in a different city. We usually see each other on the weekends, but I know I am not the only girl who visits his place. He was my first real boyfriend. Mali has somehow changed my perspective on our relationship. I guess a bit of distance can do that."

Kano was having trouble holding down a smile. "Changed your perspective in what way?"

"Well, I always thought what we had was normal, because for me it was." She finished her wine and rocked the top-heavy glass in circles. "Coming here, I have seen people live their lives in such a pure and open way, devoid of the masks Westerners wear. I realized my whole relationship with him has become a mask. It is a thing of convenience. People don't expect me to be single, so I am not. It allows me to keep my distance from other guys."

"And why would you want to keep your distance from other guys? Waiting for me to come along?"

She rolled her eyes. "There are more important things in life than flirting and whatever comes after that. In regards to boys, I don't need to sample every one that comes along to figure out who I want to spend the rest of my life with, even though it is the most important decision I will make."

They paused as the waiter discreetly came to pour them more wine.

Kano took a large sip and then plunged in. "The rest of our lives? What are we, thirty-five years old? I have learned a few things from living in this country too. Malians are the happiest people I have ever met. They don't think past tomorrow. One day I was walking around Siby and I came across a rusty contraption which looked like a cross between a UFO and a backyard barbecue." He formed a big circle with his arms for emphasis, almost knocking the bottle off the cluttered table. "Apparently it was a gift from an NGO—some random development organization. Then I had to ask what it was for, and they told me it was to dry mangoes."

He shrugged a shoulder and continued, "It hadn't been used since it was first dropped off in the village. Theoretically, the vitamins and calories stored in dried mangoes could really help people get through the dry season. In practice, I had yet to see an example of a Malian planning for the future, other than the necessary farming tasks. The concept of saving money doesn't exist. They can't even set up meetings—if you say two o'clock that means sometime before tomorrow. America is supposed to be the land of the free, but I have never felt *this* kind of freedom before. You want to worry about the rest of your life? I want to enjoy today."

Johanna paused to take in this little speech. It was more words than she had ever heard from Kano at once, but the sparks in his eyes showed he meant them. After carefully formulating a reply, she said, "I think we are both enjoying today. Unless you want to stay here for good or end up panhandling on a street corner, you will need to consider the future eventually." She paused again. "When you do, I hope I am a part of it."

Kano took another drink and paused to process what she had just said. "What about your boyfriend?"

"I know myself well, and I can see who you are. We come from different continents and our days in Mali are numbered. I am not investing my time with you for the sake of a good night or two. As far as Onno is concerned, I already explained that the important things dried up between us quite some time ago."

"Mmmhmm." He looked up at the ceiling. "I have been trying new things since my plane touched down. That includes you. Being honest is something I haven't really done with a girl before. Let's see how it plays out. I'll let you think about the future. I am going to worry about tonight. This doesn't go further until you have cut things off with, what was his name, Onno?"

Johanna put on a familiar flirtatious smirk. "Oh, and where did you think this was going tonight?"

"Well, I know what usually happens after a meal this good and a bottle of wine."

"What, you passed out with your clothes still on while your date hooks up with your roommate?"

Kano feigned surprise. "How did you find out about that? It only happened once!"

Johanna laughed, unintentionally showing off her perfectly straightened teeth. "Lucky guess I suppose. Was it awkward the next morning?"

"That story actually happened the other way around. My roommate, Ryan, didn't talk to me for a week." He laughed.

"Not a surprise." She rolled her eyes. "So this place really has changed you. Don't you find our slow pace difficult?"

"Strangely, I haven't even thought about it as being slow. It seems normal now. I never would have put up with it in college, though."

"Good. Just don't plan to spend the night any time soon." She took a long sip of wine.

"Who said anything about spending the night? Priority number one is taking care of this boyfriend problem once and for all."

"Consider it done, but our priority should be spending as much time together as we can, figuring out if we have a future or not."

The waiter returned to ask if they would like dessert in his best imitation of cultured French. They declined.

"Like I said, I will leave this future business up to you. My job is to show you a good time. This has been rather intense. Why don't we blow off some steam? I hope you brought enough cash with you to cover those steaks!"

Souleymane broke in to interrupt the recollection, "But why did she have to pay? I thought it was your custom for a man to pay for dinner."

Kano pursed his lips. "She lost a bet."

"Okay. I can see why this story makes you sad. You must be wanting that promising future together." Souleymane paused to sip his tea. "She was wrong about one thing though. The most important decision is not the person you spend your life with. Other people come and go. The only person you are always with is you. If you do not decide to become the one you are meant to be, what is the importance of any other decision?"

Kano's condition had improved to the point that he could talk during the excursions through scorching sands. In spite of this ability, last night's conversation kept him rather quiet. Souleymane respected the silence and they traversed the dunes together without speaking.

Kano tried to wrap his mind around the fact he had actually opened up to his captor, the very man whose job it was to make sure he never had the chance to escape. His prison guard had somehow secured the confidence normally confined to friendships. *How was this possible? Why am I no longer constantly looking for a way out? Have I given up? Have they broken me?* He didn't feel broken. In many ways, he felt healthier than ever.

He reflected on the positive results of being open and honest with Johanna. Perhaps he could try the same tactic with his captor. Once their route began to arc back toward the compound, he attempted to voice his thoughts. "Is this all part of my training?"

"What? Of course! You know without physical conditioning your soul cannot achieve balance."

"No," Kano shook his head with a smile. "I mean, I told you those stories last night. Is The Scholar trying to make me confide in you?"

Souleymane lowered his voice and spoke in a very serious tone. "The Scholar has said nothing of the sort. In fact, I haven't mentioned it to him. I do not think I will. He may not approve."

Kano continued to jog in silence, realizing this admission somehow solidified a twisted sort of friendship. He felt himself surrendering one of the few things within his control. He could choose whether or not any element of friendship existed in this relationship.

A large part of himself screamed not to do it. It could lead to total surrender. *How could I ever give in to people who denied my freedom? Killed my friend? Destroyed my family? Hijacked my future?*

The battle raged within, but on the outside Kano maintained calm. His poker face masked the turbulent struggle. He barely muttered a word to Souleymane for the next week and avoided all eye contact. Then he got sick.

Fever set his skin on fire. His blood felt like it was boiling. Gelatinous bones threatened to melt completely, aching as though thousands of termites were mining out the very marrow itself.

Then he plunged into the depths of the ocean. Fever quenched. Darkness and chills grew hand in hand, racking his body with spasmodic shivers. His tongue bled when the chattering white jackhammers lost control entirely.

Without warning, he would rise up again into the scorching sun, the relentless cycle of fever and chills threatening to destroy his body once and for all. It surely would have at the beginning of his captivity, when he was weak and emaciated.

Malaria-induced hallucinations warped his existence. Images of life and death, Heaven and Hell, unfathomable colors and shapes torturing his mind with an incoherent, ever-changing flood of stimulation.

Kano's life hung in the balance for several days. Souleymane never left his side. He cleaned him. Tried to keep him hydrated. Brought cool, damp cloths out for the fevers and blankets for the chills. Never slept. The death of his student spelled ultimate failure.

As Kano showed the first signs of recovery, Souleymane felt a relief far beyond his expectations. A whispering suspicion entered his thoughts that the relief he felt was more about the idea his friend might survive. *Wait. Friend. How could that possibly be?* He could never tell The Scholar about this shift in the way he viewed his pupil. Perhaps it was temporary. Part of the exhaustion.

Kano could never be a friend. He was a rich Westerner who knew and appreciated little about his culture or his people. He had squandered vast resources and was now paying the price by serving as an example to others. This captivity was just and necessary in bringing about positive changes to a world where injustice was spiraling out of control. The Scholar would see to that.

After days of uncertainty, it became clear who was winning the battle between life and death. Souleymane's exemplary care and Kano's robust physical health staved off what should have been a complete victory for the malaria parasites ravaging his body. Breaking out from their long-term stronghold in the liver, the microscopic demons entered the bloodstream, successive broods taking up temporary residence in individual red blood cells. After the ruin and scuttling of the cell, fortified numbers marched forth in search of their next target.

After a long, hard fight, Kano's immune system triumphed over the marauding invaders. Foggy delirium slowly thinned and then evaporated entirely. Quiet noises from the seemingly distant city penetrated his consciousness. A barking dog startled a donkey. Heavy breathing coming from someone in the room. He saw nothing. Perhaps his eyes still didn't work, or maybe it was just dark.

Kano lacked the strength to look around, or even to speak. A glowing gratefulness to be alive welled up within him. He drifted in and out of sleep. Dreams and thoughts and memories all blended together.

Cascading brain activity led him down a path of recollection. It was unusually strong, as if he was living through his memories all over again. He could smell dirty exhaust from Vespa scooters polluting the streets of Rome, hear the bustle and shifting of restless crowds, feel the exhaustion from a year of traveling around Europe, see sharp shadows on ancient cobblestones, and taste the bold espresso he had finished just minutes before.

Kano tried to enjoy the sunshine and the ancient city like he never imagined possible, wanting to see everything there was to see, a glorious end to a glorious journey. His travels had come full-circle, but exhaustion seeped deep within his bones like a North Sea cold that refused to be melted away by Mediterranean sun.

Kano had never been one to pray, but, *when in Rome,* he thought. He saved the Vatican for last, admitting that a bit of guidance could be useful as his long journey had ended and the next step remained elusive. He had learned many words, seen beautiful cities, won countless games of poker, slept in a different bed almost every night, often with a beautiful woman, and drank unbelievable amounts of alcohol. His liver cried out for a reprieve.

Even though it was early in the morning, the line of people loitering against sloping, castle-like ramparts barely seemed to be moving forward. The fidgety mass grew as each bus and metro ejected crowds of disoriented tourists.

After forty-five minutes of shuffling through the shadow of the massive wall, Kano paid a hefty entrance fee and started his trek through what he would soon discover to be the museum which would put all others he had visited to shame. The halls themselves exploded with beauty like carefully tended palatial gardens. Kano was accustomed to seeing the sort of art that hung on a wall inside a frame. These walls were canvases. Structural elements doubled as frames.

He was sucked into a labyrinth of passageways crisscrossing inside and out, opening into magnificent courtyards hewn with marble statues and fountains, then driven back indoors only to emerge in so many chapels seemingly touched by the divine hand which allowed paint to flourish into breathtaking images.

Kano was so visually engrossed in his surroundings, he failed to notice swirling drafts, chilled as though he had entered the catacombs. Camera flashes were forbidden, but brilliant bursts of light illuminated the bright colors, defying the laws of Man.

Marble busts lined the sides of the seemingly endless hall he had entered. They appeared to tremble as though the earth was shaking. Pressure waves caused by air expanding faster than the speed of sound due to the intense heat of a lightning bolt striking the cupola of Saint Peter's dome jolted Kano out of his swooning state. His senses became keenly attuned to the approaching storm as if God himself had escaped the confines of Michelangelo's two dimensions and was charging through the atmosphere.

Winds entered the courtyard, bending scattered cypress trees. Needles flew through the air. Branches snapped and twisted as though countless years of being locked in the same position had finally given rise to a widespread jail-break. Water from fountains temporarily flew in a horizontal direction.

Old, rattling windows shook Kano's bones as if he had become part of the elaborate structure itself. Before him stretched the colossal hall of maps, beckoning with promises of enchantment. Maps stretching from floor to ceiling. Maps of Italy. Maps from the Age of Exploration. Maps of the entire world. Kano sucked in his breath and continued. Awe of beauty transformed into lust for adventure.

His eyes darted quickly from one map to the next. Top to bottom. Scanning the ornate ceiling. Filtering out swirling curtains of rain approaching the tall windows; untold squadrons of kamikaze fighter planes packed to the gills with explosives, spiraling down toward scrambling ships.

Kano picked up his pace. Other tourists seemed to fade away as if a fog had entered the space. They shifted and fell into obscurity; meaningless driftwood piled up on a beach. Rain smashed against the windows, now breakers pushed up by a tropical storm. Maps took on a sand-like quality, moving and shifting under his darting glances. It felt as though the time-weathered hall was ready to collapse under the violence of the storm, leaving Kano as a crushed speck in its glorious rubble.

Another sonic boom, triggered by the instantaneous formation of a plasma highway temporarily allowing electrons to flow from sky to earth, shocked Kano to a halt after blinding him as if the paparazzi had just pointed thousands of cameras into his face. Gale-force winds blew the unsettling smell of ozone through poorly sealed windows, reducing them to little more than their cracks and openings.

As the hall took shape again after the bright flash, Kano saw he was surrounded by four globes clearly weighing much more than he did. An unrestrainable urge to spin one gripped him and he deftly swung underneath the thick, purple rope designed to keep tourists at bay.

He pushed with all his might and the massive sphere gave way to his force with an unlubricated protest of old age. It spun with a rebellious groan, a hollow imitation of the crushing thunder which showed no sign of relenting. Kano closed his eyes. He waited for the ancient mechanism of rotation to grind to a halt as he took in a deep breath. He somehow knew wherever his finger landed would be his next destination. Another deep breath. His mind cleared. The storm front was passing and the wind ceased its lashing of the structure;

flood-like rains filled his ears. *God is in the rain,* was the thought that entered his head, unbidden.

Slowly, with his eyes firmly clamped shut, his finger descended. The motion was nearly imperceptible. Anyone watching would have thought this seemingly marble statue was ahead of its time, adorned with modern clothing and an oversized camera. Although it felt rapid to Kano, to the casual observer he was standing perfectly still.

His finger seemed to depressurize a small part of the earth, driving a storm like the one which continued to batter the Vatican. Eyes still closed, Kano sensed the proximity diminish. Waves of energy flashed up his arm as though the globe had become an enormous Van de Graaff generator.

Suddenly, contact was made. Kano's eyes flashed open and he saw Africa had risen up to meet his finger. A closely cropped nail rested precisely on top of the dot labeled Tombutu. He blinked several times as if coming out of a trance, and wondered if that used to be the name for Timbuktu. Easy enough to check. *Was that even a real place?*

The storm had distracted the security guard, but eventually he noticed Kano standing on the wrong side of the thick rope. No time was wasted in ousting the irreverent tourist from his misplaced location.

Kano felt another tingling sensation just before the hand of the guard grasped his shoulder. His breath rushed in with a gasp and his head quickly turned toward the assailant. He pulled his index finger away from the globe as if it had strayed into the hot wax of a burning candle, and looked around in a rather bewildered fashion as the man behind him spoke with inflamed syllables. Rain now fell as a peaceful blanket of water. The security guard pulled Kano back under the rope, out into the steady, one-way flow of tourist traffic.

By the time Kano completed the labyrinth, sunshine broke though the low flying scud which trailed the thunderhead. Remoras behind a tiger shark. The downpour cleared the air of its smog, allowing scrubbed rays of light to soak into his skin with an intensity unlike what he had become accustomed to in Michigan. Even though Rome is about the same latitude as Ann Arbor, the intensity of its solar radiation reminded him of Southern California. Numerous palm trees added ample credibility to his association. Kano realized, with a few butterflies in his stomach, that he would need to prepare himself for a much hotter sun than the one currently squeezing beads of sweat out onto his forehead.

While stepping down the noisy route leading into the cool sanctuary of the metro, Kano's mind turned toward the preparations required for embarking on his journey to the edge of the Sahara. The simplest course of action would be to find a nearby travel agent who could make all the arrangements for him.

Kano barely understood the highly strung woman speaking in a staccato voice from the other side of the desk, but she swiped his card with Italian enthusiasm. While the ticket allowing him to board a flight bound for France was printing, she informed him Paris was the only European city with a commercial flight into Mali, the name of the "Countree offa Timbuktu."

She also gave him directions to a nearby clinic where he could pick up malaria medication and several vaccinations, and said he would have to work out his travel visa and find his own way from Bamako, the capital of Mali, to Timbuktu, upon arrival. She mentioned the two cities were over seven hundred kilometers apart, a twenty-four hour bus ride. He grimaced in response.

That night, Kano could barely sleep. His indefinite stay in Italy had come to an abrupt, unexpected end. The shoulder he had dislocated so many years ago hurt again, this time from yellow fever shots. He had come so far, and yet still had no long term direction.

His aching shoulder brought back memories from high school. His former classmates must think he had gone a bit crazy. He wondered where their choices had taken them after graduating from college. They had probably experienced the first year of working in the *real world*.

He could hardly remember their faces. The last five years brought about so many changes. He met an incredible number of new people. The friends and teammates he had once been close to crumbled and faded into the background. His consciousness witnessed this rapid decomposition with detached, emotionless distance. As far as Kano was concerned, he never needed to see Southern California again. There was so much of the world to experience, and so many places to live which boasted advantages easily outstripping the smoggy basin where he grew up.

Eventually, his whirring mind slowed down as it shifted entirely back into the present. He felt sad it was physically impossible for him to travel any more, but a confidence grew that he hadn't come into this confined existence by accident. The underlying anger was gone. It was as if the malaria parasites had eaten it away.

Kano looked up and out of his crumpled bed to see Souleymane's wide and friendly face recognizing his return to the present with an infectious smile. It was a wonder Souleymane's teeth looked almost perfect in a land without much dental care and no shortage of rocks hiding in the food. He couldn't help but smile back. The simple expression communicated much more than words ever could.

Souleymane had patiently spent the past week helping Kano recover. They still hadn't stepped outside, but translation duties were in full-swing. Proximity to death had worn down natural barriers between the two. Hostility and distrust faded away. A wary common purpose filled the void left behind. Friendship no longer seemed unthinkable.

Souleymane's head hurt from the strain of examining faded manuscripts with little light. He came across a partially legible but precisely scrawled phrase, '...*traveler carries with him the wisdom of many worlds,*' and wondered how it applied to Kano because he didn't come across as being very wise. He found it hard to imagine people could travel through the air like birds in a *flying canoe*, as they called it in Bambara.

He brought his thoughts into the vocal realm. "Does it feel strange to fly through the air? What did you think of Mali when you first got here?"

Kano paused for a moment as his mind transitioned from the translation to Souleymane's inquiry. Three languages: reading Arabic, writing and speaking English, and listening to Bambara muddled his recovering mind. He smiled as he thought back to that trip across the Sahara. The writers of these manuscripts would have taken months to complete the journey. He did it in a matter of hours. *What would it be like to take someone who traveled the same route five hundred years ago along for the ride? Wouldn't their reactions be fascinating?*

As he pondered this, he suddenly realized that taking Souleymane along on a journey through the Western World wouldn't be too much different from taking a traveler from a bygone century. This notion gave him more enthusiasm to tell the story of how he had arrived, trying not to spare any details. He drifted back to the morning of his departure which felt like so many years ago.

The Italian alarm clock next to his bedside table shrieked to life, rousting Kano from his cozy nest of pillows and blankets. The sun was not even gracing the horizon, but the faintest glow confirmed its promise to rise. The flight for Paris left early. The shower steamed. The clothes almost stuffed themselves into the bag. The key found its way to the front desk. Departure into pre-dawn air. Kano was on his way. He was going in the wrong direction, but it was the only connection to Mali.

Europe's second largest airport welcomed his flight of one hour and fifty-three minutes in style. Kano knew the French would never miss the opportunity to make sure the international gateway to Paris left a favorable impression. Not to be distracted from his goal, he glanced down at the ticket which indicated gate E37 was to be his next destination. He quickly confirmed this with the blue departure screens, and began a longer walk than expected, following large signs pointing toward terminal E.

As he strode forward, the airport's character changed. Colors faded, perfume and chocolate shops disappeared, and white people were suddenly a minority. He finally came to a stop behind one of the longest lines he had ever seen in a confined space. Kano slid his bag across the formerly white linoleum floor with one foot while his eyes contemplated flaking patches of paint which hung from the ceiling like solidified cobwebs. "Good thing I have a four-hour layover," he muttered to himself.

After what seemed like hours of waiting in line for a frantic push through security, Kano felt slightly violated by the whole process. The feeling quickly slipped away as the most incredible airport terminal he had ever seen opened up in front of him. A seemingly endless enclosure curved away in both directions like the shore of a large, red lake. The ceiling was one graceful arc stretching with windows and bright wooden trim.

Kano approached a wide, polished aluminum banister and realized the ceiling curved itself into a wall, and continued inward toward the floor two levels below. The effect was like walking inside a wine barrel from a land of giants that had been tipped on its side, adorned with holes, and stretched to infinity.

Regal carpeting made the barrel look nearly half full. It was not quite deep enough in color to be wine; not quite brown enough to be African soil. The color nearly matched that of the Air France blanket wrapped in cellophane patiently waiting for him inside the airplane.

Kano kept his headphones on during the safety talk that lasted for most of the long taxi to the appropriate runway. After the flight attendants safely scuttled to their jump seats, the captain gripped the thruster with his whole hand, pushing forward. This allowed the tanks contained within the wings to empty copious amounts of jet fuel into the twin Rolls Royce Trent 700 series turbofan engines. Hand-placed rivets held onto the resulting 140,000 horses tighter than a cowboy could grip his bronco.

Kano was sucked back into his seat as the Airbus a330 shot down the runway like a giant drag racer, producing three times more power than the *Titanic* ever could. When the critical speed was achieved, the back end of the aircraft dropped down momentarily, only to be pulled into the sky immediately thereafter, leaving its occupants with a sinking feeling in their stomachs. Takeoff had always been Kano's favorite part.

Drink carts rolled down the aisle for the second time. Kano asked for another Heineken. Crisp popping of scored aluminum precisely giving way under the pressure of a levered tab, releasing a slight fizz of carbon dioxide, was something so normal, Kano's consciousness failed to pay any heed. The fragility of the flying metal cocoon and the refreshments it contained did not seem important even though they were the only things protecting him from the vast expanse of the Sahara unfolding below the aircraft.

Kano was absorbed by shadows of rocks, dunes, and cliffs that the setting sun stretched out with sharp contrast eleven thousand meters below. The lack of civilization spreading before him was mesmerizing. It seemed to never end. Kano figured all of Europe could surely fit within this wasteland.

Before long, the ground turned black beneath them while the sky desperately held on to its light for a few extra minutes. Kano allowed the flight attendant to collect his partially eaten dinner and drifted off to sleep.

The ping of the safety belt warning popped his eyes open and a sinking feeling crept into the pit of his stomach. He knew the plane must be turning, but there were no points of reference visible from the window to confirm the sensation. Unsettling scraps of disorientation spread like gusts of wind preceding a storm.

Suddenly, dim lights engaged his line of sight. He was looking down on what appeared to be a settlement on Mars. Standard sodium street lamps which cast a yellow glow in the nocturnal world of the West had been replaced with dots of blue fluorescence illuminating red dirt, corrugated metal roofs, and very few patches of green. Other than a pair of headlights here and there, the roads seemed rather deserted. It was as if they were arriving at two in the morning. *Could this be a city which was home to several million people? Or was this an emergency landing somewhere else?*

The aircraft maintained its altitude for a while, as though the pilots were scouting the area, apprehensive about landing on hostile soil. The bluish glow stretching out before Kano reminded him of a heavily pixelated version of the luminescing phytoplankton which once trailed a cruise ship he had been on with his parents. Bored, he sat near the back of the ship for hours, staring at the glowing wake.

As if to jolt him from a trance, the Airbus banked sharply, abruptly obscuring the lights. Once it leveled off, Kano saw nothing but a few specks of blue contrasting a purely black horizon. They had reversed direction.

In spite of the nearly perfect touchdown, the pilots received no applause. This plane was filled with a generation and a culture unfamiliar with such traditions. After overshooting the terminal, the jet made another one hundred and eighty degree turn and headed back toward the illuminated structure, leaving the dark unknown behind.

Rollable stairs pointed the passengers toward a squat building twenty-five meters from the plane, but to Kano's worry everyone was getting onto an Air France bus. *Why? Did they have to go somewhere else to get inspected? Perhaps to a building that was not so well-lit?*

It didn't take long for Kano to stifle a bit of laughter as the bus simply drove in a semi-circle, opening its doors to the waiting airport staff. He shook his head at the bureaucratic minds mandating such nonsense.

An overwhelming number of security guards gripped fully automatic assault rifles. Their camouflage uniforms and French military berets made his head spin a little. He wondered what he was doing in Africa.

After shuffling through the slowly moving line, sweating in the nighttime heat, Kano finally made it to the customs window. The fat man behind the window said, *"Bonsoir, monsieur, s'il vous plaît passeport."*

Kano presented his passport and the official demanded fifty dollars for a visa. Or euros. The exchange rate didn't seem to matter. Just fifty of something from the West. Kano had no idea how much of this was a bribe, but one glance in the direction of the idle men with guns kept his lips sealed. He surrendered one crisp banknote.

The baggage claim triggered a feeling of claustrophobia. Military presence dominated the room. Weary travelers reeking of old sweat pushed past each other toward the conveyor belt snaking around several winding bends before returning back through the wall. There were so many people he barely caught a glimpse of the floor.

A few duffel bags popped out, followed by a partially-taped cardboard box and a hiking backpack. It was difficult for Kano to see. Height was one of the few advantages he had not been given.

The air was heavy, pungent, suffocating. Low ceilings and what he could make out of the dirty linoleum floor contributed to a sickness settling into his stomach. He knew it couldn't be food poisoning yet. *Where is my backpack?*

The slithering belt carried many haphazard belongings; few had the customary wheels and locks Kano was used to seeing at a baggage claim. Even a black garbage bag wrapped in duct tape wriggled past. After several more minutes which dragged on in agony, Kano wrestled his bright green pack onto a shoulder and away from the shiftily clicking plastic. He pushed through the crowd toward the exit.

Before he could get outside, he found himself forced into another line nearly indistinguishable from the crowd awaiting their luggage. For some reason, the bags were being loaded onto another black belt which drew them into an x-ray machine. What they were scanning for was a mystery, but the oversized group of sluggish military men loading and guarding the machine made it abundantly clear Kano needed to wait in this line before leaving the airport.

After an awful fifteen minutes, Kano stepped out into the night air. He took a deep breath to clear his head of airport chaos, but his lungs sucked in cigarette smoke, exhaust fumes, and plenty of body odor. He coughed in surprise.

His eyes took a few seconds to adjust to the dimly lit crowd standing before him. Black skin blended into a dark background and all Kano could make out were bright clothes seemingly worn by ghosts. He saw everything from ragged t-shirts and torn pants to shiny, body-length outfits on both women and men. Many of the women even displayed a matching headdress. It was as if peasants and nobles lined the street for the arrival of the King.

Kano pressed into the crowd, moving toward parked cars. They looked like they had been through a demolition-derby. Chipped, yellow paint hinted at Kano's goal: transportation into the city.

"Taxiee, Taxiee. Dix mille sanc san," shouted a small man missing two or three front teeth.

"Slow down," Kano said, "do you speak English?"

"Engleesh, yes, yes. I study University. You haave moneey for taxiee?"

"All I have are dollars and euros," Kano replied suspiciously.

"No, no, no, no good. You come. I get you *saayfa.*" He shuffled away with a big smile.

"What does *saayfa* mean?" Kano followed.

"Mali moneey, you see. Come, come," he waved with impatience.

The unease in Kano's stomach intensified when he realized the sandals the man was wearing were the exact same dirty once-white color as the floor in the baggage claim. They were worn and twisted so much Kano wondered if they provided any protection at all from the sharp gravel beneath their feet.

After a short minute of walking, they approached dingy booths lit with small, fluorescent bulbs. He started to understand the blue light he had seen from the air. Bars separated Kano from the money changers as if he were visiting them inside a prison. The taxi driver introduced Kano in an unintelligible language.

The man behind bars asked, "How much *saayfa* you want?" pointing at a sign marked with Euros, Dollars, and CFA. The casual gesture made Kano realize what they must have been saying: *saayfa* meant CFA, the Malian currency.

Kano replied, "I want enough for a few days in the city."

"O.K., dis means I geev 440 saayfa for 1 dollah," and after punching a few numbers in his calculator he said, "you geev 300 dollah, I geev 132,000 saayfa."

"You got yourself a deal, my friend," said Kano. The man counted out thirteen brand new 10,000 CFA notes along with one smaller 2,000 CFA bill. Kano was immediately struck by the beauty of the money. In spite of the underperforming tube lights, he saw bold colors and impressive designs. The dollars he had grown up with looked quite dull in comparison.

He thanked the money changer and followed the taxi driver, who had already taken his bag back to the cab. After slamming the trunk, the driver said with a crooked smile, "You geev 12,000 I take to beest hoteyl in Bamako."

"Deal," Kano said, relieved to have someone who could help him out. Even if he had known this man was charging him three times the reasonable fare he wouldn't have cared. Anything to get away from the sickening airport and those awful machine guns. As he settled into the front seat, the car creaked into motion. Crackling sounds of Bob Marley pushed their way through tired speakers. Familiar music worked to ease away the tension which had built up in Kano's stomach like rain soaking into dry, cracked earth.

As Kano returned to the present, he could still feel the last bits of tension fading away. Talking about his memories brought back physical sensations of what he had experienced; a mild version of the lucid dreams solitary confinement forced upon him.

Souleymane absorbed what he had heard in silence. Kano could see questions forming on his face, but they dutifully went back to their translations as too much time had already passed.

"Please," said Souleymane, "I would like to hear more about how you experienced my country, my people." Normally he did not speak during meals.

Kano raised his eyebrows at this unexpected departure from the routine. "Alright," he acquiesced. "But do you really want to speak while we enjoy our dinner? The spaghetti is great tonight!" Ever since

Kano mentioned how much he liked the cuisine in Italy they found more variety in their food.

Souleymane carefully set down his fork to speak. "You have practiced eating in silence. It is time for me to experience the way your culture does things."

Kano felt surprised his captor was curious about different perspectives. He kept the feeling to himself. "Well," he replied while wiping some tomato sauce from his mouth, "that usually works when we have a conversation, like now. One person can take a bite while listening and you trade off so everyone can eat. You want me to tell you another story. That means you would eat while I would talk."

Souleymane thought about this as he took a big drink of water from a thick glass with so many fine scratches it looked frosted. "I see your point. Perhaps it would be better if you spoke while we drink tea after the meal."

Kano nodded in approval and they finished the rest of their spaghetti in silence. After dinner, the tea sat on a shiny platter meant to mimic silver. Or perhaps it was silver. Kano couldn't tell; Souleymane didn't know there was a difference. As they settled into their usual three cups of tea, Kano drifted back to his first morning in Mali. He picked up his story where he had left off earlier that day.

Waking up was a struggle because his surroundings seemed like a dream. The events of the previous night came back to him in pulses as he saw the taxi driver's phone number scribbled on the back of a torn piece of paper next to his somewhat comfortable bed.

The dirt roads near the hotel had been poorly lit and full of huge potholes. Contrary to his observations, Kano vividly remembered his driver assuring him Badalabougou was one of the nicest neighborhoods in the city. His slow, rich speech overpowered the reggae struggling to emerge from tinny speakers. "Reech Malians en *Toubobous*...uuh...whiyte peeple leeve here. It is riyte ehloong de reever beetween da two breedges. Me couseen work dis hotel. You liyke veery much. Pareedayse for yuu."

Kano threw on a shirt and went to investigate this supposed paradise. There was a swimming pool near his room. The cement already felt hot from the morning sun. Not far from the shimmering blue pool, short and stubby grass gave way to suspiciously brown water—the banks of the Niger River. The opposite side was so far away he couldn't make out individual people, but Kano closely observed the curious architecture lining its shore. It was like nothing he had seen before.

The tallest building looked like an evil fortress straight from a Batman set with its horned roofline, bold colors and lack of windows. A few blocks from there, directly opposite Kano's viewpoint, loomed a blindingly white palatial structure designed for a militant sultan. He would be shocked later that day to discover the brilliant edifice to be totally abandoned and without windows. It was part of Malibya: projects funded by the ruler of neighboring Libya, Muammar Gaddafi, to gain influence in the region. *Paradise?* No, but Kano was intrigued by the view, and after capturing it in a few well-framed photographs, he couldn't wait to explore.

He brought the torn piece of paper with a phone number on it to the front desk. Nobody was there, but he poked around for a few minutes until he found the lady who ran the place. This must be the taxi driver's cousin. She started speaking a strange version of French to Kano until he cut her off, saying, "Sorry, but I don't speak much French." He could get by when he was traveling through France a few months ago, but her dialect was a total mystery to his ears.

"I no Engleesh," came the reply. Kano held out the number and it was clear enough what he wanted.

She wound her way behind the desk and dialed for him. After speaking with her cousin for a few minutes, she handed the receiver over to Kano.

Before getting a chance to open his mouth, he heard, "Heyloo...freend, how deed...sleep? Hoteyl...pareedayse, eh?" The connection was bad, and Kano missed every third word or so. It sounded like the man on the other end was driving.

"The hotel is very nice. Thank you for bringing me here. I would like to see the city. Will you show it to me?"

"I not heere yuu...louuder...driveeng," came the garbled reply.

Kano twisted the phone closer to his lips and lowered his head slightly, nearly shouting into it he slowly said, "Can you drive here? I want to see the city."

"Ahhh, yees me freende...coombing nowa."

Kano turned and handed back the phone. She chatted with her cousin as Kano wandered off toward the pool. He sat down in a chair and within a matter of minutes the heat of the morning sun lulled him to sleep.

When he awoke for the second time that day, he felt disoriented again. Tropical birds created a cacophony all around him, flying from tree to tree with dizzying ferocity. Sharply spoken syllables pierced into his skull like long, sharp beaks. The angry words stopped. He understood nothing that had been said.

His head throbbed as he brought his hands up to touch his dried out face. Putting pressure on his lips caused them to crack, adding a slicing sensation to his world of pain. The woman who was busy accosting him verbally quickly grew tired of watching her words land with no impact whatsoever and she grabbed an arm with more strength than Kano's weightlifting buddies had, yanking him to his feet. Upon releasing her iron grip, the red skin she touched turned momentarily pale.

To Kano, it felt as though his arm had been ripped out of its socket. She shoved him toward a shaded area. The woman disappeared with a few more harsh syllables and returned carrying a pitcher of water. Kano gulped down three glasses. Each one was followed by a massive inhalation as though he had been holding his breath in the swimming pool for minutes.

His agitated hostess took a jar of what looked like wet oatmeal which had spent a few seconds in the blender. She let fly several more accusations, pointing back and forth from the jar to Kano's red face. The message was clear enough. The paste smelled musty and strangely familiar, but he figured something should go on his burn as soon as possible.

He quickly realized it was a rough version of the shea butter creams his mom swore by, making him feel homesick for a briefly intense moment. As his skin brightened with an oily shine, the homesickness quickly wore off.

The woman said something unintelligible while collecting the empty pitcher and glass, but he did pick up the word *taxi*. This must be why she woke him up. His ride had finally come.

He went to his room to fetch his wallet and baseball cap, wishing he had something more like a sombrero. He wondered why people here didn't wear them. As he went for the door, the mirror caught his attention. His eyes opened wide with surprise as a flamingo-colored face stared back at him.

This African sun is clearly different, he thought, while locking his hotel room door with a crude skeleton key. He had fallen asleep for what felt like a few minutes. *How long had it really been?* In spite of the musty smelling ointment, his face felt as if he were standing in front of a furnace. Perhaps the distractions offered by the waiting taxi driver would help him forget the pain.

The decrepit yellowish Mercedes coughed out puffs of blue smoke while idling on the red dirt road in front of the hotel. Kano climbed in. "Hello my friend," he said while extending his arm for a handshake.

The taxi driver started to laugh as he gripped Kano's outstretched hand tightly. Kano sneezed as a small cloud of dust rose up from his car seat and said, "What is so funny?"

"Eat looks liyke yuu had tuu much fun nayxt to sweem poel. Now yuu look like stoopid *Toubobou*—Freench persoon."

"Well, had you gotten here faster this probably wouldn't have happened. I was waiting for you!"

"Yees, yees. Eat is liyke mye Ameerican freend teels me. Everytheeng here is deeferent tiyme zuun. West Africaan Inteernational Tiyme dey saye, or shortly, W…A…I…T." He slapped his leg and laughed infectiously before continuing in a serious tone. "Yuu must neever ehxpeect anyone to bee on tiyme."

"Right, well now we've gotten that out of the way. I don't think I've actually introduced myself. My name is Kano."

"Yees, yees. I know. Me cousin, sayd so. She see your paysport. She tell yuu me name is Modibo. Maybe she not know yuu no speek Freench. Okee Kano, where yuu want go todaye?" Modibo depressed the clutch and wormed the gearbox into first as he slowly spoke out his last syllables with complete confidence. The battered car rumbled over rocks and into deep potholes toward one of the two bridges.

Kano answered, "You decide. You know the city better than I do. Bring me to a place that you think I should see."

Modibo seemed deep in thought and after some time said, "Veery weel. Yuu weel see." After that he turned up the music and reggae pumped through the car; the low tones pushing a rumpled crackle through faded speakers long past their unassuming prime.

After driving for several hundred meters, bouncing relentlessly from one pothole to the next, the taxi shuddered to a dusty stop behind three other cars attempting a left hand turn onto a mercifully paved road. Kano looked to the left and saw the white metal guardrails of a bridge poking up like a picket fence attempting to corral the ramshackle arrangement of vehicles. Cars, buses and mopeds jammed together without regard for lanes or shoulders or even the jagged line where pavement gave way to dusty dirt, pushing and fighting to gain access to the narrow strip of road leading to the other side of the Niger River.

This chaotic mess made Kano uncomfortable, but then he looked to the right, and quickly realized they were in a rather good situation. A crinkled line of smoking traffic, looking like a more colorful version of the ridges of smoldering garbage that lined parts of the highway, stretched as far as the eye could see. Impatient drivers nosed this way and that while collectively inching toward the crushing bottleneck Modibo was preparing to wiggle into.

Mopeds and cyclists tried to weave through the cracks, regularly stopping and waiting for the jigsaw of cars to shift. An oppressive mix of partially combusted fuel and airborne red earth hung over the road like a stubborn morning fog refusing to give way to the sun.

One by one, the cars in front of Kano forced their way into the fray, poking a nose into the tiniest of spaces while most of the vehicle stuck out into the lane of oncoming traffic; the runt of a litter squeezing in for a taste of milk. Terrifyingly, Modibo hit the gas, causing the moped passing in front of him to swerve and the oncoming bus to hit the brakes, barely making it without getting clipped.

"That was close!" exclaimed a wide-eyed Kano.

Modibo shrugged and said, "Lots a ruum, an eenyway nobody sees a neew dent, so maany old unns to hiyde eet awaye." He gave a hearty laugh while lunging the car deeper into the sputtering hive of internal combustion.

One belch of exhaust at a time, the congestion narrowed into the single lane traveling north across the Niger River. Cleaner air engulfed Kano as they picked up speed with a growing sense of elation. Rising above the water, he watched the far shore grow closer through the blurred, white guardrail. Now roles had reversed, and they were the ones passing the bikers and mopeds, sequestered in their lanes near the edge.

He marveled at long, skinny boats which in a crude way reminded him of Venice. Many were even maneuvered like gondolas—upright men pushing long poles. Someone unexpectedly jumped out of a boat with a bucket in hand. Kano cringed to think how polluted the water must be and wondered out loud, "What could he be fishing for with a bucket?"

Modibo laughed again, deep lines around his dark eyes crinkling, and said, "Da deert ees good for dee farmers. Dis men geet mooney for da reever deert."

Kano asked, "How deep is the river?"

"Oh, maybee tree or four meeters."

Kano thought for a moment, processing the feat of swimming through so much dirty, brown, flowing water while lifting a bucketful of heavy dirt. "I wouldn't want that job," was all he managed to say while shaking his head incredulously.

Modibo turned the car sharply to the right after the bridge with an honest little grin, cutting off another moped driver who almost crashed into a woman riding a bike. They passed new construction along the bank of the river, every single worker looking positively Chinese.

Kano became peacefully subdued by the dense growth of palm and banana trees. He felt a twinge of hunger at the sight of colorful buckets filled with pineapple, papaya and many other unidentifiable tropical fruits. Some were magically balancing on top of the heads of women who seemed in no particular hurry to get anywhere.

After lurching down alleyways and braking for sheep here and there, the taxi hit another traffic jam. The mixture of exhaust and dust drifting through the open window brought with it a new smell, rotten and disgusting.

Kano searched for the source. Just on the other side of the open sewer, he spotted a ragged sheet of black plastic with a mound of stinking fish nearly waist-high. They were brown and shriveled up, about the size of small mice. Kano had a sudden urge to vomit. He quickly averted his eyes and said, "People don't actually eat those rotting fish do they?"

"Oh yees," smiled Modibo mischievously, "veery taystee in sauce weeth riyce."

"What about the bones?"

"Eextra cruuncheee!" he exclaimed.

"Right, well, give me fair warning if anyone tries to feed me that—I think I will have plain rice." Kano tried not to breathe for a minute.

By the time Modibo pulled his taxi into a small parking lot, Kano could feel a substantial layer of grimy dust on his sunburnt face and he had to peel himself from where he sat. The threadbare seat soaked up a good amount of sweat; his shirt tried to stay behind. It quickly realigned itself to Kano's back, clinging on for dear life as if afraid to leave the relative safety of the car.

Kano followed Modibo asking, "Where are we? What is the plan?"

Modibo turned back to Kano with a crooked grin and said, "I hoope yuu hayve lots of mooney...yuu weel want to leeve eet heere."

Kano flashed back a quizzical smile and decided to be surprised by whatever lay ahead of them. Before he knew it, the dizzying atmosphere of the street transformed into an enclosed shrine. Frantic traffic noise was exchanged for peaceful, age-old sounds of hand tools and relaxed conversation. Even the oppressive temperature dropped several degrees.

The sky remained bright and open over their heads. Kano was staring at a circular structure overflowing with drums, clothing, and jewelry, located at the center of a large cloister lined with all varieties of Malian artwork. There was very little space to walk. Kano could barely make out the sandy color of the walls through small gaps between items on display.

His eyes gradually grew larger. The last time he had seen so much artwork in the same place was inside the Vatican. The order and reverence of those galleries stood in stark opposition to the wildly colorful chaos spreading before him.

Modibo greeted an old friend and they sat down for tea. Kano, without realizing his rudeness at declining their offer to join, wandered through the maze of carved wood and stone, bold paintings, and every sort of leather imaginable.

He walked from one area to the next, hypnotized by the chaotic beauty surrounding him. Many of the typically aggressive sellers took a pitying step back as they watched this red-faced person wander around in awe.

After fifteen minutes, Kano developed a good feel for the layout of Artisana, the largest collection of Malian artwork, and a tremendous thirst gripped him. Almost in panic, he rushed back to find Modibo sipping his third cup of tea out of what looked like a slightly oversized shot glass. Kano said, "Modibo, you were right, I should have brought more money, but now all I need is water. I think I could drink a whole gallon."

"No probleem mee freeind, seet weeth us. Yuu weel hayve *ice coold* waatah." As Modibo spoke these words, the downturned palm of his hand extended toward a random young boy and he clasped and unclasped his fingers, as if waving to a toddler. Kano puzzled over the signal as the boy came running over.

Modibo placed one coin into a small, outstretched hand and rapidly spoke a few harsh words to him. The boy ran off and within a minute returned, his dirty hands dripping with condensation from the four plastic bags of water. He tentatively handed them to Kano as Modibo dismissed him with a few short, condescending syllables.

Kano tore the first bag open with his canines and squeezed the deliciously cold fluid into his mouth with such force he could barely swallow it fast enough. The world around him disappeared as he inhaled the first bag of frigid water and went after the next.

Halfway through, his face contorted in pain. Modibo and his friend, who had been watching Kano with rapt fascination, burst out in laughter. Kano's eyes showed a mixture of fear and agony, his whole throat locked with cold. Pain shot through his skull as if a dull knife sliced into his brain. His vision blurred.

Modibo and his friend laughed even harder, and with considerable effort between gasps, Modibo managed to say, "Coold...as...iyce. Dreenk sloow."

After a considerable amount of help from Modibo, Kano's purchases were scattered across the back seat: a painting of the sun setting over a group of mud huts, a polished ebony statue of a rhinoceros that seemed heavy enough to be made from cast iron, two Tuareg daggers sheathed in opposing handles made from purple camel leather to hide the blades, and a pile of carved knick-knacks. His small wad of cash had gone much further than expected, but then, Modibo did handle the negotiations.

Kano had understood nothing of what the men bantered on about. In the end, they almost always made a deal. Even though he was thoroughly entertained by their animated dialogue, he felt dizzy and exhausted. Burning sunshine thoroughly dehydrated his body in spite of the water that had tried to freeze him from the inside out.

Suddenly, they were back on the bridge, this time without a traffic jam, and Kano's pupils dilated as the white guard rail blurred him into a state of detachment. Before he knew it, the whiteness of the rail morphed into a new form: an uncountable number of white eggs layered between cardboard which was somehow attached to the rack of a slowly meandering bicycle.

The improbable mode of transportation brought Kano out of his daze. Time seemed to slow down as he focused all his attention on the fragile tower quickly growing closer.

Kano had no way of knowing the rider of this heavily laden bicycle was lulled into a minor trance himself. The weight of his cargo and the poorly-maintained state of his bike rack conspired to produce a rhythmic swaying accompanied by a friendly metal-on-metal squeak which rocked this seasoned transporter into a mental state of pure vacancy.

He did not notice the scrap of glass cracking under the relatively minor weight of his front tire. One of the newly created shards realigned ominously toward the heavens, lying in wait for the bulging rear wheel. Unstoppable, it came with a certain sense of doom. The force produced by the bang of sharp glass puncturing the tire was immediately followed by a dangerous shift in his fragile cargo. Surprise coerced the cyclist into jolting his crooked handlebars just enough that he lost control and rammed into the minor curb separating the biking lane from the walking lane.

His strong muscles and acute sense of balance prevented the ramshackle egg crate from completely tipping over, but the impact with the curb sent more than a few white missiles out of their resting places and into various skyward trajectories.

When Kano saw the explosion of eggs, their taxi was nearly upon the cyclist. One egg smashed into the windshield while another whizzed past Kano's right ear, smacking into the tail end of his newly purchased rhinoceros.

The egg triggered Kano's reflexes and his head moved away from the window, turning slightly in the direction of the now stationary bicycle. He continued this swiveling motion to see where the egg had landed, but his vision was arrested by a speeding moped driver who was at that very moment swerving around the stopped cyclist. The moped driver's brain was focused on avoiding the obvious stationary threat and failed to distinguish a white, falling egg from a small cloud which floated precariously above it—a fatal filtering error. He swerved directly into the downward path of the parabolically inclined egg. Yolk, white, and shell exploded across his unprotected face with a force which instantly drew the first drops of blood.

The swerve turned into a slide and the moped's front wheel smashed into the taller curb designed to separate car traffic from the narrow lane reserved for two-wheelers. The typically bald tire popped with a second bang. A millisecond later, the rim deformed as it hit concrete, absorbing much of the energy of impact while imparting some in opposition to gravity, lifting the back end along with its rider off the ground, sending the helpless individual catapulting through the air, just behind Modibo's taxi.

Kano watched with open-mouthed, boyish awe as the airborne man's path was violently deflected by the green bus which had been riding the taxi's bumper. Impact occurred on the front right side of the windshield, shattering the glass and bending the hopelessly chipped metal frame inward.

The unintentional acrobat was nearly sliced in half by the blow, and he left brutal patterns of sprayed blood behind as a small part of the van's momentum was effectively transferred, sending him flying over the hypnotic, white guardrail into the roiling brown waters below.

Kano's jaw would not close on its own accord. He was not even aware it had been left hanging open. Awe and fascination mingled with muted horror. Modibo's exclamations didn't even register. *Did that really happen? Or was it a hallucination after too much sun?* The bits of egg plastered across the windscreen confirmed the reality of the event as the pair continued in a stunned silence until reaching the front of Kano's hotel.

Echoes of his initial shock traveled through Kano's voice as he finished telling the story. Souleymane shook his head with sadness, "Yes, yes, this is the Bamako I know. I spent many hours watching. The bus is a safe place to be because it is bigger than everything else. I have seen people die too. It happens every day. The streets are dangerous, but the people do not have bad intentions. They simply want to get to where they are going."

"Some streets in America are dangerous as well. Not so much because of traffic. People there want to kill each other with guns."

Souleymane clucked and shook his head. "Why would people want such a thing when your country has so much to offer?"

Kano thought carefully before responding. "Here people tend to help each other when they are in trouble and can't get by. They willingly share what they have so there is enough for everyone. Where I am from, many people do this too. But others simply take what they want. This causes anger, distrust, and violence. They become trapped in a cycle and can't see a way out."

"Indeed. This is one reason why The Scholar works so hard to preserve and share the light and wisdom of these books and scrolls. The thoughts and ideas locked within can break evil cycles. Speaking of this reminds me that it is nearly time to begin our evening of translation. You will start your meditations while I collect the materials we require to proceed."

In spite of the demanding routine, Kano had energy left after dinner the next day, the time when his reserves were usually depleted. As they sat on uncomfortable wooden chairs to drink tea, Souleymane made a request. "Will you continue where you left off yesterday? I enjoy hearing the ways in which you have experienced my country."

Kano started up with a smile, happy to speak with an extra spark in his voice. This could go on for a while tonight, he thought. A nice distraction from the translations. He quickly drifted back to the hotel next to the river.

Plenty of sunblock was involved with the second morning by the water. As the hours blurred, he heard voices approaching. Syllables carried well enough into the pool area and Kano quickly identified the French language, but it sounded different from the lady who ran the place. This was faster and far more articulate.

The voices stopped briefly as they made visual contact. Then they burst out laughing. Kano heard a quip in French tossed in his direction. He replied with a squint, "Sorry, my French isn't the best."

"Ahhh, an American," said the taller one. "I don't mind speaking English so long as it's not to an Englishman! We were just laughing about your sunburn. Forget you were in Mali?"

"No, but I did manage to fall asleep by the pool. How did you know I was American?"

The tall guy rolled his brown eyes. "I can smell an American a mile away. Your accent, clothes, sunburn, you name it."

"I only said five words to you, and I bought these shorts in Italy!"

The guys dropped their towels on a nearby chair. "Well, they do have that surfer style to them. Let me guess...you are from California?"

Kano shifted uncomfortably. "Yeah, two for two. So what happened to your accent? You almost sound like you grew up in the Midwest or something."

"I went to school in Chicago, so that might explain things. Say, you don't mind if we hang out here? That pool is looking good!"

"Knock yourselves out. Good thing you brought flip-flops because the cement is hot enough to burn your feet." Kano took a big gulp from his water bottle.

"In that case..."

The tall guy ran across the pool deck and did a front flip, plunging into blue water and soaking everything with the splash. Kano was glad he had left his camera inside. The shorter man with intensely blond hair and ice-blue eyes took off his flip-flops just like his friend, but instead of jumping in, he walked toward Kano and sat down right next to him, strangely oblivious to the hot cement. He didn't say a word.

The tall man got out of the pool and shook out shaggy brown hair like a wet dog. He seemed to aim for his blond friend.

"That's Marcel. He doesn't talk much, especially in English. He also hates getting wet. My name is Caleb." A long, dripping hand extended toward Kano.

Kano took it warily and said, "Kano."

"Good to meet you! What brings you to Mali?"

"Spun a globe. Finger landed on Timbuktu." The sound of dripping water was quickly drowned out by flapping wings and loud calls from a few oversized birds fighting over nearby branches.

"Ahhh, my kind of guy! Marcel and I are both geologists. Working for the enemy. Some oil companies got the idea there might be black stuff hidden under all that sand up North. Our outfit wanted someone on the ground to see if the rumors are true. The only reason I came is for the cliffs, though. Hard to imagine, but they say some of the best rock climbing in the world is just a few miles from here!" Caleb sat down on the other side of Kano, the metal legs of his chair grating against concrete.

"Rock climbing, huh? Some of my friends in college were into that, but Southeast Michigan doesn't have much to offer. They took an ice climbing trip to the Upper Peninsula. I wasn't too interested in death or frostbite, being from California and all."

"Right. Ice climbing is not my thing either. Where did you go to school?"

Kano hesitated to answer because at that moment Marcel looked so bored he abruptly stood up and took off his t-shirt as if the *Baywatch* cameras were rolling. A sharply toned body revealed he was no stranger to the gym. He stepped out of their shaded corner toward the pool, ignoring the sizzling concrete and gingerly hopped into the water feet first, like a monkey with no choice but to cross the stream.

Caleb shook his head. "Marcel lacks a few skills in the social department, but he is one of the best climbers I know. Wouldn't want to be anchored to anyone else. Anyway, Southeast Michigan?"

"Yeah, I went to the University of Michigan. Great school. Glad to be out of that world though. Couldn't stomach the thought of working in an office. Too much to see and do."

"I hear you, brother. Putting up with this job in exchange for exploring a few uncharted places in this world is totally worth the compromise. Some days I feel like I have more in common with your Wild West characters than my French friends and family back home." He tipped an imaginary cowboy hat.

"Is that so? And who would you wanna be? John Wayne?" Kano let out a little chuckle.

"Nope. I'd be Clint Eastwood from *The Good, the Bad and the Ugly*. Always one step ahead. Never letting the other guy know what you're thinking."

"Fair enough. And Marcel?"

Caleb contemplated for a moment, and then a sly spark brightened his green eyes. "Marcel is not quite so old fashioned—more like Steven Seagal meets Val Kilmer. I've never seen him actually killing anyone, but I wouldn't put it past him. It's the quiet ones you need to watch out for. He always climbs with a knife in his belt. Says it's for snakes or scorpions. I am pretty sure the real reason he has it is so he can cut the rope if I fall and he can't support me any longer. I know he would see it as a last resort, but he wouldn't think twice about doing it."

Kano lowered his voice. "You must admit he looks way too much like Iceman from *Top Gun*. You still want to climb with the guy? He doesn't seem like buckets of fun."

"Like I said, he's got my back a hundred percent unless the danger to himself becomes unacceptably high. Life is a series of calculations for him." Caleb glanced at Marcel who was swimming in perfectly straight lines from one side of the pool to the other. "I know right where I stand, so his presence makes me feel safer. Never have seen him get into a situation he didn't see a way out of."

Kano reached down and took a sip of water. "Okay, but let's say you are up in the sandy North looking for oil. Say you find gold instead. Lots of it. Is this guy going to split it with you or slice out your guts and let the blowing sand erase any trace?"

"Hmmm...never thought about that scenario. They do mine gold up there..." He let the thought hang in the air for a moment, then bounced it away with a shrug. "I guess I always assume the best in people. In this case, let's hope we don't find any oil or gold."

Kano took out his copy of *Lonely Planet* and paged through it for a while. Caleb closed his eyes and pretended to sleep while Marcel returned, dripping, from the pool. Several hours of small talk, reading, and jumping in and out of sparkling water ensued.

Sunset arrived and bellies rumbled. The trio went inside for a change of clothing. Caleb poked his head into Kano's room and spotted the ebony rhinoceros on the dresser. He asked, "Wow, where did you get that?"

Kano pulled a clean shirt over his head and let out a nervous chuckle. "Artisana. Every time I look at it though, it makes me shiver. Bad memories of the ride back."

Caleb raised an eyebrow and picked it up, scratching at dried bits of egg. "Is this thing made out of wood or stone?"

"Ebony. Do you like it?"

"Yeah! I will have to go find one for myself. I can't believe how heavy it is. Must have taken forever to carve."

"Keep it."

Caleb looked up at Kano with surprise. "Really? At least let me buy your dinner tonight in exchange."

Kano nodded in agreement and they left the room together. Caleb dropped off his rhino, picked up Marcel, and asked the hostess if they could find grilled meat nearby. Following her vague directions, they made their way through reddish dirt streets avoiding muddy potholes.

Caleb said, "I suppose you get used to it if you live here, but can you believe this is one of the nicest neighborhoods in town?"

Kano snorted slightly and replied, "That is what my taxi driver told me. Figured he was just helping out his cousin at our hotel. Did you catch her name?"

"Nope, didn't think to ask."

"Me either. I mean, if this isn't the ghetto, I don't know what is!"

"I guess this is your first time in the Third World. Mali is one of the poorest countries out there. We are in the Beverly Hills of Bamako." The thought made Kano laugh.

"The *Lonely Planet* did talk about poverty here, but this is different from what I saw in Mexico." Odors wafting up from a plugged section of open sewer put their appetites on hold. "At least Mexico has lots of resorts and nice hotels. Plenty of rich drug dealers too."

Caleb thought for a moment. "I know what you need! You should see what a village is like. Get out of the capital for a bit." A group of barefoot children came running toward them and Marcel quickly stepped out of their way. "This country is a beautiful one—if you are in the right place. We want to go climbing tomorrow; you can tag along if you like."

"Seeing something outside this city sounds great. I don't need to deal with any more traffic here." Kano shuddered imperceptibly.

"Perfect! Oh, and this must be the place she was talking about."

They were standing in front of a tall concrete wall with a pointy iron fence on top. There were crude paintings on the side and a few smoky voices wafting over the top. As they opened a squawking iron door and stepped into the courtyard filled with sandy dirt, Kano said, "We came here for what? Food or drugs? This place looks sketchy."

"Nah, out here we are fine. I wouldn't go inside though. I think those red curtains at the end of the hallway mean what you think they mean." Caleb nodded his tousled head to the building on the left while heading toward an open spot in the corner of the courtyard.

The group sat down on a whitish set of plastic patio chairs surrounding a similar table which didn't quite match. On the other side of a small tree was another table and in the fading light they saw beer bottles scattered all around it. Loud voices with South African accents drowned out the soccer match blaring from a small TV propped up on a chair.

Kano spotted a charcoal fire in a nearby building. Before long, a woman carried sizzling plates of meat and fries smelling like heaven toward the South Africans. "There it is!" One cried out.

"Is it?"

"It is."

"Bloody Hell, it's been an hour. Meat better not be all gristly like last time. These dirty Malians don't know how to have a proper braai." He pulled up his chair, bumping into the table and nearly knocking over the remaining bottles of beer.

"Oh, and you do, Charlie?! Last time you tried your coals were so weak our meat was raw."

The gangly guy pronounced his words with a fist in the air. "Yeah, that's the best way for it. Keeps the flavor from cooking out!"

His smaller companion shook his head knowingly. "Meat in this country is best cooked well, mate."

"Oh, and whadda you know, Jerry? You hardly eat the stuff. Must be why you look skinny as those village monkeys you spend so much time with."

He rolled his eyes. "I go there to spend time with rocks, *Charlie*. I climb. That's how I stay fit. Sometimes I fly the model airplane I made and the kids love it. And besides, those *village monkeys* you talk about are the best people around. If you guys would come out with me more often you would know. The waterfalls will dry up soon and maybe if you quit parkin' a tiger you chunderheads would learn how to have a good time!" He slapped the table for emphasis.

Charlie tried to talk through the food he had stuffed into his mouth. "There's plenty...around this dodgy place. Lots...movies to download. We don't need...go somewhere worse. Probably get poisoned or kidnapped up there."

The small guy set down his kabab and started to get angry. "Whattryu talking about you stupid dof?! This is like sixty kilometers away, not six hundred! You should know by now that around here everything is fine. The villages are safer than the cities, and this city is much safer than your beloved Jo'burg—you showed me pictures of that maximum security house you grew up in. When things get sandy that's when you need to watch yourself, bru." Jerry shook his head condescendingly.

Caleb, Kano and Marcel couldn't have much of a conversation over the animated voices, so they listened in with amusement to the whole exchange. Caleb took the brief pause as an invitation to introduce himself. He turned toward the noisy table and said, "Jerry, is it?"

"It is."

"I'm Caleb. Couldn't help but hear you like to climb. You are talking about Siby I assume?"

Jerry beamed with surprise. "Yeah, that's it, mate!"

"I came to climb. My buddy Marcel and I are all about it. We were thinking about heading out there tomorrow. Our man Kano might want to tag along too. If you need someone to belay, maybe we could all ride out together."

Jerry nodded his head up and down vigorously. "All right, bru! How're you getting out there?"

Caleb shrugged. "We were gonna grab a cab."

With a wave of dismissal, Jerry replied, "No need, I got a truck. She'll get us there. Got an early morning flight to Kayes though. I'm up at four-thirty. Should be good to go by eleven. Where you blokes stayin'?"

"At the hotel on the river, just around the corner, the Villa Soudan."

Jerry lifted his beer in a toast. "Okay, Villa Soudan it is. Pick you up there at eleven. You want to pull up your table? Andrew here is new to Mali so he doesn't talk much yet, but Charlie is a real idiot and the stupid things he says might keep you entertained."

Charlie instantly took offense. "Yeah, and Jerry's a flipping biscuit, eh? Probably get ya' killed on the way out there 'cause of the way he likes to drive..."

The next morning, Marcel noted the time was 11:14 as Jerry pulled up in a white Toyota Hilux with a thick chrome roll-bar. A black plastic air intake rose to the top of the cab, enabling the vehicle to drive under water. Enough dents and scrapes to keep a body shop in business for a month enlivened the grimy paint.

As the truck crunched to a stop over a patch of gravel, Marcel observed the cab only had room for two. Social convention dictated Caleb would sit up front as he had initiated contact with Jerry.

Marcel threw the climbing bag in the bed of the truck, just behind the cab. It would make a better seat than nothing. The driver's side was marginally safer, and Kano would require space to sit next to him. The bag was only big enough for one.

Marcel had no interest in Kano because those narrow eyes glowed with an uneasy mixture of condescension and cunning Marcel didn't trust. At the very least, it meant Kano thought he was smarter than everyone else, but his actual level of intelligence remained inconclusive.

Marcel didn't buy the story of coming here by chance. Nobody came to this godforsaken country on a whim. Kano felt dangerous. After the minimally acceptable amount of greeting, he hopped nimbly into the back of the truck.

Jerry raised an eyebrow and said, "Well, someone's ready to roll, so let's hit it!" He quickly grabbed a cushion for Kano and tossed it in the back.

Caleb squeezed his lanky frame among the bags which took up much of the cab space. Jerry slammed the door and said, "Sorry I have so much junk in here. Not used to taking passengers. Watch that bag by your feet. It's got our lunch in it."

These were the last understandable words Marcel heard for the next hour. He projected clear non-verbal signals that he had no interest in conversation, so Kano kept his mouth shut.

After ten minutes, Marcel was quite glad to be facing backward. His blood pressure rose to unacceptable levels. Charlie was not kidding when he said Jerry would get them killed. The Hilux weaved across the road, avoiding enormous potholes, and barely missing Malians on mopeds and bicycles. Food vendors cluttered wide swaths of the street along with donkey carts and the occasional barnyard animal. All these obstacles turned Jerry's driving into something which resembled a rally sport. There were no marked lanes, so cutting into oncoming traffic was clearly a viable option.

Once they got out of the city things calmed down. The two lane road was wide, smoothly paved, and new. *Probably thanks to Africa's latest colonizers, the Chinese.*

Before long, the topography changed. On the right side of the truck, cliffs rose up from the plain, promising world-class climbing routes. On the left side, Marcel couldn't help but stare at a hill which looked suspiciously like a woman's breast. He wondered if this formation had come into existence entirely by chance. Surrounded on all sides with flat ground, it protruded like a turtle shell rising above the surface of a calm lake topped with a tall nipple of rock. *Could this simply be the result of erosion?* The shorn cliffs on one side of the hill revealed it was once even truer to the half-sphere it resembled. *How did it get there in the first place?* He was sure the two up front would be joking about it.

Soon they came to a village. Jerry drove fast enough over sporadic undulations in the dirt road to send the two in the back airborne several times, so they both stood up, faced forward, and gripped the roll-bar. Marcel liked this outlook better anyway, now that the streets weren't so busy. What he saw before him was an expanse of dusty mud huts topped with thatch and corrugated metal stretching toward what looked like an unending three hundred meter bluff. Shea trees dominated the landscape and recent, heavy rains allowed crops to grow.

Dirt-caked children wearing clothes hanging off of their wiry frames like rags ran after the truck; suddenly Marcel was quite glad Jerry seemed to enjoy pushing his Hilux to the limits of the road. He breathed easier with the thought that those disease-ridden kids couldn't keep up.

After a few minutes, Marcel thought they should have reached the base of the bluff, but it still loomed ahead of them. He concluded this meant it was bigger than his brain could accurately process. Gauging distance was usually not a problem for him.

The road turned into what looked like a dried up stream bed with a deep crevasse running roughly down the middle. Various sizes of rocks and boulders had scattered themselves everywhere. Marcel analyzed the switchbacked route before them and hoped Jerry knew what he was doing. At least he could jump out easily enough if things went wrong.

The 'road' seemed to be used more as a footpath than anything else. Women dressed with intensely bright fabrics carried impossibly large bundles of rubbish on their heads. The Hilux ground to a stop in front of a group of four women and several kids scampering to keep up with them. To Marcel's horror, Jerry said a few words to the women and the youngest one opened the tailgate. They placed their bundles carefully inside, then lifted the kids, and crowded into the bed of the truck.

They didn't smell quite as bad as expected; Marcel stayed focused on the road ahead. He tried to pretend he wasn't sharing space with *village monkeys,* as Charlie had so aptly put it last night. The truck plodded along slowly, roughly, making full use of any marginally drivable surface, mechanically dominating the terrain.

To Marcel's great surprise, Kano began communicating. Out of the corner of his eye he saw him turn part way toward the back, point at himself, smile, and say, "Kano." The ladies went around saying their names in return.

Miriam, the shortest one with wrinkled skin and a few missing teeth, slapped the truck and said, *"Mobili a kayne, kosebé!"*

"Mobili a kayne?" replied Kano.

"Oui, bon auto," said a different lady, translating Bambara to French.

"I see, I guess you like the truck. In English we call this a truck." The ladies looked to each other for understanding but none of them had a clue what Kano was saying. He slapped the truck a few times like Miriam had and said, "Truck, truck, truck."

Miriam mimicked him, "Truck, truck." All the ladies laughed. Then Miriam slapped the side of the bed again and said, *"Mobili, mobili."*

Kano tried it. *"Mobili."* The ladies showered him with praise. The children laughed. Kano smiled.

Marcel's frown deepened. Increasingly repulsed by such close proximity to *village monkeys,* he resisted the desire to jump out and walk. Abandoning his gear was not an option. He assumed they would break or steal something if he wasn't standing guard.

Miriam and Kano ignored Marcel and went back and forth for the rest of the ride up the bluff, teaching each other words by pointing and touching. The children kept trying to join the game but Miriam wouldn't allow it. Eventually, one of the persistent ones got through as Miriam was running out of things to name.

He must have been about four years old. His hair was cut so short it almost looked shaved and yet what little was there still managed to curl into a tight, neatly rounded pattern. Crusty streams of dried snot fell from his nose. He held up two grubby fists in Kano's direction as if offering him a present. One of the women grabbed onto his shirt so he wouldn't fall.

The boy stuck up his thumb and said, *"Kelen."* He then stuck up a stubby index finger and said, *"Fila,"* the third finger was *"saba,"* then, *"naani, duruu, woro,"* continuing until all ten digits were up in the air.

Marcel, along with the ladies in the truck, were taken aback when Kano repeated precisely what the boy showed him with nearly perfect pronunciation. *Has he studied this language before? He must have. So why was he here? Why was he faking ignorance? Or was he actually smart enough to learn so quickly?* The children cheered and wanted more. Kano happily obliged.

At the top of the switchbacks, the women climbed down from the bed of the truck, children scampering behind them. Kano yelled, *"Kan bey,"* as they walked away, assuming this meant goodbye. They had all said it, along with a few other things as they left. He also heard them say, *"In ee chey,"* so he said, *"In ee chey, Miriam,"* with a wave. She sputtered something off to him with a big, toothy smile as the group placed baskets and bundles big enough to be hiding goats onto their heads and ambled away.

The Hilux sighed to a stop in a relatively flat clearing surrounded by brush. Four climbers grabbed their gear and started hiking further up the slope. A massive rock arch dominated the hillside and Jerry said, "We can eat under there. The breeze is always nice and you get quite the view."

The group walked mostly in silence, taking in the surroundings, careful with their footing. As the arch neared, they passed several caves and Jerry paused for a moment to explain. "This is animism at its finest. If you can see into the darkness, you should be able to make out those long, flat rocks stacked on top of a pile of smaller rocks, kind of like a caveman's coffee table. If it reminds you of an altar, that's because it is one. What they sacrifice I don't want to know, but I do know it is still in use."

They were approaching the arch rather indirectly, but as they got closer, Caleb laughed out loud and said, "Is that for real? I mean, first we drive by the world's largest booby and now this?!" The three others looked where he was staring and started laughing too. A towering rock formation captured their attention, looking either like the Loch Ness Monster staring intently into the future or an enormous gentleman's sausage.

"No wonder they make sacrifices here, this must be the home of the Fertility Gods! I think I might like this place," Kano said with a grin.

After a windy lunch under the soaring arch, Kano gave climbing a try, but got bored quickly. If he wanted to get to the top of the rock he would find an easier way—one which didn't crush his groin and make his fingertips bleed.

What better structure to climb than the arch? He imagined the view from the top and felt drawn upward, so he wandered around looking for a path. After poking and prodding, pushing through brush, and jumping across a rift or two in the rock, he made the forty-five degree ascent up the backside of the geologic marvel.

The top was much bigger and flatter than he had visualized. One could even camp up here if the wind wasn't too intense. Beautiful cliffs rose around him. In the direction of the endless plain dotted with stubby trees, the village spread below like grapeshot. It looked peacefully locked into the past, as if nothing had changed in one thousand years, save the addition of a metal roof here and there. The people depended directly upon their land. Crops were growing strong. Domesticated animals roamed with freedom except for the few unfortunate ones stuck in crude pens.

Kano heard nothing but wind. Looking down over the tranquil village of Siby he felt like an ancient God. His vision seemed incredibly strong, as if he could almost view what was happening inside the mud huts. Though he knew little about the people here, he felt they were in some way his people, that he had known them forever, that he belonged, and that he had a responsibility to watch over them, teach them, direct them.

Thoughts and emotions were building up inside, interrupted by a gust threatening to blow him away. His observations told him these people needed and wanted little. They were happy and content. Rationally, he knew they must be struggling to stay alive, in desperate need of nearly every improvement technology could offer. Try as he might, the two contradictory strains of logic refused to merge, piquing Kano's curiosity. Happy and content, yet in desperate need.

He knew his finger landed on Timbuktu, and he also knew he would get there one day. This timeless village tucked beneath the endless bluff pulled at him like nothing had before. It was as if a part of himself had awakened, sprouting like the fresh new crops below.

Hunger set in. Caleb scrambled up the rock to grab the last carabiner. Before long, the truck was in sight. Jerry spoke. "We can't make it back to Bamako on empty stomachs, so let's grab dinner in town. I know a touristy place that shouldn't get us too sick."

They bumped back down switchbacks, wound through narrow gaps between houses, and pulled up in front of a large, medieval-looking gateway. Two towering obelisks dominated either side of a rounded arch. The space above the arch showcased a pattern of geometric shapes. Protruding timbers tapered into a row of spiky pyramids worn down with age.

Beyond the imposing entrance was a well-built pavilion: a concrete slab sheltered by a thickly thatched roof. Large, wooden picnic tables rested under dirty, unbalanced fans swinging precariously to and fro like upset spiders caught in their own webs. Kano said, "I'm surprised they have any electricity in this village."

"Quite a number of tourists come here," replied Jerry, "and this highway brings more than just cars, you know." He nodded his head at the line of concrete poles which held power lines tracing back to Bamako and continued, "The food is okay, but they usually only have two options—yassa and mafé."

"And those would be...?" asked Kano.

"Yassa is actually from Senegal. It's an onion sauce with chicken over rice. Mafé is beef or goat in a peanut sauce with rice or couscous. Even though this place caters to tourists you will probably still find bones in your meat. Maybe a rock or two as well. We are in a village, after all."

Caleb exclaimed, "I don't care if there are still feathers on the chicken. I am so hungry I would eat anything!"

"Don't speak so boldly, mate," cautioned Jerry. "You don't know what people eat in these villages. Pretty much any form of protein goes," he said with a wink.

After an excruciating wait the food finally came. The mystery meat in the mafé was swallowed without much chewing because it had the texture of car tires. After they were finished, Kano asked, "You say this place is for tourists. Do they have rooms as well?"

Jerry continued to act as the tour guide and replied, "I imagine so, although it won't be anything like what you have gotten used to at the Villa Soudan."

"I haven't really gotten used to anything. My plane landed a couple of days ago."

"Well, expect to have camping-like elements mixed into wherever you stay here. Do you want me to ask if they have anything open?"

"Yeah, I could use a break from the city." He shuddered with the images of what had happened on the bridge the day before. "I wouldn't mind spending some time exploring the countryside."

Marcel let slight signs of relief slip into his typically masked facial features as Caleb laughed and said, "You are a brave man! After a day of climbing, this so-called dinner filled my stomach, but if I had to choke it down after any other day I would never forgive myself as a Frenchman! I eat in the city whenever possible so I can get something resembling food." He raised his sweating glass bottle of Fanta for emphasis.

With little effort a room was arranged. Jerry gave Kano his phone number in exchange for money to settle the hotel bill along with his room key so he could grab the rest of Kano's things. They agreed to touch base in a few days. Jerry promised to come back soon so they could check out a waterfall together.

As Kano settled into his round, thatched hut, the indestructible Hilux rumbled toward the sprawling chaos of Bamako. He couldn't wait to see what life in the village was all about.

After a brief pause, Souleymane broke into the monologue. "How did you know they would come back for you? Or take care of your things? I have been told white people have no trust for each other."

Kano laughed out loud. "Well, I suppose that is usually true. But once we get to know one another we do develop plenty of trust. You quickly get a feeling about who is trustworthy and who isn't. I never would have asked Marcel, but Jerry was a no-brainer. Caleb seemed…unreliable. And besides, the only things I really cared about were my camera, passport, and wallet, and I kept those with me the whole time."

The tea was long gone but Souleymane wished there was more. This desire helped him realize their translation time had been diminished. Chastising himself, he silently rose to fetch the supplies without another thought.

The next morning, Souleymane thought about how he could hear more of Kano's story without sacrificing their routine. He wanted to know how a *Toubobou* would deal with life in a village similar to the one he had grown up in. *How did he get by without speaking the language? Did the food and water make him sick?*

Many of the white passengers he saw on the bus seemed sick, uncomfortable, or a combination of the two. Perhaps Kano was fit enough to talk again during their excursion into the dunes. He happily decided to slow down the pace so more could be told without The Scholar noticing a dip in productivity.

White cloth wrapped around their heads helped to keep sun and sweat out of their eyes as they ventured forth into the baking Sahara. Kano didn't mind talking while moving through the sand. It would seem the physical depletion caused by his devastating encounter with malaria had been totally replenished. It felt good to have his energy back again.

As Kano dipped and rose from one dune to the next, his mind drifted back to his naivety with a smile. He resumed the story with a small laugh at his own expense.

From the top of the arch, Kano had seen the village of Siby as a tranquil place. Not a single sound or smell wafted up to his lofty, windswept perch. Kano's first night of sleep in the village hostel was like jumping into a pristine alpine lake where the serene view is instantly forgotten as frigid water shocks the body into reality.

In direct opposition to the very thought of an icy plunge, the temperature never seemed to drop. Sweat continued to flow even after lying nearly naked for hours. Oh, how he wished for the air conditioner back in his comfortable hotel room!

Every metal support could be felt through the thin mattress, and either mosquitoes were finding their way through the ragged, dusty net which sagged above him or something else was biting. Large vehicles blasted their horns and pummeled the asphalt with off-road tires all night long. Surprised donkeys brayed with the startling force of car alarms. *Didn't they sleep?* At least the innumerable roosters stayed quiet until tinny sounds from the mosque's cheap megaphones rattled through the village. Kano could still see stars through his small window. *What on earth would motivate people to rise so early in such a peaceful place?*

It couldn't have been more than a few minutes after the discordant call to prayer that the pounding started. It came from several directions. Kano imagined a circus had come into town and heavily muscled men were driving tent stakes into the ground with giant, cartoonish mallets. Later on, he connected the sound with a woman in a nearby courtyard who was pounding grain with a giant mortar and pestle.

The entire community was up before daybreak, but it was the whining of mosquitoes giving way to the buzzing of flies which served as the final straw, impelling Kano from his squeaky bed.

After a refreshingly cold shower, he poked around for a bit of breakfast. The waitress from yesterday was busy preparing a few things, but brightened up when she saw him and said warmly, *"Ah nee sogoma, bonjour."*

Kano figured he would continue repeating what he heard, just like the day before in the truck, without bothering with the French, so he smiled and said, *"Ah nee sogoma."*

"Eh? E bey Bamanankan men?"

Kano recognized a question by the curious intonation in her voice, but tilted his head slightly to the side and looked at her quizzically in response. After a brief pause he said, "I don't speak much French or your language, Bambara according to my *Lonely Planet.*"

Her lips drew together slightly as she replied, "Hmmm...me no Engleesh. Seeet. Fod." She gestured toward the picnic tables where they had eaten the night before. A minute later she brought him part of a white baguette with jam and tea. Kano had trouble slicing it with the dull knife. The crust was incredibly chewy, but it filled his rumbling stomach.

He let his mind wander until she eventually returned wearing different clothing. She said, "Yuu. Cooma." Her gestures indicated she wanted him to follow her. She led him away from the main road and into the village. They walked for what felt like a long time, gathering many curious looks, mostly from children.

When they reached the outskirts, she stopped at a small, walled complex with a door made of corrugated metal nailed to a few rough scraps of wood. The wall was short enough for Kano to see over and he noticed a small thatched structure with chickens pecking about nearby. There was also a larger thatched building he guessed was a kitchen, and a small house with a tin roof. Extending the roofline, a raggedly covered lean-to made from woven grass blocked most of the sun and effectively doubled the living space of the tiny house, as long as it wasn't raining.

She knocked on the door and called out, "*Koninba, e bey yan?*" Kano heard an unfamiliar noise in response that sounded like a cross between a cooing pigeon and a cat's meow. He was startled to see a reddish-brown monkey perched on one of the twisting branches that supported the weight of the thatched lean-to. Monkey and Man appraised each other while waiting for a crude screen door to swing open. To Kano's further surprise, a white man ducked out through the undersized doorway and smiled at them. "*Ah nee sogoma, Fanta,*" he said while approaching.

The woman spoke with him animatedly for a couple of minutes. Kano had no idea what they were talking about. He reached out toward the curious monkey who grabbed his thumb and turned his palm up to see if it contained any food.

After the disappointed monkey lost interest, the man stuck out his hand and spoke in English. "Hi, I'm Tim. My Malian name is Koninba. She was explaining why she brought you here. Said your friends abandoned you last night and you don't speak French. She wants me to translate a few questions for you."

Kano smiled with understanding. "Ok, that makes sense. What doesn't make sense is what you are doing here. This is your house?"

"Yeah, I am a Peace Corps Volunteer. Wrapping up my tour. Three weeks left. Can't wait to get home and go on a fast food binge! Never really liked it when I lived in the States, but believe me, it is surprising what you miss when you can't have it."

Kano laughed. "Right on, I don't think I would miss the burgers though. I bet not being able to get a decent burrito will be the worst for me."

The monkey jumped up on Tim's shoulder to sniff his breath to see if he had been eating anything. "Fair enough. Anyway, Fanta wants to know why you are staying at her hotel and for how long."

With a raised eyebrow he replied, "She calls that place a hotel?! Well, I don't really know. Came out yesterday with friends to go climbing and the village had a certain...draw. I wanted to stick around. Seems like these people could really use someone who knows how to solve their problems."

Tim laughed uncomfortably and responded, "What do you think I have been doing here for the past three years? And what makes you think these people want *you* to solve *their* problems? It might be hard for you to imagine, but most of them are quite happy with their lives. Friends and family are much more important around here than trivial things like clean water and proper sanitation."

Kano pondered this for a moment, realizing he may need to adjust his perspective. He kept the conversation going on a new tack. "The guy who brought us out here, Jerry, said he would be back in a few days with my things."

Tim laughed again and said, "Jerry, like South African Jerry? I guess it couldn't be anyone else. He likes to make promises, but who knows when he will show up."

"Okay, so how do you know him?" Kano asked with frustration creeping into his voice; he was under the impression that Jerry was reliable.

"We have both been here awhile and he likes to come out to Siby. When you are white in Mali you tend to meet the other white people. I went climbing with him a few times and he loves the waterfalls I showed him. I stay with him when I come to Bamako. Give me a moment to translate."

Tim turned toward the woman and spoke rapidly in Bambara. Kano listened closely to the sounds of the language and then Tim switched back into English. "Okay, so Fanta wants to know what kind of food you like to eat and if the room was all right."

"Fanta, like the soft drink?" grinned Kano.

Tim rolled his eyes. "Yeah, that is an easy one to remember. People here love it if you know their names. You should introduce yourself," he said with a hint of admonishment in his voice.

Kano did, somewhat sheepishly, realizing he had been rude, and wondered at the same time if Fanta was after his money or if the concern she showed while talking to Tim actually indicated she wanted to help. "Tell her the room is fine and I want to try Malian food. What we had last night was good but the meat was too chewy. She can surprise me. The spicier the better!"

Tim replied with a knowing chuckle. "A dangerous statement. Make sure you don't get too adventurous. Get your food *only* from her and bring a water bottle with you *everywhere* you go so you don't have to drink *anything* the villagers offer you. She knows how to cook for Westerners. You will get really sick otherwise."

He translated again to Bambara and then said, "Look, I am happy to show you around the village some other time if you want to get to know the place. Right now I have a meeting to get to. Malians don't care about being on time, but I do. You can always drop by to see if I am around or just ask somebody where to find me. Any random person seems to know where everyone else is."

"Sounds good. Maybe later you can teach me a few things in Bambara."

"No problem, and enjoy Siby," Tim said with a genuine smile and a firm handshake, effectively communicating that usefulness was something he took pleasure in.

Tim told Fanta he would see her later, "*Kan bey kofé,*" and Kano memorized the phrase before following her along the dusty, twisting path back to the hostel.

Kano slipped into something that resembled a routine over the next few days. He ate his breakfast alone and then spent the morning wandering through the village, followed by curious stares and exclamations of, "*Toubobou, Toubobou,*" from dirty children. Tim would later explain to him *Toubobou* meant a person from France, but most Malians didn't know there was a difference between a French person and a white person with another nationality. Kano thought this ignorance to be rather akin to the way many Americans thought of Africa as one big country.

After wandering constricted streets aimlessly, he would stop to attempt a bit of conversation. Invariably, the invitation for tea would come. Taking part involved a potent brew heated over charcoal. They drank it out of shot glasses. Enough sugar was added to force heavy bitterness into submission. The tea gave Kano even more of a stomach ache than the food they shared with him for lunch. He fully ignored the stern warning to stay away from local cuisine.

Always, he would try to talk with his hosts, only needing to repeat a word he wanted to learn once or twice before it stuck. By the end of the third day, he had learned everything that could be pointed to. After an afternoon nap, he would take a long hike up and down the bluff, careful to avoid hidden snakes and scorpions. Every night, Kano bought his favorite Peace Corps Volunteer dinner in order to fill in any knowledge gaps from the day.

On the third night, Tim said with worry in his voice, "Jerry called me a few hours ago. One of their captains went back to France for an emergency. He has to fill in. Won't be back here for another week or two."

Kano shrugged his shoulders. He was happy.

"Do you really think you can hold up for that long? If you need to, we can always put you on a bus headed for Bamako."

Kano smiled tiredly, giving Tim a peaceful, contented dismissal. "I figure that by the time you leave I will know my way around well enough. Sure am glad I came when I did. Without your help, figuring this place out would be a lot harder."

It wasn't long before Kano lost track of the days. His quick memorization of words and phrases grew into a useful set of vocabulary. Food stopped tasting so bad and he hadn't been sick yet. The heat and sounds which kept him awake for much of the first night became manageable.

One day, he was enjoying tea with a family in a small compound on the outskirts of the village. Suddenly, the children ran out to investigate high-pitched honking followed by slamming car doors.

The small crowd came back excitedly, leading Jerry and his companion. She was a young woman so attractive Kano almost dropped his half-filled glass. His world melted away like sugar crystals dissolving into hot tea water. The only part of his field of view which stayed in focus was the female form walking toward him, dressed for adventure.

He hadn't seen a white person other than Tim for quite some time. He hadn't slept with a woman for what seemed like an eternity, although that hadn't bothered him.

She definitely would have caught his eye had they been on a beach in Southern California, but here in Siby, the effect of her gracefully athletic walk, perfectly toned body, and gorgeous smile captivated him in a way that he had never felt before.

As the group crossed the small courtyard, Kano's mouth hung slightly open and he didn't even hear what Jerry had said, so Jerry tried again. "You alright there, Kano? Forget how to speak English after so much time in the village? Sorry it took so long for me to get here! One of our captains is still in France and the new American pilot got malaria, so I had a lot of flying to do. Figured you would have called if you needed something."

Kano stammered, "No…no…Tim has been keeping my English fresh. Filling me in on the locals too. How is this…this…American doing now?"

"He will be fine. Good thing he was taking his pills. They keep the symptoms relatively minor." Jerry smiled at the kids who stared up at him with wonder. "Glad you hooked up with Tim. He is leaving the country tomorrow—called me for a ride back to Bamako. Figured I could kill two birds with one stone and check in on you too. How is he doing?"

Kano desperately tried not to stare at the slender blonde with crossed arms, as if she was waiting for something. "Ummm, he's just fine I suppose. Excited to head home."

"Good, good. By the way, this is Johanna. I promised I would show her the falls. Three birds with one stone, I guess. Tim wanted to go one last time. Feel like tagging along?"

"Ummm, yeah, great…sounds great." For some reason Kano continued to avert his eyes from Johanna. Shyness around a beautiful girl was an entirely new sensation for him. After an awkward handshake followed by a pause he continued, "Why don't you run by his office and see if he has wrapped things up there. My room isn't too far, I will walk back and get changed. Pick me up at the hotel as soon as you are ready."

Kano turned to the family and said, *"Haketo, n be taa sisan. I ne che for la thé. N be naa kofe. Kan ben!"*

Everyone from the family offered their parting blessings in an unintelligible harmony. On the walk to the truck a visibly impressed Jerry said, "Wow, you have been picking it up quickly. What did you say to them?"

"I told them this big hairy ape and his new girlfriend need my help finding their way up the mountain." Kano looked back and waved.

Jerry laughed and said, "Johanna and I just met. We aren't dating. How did you learn to say all that so quickly?"

He shrugged. "I guess I am good with languages, and Tim has been helping me out, so it wasn't hard. Greetings and goodbyes I learned on the first day. All I really said was that I had to go and then thanked them for tea. No idea how to introduce you as a big hairy ape. Nice that nobody here laughs at your mistakes like they do in Europe—they are simply delighted you try to speak with them. Kind of like being a rock star."

Johanna forced Kano's attention by turning to him and speaking with an oddly sarcastic accent and a smile. "It was nice to meet you. See you soon!"

The smile disarmed Kano and he returned it with a confused, happy expression much more genuine than his standard mischievous grin reserved for women who captured his interest. The only thing the foreign butterflies in his stomach would allow him to say was, "Yup, see you soon."

He involuntarily leaned toward her as if pulled in by the magnetic field quickly forming between the two. Given a few moments longer, the tropical air would have crackled with its growing force. Jerry broke off the connection with a thunderous slam of his Hilux door. It was the only way to get the latch to catch.

On his walk back to the hotel, Kano quickly shook off the lingering haze, and was able to place Johanna's unusual accent. As soon as he did, memories of delirious nights spent in Amsterdam and Utrecht flooded back like a dream from a different lifetime.

"So, wait, wait, wait." Souleymane had stopped dead in his tracks. "This is the girl you took to dinner, right? You told me about her. It made you feel so sad. This is how you met?"

Kano responded with a touch of longing in his voice. "Yes, this is how we met."

"And those pills the American pilot took, did you bring some with you? Would they help with your malaria?"

Kano brightened slightly from the unexpected concern, and answered, "I left the pills at the hotel room where I was staying when you kidnapped me, but I guess the damage has already been done. No point in taking them now. We have wandered out pretty far into the sand today. Shouldn't we start making our way back to town?"

Souleymane pursed his lips and said, "I suppose you are right. I would be ruined if you end up collapsing in these dunes. White people cannot handle this type of excursion. Please, continue your story as we head back."

Once again, Kano's thoughts flooded back into that glorious day. It only had taken the battered Hilux about thirty minutes to get up the ridge line and back to the waterfall. Normally the trip would last an hour. It was a miracle they didn't get completely lost as Jerry deftly followed the maze of donkey cart trails and dried up streams. He needed a bit of help navigating, but Jerry's rally-style driving got Tim so carsick he ended up being of little use.

Feeling like a cowboy in a rodeo, Kano got to ride with Johanna in the back. There was an oddly light remark exchanged here or there, but the ride itself demanded constant focus. They stood behind the cab, facing forward. The roll bar provided something solid to latch onto.

Jerry tenaciously pushed the Hilux so there was a constant wind buffeting their faces; sometimes this moving air brought a bug or two along with it. They quickly learned to keep their mouths shut. Buckling their knees to avoid being ejected by the bumps was a shared technique, hastily mastered. Both adopted a wide stance and were keenly attuned to the ground ahead of the truck.

Eventually, Jerry skidded to a halt in a shady spot. Tim dizzily exited the car while Kano and Johanna decoupled themselves from the roll bar and gingerly hopped over the tailgate. They could hear rushing water through an unusually tall copse of trees.

The group pulled themselves together and grabbed everything they needed from the cab. Out of habit, Jerry double-checked to make sure nothing valuable was left behind. The locks had stopped working years ago. A short walk under the strangely closed canopy led them to tropical paradise. It was as if ancient gods had taken pity on this relatively barren region and transplanted a hidden waterfall from the rainforests of the South.

Kano imagined they were entering the remains of a temple built around the same time as Atlantis. Two waterfalls flowed over bulky blocks of tan and black rock, worn smooth with time. The distant cascade was tall and dropped nearly vertically while the other broadly spread out across what could once have been a grand staircase or the seats of a small amphitheater. In his mind's eye, he could see mythical rulers determining the fate of the continent from these sacred steps.

A mild roar from the tall falls echoed against the sheer face of a ten meter platform which lorded over a deep pool like the prow of a war-torn battleship. The surface area of the water below was minimal; the same footprint as a small country church. It quickly changed color from narrow brown shores to unknown depths of greenish-blue mirk.

An unexpected noise startled Kano from a state of enraptured silence; the exquisite beauty of the oasis had struck him motionless. A plummeting shout from Jerry was followed by a sharp crack as his body broke the surface. An unclean animal battering its way into the holy of holies.

Water sprayed up in protest, sullying the walls of the cliff Jerry had so wildly thrown himself from. As he resurfaced, small waves broke against towering rock, mingling with scattered droplets coloring its worn surface. The young man in the forbidden pool allowed his voice to travel up from the waters, inviting his fellow desecrators to partake in the afternoon of pleasure dangling irresistibly before them.

Not knowing the history of the hidden oasis or the mystery of its waters, they didn't hesitate to soak in the offering of bliss. Three dry companions followed the path Jerry had taken. They peered down onto the happy figure treading water below like birds of prey honing in on a field mouse. Jerry's voice echoed up, "What are you waiting for?! The water is great! Jump off! Just don't aim for me!"

Tim replied, "Ask and ye shall receive." As Kano and Johanna shared a worried glance, Tim's t-shirt flew through the air in one direction while his body launched itself in the other. His arms and legs flailed like a spastic sprinter. Pre-ordained laws of gravity directed his trajectory to within a meter of Jerry, whose eyes opened wide with fright as he tried in vain to push himself backward.

After a worrisome amount of time, Tim spurted to the surface, gulping air, and yelling, "I almost had it! I saw the bottom!"

Jerry said, "You idiot! I don't know what was scarier—jumping off that cliff myself or watching your crazy karate moves as you tried to land on top of me!"

The ensuing argument faded as Kano and Johanna turned their attention toward each other with disarming smiles. He searched for flaws among her fine bone structure and the few he found made her more attractive. The light spattering of freckles drawn out by sunshine spelled the essence of youthful beauty. Kano noticed one ear was slightly higher than the other. She also had a striking nose—it was the right size for her face, sloping perfectly between her wide, light blue eyes, but the angle steepened as the strip of cartilage ended, coming to a slightly pronounced tip. This, in combination with thin lips made her seem as though she had walked out of a mail order catalogue from the 1950s. Kano realized what some would consider imperfections were what he found most beautiful about the face gazing back into his. Anything too perfect risks becoming boring.

He said, "Are you ready to jump?"

"Not yet. Maybe after those, uh, clowns down there calm down. How about you?"

Sensing her reluctance, he played along. "I don't think so. My family jewels are too precious for that type of abuse. Besides, we don't know how deep the water is or if something might stick out of the bottom. It would take a couple of hours to get to the nearest hospital. Not worth it." He paused to scan the rocks. "The water does look great, though. Shall we take the long way down?"

"Sounds good to me, but I bet Jerry could get you to the hospital faster than that." She followed him down the staircase of giants, the inviting smell of tropical sun drying wet rocks growing stronger with each step.

"Yeah, he would get us halfway there in record time, and then someone else would need to rescue us from what is left of his truck after he rolls it over," said Kano with a playful smile. He continued in feigned ignorance, "I have been trying to figure out where you are from. The clothes definitely aren't American and neither is the accent. It's not French or German or anywhere further South. It sounds very European but that's the best I can do. Care to enlighten me?"

Johanna's small frame deftly navigated the smooth rock. "I have been working on that accent. Happy to hear it isn't too specific. I am Dutch, from the Netherlands."

"I thought the Dutch were from Holland." Kano almost slipped as he failed to focus his attention on the uneven terrain.

"People say that, but it is only true some of the time. During our Golden Age a few hundred years ago, traders left from Amsterdam and Rotterdam which are in North and South Holland: two of our twelve provinces. Truthfully, they said they were from Holland, and the people they traded with assumed this was the name of their country." She paused to watch Jerry and Tim push each other underwater as they struggled for the shore. "I grew up in the east of the Netherlands, closer to Germany. Right now I am living in Utrecht, and that isn't far from Amsterdam, but still not quite in Holland."

"Thanks for the history lesson." He rolled his eyes. "Better watch out!" Kano nodded his head toward Tim and Jerry who came running straight for them, sprinkling drops of water and condescending smiles on the two chickens while racing back to the top to see who could jump first.

Kano and Johanna's continuing conversation revealed they were on a similar intellectual level. Kano was often bored when talking to others, but she seemed different. Perhaps he gave her too much credit for growing up speaking a language other than English, but Johanna understood the subtle meaning in between Kano's words which most people missed.

She never would have been attracted to Kano a year ago. Or perhaps even a month ago. The predatory sheen in his eyes had dimmed to a dangerous flicker. Expressions which recently flashed malevolent superiority now radiated open curiosity, although he still spoke with patronizing strains laced into his tone.

Sparks of their initial attraction mixed with the glow of shared adventure and grew into an energy which seemed to heat them almost as much as the African sun.

Flip-flops protected their feet from hot, dark rock as they carefully descended the few remaining meters. When they reached the point where the broad falls met the chilled pool of water, Kano didn't hesitate to shed his shirt, revealing what was for him an atrophied display of muscle. The results of his former dedication to the gym remained to a degree, fulfilling Johanna's stereotype of the solidly-built American Man. Most Europeans didn't appeal to her physically; she imagined centuries of devastating warfare deprived Western Europe of its masculinity.

Johanna was slower to slip out of her shorts and then lift the faded tank top up, over her head in one gracefully fluid motion. The deep blue bikini gripped the remaining mystery of her body tightly and Kano couldn't help but marvel at her taut stomach as the shirt momentarily covered her eyes, leaving her vulnerable to his gaze for a split second.

Time itself seemed to slow down as the beauty before him etched itself into his consciousness. Her legs were athletically honed and had more muscle than he was used to. He wondered if this was from riding a bicycle instead of driving a car.

At that moment, the attraction between the two became too intense, and they solved the problem by jumping into the beckoning water. The danger lurking within its depths remained, by design, entirely undetectable.

Six weeks before Kano and Johanna followed their flailing friends in the forbidden pool, a wildly successful hunter by the name of Amadou paused by a stream whose waters fed the hidden oasis. His hawkish eyes spied movement in the branches of a tall tree opposite the flowing water. He lifted his gun, but the monkey managed to scamper down the far side, escaping neatly through jagged grass below as if it could sense Amadou's lethal intentions.

The hunter's fame was known throughout the region; his greatness allowed him a large family. He had four wives and twenty-three children. He strongly believed monogamy was something reserved for the weak and the poor. There was no way for him to know that monogamous relationships happily existed within his very own body.

Nearly a decade ago, two eager worms about one centimeter in length pledged their lives to each other when the female nestled herself into a long groove shaped just for her—the male hugging her tightly for the rest of their privileged lives. The two had joined together to become one.

This particular couple weren't the only ones to claim a prime piece of real estate and settle down within the hospitable confines of Amadou's bladder. Without restraint, they entered into the family business of reproduction. Over the course of their lifetime they were destined to produce an astronomical number of offspring. The vast majority would suffer a multitude of deaths before reaching maturity.

On this particular day, as Amadou stood by the stream, frustrated by the escape of his prey, calmly flowing water stimulated an urge to urinate. Naturally, he pointed the fluid flowing from his body into the larger stream before him. Hundreds of eggs were released, compliments of the cloistered monogamy within.

Eggs quickly transformed into miracidia: mobile organisms propelled by tiny hairlike protrusions known as cilia, looking for a specific creature. They had less than twenty-four hours before their energy would be depleted, so they searched desperately for the perfect host. They all failed—except for a single miracidium who found its target: a Bulinus freshwater snail, clinging to a column of plant material about one hundred meters downstream. The miracidium did what Nature had programmed it to do, burrowing into the unsuspecting omnivore. A second transformation then occurred which very nearly brought death to the struggling snail. Sporocyst formation. A rounded factory designed to produce a small army of cercariae.

Cercariae are tiny creatures with a devilishly forked tail. They emerged from the spent snail around noon, six weeks after the monkey escaped from Amadou's sights. Being only a millimeter long, they swam four meters per hour. There was no way they could have made it to the other side of the waterfall by the time Kano and Johanna jumped into the pool without a great deal of help from the gentle current.

Furthermore, it is impossible for cercariae to live for more than a day in the water. Once again, most were born to a quick death, but several happened to be perfectly positioned to intercept two invigorated hosts.

Unbeknownst to the swimmers, cercariae were clutching on for dear life. Kano and Johanna eased their way over to Jerry and Tim who treaded water with boundless energy. "Too chicken for the high dive?!"

"No," answered Kano, "I just don't need some moron landing on top of me."

In reality, Kano was dying to jump off, but didn't want Johanna to feel alienated. The afternoon progressed like a dream, and when Kano and Johanna were a bit pruny, they climbed out of the water. Johanna remembered a tip she had read in her travel guide and toweled off immediately. Kano preferred to let the sun do the work. This preference would nearly cost him his life.

The towel removed the cercariae from Johanna's skin. Those remaining on Kano managed to burrow in. Before long, they shed their forked tails, became schistosomulae, and penetrated Kano's bloodstream. As they grew into the adult worms they were designed to be, they migrated to his digestive system.

Kano would experience no physical symptoms of his transformation into an egg-factory. Unfortunately for him, not all the eggs produced would make their way out. Some would enter his blood vessels and get caught up in the brain's strong granulomatous response system.

Inflammatory cells would surround these intruders like sentries, watching imprisoned eggs die and gradually calcify. Job well done. It would take more than twenty years for this cerebral granuloma to grow to a size large enough to produce seizures—the first and only symptoms of his monogamous parasites.

It seemed to Kano like they had just arrived at the oasis, but the afternoon was waning. Rapidly approaching booms of thunder could be heard over tumbling water. Kano's stomach echoed this rumbling sentiment. The group gathered their belongings and made it back to the truck in time to see scorching sunshine blotted from the sky as if the ancient gods were chasing the desecrators away from their forbidden sanctuary.

Blackness boiled. Immediately upon the truck's departure from the sheltering stand of trees, a tropical tempest descended upon the earth. Windshield wipers became useless and Tim's navigational tips required shouting to be heard. Feeling both blind and deaf, Jerry slowly pushed into the unrecognizable landscape. After the brink of the storm passed overhead, the deluge diminished, but the damage had already been done.

What were once donkey trails transformed into rivers and streams. Jerry had little way to gauge their depth. Even if he could have remembered the specific dips and furrows, the water flowed brown with change.

He cautiously enjoyed the challenge while Kano and Johanna couldn't stop shivering in the back. At least the giant raindrops which spattered and stung like hail were behind them. The thrill of the storm started to wear down into a penetrating cold. Neither had felt the least bit of a chill since they stepped onto Malian soil; the unexpected goosebumps now felt as foreign as their first impressions of the country.

Standing up in the back, they saw the route ahead much better than the two dry ones in the cab. Jerry became slightly overconfident in his skills and was going too fast to respond to the shouting and banging above his head. The front wheels of the Hilux lurched into a water-filled trench so deep the bumper crashed into the other side, supporting the weight of the front end.

Water quickly piled up against the door, flowing over the hood and into the cab. Jerry knew enough to keep the vehicle running; the elevated air intake was designed to prevent the engine from flooding.

Kano observed a pitted rock the size of a cannonball break away from the steep bank, smash into the fender of the Hilux, and scrape its way along the hood. This gave Kano an idea. He hopped out of the back and offered Johanna a hand down. Four wet companions met on high ground where Kano presented his solution.

They quickly dispersed in search of rock. After fifteen minutes of frantic lifting and dragging, a decent pile emerged upstream from the truck that was still patiently idling as if nothing was amiss, even though much of it had disappeared completely under the muddy current.

When Kano determined enough had been gathered, he directed the largest specimens to be dragged first into the flowing water at a forty-five degree angle to the direction of the flow. This made the water angry, turning it from brown to white. The group hurried to drop in melon sized rocks next, and the water reluctantly shifted its course. A shallow rivulet behind the truck started to swell from the revised flow.

The hood was still submerged, but the remainder of the pile stopped the gaps and most of the water redirected itself. Before long, sediment completed the dam, and the left wheel became fully exposed. Water poured out of the cab for a minute or two as the team observed the full extent of their predicament.

Going forward would be impossible unless they had tools to dig out ground so hard that flash-flooding couldn't make a dent. The freshly formed stream was quickly eating away the ground not far behind the truck, so backing up would not be possible for long.

Jerry directed Tim to push from the front while Kano and Johanna jumped up and down over the back axle. After burning a couple of years off the clutch, the Hilux lurched out of the hole in reverse, giving Kano and Johanna a few bruises as they tumbled toward the cab. A wet cheer went up as the group quickly prepared themselves for a return to civilization.

After backtracking to cross the flow upstream, Jerry took on a reformed level of caution which still reeked of madness to the uninitiated, but they made it down to the village.

Kano and Johanna felt their teeth chatter uncontrollably. The rain hadn't stopped. It wasn't mere chilliness they felt but raw cold seeping into their bones. Hand muscles welded to the roll bar, the truck rumbled to a stop in front of Fanta's restaurant. They struggled to unclasp themselves and move their joints. It felt like fighting against the rusty hinges of an old gate. Kano glanced over at her, and their eyes met, unlocking something deeper than the natural bond forged by their shared experience.

After the city-dwellers drove off, Kano went to bed early. For the first time, he slept through the village cacophony without waking once. He didn't even remember a single dream—a rarity for him—it was as if his whole being ceased to exist for eleven hours and thirty-seven minutes. Time was one of the only Western things he was still able to monitor, so he kept close track.

The sun was hot in the sky when he finally stepped out into daylight. After a quick breakfast, he departed from what had become his standard, slow pace and walked purposefully to the general store. The man who ran it had a friendly smile, always happy to see white people in his shop.

Kano rushed up with beads of sweat running down his face and said good morning to the store owner. "*I ni sogoma,* Drissa."

Drissa paused for a moment in surprise, related the standard greetings, then replied to Kano in Bambara, "I have seen you in this village for quite some time. Why is it only now that you come to my store?"

Kano spoke without too much of an accent, although his grammar needed work. "Ahhh, it because you are Djarra and I no like what beans do to the air in you shop. Also, you wife look like donkey."

Tim had given one final piece of advice to Kano the night before, as he packed his things into Jerry's truck: the best way to make new friends was to insult your *Joking Cousins*. Family lines had a long caste history in Mali and certain ones had special relationships with others. Greetings often included plenty of disparaging remarks, which resulted in laughter and more jokes. Conversely, when a problem popped up, they were always there to help each other based on nothing more than a last name.

Kano's comment worked as promised, causing everyone within hearing distance to erupt with infectious laughter, then they all started talking at the same time. After throwing insults around for a while, the group allowed Kano and Drissa to get down to business.

Drissa said with a smile, "So my bean eating friend, what are you looking for today?"

"I need telephone."

"You can always use mine." He slid the scratched Nokia across the counter.

The friendly offer made Kano smile. "Thank you, but my phone need."

Drissa pointed to the orange packets of plastic hanging from a dark and roughly-cut rafter. "I only have phone cards. To resupply your minutes. I can get a phone for you from Bamako." Kano scanned the worn shelves impatiently.

"How long it take?"

He shrugged. "Maybe this afternoon or tomorrow. I will make some calls. What kind do you want?"

"Something that no break. And battery no die."

"No problem. 20,000 CFA and I can get you a good Nokia even newer than this one." He gestured at the purple device lying between them. "Not one of those awful Chinese things. The battery will last for two weeks and the only way it could break is if a donkey steps on it."

"Perfect. I need fast possible." He pulled two, crisp 10,000 CFA notes out of his wallet and tried to pass them to Drissa.

He shook his hands in protest. "No, no! First I will get you the Nokia. If you like it, then you can pay. If you don't like it, I can get you another one. Now we must drink tea."

Kano carefully returned the bills to his wallet and smiled. "Okay, tea drink!"

Suddenly, it was Souleymane's turn to feel sad. He interrupted the narrative to say, "Your story makes me miss the place where I grew up. I wish it would thunder and rain here like it does in the South. I wish the tea tasted the same. I wish the people here were friendlier. Oh, what I would give to be able to pick fresh mangoes from a tree!"

Kano laughed out loud. "You miss home?! You can go any time you want. Just hop on a bus. I am the one who is a prisoner. I am the one who needs an airplane to get out of this dust bowl back to where I belong." He ended the sentence with a bitter tone.

Souleymane shook his head slowly as he formulated his reply with caution. "I don't think you truly understand my situation." He stared down into the blinding sand before his feet. "I have no money. I cannot leave. How would I eat? How can I buy a bus ticket? Only The Scholar can choose my destiny. I have never thought of myself as a prisoner, but leaving this place with dignity is not possible for me."

Kano walked in silence, realizing that perhaps Souleymane was right, and they were both prisoners. "But surely you must have chosen to come here. One does not travel so far from home accidentally."

"That is true," said Souleymane sadly. "It was not an accident. I was curious about the people who live here. People who are so different from me. I was not happy with the way I grew up. I wanted something more exciting. The Scholar offered me this. He has taught me so much. I am content and I want to stay here. But I cannot leave."

Kano knew speaking negatively about The Scholar would cause another conflict, so he didn't reply. They had already arrived back at the compound. It was time for lunch.

The next day, Kano continued his stories as they trekked into the dunes. Souleymane listened carefully, his companion's words stirring up longing for the region he grew up in. He could visualize everything happening in his mind's eye.

True to his word, Drissa quickly provided Kano with a phone whose battery put the Energizer Bunny to shame. Over the course of its first few days in use, it had been rained on and then dropped more than a few times without any ill effects. Although Kano hadn't missed having a phone in his pocket, he kept this one with him constantly so he could read each text message an instant after Johanna sent it.

His reply always took time even though he knew what to say right away. Something about this village and its culture changed the way he approached social interaction. Or perhaps it was just that he had never met such an intriguing individual. Normally he would jump right into bed with her at the earliest possible opportunity, but instead he decided to savor every moment, each little step forward.

Text messages turned into phone conversations, and he ended up giving Drissa plenty of money for phone cards. It took time, but eventually, Kano decided he was ready to head back to Bamako. His long distance tactics could only stretch so far.

The beauty of the scenery had lost its novelty. He had learned enough from his friends in the village. A certain peace settled over his character, but he also itched for some alcohol and a card game. The biggest pull was, of course, the voice who talked to him from the other side of the telephone.

Slowly but surely, and without fully realizing it, Kano had become a pleasure delayer. Growing up, everything had been at his fingertips. Instant gratification defined his way of life. After living in the village, he came to know the value of drawing out the journey.

This change came precisely in time for Johanna. She even played a role in bringing it about. She was not what Kano was accustomed to; she would not be rushed. Once he got back to the capital, he had to force himself to settle in at Jerry's place before giving her a call.

The captain sharing Jerry's apartment had gone back to France in a rage. He quit because the aviation safety regulations weren't being followed and he was the only one who seemed to care. All the other pilots were from America or South Africa and they laughed and made fun of his ridiculous accent when he got upset about it, although they were secretly worried too.

It would take time to fill the position, and Jerry didn't like living on his own. He insisted Kano take the extra room—rent free. After catching up in the spacious, tiled living room, Kano asked, "What is your night looking like? Want to find a bar or something? Any pool tables or card games in this town?"

Jerry shook his head. "Would love to, but I am flying in the morning so I'll have to pass on that one."

"Ahhh, come now, drinks are on me. Coca-Cola if you want to be a stickler for the rules." He lifted a glass of water to toast the air between them.

"When I say *the morning*, I mean I need to be outta here at four." Jerry glanced toward the door with a grimace.

"Ouch. Well, you can leave early then. Just a game or two of pool?"

Jerry groaned. "Alright. If we go now I can grab a bite to eat and get home for an early bedtime. You will have to take a cab if you want to stay later. Let me give Charlie a call to see if he wants to tag along."

"Right on! Have you seen Caleb lately? He was a pretty chill dude. That Marcel guy creeped me out though…"

With a nod he replied, "I ran into Marcel at the gym about a week ago. He said they hadn't found anything up North yet, so they were taking time to relax in the city before heading back. Charlie flew a crew in that direction yesterday. It must have been them." He reached over to grab his phone.

"Bummer! I will see if Johanna wants to meet us and then we should go. What is the name of the place?"

"I had *Le Campagnard* in mind. The pool table is decent—once you learn to play the curves. Food is not bad at all. You run into lots of industrial types and Peace Corps Volunteers there, which can make for entertaining clashes."

Predictably, Charlie refused to miss the latest episode of *Top Gear*, stunned and angered that Jerry was willing to do so. They swung by to pick up Johanna on the way. Traffic chaos left them all sweating, but they eventually walked into the bar. The pool table was taken. A tall guy with shaggy hair was bent over in deep concentration. He sent the cue ball on a terribly slow journey across the warped table where it barely had enough energy to tap the only remaining stripe into a corner pocket.

As he jumped up triumphantly, Jerry and Kano realized at the same time that it was Caleb. He had grown a beard and his skin was browned to a desert-dwelling shade, but the twinkle in his eyes couldn't be mistaken.

"What are you doing here?" asked Jerry incredulously. "I thought Charlie flew you guys back up to sand-land yesterday."

"He did! I flew back down with him too. Ended up spending too much time on the can during the flight up. I'll save you the details of what happened when that idiot friend of yours decided a thunderstorm looked a lot like an amusement park. Anyway, the company won't let you stay unless you are healthy. Costs 'em too much to fly you out if need be." He methodically chalked the end of his cue.

"You look fine today," said Kano. "Lost without your buddy Marcel?"

"I feel like I can breathe again." Caleb set the small blue cube back on the edge of the table. "Seems like he is always peering inside my soul, although you would never guess what he thinks about with those blank expressions he loves so much."

"Yeah, something traumatic must have happened to him as a child. Heck of a climber though," Jerry said as he searched the rack for a cue that wasn't too bent.

Caleb lined up his next shot. "That's for sure. I probably would be in the hospital or even the morgue if it wasn't for his help. He can see routes up a glass skyscraper."

Kano chipped in, "You should have told us you were looking for someone to hang out with. Playing pool alone makes you look desperate." He smiled mischievously.

"Guess I didn't have to. You showed up anyway. And besides, the solo game is temporary—waiting for my date to come down from her room. She just got in from a little town down South. Peace Corps Volunteer. Probably needs about as much time in the shower as I did when I came back from a few weeks in the Sahara."

"Right on. While you are waiting for her to clean up, let's clean this table up. We have four and can make a game of it."

Johanna was listening intently. "You and me?" She turned to Kano.

"I doubt the two of you would have a fair shot," Jerry nodded at Kano and Johanna.

"A fair shot?" Kano raised an eyebrow. "Let's do this: losers buy drinks for the rest of the night."

"Just drinks?" said Caleb, "I'm hungry. You can buy us dinner too when you lose."

Johanna was hoping for a free meal as her research budget was wearing thin, and Kano didn't seem to be one to make a bet he might lose, so she said, "Fine, and if that happens we will buy your date dinner too. It would be fun to meet her. But if you don't win, you buy us dinner *and* take us golfing tomorrow."

"Golfing?! This is Mali!"

She put a hand on her right hip and tilted her head to the side for emphasis. "And your point is?"

Caleb adopted a smug expression and replied, "What makes you think there is even a single golf course anywhere in this pitiful country?"

Johanna's eyes narrowed. "Think? I know. The other day I was in a taxi riding past a bunch of women trying to sell fruit. They were next to that tall wall protecting the Laico Hotel from the rabble. I watched one of them almost get hit by a golf ball that came like a missile from the other side. Quite a shock to us both."

Johanna took a step forward and continued, "Also, your tan tells me that you were wearing a glove on your left hand but not the right. Clearly you are right handed based on what I saw from your pathetically lucky little corner shot when we walked in."

"Alright, Sherlock. But the shot was brilliant, not pathetic. I played the table perfectly." He tapped the felt with his cue.

"Why play the curve when you can use a bit of power?"

"I am all about finesse, sweetheart. Pool is an art—just like golf. No chance you can beat that, but if you do, I suppose we can go to the driving range tomorrow."

"Spoken like a true Frenchman, although *true* Frenchmen don't speak so much English." She grabbed a random stick from the rack. "And don't try calling me sweetheart again. We will see tomorrow if your golf swing is as lame as your pool game," said Johanna, drawing the last syllables out into a flirtatious challenge.

As Kano rapidly fell even more in love with Johanna, Jerry gathered the balls into a chipped plastic triangle, clicking them back and forth over the threadbare patch of felt several times to get a nice, tight formation. "Ladies first?" he asked with a sly grin and his best aristocratic accent.

Transitioning from hot, chaotic streets to the lush refuge of a well-maintained golf course felt like a dream. They decided to irritate Caleb by sharing his clubs instead of renting extras. After all, he was the one who had lost the bet.

To Johanna's dismay, the three guys made another bet. Whoever could drive a ball over the wall first, just like she had seen the other day, would get to choose the lunch spot and didn't have to pay. She was worried about what they might hit on the other side, and felt guilty her innocent statement would be the cause.

It didn't take her long to realize she had nothing to worry about. Jerry could barely get a shot up in the air. Kano sliced so badly it looked as if he were hitting into a hurricane. Caleb got the closest after hooking one through wispy trees and over the side wall. Johanna held her breath and listened but didn't hear any yelling or breaking glass. Her shots went straight up the fairway, but not very far. She said, "If you guys would stop pretending this was baseball you might have more luck!"

Her comment goaded Jerry into a few desperate Happy Gilmore swings. The best contact he made nearly chopped the top off a ball, so he gave up on the wall and proclaimed a new challenge. They all followed him to the chipping green.

He slowly dropped three balls in front of each competitor and spoke dramatically. "I talked to the captain earlier on this beautiful Monday morning. Thursday we fly to Timbuktu. He said we have space for one extra passenger. You have three balls in front of you. Whoever gets closest to the pin can ride along. If I get closest, whoever wants to buy me the nicest dinner can come."

Surprise and excitement showed simultaneously in their faces. Kano's heart leapt as this was the city which had drawn his finger to the spinning globe at the Vatican. The memory seemed to arise from a different lifetime. He was not looking forward to a twenty-four hour bus ride, and this would make for the ultimate shortcut.

One by one, irons collided with spiky grass and dimpled spheres, sending the balls in the general direction of the pin, most of them falling victim to the heavily sloped green, coming to rest closer to the sand-trap than the hole.

Caleb was poised to win by the time they had arrived at the final ball. He could not contain his excitement about the idea of visiting the historical mecca which had captivated his attention for years. Before setting foot in Mali, he had vowed to stay in the country until he had seen the ancient city and its renowned manuscripts in person.

Oblivious to Caleb's excitement, Kano relaxed his entire body, and entered what could be described as a meditative state. Calmly, he shifted his weight and let gravity do most of the work. The ensuing trajectory reminded him of a Hail Mary pass thrown too deep into the end-zone.

After landing directly in front of the hole and bouncing strangely high into the air, the ball struck the pin on its way back down to the green with a cacophonous clang and settled inches from its intended destination. This stroke of luck filled Kano with a nearly uncontainable joy. Caleb sank to the ground in dismay, raised his hands in the air, and shouted, "Noooooooooooooooo!"

After chowing down on uncomfortably thick burgers at Broadway Cafe, they all went to Jerry's place to hang out around the pristine swimming pool. One of the other pilots, Tristan, managed to get a baby monkey from a nearby village. The group freed it from a stake in the grass and the tiny creature clung onto Jerry's chest as if he were its mother.

After the shakes of fear subsided, their furry friend got curious and captivated Johanna with soft, cooing noises. At the pool it would run in and around the legs of chairs and sometimes into the bushes nearby, but it would never lose sight of the group who became its foster parents for the day.

Caleb was running out of ways to irritate his friends, so he decided it was high time to see if the monkey knew how to swim. He picked up the tiny primate and started swinging it by the tail. It didn't mind this motion particularly, simply taking pleasure in the fact someone was offering attention.

The baby monkey did mind, and let everyone know with a piercing scream, when the amplitude of the swing suddenly increased and the gentle hand holding its tail held on no longer. The ensuing trajectory ended in a terrifying splash. Caleb cannonballed in just after the scream ended, adding what must have seemed like a tsunami wave to the monkey's first swim.

Johanna jumped in at the same time to rescue the poor thing. Surprisingly, the baby swam as if it had practiced since birth, even though the only other time it had been wet was during a thunderstorm. It hated water. Whenever the rain began it would quickly duck under a branch, the only shelter its rope and stake allowed. Had Johanna known this she wouldn't have stopped to admire how well it was swimming.

Johanna's eyes narrowed and she said, "That was mean. You scared her just when she was getting used to us!"

Caleb shook out his dripping hair, spraying her in the process, and answered, "Look, this little guy is amazing in the water! He was born to it!"

"How do you know it is a he?"

"Could a girl monkey swim this well on her first try?"

"Of course," she spat with a bit of venom, "and I would swim laps around you any day."

"Then why don't you prove it? Right here, right now!" A sharp crack echoed as he slapped the water with downturned palms.

"Because I don't need to, and this pool is too small, you imbecile. It is not even a rectangle; a real race where you would be embarrassed again is impossible."

He splashed at her playfully, adding to the irritation. "I will find a bigger pool. In the shape of a rectangle if your little heart so desires. I will even dye the water pink should that be your wish. We will race and the loser has to take care of this monkey for an entire day."

"Deal. I will happily rescue the poor girl from your tyranny when you lose."

"Who is being tyrannized now?" Caleb laughed and simultaneously grimaced with pain.

Amid the bantering, the monkey swam toward him and climbed out of the water, first onto his shoulders, then wrapping its arms, legs, and body securely around his head. Tiny fists clenched Caleb's scruffy sideburns while toes curled their way into the dripping hair which hid the deep tan of his neck. The straddled creature looked like a wide-eyed horse jockey frozen in position, every muscle tensed, waiting for the gates to crash open.

Jerry cannonballed into the pool on his own rescue mission, naturally doing his best to splash everyone else in the process. He swam his way over to Caleb and had to pry the monkey off his head one digit at a time. Eventually, the baby released its vice-like grip and was shivering in Jerry's hands. He felt bad for it and deposited the little wet furball in a sunny patch near the edge of the pool. Johanna got out and headed back to her seat. The monkey quickly scampered along behind her, as if it now understood she was the true benefactor.

Kano had been relaxing in the spot next to hers the whole time. He laughed as the monkey jumped up on her chair before she could. "He likes you!"

"That's because he is a she and I am the only other girl around here!" She shifted her irritation into flirtation.

"I noticed." Kano paused with a sensation of shyness, something he hadn't felt many times before. It quickly faded. "By the way, why don't we settle this he/she business once and for all? Let's take a look at what is hiding in between those little legs."

"I don't think so. No need to poke our noses into her personal business. Besides, I like the mystery of not knowing. More fun to try and figure it out." She gently picked up the monkey and eased herself into the chaise lounge.

"How could you figure it out? I mean, you would be hard pressed to tell a human baby boy from a baby girl if they were dressed the same."

"Depends how old the baby is, I suppose. Speaking of babies, what do you think of them?" She tried to dry off the shivering creature but it resisted.

"Are you asking about those two clowns in the pool or if I want to have kids with you?" Johanna turned bright red and they both laughed, melting the awkwardness. "I will take that as a yes."

"I didn't say yes. We just met."

"Then don't you think it's a bit strange to start talking about kids already?" He stared up at the wide leaves overhead to avoid turning red himself.

"Well, we were already talking about babies so I didn't think it was *that* much of a stretch."

"Right. How very Dutch of you. I hear they like to be direct." He took a sip of juice. "Well, to answer your question, it is something I haven't really thought about. I suppose I am more in the exploration phase at the moment. Settling down seems like something adults do."

"But when you do settle down, what kind of family do you want? Or don't you want a family?"

"By the time I settle down I will be a much different person than I am today. You will need to ask that person."

"Well, I can't, that's why I am asking you." She covered the shivering monkey with her towel but it pushed it away.

"You won't let this go, will you?"

"We could discuss it further over dinner tonight."

Kano's eyebrows perked up as a slight breeze sent a rustle through the leaves. "Hmmmm. That means we would need to figure out a way to ditch these idiots," nodding toward Jerry and Caleb who disappeared under the surface, in a contest to see who could hold their breath the longest.

"Shouldn't be too hard."

He replied with a chuckle, "I wouldn't count on it. Those two would kill to have a girl around to show off in front of. That means I will need to watch my back if I take you away."

"They don't have to know you are taking me away."

"I bet they can put two and two together."

"I bet we can come up with a plan so they don't."

"I like where this is going. What do you have in mind?" He tilted his head slightly with curiosity.

"Well, I can get away easily. My reason to be in this country involves getting work done. You, on the other hand, still haven't told me why you are here." The monkey finally stopped shivering and looked intently back and forth between its two foster parents.

"Who says I know why I am here?"

"How could anyone just stumble upon Mali? It's not like it's on the way to anything." Caleb breached the surface with a loud gasp.

"It used to be. Timbuktu was the center of the world's main trade routes back in the day."

Caleb broke into their conversation, short on breath. "Are you talking about the…history of Timbuktu? That is one of my favorite subjects! One of the main reasons…other than climbing…that I wanted to come here. I can't wait to check out the new library the

South Africans are building to store those ancient manuscripts! So many mysteries to uncover."

Johanna rolled her eyes. "I didn't ask for a history lesson from either of you. Let's get back to the point." She turned to Kano, ignoring Caleb.

"I thought you liked a mystery," taunted Kano with a boyish grin.

"Sure, when it comes to monkeys. Are you a monkey?"

"Depends on your definition." Caleb took the hint and turned his attention back toward Jerry.

"Well, this monkey can do things you couldn't dream of as a baby." She held its hands and danced with it. Tiny feet left white prints which quickly faded from her sun-kissed stomach.

"True, but it won't be dining with you tonight, and I doubt he will be much of a conversationalist later in life."

"I suppose you have her beat there. Did you come up with a good excuse for tonight?"

"No, I am not much of a multi-tasker. Talking to you requires my full attention." He paused and smiled.

"Should l take that as a compliment?"

"It was meant to be one."

"Your compliments need work then."

"Thanks.....*not.*"

"Didn't people stop saying 'not' at the end of a sentence in the 90's?"

"Yeah, but then *Borat* brought it back."

Johanna made a face as if the monkey had pooped all over her. "*Borat?* Don't tell me you actually think that movie is funny."

"Funny? No, not funny. More like hilarious. Ask those two in the pool. One is from France and the other South Africa. *Borat* is an international phenomenon. Any guy will tell you."

Johanna let out a little laugh. "Key word, GUY. None of my friends like that garbage."

"Have you asked them?"

"I don't need to."

"Then I don't believe you. Some girls think it's funny too."

"I know my friends well enough."

"I bet at least one of them likes *Borat.*"

Kano let a smile creep across his face. "How much do you want to bet?"

"Loser buys the best filet mignon in town for dinner tonight."

"Very feminist move. Paying for dinner on our first date. I accept."

"First date? Does that mean you think there will be a second?"

"Think? Just like I think that you will pay for dinner. Almost guaranteed." He took another sip of juice and laughed as Caleb let out a war cry, put Jerry in a headlock, and dragged him back under the water.

Abruptly, Souleymane brought Kano back to the desert heat with a rare interruption. "Okay, wait a moment. So this is the dinner you told me about before? She ended up paying for it, right?"

Kano smiled with the memory. "She did, and she wasn't happy about it."

"So one of her friends actually liked this *Borat?* What is *Borat*...?"

He laughed, realizing how little Souleymane knew of his culture, and wondering how much of what was spoken he could truly follow. "He is a movie character who makes fun of certain groups of people. Viewers either think he is really funny or they hate him. Do you even know what a movie is? Have you seen one?"

"Sometimes they have movies on TV here." He paused for a moment and then continued with a condescending frown. "We do have television, you know."

Kano chuckled. "Of course. Usually in black and white, though."

"The one in Bamako's bus station was in color. That was magic the first time I saw it." He nodded his head toward the emerging rooftops spotted with the occasional satellite dish. Kano vacantly wondered if he could use one to get a message out. This uncommon thought of escape, no longer attached to emotion, quickly drifted away as Souleymane continued. "We are almost back. Perhaps you can tell me more tomorrow."

Souleymane enjoyed listening to Kano's stories. The more English he heard the more he could follow. His innate desire for understanding seemed insatiable. Many things existed in his own country which he had never heard of before and could barely imagine, such as swimming pools, ice cream, and strange games like golf.

His pride nearly always overpowered even the strongest bursts of curiosity, ensuring silence while Kano spoke. Even though he wanted to ask about almost everything Kano said, he simply could not allow himself to look foolish in front of his student. Every once in a while he allowed a solitary question or remark through to show he was listening.

That night, while falling asleep, Souleymane thought about this special friend Kano had made and what had become of her. Perhaps their bond never solidified. *But what if it had? How did she feel about his disappearance? Was she still in Mali? Could he somehow make contact with her to say that Kano was okay?* His mind went in circles as a sensation of guilt grew and blossomed like a stain, preventing sleep from coming.

Tossing and turning, eventually he resolved to listen carefully to the rest of the story to avoid any misguided conclusions. After it was finished, he would decide what to do with his feelings, although he realized any message sent from him about Kano could only result in trouble. The Scholar would never allow it.

As they walked into the desert that day, Souleymane was rather low on energy. Kano noticed and decided to take advantage of the opportunity. "Shall we race? It seems like you had a bad night. Maybe I can outlast you for once!"

Souleymane laughed. "At least you have your sense of humor. I could stay awake for three nights in a row and you still wouldn't have a chance. Why don't you continue with your story as we walk, and when we have gone far enough, let us see who can make it back first. I will demonstrate your weakness to you once again."

Kano nodded in agreement, tapered his stride, and lowered his voice to conserve energy. "Okay then. Let me think back to where we left off…"

Kano and Johanna became fairly inseparable. Somehow they got to know each other better in that short time period than some couples do after years of living together. Kano knew his trip to Timbuktu would be a good chance to reflect on the whirlwind Johanna had swept him into. Never had he felt so upside-down, inside-out, and altogether shaken up.

Living in Siby, the town nearby the hidden oasis, had definitely changed him, but this was something else altogether. It was as if he no longer recognized himself. Perhaps it was like being drunk, he thought:

short-lived pleasure, and after enduring the hangover, back to business as usual.

His usual business presented itself as an itch that hadn't been scratched since he came to Mali. An ever-present pull he felt drawing him toward a card came and a glass of whisky. It somehow evaporated in her presence.

Yes, Timbuktu would be the adventure he had come for, but a strange sense of dread welled up from an unknown place when he thought about going without her. There was no time to analyze this or any of the other foreign thoughts and feelings he was experiencing.

After having a lunch so spicy at a place called African Foods that even the powerful fan couldn't keep his forehead dry, Kano and Jerry went to get Tristan. They took a moment to harass the tiny, forlorn monkey who was tied up in the front yard before knocking on the door.

Tristan appeared, sharply dressed in his captain's uniform. He tossed his neglected pet a couple of bananas and swiped peanut butter on a nearby branch before climbing into the filthy Hilux, scrunching Kano uncomfortably into the shifter while complaining about the mess inside.

Swerving through chaotic streets until the highway appeared, eventually they neared the service gate on the side of the airport. Jerry said, "Stay quiet. Just let me do the talking."

They pulled up to three militant guards brandishing fully automatic weapons. Kano's heart rate went up perceptibly as he flashed back to the night he had arrived on the continent. The biggest lumbered toward the truck and in a gravelly voice addressed them in French. "I see two pilot badges but three people."

Jerry spoke back in French with a smile. "Of course, my friend. This is our new intern. He is coming along with us to Timbuktu today."

"And why doesn't your little friend have a badge?" His eyes narrowed suspiciously.

"Like I said, he is new. The company still hasn't arranged one for him." Jerry shook his head and pursed his lips in an attempt at looking annoyed.

"Very well. Be sure he has one next time."

"No problem, friend."

The big guard frowned and then nodded to his colleague who opened the gate allowing Jerry to drive toward the hanger. He switched back to English. "Security here is a joke. As long as you are white you can do whatever you want at this airport."

Tristan laughed. "Or anywhere else in this country! When I get a real flying job I will miss being a rock star."

"Right," said Jerry, "anyway, Kano, you can keep on playing the intern. No stewardess on this flight so you can hand out drinks and sandwiches if you want. Otherwise I will. This is a charter for a South African film crew. They are working on commercials for the World Cup."

"Sounds good. Do I have to show them how to buckle up?"

"Nope, not many rules on a chartered flight." He pulled out the key and opened his door. It groaned in protest.

"Do we have time to check out the aircraft control tower?" Glancing over at the relatively tall, awkward structure he continued, "You said we could do anything at this airport."

"No time now, but we can on the way back. The guys up there are pretty cool."

After checking the weather, the uniformed pilots walked up to a Beechcraft 1900 with Kano in tow. This airplane had been out of production for almost ten years but was still commonly used as a regional commuter. It transported up to nineteen passengers with two rather basic turboprops.

The pilots settled into their pre-flight checklist while Kano watched intently from the first row; there was no jump seat on the plane. Two Pratt & Whitney Canada PT6 engines spooled the propellers into a throaty roar which reminded Kano of giant hummingbirds. They fueled up and taxied to the private portion of the terminal. Camera equipment and suitcases were casually stuffed into the baggage compartment and the film crew climbed the steps. Kano greeted all of them with a handshake and a smile.

Once they were settled he introduced himself to the mostly male crew in a slightly overdone style. "Hello and good afternoon ladies and gentlemen. I know you probably expected someone much prettier up here with a uniform and larger breasts. My presence is not exactly standard, but I am considering taking a job flying for this company and wanted to see what the routes were like before signing the papers. If I can get you a drink or a sandwich or answer any questions, just say the word."

Kano passed out a few warm cans of Fanta and Jerry handed him a headset before pulling up the stairs and commencing the taxi toward the end of the runway. The sky that greeted them was dark blue, spotted with quickly rising clouds. As they traveled toward Mopti, a city halfway between Bamako and Timbuktu, green vegetation which cloaked much of the red earth began to spread thin.

While cruising at just under seven thousand meters, Jerry interrupted the meaningless chatter on the radio. "Tristan, do you see what I see?" The horizon directly in their flightpath had grown a few shades darker.

"Yeah, looks like we may need to take a detour."

"A detour? Didn't you see what this plane looked like? My truck can't get much dirtier when I take it up those dusty roads around Siby. The condition of this aircraft is an embarrassment to our well-paying customers." He gestured toward the back of the plane with his thumb. "What I see is a super-sized plane wash sitting directly in our path. When we land in Timbuktu our trusty Beechcraft will shine like the day it came off the line."

"You sound way too much like Charlie. I don't think anyone should *ever* copy that guy. Let me explain things to our boy Kano here. As pilots, we have three main things to worry about when we are up in the air. First, we worry our mechanics have screwed things up or fallen behind on their maintenance checklists. Second, even though we live in the hottest place in the world, up here, iced wings are a major problem. Finally, we worry about the weather. We don't know what is inside that dark devil up ahead. What is the point of unnecessary risk?"

Kano spoke as quietly as he could into his headset as he didn't want the film crew to catch wind of their conversation. "With all due respect, Tristan, you signed up for more than your fair share of risk taking when you took this job—don't forget you are living in the hotbed of some of the nastiest tropical diseases out there. I, for one, would rather go down in a thunderstorm while having a bit of fun than have a fever fry my brain in a stifling hospital."

Jerry laughed into the microphone, "Sorry to hear you have a death wish, mate. Doesn't mean the rest of us do. We are at altitude, so that *does* give us plenty of room to maneuver. I don't think this storm is big enough to be a real risk, do you, Tristan?"

"Storms are always risky, but that is indeed a smaller one. I will let you fly us through it for the sake of gaining experience, and so that you will steer clear of the next one."

Jerry exaggerated a salute and exclaimed, "Ten-four, good buddy." He then switched over to the intercom and announced to the passengers, "Good morning everyone, this is your co-pilot speaking. Hope you are enjoying the flight so far. In about thirty minutes we will land in Mopti to refuel the plane, but we do have nasty looking weather to get through first. Please buckle up and prepare yourselves for some turbulence."

Had the South Africans seen the storm filling the entire windscreen they probably would have taken this warning more seriously. What Jerry expected to be a bumpy car wash turned into a garbage disposal. The turbulence was so bad Kano couldn't understand how the wings were still attached. After what felt like an eternity of being shaken to bits by the weather gods, the plane hit a massive downdraft knocking them into a free-fall.

In a brief moment of eerie silence the airplane itself seemed to hold its breath. Kano noticed his unopened can of Fanta floating in front of his face as if advertising the fact it didn't care whether the plane crashed or not. Before the shock of weightlessness could pass, the Beechcraft slammed back onto what felt like the tracks of a deranged roller coaster and Kano heard a few screams along with what he feared was vomiting coming from behind him.

The wall of cumulonimbus spit out the shaken craft like a watermelon seed. Wide-eyed pilots were nearly blinded by bright skies ahead. Their path to Mopti shone with the clearest blue anyone had seen for quite some time. All the pervasive dust had been sucked from the atmosphere by the giant vacuum cleaner of a thunderstorm.

Inside the plane, the stench of fear and *chunder*, Jerry's word for vomit, still lingered among the passengers. The pilots radioed ahead to get someone on board who could clean up the mess.

Tristan didn't say anything until his eyes narrowed upon their approach. "Isn't the tarmac missing something?"

"What do you mean?" Jerry asked with a slight tremor present in his voice.

"Where is the King Air? It hasn't been flown back yet." He pulled back slowly on a lever to decrease engine power.

"Right, the mechanical failure last week. Charlie had to take a bus back to Bamako. He has been whining about it ever since."

"Yeah, our mechanic isn't supposed to be done fixing it until tomorrow." Both pairs of eyes nervously scanned the terrain ahead.

"Well, it may not be on the tarmac, but it hasn't left Mopti. Look on the far side of the terminal in the scrub."

"Uh-oh. That must be her. At least she is still right-side up. Looks like our mechanic will have to stay up here awhile longer."

After skittering to the ground across an unusually wet runway, the plane taxied toward the tiny terminal and Kano addressed the film crew. "Sorry for the bumps back there. We will get things cleaned up for you while our tanks are topped off, so feel free to get out and stretch your legs."

They were met with unconscionably hot sunshine and the smell of steaming rain mingling with jet fuel. The passengers may not have given the odors a second thought but the pilots surely did. Jerry asked one of the ground crew in French, "Has there been a fuel leak?"

The short, stocky man with a shaved head and an orange vest replied slowly and deliberately, "Not our truck. Much worse. Airplane blow away. Me show you." They followed him over to scattered supports which had been holding up the wings. "I saw wind shaking plane up and down. Then poles slipped and went through wing. Whole plane start roll away."

Kano couldn't understand much of what was being said, but he added to the conversation anyway. "Is it just me, or does it smell even more like jet fuel over here?"

Tristan eyed the glowing charcoal left scattered after brewing the most recent pot of tea. He addressed the short man curtly in French, "Someone might want to put that out. Also, tell your crew not to be smoking any more cigarettes around here." He gestured to a few butts lying near the charcoal. "At least not until we figure out where the spill is. That thunderstorm may have soaked everything, but jet fuel can still burn."

The group stepped over the overflowing trough cut into the edge of the cement on the way to the wayward aircraft. Jerry and Tristan looked up at the punctured wing, their fears simultaneously realized. They looked at each other with wide eyes and Jerry said, "Let's get out of here now!" He turned to the short man and barked orders in French while Tristan explained to Kano what had happened.

"The support didn't just go through the wing like he said. It severed the fuel line! Hundreds of gallons must have leaked out. The ditches around the tarmac where those morons were playing with charcoal and smoking cigarettes are not filled so much with rain water as jet fuel. Good thing we parked our plane at a relatively safe distance, but Jerry is right, the minute the truck is done pumping, we need to get back in the air!"

The rest of the journey was uneventful, and the shiny aircraft landed safely in a world of sand. Drifts piled up everywhere, even over the edges of the runway. The terminal looked like a giant sandcastle. Streets and houses seemed to be an extension of the desert, shaped by man. Several people wandered about, caked in a layer of dust.

The sand was finer than any Kano had felt before. It sifted through his fingers like powder and scattered into the wind, much of it nearly lighter than air. He realized it had been here for a long time. Sand without a sea has no better way to spend its time than to endlessly hone itself into smaller and smaller grains.

After a few minutes of waiting, a car picked them up. The older, dark blue Mercedes wound through a city which looked like it hadn't changed much during the past centuries. The only things out of place were satellite dishes and electrical cables slung haphazardly as if a giant, drunken spider had tried to build its web at night. Air conditioning blasted out of the dashboard, but two pilots and their 'intern' were still soaking their seats with sweat. Every once in a while Tristan would point out a landmark like a tired tour guide. The driver remained silent.

Kano longed to explore the city even though the outside air burned as it entered his lungs. Perhaps this car ride would need to suffice until the raging sun offered a respite to their timeless surroundings. He asked Tristan, "Why did the river look so far away when we landed? Wouldn't they want the city closer to the water?"

"Of course. It used to be closer to the water, but the water moved. The Niger River is about thirteen kilometers away. Not a big problem as the water table is still so high. Digging a well doesn't pose a huge challenge."

"Can't be easy to dig through this kind of sand." Kano imagined trying to do so under this blazing sun.

"Not much is easy when you live on the edge of the world's largest desert. It might not look like a lot has changed here in a few hundred years, but believe me, it has. Not just the river has abandoned this place. Five centuries ago, twice as many people lived here, and a quarter of them were scholars. It used to be a pillar of the intellectual world—it had the largest university on the planet back then.

Most of the manuscripts have long since disappeared. Jerry's government is building that monstrosity at the central square to house the remainder. They used to sell books at vibrant markets. Now nothing but useless trinkets, junk from China, and what they call food."

Jerry piped in, "It is still a pretty cool place. If we have an early dinner we can check it out when the sun is going down. Maybe even head out to the sand dunes."

Tristan said, "Count me out. I've seen the dunes before and I don't need to be wandering around after dark. Maybe I didn't mention it, but something else about the city has changed too. It used to be a respected center of Islam, now it serves as a backwater for Al Qaida. If you go, don't wander around at night."

Souleymane hung his head with sadness. It was as if he had just heard from a ghost. The one who had been killed was never real to him. Now he had a name, actions, words.

He could no longer handle the guilt rising up from within, so he broke into Kano's narrative. "I think I know how it goes from here. It is time for us to run." He punished his body, pushing it beyond its incredibly high limits. Kano had no chance. He was left far behind, completely on his own, but the thought of escape failed to even enter his mind.

The foolishness of goading Souleymane into a desert race captivated his consciousness. Challenges seem to lose their purpose if one has no way to win, he mused, realizing that he couldn't remember a time he had ever been on the *losing* side of an unwinnable challenge.

Phase Four: Sublimation

Sublimation   *noun*   / ˈsʌblɪməʃən /
*Base instincts that have been diverted or modified into a
higher form of activity.*
Transforming from a solid directly into a gas.

August 2011

Nearly two years passed peacefully. The only contact Kano made with the outside world was an occasional video call to his comparatively disheveled parents in California. Any outsider witnessing these conversations would assume they were the ones being held hostage.

His parents requested repeated confirmation Kano was still alive as they worked hard to collect every dollar they could to secure his release. Their grand total still wasn't enough for The Scholar. Or perhaps the time had not yet come.

Kano's mind and body were honed and sharpened into a condition he never dreamed possible. Even prayer and meditation yielded fruit as Souleymane guided his connection with the spiritual realm. Kano regularly became flooded with powerful emotions he had never experienced before. He trusted these encounters as a force which was revealing itself to him, a force with the potential to guide and protect him. A force which, according to The Scholar, had led him to Timbuktu.

Three thousand kilometers northeast of the ancient city, on the other side of the Sahara, what looked like an oversized Bedouin tent was firmly staked into desert sands. Winds whipped violently around it, but no more than a rustle was heard within the luxurious interior.

Many years ago, as a revolutionary and a young leader, the tent's owner would often take times of solitude, communing with the sands of his ancestors, gaining wisdom before making choices which would impact his own people or countries across the sea. In the early days, his tent was little more than it appeared, reminding him of his former life as the son of a goat herder.

Decade by decade, aches and pains of old age mingled with the pleasure and extravagance he had grown accustomed to. The tent which once had the sole task of sheltering him from the desert could now fend off stray bullets. It bristled with firearms, comforts and amenities.

After the prescribed period of solitude, a most trusted advisor was the first to speak to the aging dictator. The battle-hardened Tuareg warrior silently entered the tent and sat before Africa's *King of Kings*, a title bestowed upon him by other leaders in support of his desire to unify Africa's separate states into one great nation. Tea was poured, and after a moment of silence, the Tuareg quietly began in a dialect of Arabic. "*Amghar*," meaning chief in his native tongue, "your people have turned their minds against you. They have been poisoned by the lies of your enemies. You must show them your greatness. Take up your sword. The Tuareg stand behind you."

The great leader looked up with a sad expression on his face. "But they are my people. I love them as a father."

"And a father punishes his children when they wander astray. A father demands respect with the force given to him by the Most High God."

Sadness slipped into confusion. "Why have they turned against me? Do they see my age as weakness?"

"Perhaps so, *Amghar*. All the more reason to show them this is not true. You are the Supreme Leader of our great nation and destined to be so much more. How can you reach for your destiny if your people are not showing you the respect you have so fearlessly earned?"

He took a sip of tea and allowed the delicate cup to rattle back into its saucer. "And how is it you know my destiny?" His eyes penetrated with a challenging fire.

"It is written in the stars that light the desert, *Amghar*. You have the heart of a lion and the wisdom of ancient kings. We are sure to fall into chaos without your strong hand to guide us. Not only our nation but all of Africa. The continent calls you to become its ruler."

He shifted uncomfortably. "This is what the other leaders have said. But what do their people say? How can I rule many countries if my own turns against me?"

"You must not allow them to do so. You are their Father. Force them into submission. My Tuareg brothers will be your sword. Together, we will show the world the heart of a true leader."

In the moments after the warrior left, the old man felt as though he was the last person alive. Immense weight of decision crushed down upon him, driving him further and further away from the people he loved. Only the whispering sand remained. The tent itself seemed to evaporate into the night. He knew the Tuareg was right. There was no alternate path.

Without his position as Supreme Leader he was nothing; nothing he knew he was not. Therefore, he must fight for the leading role he had starred in for so many years. He must fight for his people, fight for Africa. He would rally the Tuareg and silence all those who stood against him. The time had come to bring order to his household.

The Scholar listened to news reports with growing concern. The powerful man who had brokered peace in Mali now spread war in his own country. He knew the Sahara had never been wide enough to stop the chaos expanding through Libya from entering his beloved city. Three thousand kilometers meant very little when modern technology allowed the foreign cancer to spread faster than ever before.

On the 22nd of August, 2011, The Scholar listened in shock to radio reports of rebel forces entering the Green Square in central Tripoli. He could no longer hope Gaddafi could recover from this crushing defeat. He knew the conflict could not be contained, and the darkness of war would seep across the sterile desert like a rotting corpse thrown into a well. Nothing could stop it from blighting and corrupting one city after another, spreading faster and farther than an outbreak of cholera.

Preparations needed to be made. The Scholar held secret meetings with the keepers of other ancient libraries throughout the city. They agreed upon the details of how and when they would protect their treasures. Some had hidden compartments and chambers built into their houses specifically for this purpose. Others would need to carefully catalogue their manuscripts and smuggle them in a southerly direction, although it was argued the humidity would pose too great a threat. All would contribute a few insignificant portions of their collections to create a red herring for South Africa's new Ahmed Baba Library in the city center.

It was also agreed that the work must be done in absolute secrecy, trusting as few people as possible. This translated into months of meticulous labor for a small group of individuals who set out to protect and preserve the historical soul of their city.

November 2011

After ten weeks of preparing manuscripts, The Scholar knew the time had come. Dry season was descending upon Bamako. Keeping brittle parchment away from moist air was paramount. This meant it was also time to collect his ransom. He would never allow his brilliant captive to fall into the hands of an uneducated psychopath who happened to control the largest arsenal; his conscience still kept him up at night whenever he was reminded of Jerry's fate, even though he knew there had been no alternative.

The pending exchange was about more than money. Kano had become a valued pupil. A member of the household. He could offer something to the world which had not been possible before. His unprecedented levels of intelligence enabled a top-notch Western education to meld with ancient wisdom contained within carefully selected manuscripts. A connection to the creator had been cultivated, transforming Kano into a conduit with the unique abilities and perspectives required to usher in a new way of life. The Scholar smiled at the premonition that he had helped create a spark of light to shine against the looming destruction and collapse of the precious world he knew and loved.

Whenever The Scholar initiated contact with Kano's parents, Jack and Lina, it appeared to be through an encrypted connection somewhere near Lagos, the capital of Nigeria. Continuing to follow strict protocol, he spoke with a nearly flawless Nigerian accent after the phone rang several times. He made a concerted effort to skip the standard greetings. "How much have you collected for the ransom of your son?"

A haggard voice, thick with sleep, answered from the other side of the globe. "Ummmm, we now have two million dollars. Surely this has gone on long enough."

"Indeed, the time has come. Two million dollars will be sufficient for my purposes. Nigeria is not a safe place for an exchange. Suspicion and corruption are too deeply rooted here. We must meet in a more trusting society."

There was a long pause on the other end of the line. "What do you suggest?"

"Bamako, Mali has a very low crime rate and white people are welcomed with open arms. Not one of those ignorant fools will suspect our true purpose."

He sluggishly cleared his throat again. "Alright. I will allow our agent to handle the details."

"That will not be acceptable. You and your wife must come on this journey together. Alone. If something is not correct with the money I receive, I want you to be there to watch your son die with your own eyes. You will bring with you ten thousand United States dollars and your wife will carry ten thousand euros in cash. The rest must be ready to transfer electronically to an account of my choosing. When everything is in order, you shall be reunited with your son."

"Wait a moment." He quietly conferred with his drowsy wife whom he had summoned from a different room. "We would like time to discuss this plan."

"Very well, I will contact you again in six hours to make our final arrangements." The connection died. Kano's father immediately woke his agent to probe the situation for any last hope of recovering their son without becoming destitute.

Every possible scenario was played out over the next few hours, from contract killers to banking magic. Nothing seemed feasible enough to attempt the risk. The Scholar held his cards too tightly. Soon he would hold more than a lifetime's worth of hard-earned money. While they could never abandon their son, deep down they knew they could also never forgive him for ruining their lives by walking into such a dangerous situation.

They didn't know their money would actually serve a noble purpose. It was providing their son with an education far more transformative and valuable than the one they had already bought for a quarter of a million dollars from the University of Michigan. The funds would also provide the means to preserve ancient historical treasures.

Without this knowledge, all they could do was look at each other one last, desperate time before all hope for the future drained away.

Out of options, the only thing they felt was the torturing blackness of despair.

The final arrangements fell into place quickly even though it felt like an eternity. Pushing from one minute to the next took all the willpower they could summon. Inevitably, Jack and Lina Griffin found themselves over the Sahara, following the same flightpath their son had taken more than two years before. A stack of valuable paper about as thick as a deck of playing cards pressed through each of their money belts making the already uncomfortable seats even worse. Flying coach was something they were not accustomed to.

Sleep proved impossible in spite of the pills they took. The long flight across the continental United States and then the Atlantic was taken up with tension and avoidance. Above Africa, things started to change. They spoke about how they missed their first years together, and the ways in which their respective careers had pulled them in different directions.

The crisis they were thick in the middle of had somehow yet to become real, although the sands stretching below were beginning to make an impression. Only by talking about the situation facing them upon landing did the entire emotional nature of what they were about to do rear its ugly head.

As fear crept over her like a shadow covering the moon, without thinking, Lina reached over and gave her estranged husband's hand a squeeze. A pulse spread from that contact, manifesting into a surging wave breaking over a rocky beach. Both souls awoke and suddenly felt connected to something greater than themselves, not as individuals, but as an ancient, rusting lock must feel when its key has been found at long last; the completed mechanism turning smoothly to reveal long forgotten mysteries.

Something akin to silence spread through the half-empty airplane. Jack and Lina sat in rapt wonder as the energy traveled through their bodies, tingling their fingers and toes as it dissipated outward. Before long, they both fell asleep. It was the sort of deep sleep borne from built up exhaustion and the release of heavily compounded worry.

They awoke to what seemed like a dream. The airport terminal was a broken semblance of what they expected it to be, filled with a strange sort of people and a different kind of language. The taxi they stepped into was a far cry from their mental image of one. Fields revealed themselves through grubby windows. The only apparent crop they yielded was smoldering garbage. Endless, stinking piles. Hellish snowbanks. It was the world they imagined after the apocalypse.

This dreamworld seemed like a nightmare at first, but city colors began to present themselves, and the hotel they shakily arrived at positively glowed with warmth and a style they had never before encountered. They changed their reservation from two rooms to one, and without speaking tried to enjoy one last night of wealth and indulgence before they were plunged into poverty by the recklessness of their son. After one drink and a few bites to eat, tension about the day to come overwhelmed the mood, and they did their best to get as much sleep as possible.

Morning light struck Jack and Lina with the force of a powerful hangover. Sunrise in Bamako came not long after it set on California's coastline. Jet lag from an eight hour time difference slowed their already frayed minds to a torpid crawl.

Showers helped, but their heads still pounded as if they had finished the entire bottle of Havana Club Anejo 7 which lingered nearly untouched on top of the minibar. The light brown liquid seemed to glow with an intensity of its own in the early morning light.

Somehow, they cleaned themselves up and tried to keep their vision in focus as the elevator took them to the front desk where they arranged for another cab ride. The meeting with The Scholar took place in an hour, and although they were told it was nearby, they wouldn't dream of showing up late.

After a short but dusty drive they were led into a diner called Broadway Cafe. A rather overweight man greeted them with a friendly smile and introduced himself as the owner. He spoke with a cheerfully heavy accent, "I am always happy to practeece English I learn in New York. I see we have mutual friend. You are here to discuss his books, yes? He say you interest in helping save dem. A, what is dee word...noble ting to do."

Jack answered guardedly, "I don't think I would call him a friend, but yes, we are here to meet him."

The owner's eyebrows rose with surprise. "I see," even though he clearly did not, "well I give you comfortable lunch, even though it still early. Maaany Americans dat come here order hamburger and of course we have Coke. Dey say Coke is better here because it have real sugar. Please tell if I can do anything for youuu."

Lina was momentarily lulled into the genuine display of friendly hospitality, and replied in an automatic tone which tiredly mirrored his radiancy. "Thank you, we will."

The Scholar awaited them at a plush, vinyl booth which looked like it had come straight from the 1950s. He stood and held his head high upon their approach. His luminescent, deep blue robe shone in the dim light as if he had brought the sparkling ocean itself into this dingy realm.

He delicately approached the couple and softened his Nigerian accent. "You must be Jack and Lina. I am happy to see you have arrived safely, and I trust you will depart today with your son. I must say he is an extraordinary student and his work on the manuscripts has been impeccable."

Jack and Lina allowed their mouths to hang open slightly as they looked to each other for some sort of understanding. Neither knew how to respond. Similar questions rushed through both of their minds. *Was this the man who kidnapped our son and is about to steal everything we have worked for? Why was such a horrible criminal acting as though he was the principal of an expensive private school? What do books or manuscripts have to do with anything?*

The Scholar endured the rude pause and continued humbly, "I am sure you would like something to eat as you come to the end of what must have been a trying journey. I have taken the liberty of ordering you hamburgers, which happen to be my favorite thing on the menu. Cokes are on their way. Please have a seat." He made a sweeping gesture toward the tacky booth which exuded an appearance of stickiness.

Jack and Lina cautiously sat, trying to adjust their expectations to their surroundings. *Hamburgers for breakfast?* The intimidating men with AK-47s and turbans waiting for them in an underground lair that they had expected to encounter did not mesh at all with this strange twist on a retro diner and a somewhat regally dressed, well spoken, aging gentleman.

After Jack slid into the booth, his head cleared, and he asked, "I thought Al Qaeda was anti-American. Why are we sitting at what must be the most American place in Bamako?"

The Scholar placed his hands on the table submissively. "Al Qaeda *is* strictly anti-American, but I do not subscribe to all their notions. I assumed your journey to be difficult enough and did not wish to subject you to uncomfortable surroundings."

Lina sharpened up and leaned forward. "The important thing is that our son is healthy and returned to us today."

"You have my word. As soon as your funds are received by my bank in Nigeria, Kano will be released into your custody."

Jack squarely donned the persona he used whenever dealing with powerful businessmen and probed, "My wife is right. Getting Kano back today is the most important thing. This meeting is not what we expected. You do not seem like the person we spoke with on the phone. How do we know Kano is well and nearby, and what do you plan to do with our entire life savings?"

The Scholar gestured to one of his young bodyguards standing alongside a brown steel door not far from their booth. He turned to Jack and spoke thoughtfully with many pauses. "You very well know it doesn't matter what I say about where your money is going. Any assurances I give you will mean nothing because you see me as a terrorist. We have little basis for trust." He paused to take in their confused expressions.

"I have taken the pleasure of educating Kano. You will soon see he has become a new sort of individual. I think you will find the changes are for the better." He shifted his glowing eyes to Lina and paused again before saying, "I believe he is much healthier now than he ever has been before."

She crossed her arms and replied with a harsh tone, "Why, because he has been brainwashed with your crazy ideas?"

Jack put his hand on her thigh, a place it hadn't been since long before this ordeal had begun, and said, "Lina, we are here to do business. Let's stick to the point. I still want to know where our money is going and…"

The Scholar cut him off by raising a finger and replied, "Very well. Part of your financing has provided for the education of your son. Another part will go to the greater Al Qaeda organization. Finally, some will be used to preserve a bit of endangered history."

Jack nodded as he saw truthfulness in The Scholar's eyes. "At least it won't all be used to fund terrorism."

"On the contrary, I plan to make that the smallest part," The Scholar said with a glint of a smile.

At that moment, the creaky steel door opened just enough for Kano's head to pop through. He beamed at his parents with tears in his eyes and said, "What took you so long?"

Lina was overcome with emotion and couldn't find a single word, but Jack felt a spark of anger grow. "I could ask you the same. We haven't seen you in over three years, and a good chunk of that had nothing to do with being held hostage!"

Kano wasn't given the chance to reply as his head was yanked back through the doorway. The Scholar broke the following silence. "I see the tension Kano once mentioned to me. Perhaps you will be able to talk some of it through after this is all over."

Jack replied with icy dismissal in his voice, "We did not come here for family counseling. There is a transaction to be made."

"Yes of course," came the oddly lighthearted reply, "but we will enjoy our hamburgers first."

It wasn't long before the greasy food came. Tense conversation centered on what Kano had been doing for the past two years. The Scholar explained the many ways he had grown and the valuable contribution he had made to the translation of precious historical documents. He brought home the conclusion that Kano would never again be in a stronger physical, mental and spiritual condition.

The chunky, half-eaten burgers were soon cleared away, although they would not go to waste. "It is now time. First I must ask for the cash you have on hand." Jack and Lina both produced stacks which had become damp with sweat. The Scholar quickly flipped through them, easily assured all was in order.

A laptop emerged and numbers were entered. Every penny they could scrape together, enough to match the income of a large Malian family for two thousand years, departed from Los Angeles and instantly arrived in Lagos, where it was split and routed to several other banks throughout the African subcontinent. It eventually came to rest, rather untraceably, into multiple accounts scattered across Bamako.

The thoughts and feelings traveling around the table in silence as the fortune made its complex journey were as varied as the people sitting together. Jack felt an emptiness like never before. All he had worked so hard for slipped away electronically, unseen, gone in an instant like an irreversible magic trick.

Lina felt a deep sense of relief as her one and only son was nearly within her grasp. It momentarily blocked her view of the pit of uncertainty which tormented her thoughts of the future. The Scholar felt sadness because the situation demanded such difficult measures, his soul reaching out to those before him while the shadow of a smile crept in from behind at the assurance that his history and household could now stand up against the onslaught the desert would surely bring.

Kano waited in silence with Souleymane for the transaction to be completed. His mind wandered over two years of captivity in Timbuktu. He knew the experience would shape the person he was becoming more than anything else could.

Those first weeks crushed his spirit and scrambled his mind, but once the routine dominated his existence, he felt the slow strengthening of body, mind and soul permeate throughout.

After the first year, he lost track of days and time; the number of manuscripts he had translated seemed too high to count. When The Scholar told Kano the invaluable collection had fallen under threat, and the only way to preserve it was to smuggle the contents to Bamako where funds from his family could ensure safekeeping, Kano reacted with joy that a solution had been found.

Kano took pleasure in helping with the massive undertaking of organizing, cataloging, and packing up nearly forty-five thousand brittle and crumbling pieces of history ranging from academic subjects such as astronomy, medicine, law, art and philosophy to everyday advice about women and fortune telling. A small portion was set aside to serve as a diversion for the invaders, allowing them to destroy something relatively insignificant so their uninformed efforts to find the true collections would cease.

This small window of reflection allowed Kano to realize Stockholm syndrome had set in as if it was the only natural course of things, like the slow shifting of the Niger River, a modern traveler never imagining the water used to flow somewhere else. He not only identified with his captors, but learned from them, worked with them, and developed a strong sense of belonging among them.

During the nearly month-long trip up the meandering Niger among dented metal trunks and shoddy wooden boats belching black fumes, Kano never gave a fleeting thought to the idea of escape. A slight pang of guilt accompanied this realization. Although it would have been possible, he had somehow become a part of the mission and knew that without his parents' money the manuscripts would quickly rot in Bamako's humid climate. The beauty and wisdom of some of the things he had translated affected him deeply. Imagining the abandonment of such treasures twisted his stomach into knots.

The financial security of his parents and his future inheritance meant very little to Kano in comparison. He knew beyond any doubt they would find a new way forward, and he had a sneaking suspicion this whole experience would actually bring them together in a way which was different and better than the comfortably superficial existence they had become accustomed to.

Dilapidated structures and piles of garbage clogging the dusty surface of the ramshackle city became smaller and smaller as the Airbus a330 gained altitude. Terror which had engulfed her in Bamako faded away as barren land replaced impoverished sprawl. Lina could not let go of her son's hand.

She noticed her pulse return to a more normal rate for the first time since she had arrived into that nightmare of an airport two days before. So much had changed. Two years of pent-up rage, fear, frustration, and helplessness all suddenly found cracks to seep through. It started with a trickle which quickly gave way to a torrent of tears.

The raw display of emotion broke through simmering outrage burning within Jack. He didn't think he could ever forgive Kano for ruining their lives until that very moment. The first glimmer of a possible reconciliation formed with the image of Lina's tears. Her knuckles had whitened from gripping Kano's hand so tightly.

Jack took Lina's other hand. The touch brought her head to his shoulder, and for the first time in their twenty-five years of marriage, they felt the strange sensation of melding together as one.

Like muddy water spilled onto desert sands, the assumption they would go their separate ways evaporated. The life they had built together crumbled and dissolved completely in their minds: a mud-brick wall without a roof, eroding and collapsing under a torrential downpour. It hadn't taken much to fray and snap the tenuous, shallow relationships which had kept them rooted in their environment much like a tumbleweed, ready to roll away as soon as the water dries up.

Their security of wealth had been swallowed up in one gulp by a giant crocodile. For a brief moment she felt dizzyingly free.

It wasn't long before a chasm of fear and uncertainty opened Lina's eyes a bit wider. Her tears stopped as she looked at Jack and said, "What will we do?"

He peered back into her eyes and replied thoughtfully, "I have no idea. There is nothing left for us in California."

Kano looked over at his parents with a smile and a glint in his eyes. "Of course not. Why would there be?" He paused. "Now that we are finally together again, why go back to a place that isn't our home anymore? The Scholar always assumed I didn't have any money for the ransom he needed. He was…"

Jack interrupted with an angry tone laced in condescension. "You don't. We had to pay a lawyer to help us, but we drained all your accounts for the ransom."

Kano chuckled. "You didn't get them all. I checked before we left. You assumed my year in Europe was all about spending money and having a good time. Of course it was, but you missed the fact the poker tables were good to me."

Lina spoke up, "Poker is just a game, honey. We need a place to live. Food to eat. A car to drive."

"I know, Mom. People do make a living from playing poker, though. Believe it or not, the language barriers made it even easier for me to take their money. They all seemed to think that not understanding what they were saying meant I was at a disadvantage. The opposite was true. I wasn't distracted by their pointless words, so I could read body language even better."

Lina always wanted to get straight at what was relevant. "So how much do you have? Where did you hide it?"

"I have enough to float the three of us for a while. I always wanted a Swiss account, so at the time I figured, why not? Looks like it wasn't such a bad idea after all!"

Jack rolled his eyes and said, "You make yourself sound like a criminal."

"Perhaps I was one. I am sure Los Angeles is what your ticket says, but let's get off in Paris and forget about the connecting flight. I can handle our travel expenses. There is someone I want you to meet in the Netherlands."

Kano rubbed his left cheek. It turned bright red. His ears still rang from the slap.

She didn't care who was listening. "How could you DO THIS to ME!?"

He looked down at the dirty, cracked linoleum under his feet. Bright expectations of a joyous reunion shattered before him like a crystal wine glass.

She seethed, "I can understand why you disappeared without warning, but to show up here without ANY?!" Her back was straight while her hands clenched her hips. "How did you even know where to find me?"

He kept rubbing his cheek in shock. "Didn't you want me to find you?"

Her voice ominously dropped a few octaves. "I asked you a question."

Kano sighed. "You know that friend of yours, Roos, the one who liked *Borat*...?"

"I haven't seen her in a while." She bit her tongue hard enough to draw blood.

"I told her I would send you a letter. Needed your address. Said it was meant to be a surprise."

Her head shook with indignation. "And how is that surprise working out for you? What if my boyfriend was here? What if I…wasn't?"

Kano allowed the slightest of smiles to slowly overtake his stunned expression. "If you weren't here, I would have waited. I have gotten good at that. If your boyfriend was here I would ask him to leave."

"And what if I didn't want him to go?" Her eyes narrowed into slits.

Kano looked at her quivering face intently. "Do you even have a boyfriend?"

Her fury broke down, giving way to a rush of sobs. She left her hands at her sides as he stepped forward to embrace her. He felt her body shudder at his touch.

Before long, his shoulder was wet, and his face still stung. He managed to push the crooked door closed and they sat down on the numbingly cold floor, backs up against the ladder-like staircase. They sat in silence for what seemed like hours. Kano wanted to speak but knew he had to wait.

Unexpectedly, she stood up, opened the door, and politely told him to leave. "I need time to process this all alone," were the last sounds he heard before the door slammed in his face. He stood there staring at chipped cracks in the paint until the thought entered his head that she might get hungry after a few hours of processing.

He was almost there. Shivers of excitement and apprehension spread and paled within him, pulsing like northern lights. Narrow, bustling city streets gave way to wide open space in the Griftpark.

Following an abruptly awkward separation, Kano had spent the last two hours buying nicer clothes and cleaning up in the hotel room next door to his parents. She had sent him away much too soon after his arrival. It was as if she had pushed him off the top of a mountain and he was still tumbling.

Even though dizziness swam through his head and mingled with the butterflies threatening to float his stomach away, he knew he needed to try again. One foot after the other. Souleymane had taught him to march through the blazing Sahara. Kano knew he could handle what felt like the coarsest cobblestones of Europe.

There must have been one thousand layers of paint on the door hanging before him. He stared at the uneven, cracked up surface for a full five minutes before his brain was able to command his finger to press the doorbell. It didn't work, so he tried knocking.

Years spent perfecting his poker face were unable to mask disappointment when a tall guy about his age answered the door. He looked down at Kano through a mass of scraggly hair and said with an unfriendly tone, "*Ja, wat is er?*"

Kano looked down to avoid eye contact with obvious unease. "Is Johanna still here?"

The tall guy squinted as though it were bright outside. He spoke slowly with a heavy Dutch accent. "So you are the reason she won't come out of her room?"

Kano glanced up for a brief instant. "I guess so. Can I see her?"

"Hmmm…maybe you will have better luck than I did." He nodded up the steep staircase wrapped in thin, tattered carpet grimly holding onto the vague idea it was designed to be green. "Second door on the left."

Kano felt the railing pull away from the wall with a squeak as he climbed, so, like a small child, he kept his hands on the steps in front of him to steady his progress. Shakily, he knocked on her door and said, "Will you just let me take you to dinner? I can explain everything."

He waited in silence for what felt like ten minutes with the tall guy looming nearby, arms crossed. A damp smell of spoiled food and unwashed laundry pervaded the uneven hallway. Eventually, a small, unsteady voice penetrated the door. "Go wait in the park. I will come down when I am ready."

Kano released a deep sigh as if he had been holding his breath the entire time. "Okay, see you soon." He nodded appreciatively to the tall guy and gingerly made his way back down to street level.

Kano felt several hairs turn grey before their time as he struggled through his endless sentence on the park bench. He never would have managed without his training in Timbuktu. The unmoving door he stared at from across the street would have been a smoldering pile of ashes had he possessed any sort of telekinetic power.

His body would not allow him to sit still, so he paced, did jumping jacks, even a few sit-ups before realizing his new clothes were probably getting dirty. It felt as if he were locked away again, back in the claustrophobic chamber of insanity. In spite of the late November chill, memories cloaked in heat surged through him. He began to sweat profusely.

Finally, the door he focused on so intently seemed to come alive. Slowly at first, it swung inward until a form appeared. Kano's vision swam with pure panic as blond hair glinted in the setting sun. A slew of thoughts crashed into his consciousness all at once; a bottleneck stunning him into a stupor. *How can I explain it to her? What if my clothes are dirty? The sweat will make me smell bad. What if she sees me and keeps walking?*

The figure wore a long, black coat which hugged her as if it had been tailored to do so. Her steps drew her to him in a reluctance resembling slow motion, as if walking into a funeral. Every foot-fall fell flat with despondency. The thoughts flowing through her during this grim approach were the same ones that had looped unrelentingly since he had appeared out of the blue just hours ago. *I finally let go. My life is on track again. This isn't fair. How can I speak to him?* And one bit of heavily repressed curiosity which pushed her forward. *What happened?*

Kano approached with shaking arms outstretched like Frankenstein, not sure if he could take another step without vomiting. Somehow this fear triggered a memory of Charlie explaining, in great detail, one after the other, all the embarrassing moments when he had *chundered.* If Kano were to throw up at this moment, he would have all Charlie's exploits beaten. Hands down. The slightest of smiles escaped with the thought.

It was his smile which broke through Johanna's protective veil. She ran the last few steps and for the long moment she was wrapped in his arms her anger melted away.

Kano grabbed her slender, gloved hand tightly as they began to walk, feeling a slight shudder in response. He broke a long silence with a question. "Aren't we going the wrong way? I thought all the dinner places were back there, toward the center." He nodded his head off to the right.

"Not all of them." Her eyes reflected a slight twinkle as the street lights slowly began their pinkish glow toward life.

He moved forward with somewhat jerky, drunken steps. "I hope it isn't too far. I haven't eaten since this morning. Not sure if my stomach will let me eat yet, but my head is dizzy with hunger."

"It is only a few blocks from here." They continued in silence for minutes.

"Are you sure we are going the right way? It seems like these houses go on forever!" His stomach growled angrily.

After ignoring him for a few seconds, she slowed down. "Here we are, my favorite Greek place."

He let disappointment creep into his voice. "Looks like someone's living room."

"So it does. Not many people know about it. Shouldn't be too busy yet." She peered through the glass. "Table by the window is open."

The shot of ouzo promptly placed before them acted like a wrecking ball punching a hole into the emotional barricades they had erected over the past two years. It allowed rays of light to shine through.

"Start from the beginning," she whispered with a faint smile. "All I know is what the BBC article reported about a South African pilot and his American friend who had been taken by Al-Qaeda." She held back the sobs, but a few tears still managed to escape. "They said Jerry was beheaded to make an example. After that I could barely continue."

Extravagant smells wafted in from the kitchen to fill the small space. When giant prawns and steaming moussaka finally materialized, they promptly disappeared without really being enjoyed. Kano was so hungry he burned most of his taste buds on the first bite and Johanna was hanging onto every word, paying little attention to the exquisite flavors.

By the time Kano's story was coming to a close, they were the only ones left. The owner politely appeared to ask them to leave, surprising them both. Walking hand in hand back toward the park, they were filled with a warm, bubbly joy which had been completely absent for the past two years. The hidden Greek oasis reduced their fortified barricades to rubble.

Phase Five: Condensation

Condensation   *noun*   / ˌkandənˈseɪʃən /
The fusion of multiple images or ideas into a singular result.
Transforming from a gas into a liquid.

December 2011

Kano finally found the time to sit down at a computer. He opened his email. Seven thousand, one hundred and forty-three unread messages. He laughed. Word must have gotten out that he had been in the hands of Al-Qaeda. He imagined everyone wanted their own little piece of the adventure.

One of the messages on top caught his eye; he hadn't thought much about his old college roommate since his first days locked away, trying to imagine what sort of brilliant engineering solutions Ryan would come up with to break out of that concrete pit.

from:	**Ryan Vandenberg**
to:	Kano Griffin
date:	Sun, Dec 4, 2011 at 10:24 PM
subject:	Week 116

Introduction - copied from Week 1: I finished watching *Band of Brothers* for the sixth time. Just got word from your parents that you are a 'Prisoner of War'. I had no idea where you would go after Michigan, but this news is way beyond anything I had imagined. Back in the Second World War letters were at times the only thing that kept prisoners going. I promised your parents that I would write you a weekly letter of support even though you don't have access to email.

I guess this is more for me and for them than it is for you. Hopefully someday you will be able to look back on these weekly updates to see what I have been going through. It will be a journal of sorts for myself, a chance to reflect on things and process life. Your situation certainly puts mine in a different light...

Week 116

I know we have been through this before, more than a few times, but I can't help coming back to it. You are a prisoner. You could be dead for all I know, or starved to the edge of death. Perhaps you have gone crazy. I know I would have by now.

I have all the freedom imaginable. I can hop in my car or get on a plane and be anywhere in the world. Maybe it is just that we haven't seen the sun in ten days. Seattle can be depressing this time of year. I hate the rain. Is that why I feel trapped?

I got the dream job. Working for Boeing was great at first. Made it to the big leagues straight out of school. Now it feels like that Blink 182 song you used to listen to, *"...but every day's the same..."* How could I find a better job when I already have the best one out there? I have some money saved up, but not enough to do anything real with. Four years and what do I have to show? I feel like I accomplished more at Michigan.

Work takes all my time and energy. Haven't been able to keep a relationship together. I need to get out but I don't know how. I am still hopeful that you will get out one day. Perhaps when you do, you can advise me on the best means of escape.

Stay Strong,

Ryan

If Kano had received an email from a friend a few years ago, he might have quickly typed out a superficial reply, or, if he had better things to do, which was usually the case, he would have simply moved on. That sort of response seemed unreal at the moment. He reflected on the fact that someone who had lived nearly the same life as him for a time was now worlds apart.

His words could reach across the ocean instantaneously. How utterly different from the timeless toil of working with ancient, crumbling manuscripts. Ryan sounded unhappy, insecure and tired, even though he achieved everything he had worked so hard for. Kano had nothing and yet he felt ready to take on the world. He closed his eyes to meditate on this unexpected disparity for several minutes. Upon opening them, the laptop came to life, keys like magnets, pulling his fingers toward them with blurring rapidity.

from:	**Kano Griffin**
to:	Ryan Vandenberg
date:	Mon, Dec 5, 2011 at 10:24 AM
subject:	Freedom...?

Ryan my friend,

Has it really been 116 weeks? Hard to imagine that many have gone by. You always were one with numbers, though. I am sorry to hear you are feeling trapped. I also felt that way, more than you can possibly imagine, for the first few weeks. Somewhere along the road that burden was lifted, but that's a long story. The important thing is that I feel free. More than ever before. Just like I did while I was still a hostage.

That must sound strange to you. It feels strange to type it. I don't know how you could possibly understand if I don't really understand myself. Can you imagine, that at the end of it all, I had the chance to escape, but didn't take it? What does that make me from your perspective? I am sure that if my dad found out, he would disown me once and for all. Try not to mention it to him.

Maybe you do understand. Don't you have the chance to escape too? What is keeping you at Boeing if you hate it so much? Why does it matter to you that it is the most prestigious place to be? Maybe you explained all that before, but I only read your latest message.

Do you remember when that boring, monotone professor was talking about Stockholm syndrome in our psych lecture? I think I fell asleep for the second part. I am sure you were awake. Wish I had paid more attention. Maybe I need to read up on it. Seems like I may have identified with my captors a bit more than I care to admit to you, or anyone else, myself included. What does that make me?

I met someone right before I got kidnapped. Her name is Johanna. She was less than thrilled about me disappearing for a couple years since we hit things off so well. It took her a while to come around, but I think it will work out. She is Dutch, so I am here in the Netherlands. So are my parents. Not sure what they will do now that I helped clean them out. You say you can hop on a plane and be anywhere. Perhaps you would like to join us? Time for a European adventure?

With Peace,

Kano

Just as Kano pressed the blue *Send* button, in the room next door, Lina reached across the breakfast table and took Jack's oversized hand. She looked him in the eye. He looked back without blinking. The connection between them had deepened since their experience in West Africa.

"We need to figure out what comes next. Kano's money will run out soon enough."

Jack rolled his eyes away from hers. "Hah! He wouldn't even tell us how much he had squirreled away. He has spent what, about a grand on us now? If he does that a couple thousand more times we can call it even."

Lina pursed her lips. "You know we can't stay here forever. This hotel is already getting old."

"So are we." He let go of her hand. "I don't want to go back to the lives we had before. You say we can't stay here forever, maybe not in this hotel, but why not in this city? It is a beautiful city. We have had more fun here than anywhere else I can remember!"

She paused to take a sip of her freshly squeezed orange juice, averting her gaze as the thought struck home. "Maybe you are right. Maybe this is our chance to start over. I don't want to go back either. I think there is someone I used to work with here at the university. Perhaps they could use an economics professor."

He raised his left eyebrow. "Yeah, and there are enough companies with bricks in Amsterdam that I have done business with. Should be able to find something."

Lina felt her pulse increase and a slight dizziness blurred her vision. Naturally, she kept the sensations crisply masked, but allowed her thought a verbal outlet. "So we stay," she wondered aloud. "Why not?" A smile crept across her lips followed by a little giggle. "Would we have to learn Dutch? It sounds so ridiculous when they speak it. Like everyone has something stuck in their throats!"

Jack grinned too. "I don't know, everybody speaks some sort of English. What was it the bartender was trying to say about me last night? Something about looking too deeply into my glass?"

Lina put her petite fingers in front of her mouth to cover up another giggle. "Yeah, and then the guy sitting next to us said the bartender was totally in the war! What war?! He couldn't have been twenty-five!"

"I have no idea what they were talking about, but these Dutch people sure can be entertaining. Maybe it wouldn't be such a bad idea to learn a bit of their language…"

"You should see a psychiatrist. I know a good one." Johanna stared straight into Kano's averted eyes.

"Why? I haven't lost my mind. I am still the same person I was before I left for Mali." Kano took a sip of his freshly squeezed orange juice.

Johanna bit her tongue with annoyance. "You can't seriously believe that. I don't think you have lost your mind, but you are not the same person I met in Mali, and you told me that person was much different from the one you were before traveling there in the first place."

He chewed on a bite of French toast and continued to stare out the window. "I guess you have a point. Just because I have changed doesn't mean I need to see someone though. Everybody changes."

She rolled her eyes and allowed her tone to become more condescending. "Of course everyone changes, but not in the way you have. No matter how many ways you try to rationalize it, I still can't get over the reality that you had the chance to escape and didn't. You don't have to see the woman I know, but if you want this relationship to go somewhere, you need to start talking to someone."

Kano reached across the table and took her hand. He lowered his gaze. "If you feel that strongly about it, I will find someone." He paused and looked into her gunmetal blue eyes. "Don't you dare threaten to abandon this relationship if you don't get your way again. That negotiating chip needs to be taken off the table. I am not just here to have a good time. I am here because I don't see anyone in my future other than you. I am here to build a foundation with you that will last for the rest of our lives."

Her eyes moistened as her heart pounded, but she kept the tears at bay. "Kano Griffin, words don't mean much to me. You will need to prove what you just said."

A smile slowly spread across his face. "No, we will prove it together. I think of you less and less as an individual and more like an extension of who I am."

"Are you saying what I think you are saying?" She spoke with mock outrage. "I don't know what you are thinking, but this is a country where men and women have equal rights! Before long you will be telling me to quit my job to take care of your kids!"

He laughed. "Who said anything about kids? It's still too soon for that topic!"

A mischievous look crossed over her face. "All I am saying is that we need more practice."

He raised his left eyebrow. "Practice making kids…? I have never thought about it that way before. The more practice we put in, the better looking the kids will be, right? Isn't that how it works? Let's assume so." He abandoned his orange juice.

April 2012

Caleb's hair changed. It became frizzier. The humidity was, ostensibly, the culprit, gradually rising alongside the temperatures in a subtle attempt to suffocate the chaotic city. Rain clouds were a distant memory and would not make another appearance for at least two months. The dreaded hot season was upon them.

He slipped into a lethargic state, unwilling to leave the bar at the hotel which had become his home in Bamako. The mining company sequestered them to the capital as the situation in the North deteriorated.

Caleb vacantly thought Marcel would make a good secret agent. Definitely not the James Bond type. Women didn't seem to interest him. Men either, come to think of it. He was always into the latest developments in the desert, upsetting the mood with one piece of bad news after another. Updates over the course of the last few months had been mostly about the Tuareg rebellion.

He recalled the first time he had asked Marcel about them. "I thought that was the name of one of those big Volkswagens," he had said jokingly.

Marcel gave him a look of contempt and answered in his standard, semi-robotic tone, "Names come from somewhere. The tribe spread throughout the Sahara over fifteen hundred years ago and came to be known as the *Blue People* due to the indigo shade of the veils and clothing they wore. They have always been nomads and fighters, giving our French colonialists a real punch in the face somewhere in the 1880s. More recently they have made big friends with Libya's Gaddafi."

Caleb had made an insult about how Marcel's left brain was really a computer, but secretly he valued his friend's extensive knowledge. It had kept them out of trouble more than a few times before. Even so, he wished he had some other friends to hang out with. Spiraling further and further into a darkening depression, it was as though Caleb's mood mirrored what was happening on the edge of the desert.

Immediately after he ordered another locally brewed Castel beer, Marcel appeared on the next stool without making a sound, as if he knew Caleb was already thinking about him. His eyes were lit up with excitement. "It is all happening so fast," he said in a hushed tone.

"What, you are finally about to lose your virginity?"

He ignored the comment along with the slur in Caleb's voice. "The rebellion is already falling apart. About two weeks ago, March 22nd, the Tuareg force seemed unstoppable. They ousted ATT, the president, a month before the elections. The North finally had a major impact on the South!"

Caleb grasped his cold beer and pressed it into his forehead. "You think I forgot? That is when they locked us down. I can't handle this for much longer."

"Several days ago, on April Fool's Day, they captured Timbuktu. Then they started messing things up with their brutality. Looting and raping the locals. Bad strategy for hanging onto new territory. Earlier today, the 'saviors' showed up. Wolves looking like sheep. Ansar Dine. Ties to Al-Qaeda. They want Sharia law."

Caleb mumbled, "That's where they cut off body parts and stone their women, right?"

Marcel continued to ignore his friend's idiotic commentary. "They will probably get it too, now that the Tuareg are making fools of themselves. The people will be all set for a 'rescue' in no time at all."

"I think I might need my own rescue from this place. Bamako sucks big balls in the hot season. Did you feel the metal chair you are sitting on? Did you even notice? You wouldn't notice. Of course you wouldn't notice! It feels like it has been in the sun all morning. Was it? Was it in the sun at all? No. It has been in the shade. The whole time. But it feels hot. Like it was in the sun. That means the shade is hotter than we are and it is not even eleven. I have been drinking beer all morning. Did I get up to pee? Even once? No. I sweat faster than I can drink. If this crap up North doesn't clear up soon, I am finding another job. Doing nothing but drinking and sweating is killing me!"

Marcel rolled his eyes. "When most people think of their dream job, getting paid to drink beer and swim in a pool is beyond what they can even imagine. I don't see why you are complaining."

Caleb sluggishly raised his eyebrows and said, "Well…I guess you make a point." He considered it slowly and then pointed his finger unsteadily in his blond friend's face. "But too much of anything is never good, you know!"

Caleb wasn't the only one who was sweating. A few blocks away, The Scholar felt a drop of liquid escape from his temple in a suicidal dash for the uneven concrete floor. The room chosen to hide his precious manuscripts still did not have the air conditioning he had ordered, although the backup generator arrived and was collecting dust in a corner.

He could feel humidity invading every fiber of the ancient scrolls which remained in metal trunks at his feet. The archaic material was already changing color as the brittleness defining its texture softened.

Frustration rose in him once again and he fished out a phone from the depths of his shimmering blue, robe-like outfit. His tone escalated as the man speaking to him explained exactly what he did not want to hear. The air conditioner was lost. The workers who would install it were busy. All would be well soon, *inshallah* (God willing).

In that moment, something inside him broke loose: the pin which held the window shut against the howling desert sandstorm. He raged against the man on the other side of the telephone, crushing his spirit into oblivion. Afterward, he sat on one of the many metal trunks, his slim frame distorting the already dented lid further inward. He held his head in his hands as if it were too heavy for his neck.

Everything he had done up until this point had been purely rational. Reflecting back upon the last three years, he knew his conscience was clear. Under no circumstances would he allow so much hard work and the necessarily painful bending of his principles to result in failure at the hands of lazy and incompetent Southerners. He had protected the essence of his city from marauding hordes of the desert. Now he would find a way to save it from the mordant climate of the South, at any cost.

This room dragged his spirit down with the weight of responsibility. It contained much more than his personal collection. Trunks had streamed down from the North in cars, trucks and canoes, hiding under crates of vegetables or carpets. The majority of Timbuktu's ancient scrolls were now housed under a single roof. Under his protection. Everything possible had been arranged for. Additional funding from Germany and the Netherlands was secured. Even absurd sums of money were incapable of forcing these dark skinned imbeciles to do their jobs.

He knew the manuscripts could not stay in the trunks. They needed air circulating around them. He also knew that the air could not contain more than 60% humidity, a tipping point which had already been reached. It promised to hover around 80% until the rains came.

He knew what he had to do. If they would not respond to reason or bribes, the only thing left was the threat of physical violence. He had evacuated his arms alongside the manuscripts. Southerners were not accustomed to assault rifles. He resolved to bring the fear of the desert into their homes that very night.

What he did not know is that the vast room he sat contemplatively in was once a restaurant. It had closed down several years before when a severe thunderstorm brought a meter of water into the space, destroying enough to put the owners out of business.

The water kindly receded in an hour or two, but not before saturating the porous structure. This created the perfect environment for a rather assiduous form of mold to take root. He could not smell or taste it even though every cubic meter of air around him contained thousands of spores. They had already slipped into the metal trunks and taken the first steps toward setting up new colonies, expanding their empire. Within a matter of hours their relentless efforts would become visible to the naked eye.

What the Scholar did not know as he planned his bristling offensive is that he was already in the midst of succumbing to a rather dramatic defeat.

October 2012

Hello.
> *God be with you.*

Who is this?
> *You do not recognize my voice?*

Of course, it is you, Doctor. Are things as bad as I have heard?
> *Worse. I have done something I cannot take back.*

What is it you have done?
> *I have cooperated with the Northern Barbarians. Their evil form of Islam squeezes the neck of our beloved city like a clenched fist.*

What is it you have done?
> *They asked me to give medical attention to the one that would be made an example of. I told them I did not have the right instruments. A crowd gathered. The sounds made us all sick. A small boy threw up when the severed hand fell into the sand. Such violence goes against everything we are. And yet I cooperated.*

If you had not, the example may have died.
> *He might yet. I fear infection.*

Who is he?
> *One of yours.*

Who is he?

> *Souleymane.*
> [extended silence]
> So that is why you have called.
>> *I will smuggle him out myself. I cannot bear to be in this place any longer. We only require the means. He may lose the rest of his arm or be dead in a matter of days if we cannot get him to a good hospital.*
> Very well. Speak with one of my drivers. They will find a way to get you to Mopti within 24 hours. At that time I will have a plane waiting.
>> *God be with you.*
> God willing.

It had only taken a few hours for this recording to be translated from the Songhai dialect in which it was spoken to French, and sent to Marcel's encrypted phone. His heart leapt as his mind processed the words. *Finally, a way in!*

The French were preparing for an invasion. Their goal was to minimize civilian casualties while restoring freedom to the Malian people. Marcel was given the task of developing contacts, information, and assets to help the joint strike force defeat the Islamist militants, the MNLA, who had secured Northern Mali and declared independence five months ago, in April.

He immediately called for his white Nissan Patrol and driver, ensuring they were both prepared for the ten hour ride to Mopti. He forced himself into forty-five minutes of sleep on the way up. The rugged singing of off-road tires was more effective than Red Bull at keeping him wired.

A dirty King Air 200 taxied up to the terminal, engulfing it in a cloud of dust. Shrieking engines slowly tapered off as one of the wheels settled into a chipped out crack in the concrete. The only breeze was artificial, coming from the aircraft itself. Dust hung in the air, stubbornly refusing to disperse. It shrouded Marcel's view of the stairs lurching down from the fuselage, creating a gaping hole revealing nothing but darkness.

He watched his driver approach a glinting figure that emerged from the gloom. Even though this style of clothing was not uncommon, when worn on this particular individual, it made Marcel think he was in the presence of ancient royalty. The shimmering cloth reflected sunlight penetrating the dust like an ocean. It grew brighter. Marcel stopped staring through the door and opened it, sliding across the grey vinyl bench to make room.

The Scholar did not offer a hand or even look at Marcel. The Patrol's suspension barely responded to the introduction of the old man's light frame. He spoke in Arabic with an ancient, wandering voice. "Amadou, your driver, tells me that we are to be friends. I am accustomed to sharing tea with my friends. Not hiding in the back of a truck as though something illegal were taking place."

Marcel stared ahead in a similar fashion, crisply responding in the same language. "Forgive me, but I don't believe you have done something legal to acquire the means for such a form of transportation." He gestured nonchalantly toward the airplane. "That is nothing of my concern, though. Please understand that I am here to help you. I know you care deeply about your city. I know of the efforts you have made to protect its history. We both want to see your people liberated."

A moment of silence transpired as beads of sweat developed on Marcel's forehead. The Scholar responded in a low tone. "I am listening."

"Mali has been a beacon of stability and democracy in the region for many years. We, the people of France, would like to see it return to such a state. A joint strike force is assembling to expel the Islamist occupation from the North. We need reliable information to complete this operation as quickly and painlessly as possible. I am asking you to return with your friend who treated the boy and work together to supply us with what we need to know. I will take responsibility for Souleymane. He will receive the best care."

The Scholar turned his head toward Marcel to examine his face. "How is it you have this information?"

Marcel's expression remained unchanged. "Information is the business I am in. I am good at my job."

After a moment of reflection, the Scholar knew he had no choice. Marcel's veiled threats along with the promise of liberation was enough. Now he needed to find a way to convince his friend to return. It would not be easy.

The Scholar acquiescently switched to French. "Very well. I trust the boy to your care. The manuscripts are safe for now. Please ensure the arrangements I have made for their preservation are honored."

A smile crept across Marcel's face as he thought of his depressed friend who never got the chance to visit the city he had dreamed of before the fighting ensued. "I know the right person to look after your manuscripts while you are away. He has been searching for something to do."

January 2013

It was early in the morning, the sun still far below the horizon, when Kano opened his laptop. Johanna was still sleeping in the tiny bedroom a few meters away. He planned to do some reading for the classes he had joined, but something in the RSS feed that filtered relevant news caught his attention. Several articles about Timbuktu.

He clicked on the first one. An image of dusty, Malian soldiers blending into the open back of an equally dusty, camouflaged truck. A giant machine gun mounted among them ominously lit up his screen. The next picture showed a single French soldier stepping out of an equally camouflaged, but not so dusty, helicopter. Loaded rocket launchers garnished its haunches.

Kano thought about the way these two images captured so many differences between the Malians and their former colonists. Black and white. Poor and rich. Many and few. Separate and unequal. The simple colors of their camouflage seemed to be the only thing they shared, but in this atypical occurrence, they happened to be fighting together against a common enemy. He scrolled down to read the article.

French and Malian forces recapture Timbuktu

28 January 2013

Troops led by the French military are nearing complete victory in Northern Mali. After seizing Gao on Saturday, they marched to Timbuktu, claiming the airport overnight.

French President Francois Hollande said in a press conference, "We are winning in Mali." Coalition fighters are still clearing out the historic center of the ancient city, careful to minimize damage to the UNESCO World Heritage Site.

The joint military operation commenced two weeks ago. 600 troops were sent yesterday to capture Timbuktu. Most of the resistance had already fled into the desert, explained French military spokesman Thierry Burkhard.

Islamists captured the region nine months ago. They destroyed more than half of the city's listed mausoleums and burned historical manuscripts.

Bones of saints were dug up and a mosque door that was meant to stay shut until the end of the world was torn down.

Secular Tuareg rebels initially worked alongside the Islamist groups, but were quickly sidelined. Consequently,

locals have suffered under Sharia law.
According to the UN, over 7000
civilians fled to neighboring
countries.

Authorities are unable to comment
specifically on the duration of the
French led occupation. They hope that
an African coalition will take over in
the fall, after the short rainy season.

Kano sat back in his chair, slowly sipping on a glass of orange juice. Even though there was little more than darkness outside the window, a casual observer would have thought he was staring at something fascinating.

Questions turned through his head like the teeth of a slow-moving gear. *Was Souleymane still there? How many manuscripts have been destroyed? When would the Scholar return? Did he truly preserve our work? What if I was still there?*

One line of the article became a rock thrown into his well-oiled gear of questions, grinding it to a halt: "A mosque door that was meant to stay shut until the end of the world…"

The rock shattered, its fragments forcing his thought process into a new direction as the gear began to turn again. *What if the myth was true? What if the door was destined to be opened at this point in time? What if this is the end of the world?* Over a month had passed since December 21st, 2012, the supposed end of the world according to some. Or the beginning of a new age. Depending on who you asked.

What about the cultural obsession encapsulated within so many movies and TV shows about the end of the world? What about global warming and the fact that we are destroying the ecosystems that support us? What about exponential population growth? What about the ever increasing gap between rich and poor? What about the frenetic movement of people rendering the spread of a deadly virus unstoppable? Was this it? The beginning of the end?

Kano watched the laptop in front of him close with excess force, somehow disconnected from the action. He couldn't breathe the stale air. He pulled on a jacket and unlocked the door, wandering out into the damp cold.

He disappeared for hours, his mind reverting to a state similar to that of his early captivity. Panicked. Scattered. Memories and wrenching emotions firing off in all directions, uncontrolled and incoherent. Directionless. Water was spilling into the circuitry of his mind, arcing and sparking and impairing.

Eventually the water ran its course. His thoughts started to flow again, although in a direction and a manner which felt rather foreign. *What would this new age look like? Was there a way to avoid the death and destruction which chilled his bones and numbed his mind? What is my role? Why am I still here while Jerry is not?*

Kano was unable to stop the flood of questions which made his head swim. Dizziness directed him toward a bench. Within a minute his eyes were closed. His brain escaped into the slightly less tumultuous world of dreams, just as it had learned to do in captivity.

Eremita continued with a condescending look in her eye. "Once you optimize those parameters, our update will create a six percent increase in efficiency."

One of the men sitting across the conference table spoke up for the first time. "Can you be more specific about the parameters you are referring to?"

She glowered at him, shifting uncomfortably in her seat while giving her watch a cursory glance. "Perhaps if you were paying more attention to my explanation than to your phone, I would not need to repeat myself. Let's run through it again."

As she took in an exaggerated breath through her pert, businesslike lips, barely showing the perfect teeth hiding behind them, she caught a glimpse of a familiar figure sauntering past the conference room. Her heart skipped a beat as emotions from her freshman year at the University of Michigan flooded in. She quickly closed the meeting on a rudely sarcastic note. "On second thought, have one of your *esteemed colleagues* fill you in. I am late for my next engagement."

Eremita barely caught up with him before he stepped into the elevator, holding the door for her. She took a moment to catch her breath while he said, "You in a hurry?"

She looked up at him. "You always did have a knack for stating the obvious."

He paused and narrowed his eyes, figuring out how she knew him. Characteristically, he let his surprise show and exclaimed, "Eremita! You sure look different! Not used to seeing you in anything other than that hoodie you always…"

With a slightly flirtatious smirk she cut him off. "Is that supposed to be a compliment?"

Ryan was caught off-guard. He wasn't used to being around members of the opposite sex, especially attractive ones. He stammered, "You…you do look amazing!"

She blushed slightly in spite of his awkwardness. "If it were up to me, I would still wear a hoodie, but I have enough trouble getting these morons to take me seriously as it is." She motioned back toward the direction she had come with a grimace.

The elevator doors opened and they both stepped out, greeted by an enormous plant with tiny leaves. She shifted her bag from one hand to the other and asked, "Which way are you going? I can walk with you."

He pointed through the wall of green. "Other side of that bush. R&D. Restricted access only, so you won't be able to walk too far."

The crisp clicking of her heels echoed against the glass walls as she responded, "What is it you do here?"

Ryan stopped at the card reader in front of the door. "I was thinking of asking you the same." Ryan paused awkwardly as he looked down and fumbled at something in his pocket. "I don't think we can answer all our questions before I get through this door. My trial is about to begin." He fished out his phone presumptuously and his face brightened as eye contact was made. "Will you have dinner with me tonight? I was going to get take-out, but we can go somewhere nicer to catch up if you like."

Her eyes twinkled irresistibly. "Luckily for you, my flight doesn't leave until nine-thirty." She grabbed his phone and entered a number. "Text me when you decide where and when." Eremita looked back and confused him with a wink on her way to the elevator, making him bump his head on the door as he entered the secured area.

Eremita's senses were acutely aware. She could feel her knife sever individual fibers as it trimmed fat from the edges of a medium-rare ribeye. A rash of warmth spread up her slender neck as Ryan's eyes rose from his creamy dish of salmon and linguini to probe her facial expression.

Silence came after exhausting all the standard bits of small talk. He looked down and spoke with more than a hint of shame in his voice. "I hate my job." This simple statement brought their eyes together with unexpected intensity.

"Really?" It nearly came out as a squeak. The rest flowed noisily like an overinflated balloon. "I remember when we were freshmen and you told me the reason you worked so hard is because you had always wanted to make airplanes. Ever since you were little. You were obsessed with Lockheed Martin. Remember how mad you got when that awful roommate of yours tore down the poster you loved?"

Ryan released a rare and genuine smile, meticulously cared for teeth sparkling in the low light. "He wasn't so bad once you got to know him!"

Eremita flashed him the same withering look she had unleashed in the conference room earlier that day.

He responded in a conciliatory tone, "Maybe you did hate him for a good reason. He has changed though! We trade emails back and forth. Did you hear he got kidnapped by terrorists?!"

She raised an eyebrow and listened as the story gushed out, soaked in vicarious pride over being connected to someone who led a life filled with such adventure. Eremita was entertained, and somehow this made her steak taste better. She prevented it from touching the potatoes or the asparagus, finishing it completely before moving onto the next thing.

By the time the waiter set down their third glass of wine, he had finished bringing her up to speed on the life of Kano Griffin.

Her only comment was made with a smile. "Glad to hear you have something to be enthusiastic about. Now tell me why you don't like your job. That is what I am really interested in."

Color drained from his face, chased by the shadow of guilt. "Well...I...I thought at first it was the same thing anyone gets when they finish a big project they have worked on for years. That sense of letdown. A bit of depression. I figured things would get better now that I could do what I always wanted, that I would find new goals within the company." He paused to check his watch, worried she would be late for her flight. "You know what it is?" He perked up. "I always thought building an airplane would be what it looks like in a documentary on the Discovery Channel. The problem is, my part of the documentary is only three pixels. Staring at those three pixels the whole time gets really boring."

She shifted in her chair and swirled the dark wine before taking another sip. "I am really good at writing code. I also look good explaining how it works to a room full of stupid, immature men, so that is what they make me do. What am I really doing though? I make software that allows giant corporations like yours to fire a few people because the systems I design are more efficient than the ones they already have." The glass was still in her hand so she took a larger sip. "At least you contribute to a real product. Something that allows people to fly though the air. Hasn't that been a dream of humanity for thousands of years? All I do is give wealthy people slightly higher profit margins."

"Well," he pondered, "what would you rather do then?"

His genuine curiosity was not lost on her. "I already am doing it..." she let the statement linger in a mischievous grin.

"What, having dinner with me?"

This made her laugh. "No, I mean yes, but I am working on something else."

"Care to share?"

Eremita narrowed her eyes and slowly ran her tongue along the inside of her bottom lip, showing nothing other than the bulge it created. "I don't share the specifics with anyone, but I am working on an app. It has the potential to really change the way people interact."

"Okay. I can see you making something that changes the world. You always were kind of on your own planet."

She sighed. "You say that like it was a good thing. People thought I was weird." The fluffy potatoes having vanished entirely, she moved onto her steamed asparagus.

In a playful tone he teased, "You were kind of weird, but aren't most of us engineers? Couldn't have been all bad—even Kano had a thing for you. He was always trying to get you out of that hoodie."

Her face darkened. "He was a dick. I am glad he got kidnapped. Hopefully they tortured him too. He only paid attention to me because I had more of an accent back then and I wouldn't give him what he wanted."

Ryan raised his eyebrows and thought about that for a minute. "You are probably right. I think being locked up for two years for no reason is torture enough, though."

"For no reason?!" She continued with incredulity, "You really think there was no reason for what happened? Everything has a reason. I don't mean in a religious sort of way, but this is a world of cause and effect. People make choices. Those choices have consequences, intended or otherwise."

He backpedaled, "Yeah, but you know what I mean, if you go to jail it is because you broke the law. They locked him up just for being in the wrong place at the wrong time."

She smiled and shook her head. "Isn't that a reason? Being in the wrong place at the wrong time? Look at a painting in a museum with your entrance ticket in hand and you are cultured. Go look at the same painting twelve hours later and you are a criminal. Wrong place at the wrong time.

After biting his tongue and looking down, he said, "You still like to win arguments, I see."

"Of course. That is one of the other reasons they send me into those awful conference rooms. Kano was in the wrong place at the wrong time. No respect for anyone, including terrorists, and it finally caught up with him!" She slapped the table for emphasis. "I get that you have a thing for your old roommate, and I think you understand that I refuse to stop loathing him, so let's talk more about you. If you hate your job so much, why haven't you left?"

He shrugged. "Why do most people keep doing a job they don't like? Security. Stability. Haven't you seen *Office Space*? I've looked around, but I can't find anything better."

"You could get into the construction business," she joked.

"Funny, Kano mentioned the same thing. I do like infrastructure and I want to be able to step back and design something on a bigger scale. Planning a city or some such thing." The last bit of linguini swung toward him, sending a drop of creamy sauce onto his shirt.

She let out a little laugh because his clumsy action brought her thoughts back to the dorms. "Remember that time Kano was drunk in the caf and he slurped up the spaghetti, spraying himself to the point where people thought he was bleeding?"

He smiled. "Yeah, and then he climbed up on the conveyor belt that brought the trays to the kitchen and yelled, *clean me, clean me, clean me,* over and over again."

"He ended up falling off when he got to the curve. That's when I started laughing. Too bad he didn't break anything."

Ryan's face got serious. "I want to go visit him in Europe. I keep waiting for him to come back to the States, but he still hasn't. I am telling you, he has changed. Maybe a holiday is all I need. This might sound ridiculous, but do you want to come along?"

She laughed with surprise. "I have been on a few first dates before. Most of them ended abruptly when the guy tried to move too fast. This is beyond ridiculous though. Are you out of your mind?"

Ryan felt an uncommon rush of confidence. "For once, I am *sure* this is a great idea! First of all, this is no first date. We have known each other since we met in the dorms. Second, it sounds like you could use a vacation too. It's not like we need to spend much time with him!"

She rolled her eyes. "We haven't really even talked since we were freshmen. A lot has changed in nine years. I'm not going to hop on a plane with someone I hardly know."

"Okay, okay," he radiated, "so get to know me again first. I am booking two tickets. If you don't use it, I am sure someone else will." He surprised himself with the boldness of his statement.

They were waiting outside for her cab. She kept checking her watch, ostensibly worried she would miss the flight. In reality, Eremita couldn't stop thinking about Ryan's proposal. She knew she couldn't say no, *but how could she say yes?*

Eventually, the cab rubbed up against the curb and settled tiredly into place. She stood up on her tiptoes, giving him a kiss with the sort of familiarity suggesting they had been together for the past nine years. His eyes went wide with surprise. She whispered into his ear, "I'm in," and gracefully slid into the backseat that whisked her away through the dark night air.

Souleymane woke to a slur of painkillers muddling his consciousness. He groggily shifted in his bed and a blinding flash of white pain emanated from his right arm. Involuntarily, his mind jolted back to the crowd that surrounded him as the blade came down, glinting in the sun, severing his bones to prove a point. The fear he saw reflected in their faces demonstrated that the message had been effective.

Pain gradually gave way to sadness as he felt the loss not just of his hand, but of his city, his way of life, all that he had come to know and trust. It gripped him like a straitjacket, making it difficult to breathe. The strong dose of morphine dripping into the IV gradually eroded the forceful hold on his tormented mind.

Before he could drift back to sleep, a short but powerfully built man with spiky blond hair and piercingly blue eyes entered the room, taking a moment to assess his surroundings before addressing Souleymane in French.

"The Scholar sends his regards. I am Marcel. He has asked me to look after you while he takes care of a few things in Timbuktu."

"*N be min…*" slurred Souleymane unintelligibly. Flashes of an excruciating ride in the back of a car followed by a nightmarish version of flight electrified his mind.

"I brought you to a hospital in Bamako. The doctor tells me you will be here for at least two weeks because your wound is infected. He also said it will take more than two months before it is healed. I believe this is an exaggeration due to your excellent physical condition. Most people would not have survived the journey given the severity of the injury and its subsequent infection."

Souleymane was still for a time, his consciousness pulsing to the rhythm of the open wound, slowly processing most of what he understood. "*Ça va bien,*" he mumbled with a muted acceptance, wishing for a fleeting moment the journey had claimed his life.

Marcel raised an eyebrow and continued in French, "Is there anything else I can do for you at this time?"

After another long pause he muttered, "No."

"Very well. I shall return when the doctor says you are free to go. You are in good hands."

As he took in his beloved home, The Scholar was shaken by the deathly quiet. French and Malian allied forces had driven out the barbarians from the North, but the damage had been done. He missed the yelling of children, rattling machines, mopeds, trucks, and all the other commotion which keeps a bustling city alive.

A hint of despair darkened his face as he turned toward his old friend. They reverted to the local Songhai dialect, not bothering to maintain their elite status by using Arabic. "Perhaps everyone is simply indoors, still hiding? Don't they know it's safe now?"

The Doctor looked at the ground and shook his head. "Some are, but as I already explained, many have fled, in the same way I tried to do."

"How many, did you say? I wonder if they will ever return."

The Doctor continued to shuffle through familiar sand and replied, "My current estimates are still between seven and eight thousand, about half of Timbuktu."

The Scholar looked up at the dusty blue sky and thought aloud. "What will they do? Where did they go?"

"I do not know. Wherever the men with trucks took them, I suppose. Those men must be rich by now, if they survived. Nearly everyone with money has fled."

After a pause, the silence became too much, so The Scholar spoke again, trying to reach his friend. "If money is your concern, you see too far into the future. What we must focus on now is healing this community. If we can return it to a place of stability, I have access to funds that will help us to restore our noble city, should Allah grant us the opportunity."

The Doctor bowed his head even lower and spoke in a rasping whisper. "I do not wish to speak of your ill-gotten funds. The Frenchman told me how you acquired your precious fortune."

After a moment of silence, the Scholar replied, "I understand if you would have been upset years ago when this plan was put in motion, but even now, when you see that I was right and justified in all my actions, do you judge my path ill-conceived! Our precious history would have been destroyed. Our beautiful city left damaged with no hope of repair. These manuscripts are our very spirit and soul. How could I not do what had to be done in order to protect them? The boy himself has grown beyond my wildest hopes. He can now bring light to the world in a way which was never possible before. That alone was worth some measure of sacrifice."

The Doctor shook his dusty head adamantly as they turned a corner and entered a narrow, twisting alleyway. "What about the other boy? My purpose in life is not the same as yours. You worry about old pieces of paper and crumbling buildings. I suppose someone must. I am concerned with living things. The people dwelling not just in this city, but here on Earth. My purpose is to heal, restore, and dignify their lives. You have snuffed out life itself in your quest to preserve the past. This is something I will never condone. Our required cooperation is complete. Timbuktu has been liberated. We will no longer drink tea together or share another meal. Our long friendship has weathered many heated discussions, but it shall not survive this."

Johanna did not believe in multi-tasking. She had read a few of the studies and was convinced it didn't work. Riding a bike while talking on the phone didn't count. To her, riding a bike was not much different from walking.

She also didn't believe in having the latest technology. The same Nokia had gotten her through the last few years, performing admirably even in Mali, and was not about to let her down. After pausing for a moment to listen to her friend as she bumped across tram lines, she answered back in rapid Dutch. "Yeah, Olivia, but you don't know him like I do. I mean, you have only met him once!"

"Once was enough. I don't think he is reliable, especially after what he has been through. You told me yourself what his dating history is like."

Johanna narrowly missed clipping a small dog which was trying to pull its master onto the bike lane. "Olivia. I know you still live at home, and nothing really changes there, but people do change. Look at me! Am I the same person you grew up with?"

Olivia twisted a brown curl of hair around her finger while speaking. "Of course you are! You are still stubborn, strong-willed, ready to take on the world, and prettier than me!"

"Well, I don't know about all that, but people can change! Kano has become a beautiful person, and I really don't care much about his past. What matters to me is that we are heading in the same direction, and that by doing life together, we can accomplish more than we could have individually. Also, whatever we achieve will have more meaning because we can share it with each other."

Olivia took another sip of tea as she scrolled down her Facebook feed on the laptop sitting in front of her. "Right, you always were an idealist. Don't you realize that our town is full of idealists? People who think they are a part of something bigger? Look what happened. All that idealism forced you out."

"If by idealism you mean dogmatism, then I agree. The community there is rotten, but it is a community. I miss being noticed. Utrecht is amazing, I love it, but I do want more interdependency and teamwork in my life."

Olivia continued to stare blankly at the screen in front of her, biting off a chunk of her cookie and sprinkling the keyboard with tiny crumbs. "Well, I suppose community is just a bunch of relationships, and every sort of relationship is the same on some level: you have to take the good with the bad. All I am saying is that there is more bad to Kano than you can see at the moment."

Johanna allowed her everyday bicycle to squeal and protest against her efforts to slow it down, shuddering to a stop in front of a beat-up bike rack. "Hang on a sec." She set her phone on wet pavement and locked the bike twice with fluid, practiced motions, thick chains rattling across the frame and through bent spokes. Anything with two wheels was liable to get stolen.

After wiping some drizzle from the face of the phone onto her sweater, she said, "Yeah, but Olivia, you are xenophobic like everyone else in that awful town, so of course you see the evil you have been trained to see, even if it doesn't exist. I haven't given much thought to it yet as getting through school and figuring out Kano have taken most of my time and energy, but I know that we can do something great together. I am less of a person without him. With him, life won't be what I expect it to be, and isn't that what I always wanted?"

Olivia sighed deeply with resignation. "I suppose I never expected anything different from you."

"Look, I have to go. Don't worry about me. Talk to you soon!" The sliding doors opened automatically before her.

"I send my love to you, dear. Be careful! Bye!" Olivia tore open another package of cookies, sadly realizing she probably wouldn't get to see much more of her oldest friend.

Kano was taking a break between his afternoon classes, drinking a cup of black coffee. The quality of the typical Dutch roast always let him down. *Maybe that is why almost everyone adds cream and sugar here,* he mused to himself.

Suddenly, like a bot fly growing under one's skin, a writhing lump burrowing out upon maturity, a dream from the night before surfaced into his consciousness.

The memory of this particular dream suffered from none of the gaps and shimmers which usually distorted his recollections, but remained clear in his mind as if the event had actually happened. A remnant of the warping effects of those first weeks in captivity remained; Kano still experienced episodes every now and again where reality blurred. He felt himself pulled back into an alternate realm.

His dream started with the sensation of the sun as a disconnected force he could not see or feel directly, but the sand outside his oven-like enclosure shimmered with its rays. A low metal roof flattened his field of view. He peered out in all directions through heavy iron bars which were hot to the touch, even though they remained untouched by the sun. Omnipotent heat warped and deformed everything in the world around him.

Kano's perspective unexpectedly shifted as if he were watching the dream through the lens of a movie camera. It rose above the metal enclosure and panned about.

Lions wandered aimlessly outside of his cage; a nightmarish reversal of the concept of a zoo. They paced up and down, back and forth, leaving shifting indentations in the sand where their massive paws had been. Strangely, they seemed relaxed and unaffected by the scorching sun. His viewpoint zoomed in to witness an extreme close-up of heavy pacing which rippled and quaked the desert itself.

Another abrupt shift revealed several misshapen, seemingly abandoned enclosures holding disheveled, nearly invisible humans captive. The lens of his dream traveled toward one to make out the details of a bearded man's face across seething sand.

Lions stopped in unison, almost robotically, heads raised and ears pointed rigidly toward the stark blue sky. One of them broke the collective trance and prowled toward the cage which held Kano's focus. The lion stopped short of the bars and bared his ferocious teeth in a snarl transforming into something more. The Savanna-shaking roar Kano expected to hear was replaced with staccato machine gun pops as if a clip of the soundtrack from *Reservoir Dogs* had been tastelessly dubbed over a National Geographic special about top predators.

Kano recoiled at the unexpected burst of noise and the sight of the bearded man violently convulsing as shining sand behind him soaked up a foreign mist laced with a reddish hue. His empty eyes looked just like Jerry's.

An electronic chime brought him back to reality. The laptop hadn't been open for long, but the Facebook tab was flashing, indicating Ryan Vandenberg sent him a message. He quickly shook off the terrifying invasion of his mind, as if it hadn't really happened, and clicked.

Hey, Kano!

Aren't you up too early?

I always get up early. It's called having a job.

Right. So those people do exist...

And they are about to exist in a real way for you!

You mean you found me a job? Might be tough to work into my class schedule...

Haha, you, go to class? When has that ever been a thing? I thought you just registered to get a visa.

Yeah, but I also want Johanna to take me seriously, so I go.

Right on. Well, I have some big news. Met someone the other night.

Remember that girl from Bursley who always wore the Michigan hoodie and hated you? Eremita?

Of course. I only forgot the ones I hooked up with. Is she still looking good?

Better than good. No more hoodie. Sexy boardroom outfits.

You would be into that, Mr. Corporate stooge!

You would be too, if you saw her. Speaking of seeing her, how about we come visit you?

Seriously? Why would you want to come here? I get depressed every time I look out the window. This is worse than winter in Michigan, and you know how much I hated those! Take her to Italy or to the South of France.

We can't get the time off to do everything. We can wait until the weather warms up, though. Can it really be any worse than Seattle? I always wanted to see those famous Dutch paintings. They have been renovating the Rijksmuseum for ten years and it should open up in a couple months!

The Vatican is better.

How would you know? They haven't opened the Rijksmuseum yet.

Well, it does look pretty impressive from the outside, but nothing can beat the Vatican.

It would be fun to meet Johanna too.

I get the feeling that Eremita wouldn't be excited about seeing me.

It's a big country, man. Lots for us to see and do - apart from you!

Stop rhyming, I mean it! Actually, this is a tiny country. You can drive across it in two hours.

Well, then it would be easy to escape to Belgium or Germany.

Fair enough. Let me know when you want to come. Look for an Airbnb in Utrecht. Easy to get on a train to just about anywhere.

Will do. I was thinking sometime in May. That work for you?

Should be fine.

Perfect. I gotta run to work, almost late at this point.

Take it easy, dude. Try being late once in a while! It will rock your world.

Kano scrolled through a few news websites and finished his coffee. A little spark of happiness burned inside him at the thought of seeing his old friend. Something to look forward to. The short, grey days truly were making him miserable.

May 2013

Amber sunshine whirled between fresh, new leaves and reflected off thickly undulating canal water. Dancing flashes of light resulted, causing Johanna to put on a pair of cheap sunglasses. She found herself sitting in one of her favorite spots, drinking a glass of red wine, feeling the old city embrace her as shoppers and students crowded the streets above.

The moment of perfection was jilted by American drawl trying to get her attention from across the table. Steel blue eyes and a monotone voice produced an effect which bored her to distraction. He continued to try as though he didn't notice her lack of interest. "You know, the glare wouldn't be a problem anymore if you invested in polarized lenses."

Johanna swirled her wine and shifted in her chair and said, "Sounds expensive. I would just lose them anyway. Can't seem to hold on to a pair for more than a month or two."

Ryan stared at her without flinching. "Once you try them, you probably won't lose them so easily. They make a real difference, you know."

Kano rolled his eyes, knowing where his friend was headed. "Go on then, Mr. Nye, dazzle us with your scientific explanation."

Ryan cleared his throat, pretending to address a crowd with a bad British accent. "Ladies and gentlemen, the secret of polarized lenses lies in the fact that waves of sunlight, when reflected, tend to be oriented in a single direction, vertically that is. Polarized lenses are simply a bunch of tiny slots, like a picket fence turned on its side, which block vertical waves of light. The rest, which are randomly oriented, get through without a problem! This means you can still see, but glare is virtually eliminated. If the water in this awful, stinking canal wasn't so dirty, they would even allow one to see more easily below the surface."

Eremita noticed Johanna's raised eyebrow and leaned over to pat Ryan on the thigh condescendingly. "If you keep giving these speeches we will need to dress you up like a professor. Or perhaps we should start collecting money from you every time something too sciencey comes out of your mouth."

Kano laughed. "We tried that in college. Seemed like Ryan was buying us pizza every week!"

"Hey," Ryan said in mock offense, "no problem, because nerds make the big bucks, right, honey?"

Eremita narrowed her eyes at him, suppressing a grin. "Ahhh, so that is why you pretended to fall for me. As soon as I mentioned the app you knew it would rake in the cash and you wanted a sugar momma so you could sit around and do nothing but be rich and nerdy all day!"

Ryan practiced his best mushy voice. "Yeah, but what is the point in doing nothing all day if I couldn't do it with a beautiful, smart, and somewhat intimidating woman? You are slightly more to me than a walking checkbook."

She slapped him in the face, the others taken aback and unsure if it was meant to be a joke or not. Eremita calmly went back to the salad sitting in front of her, stifling a grin.

Kano laughed out loud and said, "I can't tell you how many times I have wanted to do that! Nice to see he is finally with someone who doesn't hold back. So tell us about this app. Are you really making money with it?"

She replied curtly, "Of course, why else would I put my time into it?"

Ryan stopped rubbing his face and cut in. "Don't try to pretend you are all about the money. Why don't you tell them the real story or I will!"

Eremita wiped her mouth and paused for a minute, continuing reluctantly, "All right. It seems like this friend of yours is now capable of extending his attention up to my face, so why not?"

"A lot has changed since freshman year," said Kano with a patient smile.

"So it would seem…I guess the story is really a rather short one. I love to cook and I hate to waste food."

With an idiotic grin, Kano butted in, "Don't all Mexican women?"

She glared at him and continued with an icy tone, "I always spent lots of time searching for a recipe that used the ingredients I already had at home. Figured it would be nice if there was a better way, so I created one. First, I built up a massive recipe bank, then I coded software that allows your phone to recognize different types of food based on what the package says, shape, and color."

Kano interrupted again. "Not smell? What if it's spoiled?"

Ryan tried not to smile.

She flashed anger in his direction and went on. "That was the hard part. The next step was pretty similar to online dating software, just matching the ingredients to recipes that fit your personal tastes."

Johanna perked up. "Sounds like a good start, but I don't see the money element."

Eremita smiled and explained, "For most apps that is enough. You can charge for each download, which I did, and you can sell advertising, which I did not because I hate ads, but yeah, I took it a step further. I partnered with grocery stores to deliver, or at least set aside, the missing ingredients for various recipes. This is the lucrative part. I get a cut of each order placed with the app."

Ryan beamed with pride and enthusiasm. "It has positively exploded these last couple months! Eremita quit the job she hated and now runs her own company full time. She even hired a few people!"

Johanna lifted an eyebrow. "Wow, congratulations. Must be nice to be out of the corporate scene."

Ryan could barely contain his excitement. "Yeah, she loves being the boss, but she still won't even tell me how much cash this project has raked in. I mean, I have seen the number of downloads and those must have generated millions of dollars, but she won't do more than hint at what has come out of the stores. The darn thing doesn't seem to be slowing down!"

Eremita managed to look down at him even though he was much taller. "Someone has had too much coffee today. It is nice to be finished with conference rooms, but to be honest, I am already done with this app too. The people I hired can pretty much run the company without me, and now I am looking for what's next. Chalk this one up to the win column, and use the capital for something bigger and better. Not sure what that looks like, though."

Kano set down his glass of water, raised an eyebrow, and thought out loud. "It usually takes people a lot longer to get to that point, if at all. Most of them stick to what they created until it goes under or pushes them out. Why are you in such a hurry to move on?"

Eremita paused and looked down for a moment, deciding how much to share. "Maybe this sounds a little strange, but I guess I am disenchanted with Western culture. I wanted to make a tool that would help people connect over food and also reduce waste. Did you know that over a third of the food we produce is thrown out? People were supposed to develop relationships by sharing food, recipes and cooking techniques. Within the app, you can fill in missing ingredients not just from grocery stores, but from what your neighbors have. The problem is, hardly anyone is using that particular feature. In the corporate world, I got sick of living out of hotels, tired of spending days and weeks with lonely people. I thought maybe this could help create a bit of community. Unfortunately, the app is mostly used to save time and energy, but that wasn't my main motivation for making it. I could have stuck with my old job if improving efficiency was my goal."

They all sat in silence for a moment, picking at what was left of the food in front of them. Johanna sensed this wasn't something Eremita usually shared with others, so she replied delicately, "I am happy to hear that there is something behind that sharply dressed facade you put out there. Now I can see why Ryan can't stifle his enthusiasm."

Ryan looked a little embarrassed and stared at his girlfriend for a moment before responding. "I am thrilled to just be around her. I know she doesn't always take me seriously," he shrugged, "but I suppose that is because I don't always take myself seriously. I mean, a year ago we were sort of in the same position. Cogs in the corporate machine. She created a way out, something I try to do every day, but I am not sure that I have what it takes. I am too afraid to go on some adventure like you did," he paused to nod at his old roommate, "and I can't see computers the same way she can. I am stuck with physical materials that I can visualize and manipulate. They don't seem to be getting me anywhere."

Kano thought for a moment and responded with an uncommon level of compassion. "To be honest, I lost touch with everyone from high school, so that makes you my oldest friend. I have been thinking about your situation ever since reading through the emails you sent while I was in Timbuktu. I don't have a solution for you. All I can say is that I think you have become lost in the machine. Boeing is too big for you. You need to be part of a smaller machine. A real team. One where you can use your skills to create something that you are excited about, but you probably won't be the boss like your girlfriend here. Find a small group with a vision to attach yourself to and make sure the others see you as a collaborator, not a minion."

Ryan felt the truth of these words roll through him like a rogue ocean wave. He took a moment to respond, eyes focused on crumbs from his meal. "Believe it or not, I don't really talk to anyone from high school either, so I guess that makes you my oldest friend too. I wouldn't know how to hit up the gym, pick up a girl, or get drunk if it wasn't for you. I don't understand what happened in Timbuktu, but you have come back as some kind of philosopher. Whenever we talk I feel like I get new insights about myself or the world we live in. How do I find that vision you mentioned?"

Kano responded without hesitation. "It will come to you; all you need to do is let go of what you are clinging onto. Your life is so full that your big opportunity can't squeeze itself into the tiny cracks that remain."

Ryan processed for a moment, swallowed his glass of wine in two big gulps and slammed it down as if it were a shot glass. Luckily it didn't break. "Alright," he said, "that settles it. I am done. Out. Quitting my job! No idea what I will do, but I suppose I have to finish off my current project before I can really stop, and by then leaves will be falling off trees. Start of the ski season." He squinted and pointed at Kano's face. "Didn't you once tell me you had some connections at Tahoe?"

The corners of Kano's eyes crinkled with a smile at his friend's newfound audacity. "Yeah," he laughed, "my uncle owns a hotel up there. Maybe he could use a valet or something. I am guessing you want as little responsibility as possible, preferably with a season ticket thrown in?"

"Ahhh, you still know how to read my mind. Just let me know when I can start!" He turned to Eremita, beaming. "This way, we can be much closer! No need to fly anymore!"

She rolled her eyes at him. "Not sure if that is a good or a bad thing. Sometimes I can use a little distance."

"Four hours isn't enough?!" He continued with mock incredulity, "If you could ski through the redwoods I would live next door!"

Her voice deepened slightly as she had learned to do when confronting an over-excited specimen of the opposite gender. "If you lived next door, we would fight every day until the end."

Ryan launched right in. "So what part of that are you afraid of? Fighting or breaking up? The fighting doesn't bother me so much…at least we would be spending time together."

Kano interrupted. "Look, this is not a couple's therapy session. It seems to me that becoming a ski-bum in Tahoe, as ridiculous as it sounds for a successful engineer at a dominant aerospace company, is exactly what you need. I think it will give you both some time to figure out what comes next. Perhaps we can make a deal. Johanna needs one more year to finish up with her physician's assistant degree. That means I won't be going anywhere until then." He flashed a quick but reassuring smile at Johanna and continued, "We have to figure out our future too. Not sure I can handle the winters here. What if we all meet back in this same spot, at the same time, exactly one year from now? Maybe we will be able to find some answers together."

He looked around the table, from one person to the next, taking in everyone's reaction to the proposal. As soon as they were all satisfied, Kano said, "That settles it. One year from today. We will get our futures sorted out!" Glasses raised, they toasted in agreement.

After dinner, Johanna asked Eremita if she would like to take a walk through the city. Ryan and Kano stayed behind as the light slowly dwindled, ordering Belgian beer with a proud little gnome for a mascot.

They started to reminisce. "Hey," Ryan said, "why did our first week in the dorms, Welcome Week, make such an impression? It kind of sucked at the time, but now it feels amazing. How come?"

Kano thought about this for a moment. "You know, I read somewhere that the direction our memories shift is a good indicator of the afterlife. When your recollections take on a rosy glow and you think of them fondly, you are heading in the right direction. If you do nothing but cringe at what you have gone through then you might be in trouble."

Ryan waved his hand with dismissal. "I never believed in the afterlife. Here and now is all that matters. That is probably why this whole work thing has been such a drag on me," he reflected.

Kano took another big sip of the foamy, amber liquid filling an obese hurricane glass. Several beads of condensation dripped down onto his shirt. "During Welcome Week, could you have imagined beer tasting so good? The stuff we were drinking back then was nothing like this."

"Yeah, it was pretty terrible. Natty Light. The fraternities loved it."

"That first frat party we went to was quite something…"

Ryan interrupted him. "You mean the first one *you* went to. I would have loved to join. You never really even told me about it!"

Kano laughed. "That's right! I was so annoyed by our stupid room and what you were doing to it. I had to get out of there…"

The memories drifted back as they both smiled nostalgically and retold what they remembered. The days scheduled for moving into the dorms turned the sleepy North Campus community into a circus. Hotels were booked months in advance; restaurants had ridiculously long wait times if you could get a spot at all. Hilly expanses shrouded in trees surrounding Bursley Hall were choked with SUVs and minivans. Large blue bins on wheels provided by the dorm rattled across bumpy surfaces in regular, ant-like streams in and out of each entrance.

Ryan commandeered an idle bin which was sitting next to a dumpster and steered it toward the Acura MDX which hauled everything he needed from the western side of Lower Michigan. He was ready to move into the eastern side of Bursley Hall, but he had to do it on his own. His dad, the renowned Dr. Vandenberg, had been called in to perform an emergency heart operation. His mom was too tired to help.

She sat in the front seat listening to classical music with the air conditioning on. Everyone else around her was working up a sweat. Late August sun blazed down, threatening to kill the verdant grass in a single day. As Ryan steered his bin up to the tailgate, a friendly guy with curly sun-bleached hair asked if he could help out. The yellow t-shirt gave him away as a *Move in Maker*—an older student who got to return early in exchange for his labors.

Ryan was happy for the help because it took seven trips with the two of them to unload the neatly packed cargo filling the entire space behind two front seats. While all the heavy lifting was happening, Ryan learned that the guy helping him didn't live in Bursley. He was there to meet girls and recruit freshmen for his fraternity. When they finally finished, Ryan consented to checking out their Welcome Week Party the next night. His mom would be gone by then.

After a tasty lunch in the nearby, heavily air conditioned Cafe Marie where they had to wait nearly an hour for a table in spite of their reservation, Ryan dropped his mom off at the hotel and went back to work. Had he bothered to look out the window instead of focusing so intently on the futon manual, he might have seen an airport taxi glide to a stop near the side entrance, blocking the way for a frustrated father trying to back out his Dodge Caravan. Strangely enough, a single passenger emerged and was carrying only hand luggage. A teal Osprey backpack.

Kano swung his pack over one shoulder and quickly assessed the scene. He felt happy his parents had important meetings to attend. All he needed from them was the assurance his credit card and tuition bills would be paid in full. He quickly registered and skipped the line at the elevator, climbing five flights of stairs two at a time.

The door to his room was open, but he could hardly get inside. The floor was covered with carefully packed boxes in various stages of being emptied, futon parts, and a few random tools.

Kano said from the hallway, "Please tell me this is a closet. There is no way all this crap is going to fit in here!"

Ryan replied as he finished tightening a bolt. "It sure is the size of a closet, but with a razor sharp coating on walls that must be filled with asbestos."

Out of curiosity, Kano felt the walls and realized they were probably made this way to prevent posters and hide damage. "How can they allow people to live in this shining example of the hideousness of sixties architecture? On top of the embarrassment of such an ugly excuse for a building, the place already smells. Imagine what it will be like in a couple months when all the windows are closed because it is freezing outside!"

Ryan said, "All I can think about is how to get all my stuff to fit in this room. I hope my roommate doesn't show up until after dinner. He won't be able to unload his stuff any time soon."

"He already has. I'm Kano Griffin, and this is all I've got for now."

Ryan paused for a moment of embarrassment and then stretched his hand across the futon frame. "Ryan Vandenberg. Nice to meet you. Sorry about the mess. You said that is all you have? How is that possible?"

"I flew in. Checking luggage is a nightmare. Parents gave me a credit card. I can buy whatever you don't already have. Did you bring a car?"

"Yeah, I'm parked illegally for now, but I just bought Aaron's sticker, our RA, so I can park it in the back lot. I guess not many freshmen get a pass, so it's a good thing I asked first."

"What's an RA?"

"Resident Advisor. Two rooms down. The older student who reports us if we do something he doesn't like."

Kano finally dropped his bag and headed back out to the hall. "Okay, I will go introduce myself and then find someone who will build us a loft. Clearly that is the only way to get all the junk you brought to fit."

The long, curving front edifice embraced the main doors of Bursley Hall. Kano emerged in search of a loft. Waning afternoon sun dappled several stands just waiting to take his $400 in exchange for the simple wooden structure designed to raise their beds up to the ceiling. He made a quick deal and the young entrepreneur on the other side of the table promised to set it up the next day.

His main contribution to moving in taken care of, Kano set off to explore one of the big reasons he had come to Michigan: athletics. He set off down the hill on a narrow path winding through a tall, hardwood copse. Soon he found himself at a bus stop. After a brief look at the map, a *Commuter Southbound* approached and he conveniently hopped onto the free ride, pleased he didn't need to show his shiny, new M-Card.

The bus wound its route through choked Ann Arbor streets. As Kano passed families moving the next generation of students into stately Central Campus dorms, he was filled with jealousy. *All the action happens down here.* After about forty-five minutes, he stepped onto the parking lot of the Chrisler Center, home of Michigan basketball. He didn't realize the university was so large.

Ten minutes of walking across blacktop ribboned with patched cracks brought him to the Big House. This was his main goal. His chances of playing sports on anything but an intramural team were shot. Watching football would be amazing, though. He was looking forward to basketball and hockey, but there was something special about walking into the country's largest stadium with at least one hundred and twelve thousand other people. A shadow of disappointment crossed his face when he realized all the gates were locked.

A twenty minute walk brought him back to the edge of Central Campus and his rumbling stomach led him to Big Ten Burrito. After a long wait, he finally made it to the counter, ordered a chimichanga dripping with grease, and brought it up State Street to find somewhere to sit.

The Law Quad, modeled after Oxford, loomed ahead on his right. Geometric peaks above the windows and soaring turrets pierced the dusk sky like a medieval castle.

The foreboding structure did have something that immediately pulled Kano under one of its perpendicular-style archways: a place to eat. He sat down on the wide staircase and devoured his dinner, thankful he had left his car in California. The vehicles in front of him were stuck in a massive traffic jam mimicking the deadlocked 405 Freeway around Los Angeles.

After abandoning the Styrofoam takeaway box on stone steps worn smooth with dips and depressions, Kano wandered through the heart of Ann Arbor. He traced his way up and down busy streets, passing many crowded restaurants and noisy bars. People thinned out as he read a sign labeled Kerrytown, so he headed back toward campus.

While cutting across the Diag, a nickname for the original forty acres granted to the University of Michigan back in 1837, Kano felt rather uncomfortable. The busyness of downtown made the center of campus feel entirely deserted. Tall, dark buildings looked down upon huge trees dominating open spaces in between paths. A few strangers passed here and there on the way to somewhere else, quietly ignoring their surroundings. He picked up his pace.

Emerging on a street called South University, he felt more at home. The buzzing excitement of people on a mission to enjoy one of the last summer evenings washed over him like a perfect wave on a San Diego beach.

The chimichanga had already begun to wear off, so he popped into a place called Jimmy John's for a sandwich. The Beach Club looked good. Classic California style with avocado and alfalfa sprouts. The service was much faster than at Big Ten Burrito. He grabbed one of the last window seats to stare out into the gathering nightlife. Falling into a tired sort of trance, his eyes rolled back and forth like loose cannonballs on a storm-tossed ship as he watched the ever-increasing number of sorority girls walk by.

Unsure of how much time had passed, he suddenly sat up straight and left his rumpled paper containing nothing but a sprinkling of spouts and a few drops of mayonnaise on the counter. A particularly attractive trio of blondes approached. He wanted to figure out where they were headed.

Kano tailed them from a distance, fixated on every harsh, high-heeled step, continuing to admire their curves even though he memorized the shapes and colors the moment he laid eyes on them. The snapshot was burned into his consciousness; a beautiful thing was hard to let go of.

They turned right onto Washtenaw Avenue, heels clicking up the hill in the direction of a massive white house. Kano quickly realized the low rumble he heard must be coming from inside the well-lit, stately edifice. Near the top of the massive wooden structure hung three letters: PKA.

Tall trees surrounded the sweeping, green lawn which led uphill to crisply detailed architecture. From a distance it looked like college paradise. As Kano got closer, he noticed the colorful spots dotting the lawn were not late summer flowers poking through luscious green surrounding the mansion, but cheap beer cans and red Solo cups in various crushed and broken stages spotting trampled grass.

Kano slid into the curving line behind the girls and stuck out his hand. "Hi, I'm Kano," he said. It was the best pickup line he could think of. Simple, honest, and non-threatening. *Who could ignore a handshake?*

"Matilda."

"Rose."

"Grace."

They replied one after another, extending their slender arms to meet with Kano's. He asked, "Have you been here before?"

"To Pike? Not since last year. This is their Welcome Week Blowout. I mean, they party just about every night, but this is the first one that is interesting. Good luck getting in."

She nodded her head to the group of young men who were being turned away at the front of the line. "Did they not bring an ID, or what?" asked Kano.

She delicately covered her mouth and laughed. "They don't care about your age...I mean, if the cops ask, that is what they are checking for...all they care about is what you've got between your legs. With fifty-five guys living under the same roof, don't you think they need to compensate for a little latent homosexuality?"

He buried the smirk which would have betrayed his quickly developing condescension toward frat boys and replied with a mischievous grin, "What about the three of you? Don't you live in a sorority? What are you hiding?"

"Lots of things...but you won't ever find out what they are," one of them said smugly, "so what dorm did you get stuck in?"

"I guess it must be obvious I am a freshman," replied Kano with a hint of shame. "Bursley. I've only spent fifteen minutes there and I already hate it."

As the line moved forward, one of the blondes turned back to Kano with a look of solidarity. "Yeah, I lived up there last year and it was terrible. The food was gross and I felt like all those creepy engineers were constantly watching me."

Kano stared at her with more than a touch of lust in his eyes and said, "I think my roommate is an engineer. You should have seen the way he packed his boxes—everything labeled and organized. The entire floor of the room was covered in his OCD mess. I wish we could choose who we had to share a room with. Too bad the singles are so hard to get."

"I don't know," said the quieter blonde, "I dated an engineer last year. He was pretty cool. Ended up rushing FIJI in the winter. One of the few decent fraternities."

"Yeah, and then he dumped you for a DG," her friend replied, "I hate that sorority."

"Who doesn't?" said the quiet one.

The line was moving quickly; another group of seven or eight guys just got turned away. Eventually, two chubby males with matching t-shirts asked to see some ID. While Kano handed it over, the tallest blonde said flirtatiously, "We left ours back at Tri-Delt. Didn't think we needed any to get in. Want us to go get them?" Kano figured this was a lie, and she probably always needed the upper hand whenever a male claimed a position of relative authority. He imagined this sort of behavior served as a drug for her ego. *Without the necessary daily boost, her self-centered balloon would slowly deflate into extra hours spent in front of the mirror making herself irresistible to everyone.* He knew precisely how to use this information to his advantage.

"Tri-Delts, huh? Well, you guys look twenty-one to me. Enjoy the party. We don't let freshmen in though. Take a hike, shorty."

Kano bristled, but before he could open his mouth, the tall one kept talking with an embellished Southern accent. "He's with us, darlin', and if you want our opinion, he could be a Pike before you know it," ending her last few syllables with a friendly wink.

The wannabe bouncer dropped his eyes. "Fair enough, have a good time, *ladies.*"

Music shook the walls. Kano's sneakers stuck to the floor as his senses were quickly overstimulated. Drunk girls dancing on tabletops were like ever-changing photographs which never really changed in the flashing strobe lights. Kano took in every hypnotic drop of beer falling from their red cups down to the floor, one frame at a time.

The quiet blonde brought him a warm can of Busch Light. The good stuff. She took him by the hand and they slowly bumped and jostled their way through the packed entryway to a dining room which had been converted to a dance floor. Tall windows were covered with thick black cloth and the effect was stifling. It trapped something primal and cave-like into the raucous room. The two pressed up against one another in rhythm to a song by Akon.

It didn't take long before the lights, noise, sweat, lack of oxygen, and the alcohol pushed Kano upstairs as he became fully aware that a hand was still holding onto his own. The thuggish guy guarding the staircase let them through, and Kano was quickly pulled around the corner. She whispered in his ear, "You don't have to go back to Bursley tonight. My friend from Connecticut has an empty room in her apartment."

He was about to kiss her in response when he got distracted by something down the hall. She followed his eyes. There was someone sitting on the floor staring vacantly at a jagged hole punched into the wall with a thin string of cheese dangling from the top of it. A cooling pizza was the only thing keeping the lethargic figure company. Someone with the name *Nash* on the back of his t-shirt brusquely passed the couple, striding toward the seated figure with purpose. "Dude, what the hell are you doing?" he said.

"Sup…Nash." He talked slowly, trying really hard to sound like he was from Southern California. "I'm tuned into the house…man. It's tellin' me it's hungry…bro. Shhhhh. Can you hear it?" He paused for effect as Nash stared incredulously with a wide stance and hands on his hips. "It says, 'feeeed meeee,' over and over again. I'm hungry too bro. Figured me and the house could chill together and eat some pizzzza…bro." He continued defensively, seeing Nash remained unconvinced. "I'm feeding our house…man."

Nash started to get angry. "How many of those brownies did you eat?"

"Whoa, whoaaa, slowww down…bro. What are you, the Gestapo or something?" He shoved what seemed like half of a slice into his mouth and stuffed the other half into the hole, struggling to talk through the grease. "I told you…bro…the house is hungry, and I am feeding it, bro. I don't see…any…body…else, caring about this place where we live…bro. I mean look, we got holes…in the walls, bro. Somebody's gotta feed this house…bro…so it gets strong again…it's fallin' apart."

Nash grabbed what was left of the pizza and barked over his shoulder: "You're an embarrassment. Find your bed if you can, but don't let any more girls see you like this."

Kano shook his head in disbelief. "Why did you want to come here? We should get some fresh air. It smells."

"Let me pee first and then we can go." Kano's eyes traveled up and down the short, black dress gently squeezing her slender figure as she slinked toward the toilets. He closed his eyes and pictured the inevitability of slowly sliding it up, up, and over her head.

Ryan broke into Kano's story as the light along the canal faded. "Seriously, man? I mean, within what, twelve hours of getting into town you already picked up a girl? Do you know how long it took me?"

Kano chuckled. "Yeah, but look at you. Besides, you always wanted to treat them right. Can't do both you know. One is quick and easy, the other takes time and effort. You have always been the time and effort type."

He scowled. "I have always been jealous of the quick and easy type. How is it that everything in life is so simple for you?"

The waitress stopped by, and after ordering more beer, Kano replied thoughtfully. "Everything isn't. Getting Johanna back was pretty tough. So was figuring out how to survive in the desert. Worth it though."

Ryan laughed. "Okay, I stand corrected, you have done two difficult things before. Both were met with success."

Kano smiled. "Weren't you there freshman year? Don't you remember? Plenty of things didn't go as they should have. Thinking back on everything that happened, I am kind of surprised we are still friends." After taking a deep breath of the chilled night air, they plunged back into memories.

Two months after Kano went to that first frat party, he still hated the chaos, but couldn't stop himself from becoming a regular face in the crowd. The strategy he had discovered that first night rarely let him down. Find a few attractive girls dressed up and heading somewhere, start a conversation, and they would grant his entry. At least one would usually end up granting him a lot more.

He seldom went back to Bursley on party nights: Thursday, Friday and Saturday. If he did, it was almost never alone. Eventually, the thrill of sexual encounters waned when compared to the satisfaction of becoming a puppeteer. He knew exactly how to bend and stretch nearly any situation toward the end result he pictured from the moment he first sighted his target. It became an addiction, to the point where a girl who caught his eye would most likely end up in bed with him whether she was interested or not. But then, most of his targets were interested.

After several awkward mornings, Kano realized he was playing with fire and decided to tone things down before they got out of hand. He needed to find something to focus on that was less likely to get him kicked out of school.

Midterm results had just been published online. An outcome of a B+ on his Calculus exam was glaring at him. He felt rather disgusted since he had already seen the material in high school. What he didn't realize, because he so often skipped class, was that many of his classmates had also seen the material in high school, but the average was still a D+. He silently concluded the late nights and cheap beer were taking too much of a toll. Besides, girls were beginning to irritate him, especially now that he was developing an unsavory reputation.

He suddenly felt the need to vocalize his thoughts, so Kano spun around in his chair and told Ryan his decision. "That's it, calc results came out and my grade sucks. I'm joining your study group."

Ryan continued to stare at his screen. "What makes you think we'd have you?"

"Because I'm your roommate and you could use my help. What time do you meet?"

"Two-point-five hours from now at the tables in the main lobby. Make sure you try the problems first." Ryan spoke into the keyboard.

As Kano was about to swivel back to his laptop he said, "Yeah, whatever, I'm not even sure where my book is."

Ryan stared in silence at a screen that wasn't changing. Kano found this rather odd. "You alright, man?"

"Ummm…not really sure. My mom died last night. Part of why I came here instead of MIT was so I could see her regularly. I only went once in the past two months. All I wanted to do was get away from there. Maybe I should have gone to MIT. It's not like my dad can't afford it."

Kano paused for a moment to think as he spun his chair toward Ryan. "Whoa," he said, "Rough, dude. Sorry to hear about your mom. If you were at MIT, you never would have met me!"

Ryan let an annoyed smile begin to grow and answered sincerely, "I don't think I would be missing you. I mean, you don't spend much time around here."

After an awkward silence Kano made another decision. "We can change that. I will hold down the fort while you are gone. Once you get back, and things settle down, I'll show you why you chose the right school."

"Not sure if I want to know, but ok." He let out a big sigh which sounded like acceptance, and continued to stare at his frozen screen.

The decision to shift his focus away from girls solidified after the heavy conversation. Kano figured he could let Ryan have all the fun. The game had simply become too easy. Time for a challenge. Time for a protégé.

Could he turn his depressed roommate into something a bit more interesting? The guy was tall with the craggy looks of an explorer, although cafeteria food had softened his lines. If nothing else, the sob story would always work as a last resort when he played it right. He figured the best way to begin would be to start showing up for lectures and study groups. Seemed like school was all Ryan cared about, and to be an effective puppeteer, Kano needed to gain his confidence.

"…and if you apply these percentages to our three hundred pound offensive tackle, Jake Long, we can calculate, using current market values, that the atoms contained within his body add up to the raw material value of a fresh cup of Starbucks coffee," the short professor explained. He looked rather like a pearl on the bottom of an overturned shell curving around him. His features spoke of Edward

Norton and helped to captivate the attention of the female undergraduates comprising much of the crowd. There simply weren't enough plush stadium seats sloping up and away from the center of attention. Bodies cluttered staircases.

He continued in his slightly arrogant fashion after a sip of water. "Undoubtedly you are aware that the atoms contained within you were borne out of the center of stars and spontaneously coalesced and mutated into all forms of life we see today. While your basic building blocks are common and worthless, they have combined in a manner elegant and surprising enough to have commandeered my complete attention."

Dwarfed by colossal pillars, latecomers stood in the back preparing to take notes, trying not to disturb the audience. "The boy in me wonders who could have created such beauty, but his voice is small in comparison to my rational, scientific mind. Naturally, among untold numbers of planets and stars, life is a byproduct. This semester, we have merely been dipping our toes into the ocean of organic chemistry; the result of random chance applied over billions of years."

As the sandy-haired professor took another sip of water to patiently allow for the absorption of his words, Kano slipped in through one of the tall back doors. A truculent crash inflicted by overwrought springs closing solid oak echoed throughout the silent auditorium. This intrusion caused a multitude of startled movements among the crowd of admirers.

Kano didn't bother with a notebook, but he curiously watched others who stood around him scribbling furiously while the professor continued on with his lecture. Kano wanted to understand why so many students were here and what was so difficult about organic chemistry. He had done fine thus far just by reading the book.

The professor continued to enrapture his audience as Kano's mind wandered. He spotted Ryan on the other side of the oyster, sitting next to the aisle as if ready to make his escape. The seat next to him was empty. Surely a sin in the eyes of the sharply dressed man who spoke with apparent sincerity.

The attempt to befriend his roommate and turn him into a ladies man was not working. Ryan didn't seem terribly interested. Kano knew he needed to fill all the hours he would gain by giving up on the opposite sex, so he explored online options. One of his porn sites had an advertisement for Party Poker, which caught his eye. He clicked on the link, grabbed a bottomless credit card to start an account, and began his first game.

Kano understood the other players by imagining what they looked like and the things they were doing. Some were impatient and played quickly, others took a lot of time to think, get something from the fridge, or yell at their kids. Slowly he got a feel for who was thinking and who was distracted, who took risks and who didn't, who would go for his bait and who wouldn't.

Personalities emerged from behind the screen. He couldn't figure out how it was possible, but he had this otherworldly confidence that the characteristics he conjured were not actually made up, but from the real people he was playing against.

Although these insights helped, his main strategy was simply to calculate the odds. It took practice, but eventually he did it without even thinking. He read somewhere that anything over twenty-five percent was worth a bet. This quickly became his golden rule as the games sucked him in.

It seemed to Kano that he still had an hour before the meeting started, but Ryan closed his laptop and said, "Okay, I'm heading downstairs for calc group, you coming? Those first few times you actually made yourself useful, so it would be nice to see you there again."

"Yeah, give me a minute," was the mumbled reply.

An hour and a half later, Ryan punched his code into the door and swung it open. "Still here?! You said you'd be down."

"Oh, yeah, you started already?" The reply sounded robotic.

"No, we finished already," said Ryan, "and now I'm heading to the caf to get some food, you coming?"

"Yeah, man, give me a minute," came the vacant reply.

"Whatever," said Ryan as he grabbed his M-Card and headed in the direction of the cafeteria.

Kano didn't even hear the door close because his focus was so intense. He learned he could play four games at the same time, one in each quadrant of his screen. He was able to calculate odds for them all and had a strong feel for each personality and life behind the limited digital representations. The physical appearance of his opponents entered his mind so clearly it was almost as if they were playing around a real table: a fourteen year old redhead with acne, a skinny construction worker who only put down his cigarette to light the next, a bald guy with his belly extending under the keyboard, even a pedophile with a thin nose who made Kano's skin crawl with every play.

He was up seven hundred and forty-six dollars by the time Ryan came back through the door. "Hope you grabbed some food. Caf is closed, man."

"Closed? You just got back, and you always go when they first open to skip the lines." Kano spoke to his screen with bloodshot eyes which were unable to look away.

"Yeah, but after dinner we went down to Pierpont to play some pool. I'm heading to bed. It's late." Ryan grabbed his towel and shower caddy.

Kano didn't hear much after that. At three in the morning he snapped out of his trance, eyes opening slightly wider when he saw his balance had topped two grand. He ate a whole box of Pop-Tarts and climbed up into bed, dreaming of nothing but pixelated playing cards.

The first week in December meant exams were looming in the all-too-near future. Ryan had gotten used to having a full-time roommate. He noticed Kano was becoming the hub of the hall.

Doors were usually kept open. Some guys didn't close them unless they were sleeping at night. Rooms still held the distinct personality of the individuals who lived there, but the flow of people ebbed from room to room like groups of starfish making their way from one tidal pool to the next. 5-Lewis had become a social hall, so students from other parts of the building would filter up to hang out when they needed a break from studying.

Ryan was able to apply a principle he learned in one of his economics lectures: A-people spend time with other A-people because they like the challenge while B-people surround themselves with C-people to feel more like an A-person.

He observed most of the individuals who hung out on 5-Lewis were A-people: future doctors, lawyers, and venture capitalists. Those who kept their doors open adjusted easily to university life, played at least one sport really well, had a quick wit, and liked to party.

Kano became their idol. While he had kicked his addiction to girls, he couldn't give up on alcohol or party poker. His fake ID ensured there was never a shortage of booze. They even snuck a keg upstairs into the oversized quad (four-person room) at the end of the hall.

Ryan found it amusing that the people who flowed in and out of his room at all hours weren't bothered that Kano would often play games while they were in there. Once in a while the Party Poker addict would throw a word or two at their conversation, but generally he was focused on winning. Granted, the most he would play was an hour or two per day, but it seemed like that was just enough time spent ignoring people that their veiled, obsequious desire for his attention kept humming below the surface. It spread through the community like the greasy smell of pizza wafting across campus streets teeming with students, pulling them in for a slice.

Ryan didn't drink much and he loved to stay in shape. The extra weight he had gained in the first two months quickly disappeared. Groups of guys would regularly head across the street to the NCRB (North Campus Recreational Building) to get in a workout, but somehow Ryan and Kano became rather exclusive with their timing. Without any sort of forethought or planning, they would always go together, and fail to invite anyone else along.

Sometimes they would lift weights or play racquetball. They also became regulars on the basketball court. Ryan was taller so he could play down low. Naturally, Kano carried on with his high school position of point guard. He had a big mouth and could pass into places nobody other than Ryan expected.

One particularly cold December night, a guy walked in, threw a puffy Bulls jacket on the bench, laced up his Jordan's, and the big center on the other team projected in a baritone voice: "Yo, Tyrell, you with us, we down one." Tyrell was about Kano's size, and since Kano had been walking all over his man, Tyrell stepped in.

After a few points, Kano turned to Ryan as they were backpedaling down the court and said, "There is no way this corn-rowed gangster full of ghetto vocabulary and tattoos goes to this school. How did he get in here?"

Ryan shrugged. "Probably lives in Ypsilanti and bought a membership with his drug money."

Ryan figured Tyrell picked up on the notion that they were talking about him, because he brought the ball up the court, passed it off, paused in front of Kano, and threw an elbow into Kano's solar plexus. He moved quickly, got the ball back, and scored two easy points.

Ryan knew that fouls were usually called on Kano, not by him, and that Kano had way too much pride to stop the game. So instead, things got rough. The vocabulary worsened and Ryan knew plenty of new bruises would appear on both point guards the next day.

Ryan and Kano always left by ten-thirty. Ryan needed to be asleep by midnight in order to get enough rest for the next day's classes. Some of the guys from the hall made fun of him for this; Kano never mentioned anything one way or the other. The large minute hand of the clock partially obscured by protective bars slid past its downward limit. During a water break, Ryan said, "It's time, Dude. Let it go, he will be back another night."

Kano shot back, "No way, he needs to know how we do things here. He's the one who has to go. You head back, I will take care of business."

Ryan looked down at the floor for a moment and then said with concern, "Alright, man. Be careful."

His worry intensified when bedtime slowly arrived but Kano hadn't. The gym closed an hour ago and Kano's slender flip phone remained untouched, next to his laptop. Ryan grabbed his jacket, slipped on his shoes, and headed back across the street. No sign of Kano anywhere. The air was chilly and there were no people around this part of North Campus so late at night.

He found dark red stains frozen to the sidewalk near the entrance to the gym. They made his stomach turn. After searching for ten more minutes he realized there was nothing more he could do. In resignation to the routine, he decided to head to bed. Partway down the hallway, his heart skipped a beat when he saw light pouring out from their room.

His pace quickened and he turned the corner to find Kano sitting on the futon, slumped against a cushion, holding a compress to his forehead.

"Ahhh, you're back," Ryan said with obvious relief.

"Yeah, my head is pounding. They numbed the stitches but the Tylenol 3 or whatever they gave me doesn't seem to help for the rest."

Ryan's forehead wrinkled up with worry as he sat down in his computer chair. "So what happened?"

"Tyrell followed you out. I was worried he was gonna jump you, so I grabbed my things and left. Must have been what he was counting on. When I turned the corner outside the front door he was waiting for me in the bushes. The next thing I knew I was on the sidewalk and my face was full of blood. He started kicking me in the ribs, so I got his foot and took him down with me. Before he could get up, I grabbed one of those nasty corn rows and yanked as hard as I could against the grain. He screamed like a girl and ran off. I didn't inspect it closely, just threw the disgusting chunk into the bushes where he had been hiding. Pretty sure he won't be back."

Nausea crept into Ryan's stomach. He was thankful to have no part of that encounter. "Can I get you anything?" he managed to ask.

"Nah, man, it's past your bedtime. I'm gonna pop a sleeping pill and get some shut eye a bit early tonight."

Ryan brought their thoughts back to the present night next to the canal, happy with the relatively mild temperatures. "Yeah, you were a mess back then. Glad we never saw Tyrell again. I honestly wondered whether or not you would even make it to graduation. Now what I am unsure of is where those girls of ours went..."

Kano scanned the edges of the streets overlooking their spot by the canal. "Do you think we should give them a call? I could use a change of scenery. Tired of looking at this filthy water."

June 2013

For the past few months, Souleymane had been assisting white people, who came from Europe, preserve the precious manuscripts smuggled out of Timbuktu. He was limited by his missing hand, but somehow this problem enhanced his mental capacity.

Perhaps the rest in the hospital had simply recharged his batteries, or maybe the jagged desire to prove to himself that losing his hand did not make him less of a person provided motivation to absorb everything the Europeans did. Some preferred to speak English and others French. He could follow conversations and reply to their questions in either language. This allowed him to serve as their contact to the outside world. He arranged for food, supplies, and whatever sort of practical support they required.

Souleymane learned a lot about the techniques employed to preserve and restore ancient documents. The savagely invasive mold had covered everything, completely destroying thirty-five percent of The Scholar's personal collection. To Souleymane, the fact that the team was able to save the remaining sixty-five percent was a true miracle, until he understood the methods and chemistry behind the process.

He placed his questions carefully, ensuring the expert was in a good mood and had nothing critical to focus on. Mealtimes tended to work best, but speaking while eating was something Souleymane still had trouble with. He preferred silence during the meal, and conversation afterwards. The problem was that these experts would resume their duties as soon as they finished eating. Some even ate while working!

Eventually, a clear picture of everyone's task came to light, along with a fundamental understanding of how their technology functioned. Souleymane had to make many guesses in the beginning. One by one, almost every assumption was proven to be true.

By the time Souleymane felt at home among the scientists and technicians, something happened which shattered the inner peace he had carefully cultivated. The Scholar stepped through the door. Their eyes locked in an uncharacteristic assessment, teacher and student, father and son, one evaluating the other, searching for deeper feeling and understanding.

For the pair, it seemed to last an eternity. Souleymane felt as though he had plunged into the Niger River among a violent family of hippos. He could barely tell up from down as conflicting emotions threatened to tear him apart. A swelling sense of joy at seeing his great protector fought against the primal desire to run from the one who had abandoned him, allowing, even causing, the terror and pain of disfigurement.

Souleymane never would have tried to take back the few crumbling bits of parchment which had escaped fiery destruction had it not been for the Scholar's charge to watch over and protect all that remained of his holdings while he safeguarded the manuscripts in Bamako. The subsequent capture and interrogation directed at locating the rest of the ancient collection ended in the fruitless removal of the young thief's hand in a public square. The irony of being labeled a thief for taking back something which had been stolen seemed lost on the invaders.

The Scholar simply observed the quaking individual standing before him, waiting to see which emotions would bubble up to the surface, and in what way the highly trained mind would gain control of the volatility. He allowed sadness to seep through his eyes. Sadness at the loss of his legacy—the manuscripts. Sadness at what had happened to his treasured pupil. Sadness that the West had taken from him a sacred task. The unwelcome justice of the situation was clear. He had first taken a sacred task from the West—educating Kano.

Sadness is what plucked Souleymane from the roiling river. It restored his faith in the humanity of the man standing before him. Now he thought of him as a man. No longer Father, Teacher, Oracle, but simply a man. This unexpected leveling allowed a tiny measure of love to flow, escaping through fortress walls which had barely contained the emotional chaos.

The Scholar smiled infectiously, allowing joy to swell up and break through. He approached Souleymane, ready to place his hands upon his upper arms in a fatherly way, but Souleymane took half a step back and extended his only hand with a grin, asserting his newfound independence. The Scholar clasped it with both of his and shook it warmly. He spoke in Arabic so their conversation would not be understood. "How are you, my son? Far too much time has passed. Have you found purpose here among these infidels?"

Souleymane released the grip and held his head high. "I have. I learn to speak like them. To work like them. I learn much."

The Scholar's eyes crinkled with pleasure. "This I am most happy to hear. I have an odd suspicion this sort of learning is just beginning for you. It appears their work is nearly finished, and because they have provided their own funding, I do have something left for you, my son, should you choose to use it."

Souleymane bowed with gratitude and the Scholar continued, "I learned many things during my time of study among the sort of people you see before you today. There is a fellow professor I keep close contact with. We shared a room during my time at Oxford. He teaches in America. A God-forsaken place called Michigan, where it grows so cold the Earth becomes entombed in frozen water. It feels as though the sun itself has given up. Should you choose to venture into such a hostile environment to further your education, I will contact my old friend and provide the means."

Souleymane's heart raced and his stomach seemed to turn inside out. He was being given the chance to leave everything he knew and loved behind. Caution surfaced first, insisting that the last time he had taken a similar step it resulted in the excruciating removal of his hand. It was followed by a deeper peace, the budding realization that perhaps, just maybe, he could gain more than he had lost.

It only took a moment for his eyes to return the gaze of the man before him for the second time, something not done between a teacher and student, the sparkle revealing his answer before the words stammered out, "Of...of course. It is my...honor."

The brief moment of reconciliation was interrupted by a tall, curly-haired form bounding toward them in a lab coat which was a few sizes too small. His eyes rumpled into a smile as he stretched his long arm out to shake the hand of The Scholar. He addressed him in French, with deference. "Hello, my name is Caleb. We have heard so much about you and feel the pain of destruction alongside you. Fortunately, as you know, all is not lost. We are doing the best we can to salvage everything possible."

The Scholar bowed slightly and responded with a wisp in his voice. "Your efforts are commendable. When I saw what had happened I closed myself off from the world for a full week of mourning. I felt my soul move once again when I heard something could be saved."

Caleb beamed in the light of appreciation and naturally re-directed its rays to the nearest person, nodding toward Souleymane. "Your student has been of excellent service. He does not get in the way of our work, but his desire to know everything we do, why we do it, and how the process works never fails to amuse. He has such great curiosity. The other day, when we were eating the lunch he brought for us, he made a special request."

Souleymane bowed his head further, knowing what came next. Caleb continued, "Souleymane asked if I would speak English with him. He said he once had a friend to practice with, and wanted to further the progress he had made. A true academic at heart if I may say so."

The Scholar allowed a measure of pride to escape in the form of a smile and switched to his peculiar version of crisp English laced with a timeless Oxford accent. "Of course, Souleymane has always shown great curiosity. I can't imagine a Frenchman would be terribly excited about teaching English, though."

Caleb's mouth hung open slightly. He had not expected the old man before him to speak a word of English, let alone with such mastery. After recovering, he replied with his best American accent. "Actually, I studied in Chicago and I love to speak English."

The Scholar took one of his typical, contemplative pauses. "This is clearly a situation ordained by Allah himself. Man could not have planned such serendipity. Souleymane and I were discussing the possibility of an academic future. I have an old friend who now works in Ann Arbor, at the University of Michigan."

"We always had trouble beating them in football," Caleb said with a playful grin.

The Scholar allowed a touch of sadness to permeate his expression. "Souleymane will be unable to compete in athletics, but his mind is sharp as ever. He simply needs someone to prepare him for what is to come." He paused again, then continued knowingly, "Many pressures loom upon the horizons of his future as past experiences within a traditional academic learning environment are quite limited, although I have poured solid foundations. You seem to have the ideal capabilities for building upon that which I have started. May I offer you the position of private tutor to this young man, to prepare him in every way you are able for the rigors of student life in Ann Arbor?"

Caleb thought for a moment and then continued in English, "I would be happy to help Souleymane with his transition to America. Can you be more specific about what a 'position of private tutor' means?"

He took a moment to smile at his prized pupil and then responded, "As you know, it is too late, and also foolish, to apply traditionally for the fall semester without any academic credentials. Fortunately, my old friend happens to be the director of admissions. He once told me that a certain number of international hardship positions were made available by a conscientious group of alumni. Before us stands the ideal candidate for such a position."

The Scholar paused, choosing to resist his natural impulse to haggle and simply spoke with the friendly Frenchman as an equal. "I will, as they say in America, *get the ball rolling* with the University. Expect this young man to begin at the earliest in the Fall. That means you may only have three months to prepare him. Your current duties with the manuscripts are important, so please continue your good work here. I will match whatever salary you currently earn for your additional efforts with the boy. I believe you will find Souleymane requires little rest and will do all that you ask of him and more."

The Scholar diverted his piercing gaze to Souleymane, introducing softer tones into his English. "My Son, have you understood our conversation?"

Souleymane continued to stare at the floor while nodding and giving a humble reply in his best English, dismissing the fleeting notion of equality without a thought. "Mooch of eet, Fathuh."

"Very well. Then you know what you must do. It is no small task to master a language and fit many years of learning into three months, but your path has been chosen. Your injury brought you the necessary amount of rest to push yourself beyond anything you have ever done before. This American friend you once had," he spoke with amusement in his voice, "possessed the sharpness of mind for such an endeavor. This, I fear, is something you lack. The shortcoming must be compensated for by sheer strength of will and genuine curiosity. These are two things you possess in abundance, my Son."

That night, for one of the few times in his life, Souleymane had trouble sleeping. *Caleb was a common name, right? Could it really be the same Caleb that Kano had spoken of? Was it possible that two different Frenchmen named Caleb studied in Chicago and then came to Mali?* All the other scientists had come directly from Europe to work on this project. He had always assumed the same was true for Caleb, until he heard the word 'Chicago' come out of his mouth.

His new teacher could never find out Kano was the one who taught him English. The Scholar's heroic efforts to save the manuscripts would be condemned if it became known that he funded the task by working with Al Qaeda. Souleymane tossed and turned with the anxiety of keeping this secret.

Additionally, the mission set before him seemed immense. He had no idea what it took to prepare for the University of Michigan, but he wondered if there was any way he could possibly be ready for an academic life in America on such short notice. Fall Semester was only a few months away. Sleep remained elusive.

The next morning, Souleymane arrived at the historical preservation facility before anyone else. Typically bustling streets were dark and quiet. He had no key to gain access to the space within, so he sat on the steps outside. An occasional dog or moped disrupted the relative calm. He waited until sporadic noises gradually grew together into a crescendo of city life, absently greeting the scientists and technicians as they entered.

Caleb was the last to arrive. Souleymane watched with deepening dread as his new teacher rounded the corner and dropped a phone into his pocket. The happy halo of curly hair was backlit with morning sun as he approached. Souleymane stood and lowered his head submissively, waiting for his teacher to speak, as had always been expected of him.

Slightly puzzled at this stark change in his friend's behavior, Caleb greeted him normally, and explained slowly in English, "I was just speaking with The Scholar. He is going back to Timbuktu this morning. He talked to his friend in Michigan. There is no place for you this Fall Semester. You must wait for another year."

Souleymane looked up with relief flooding across his face. Tears formed in the corners of his eyes as a dizzy feeling overwhelmed him. He still had to keep a secret, but at least he would have time to properly prepare for his new life. Caleb raised an eyebrow in response and continued, "I am not sure if you are happy to hear this or not. I think it is wise to have more time to prepare."

Souleymane simply nodded in agreement and took in a deep, stabilizing breath before speaking. "Okey Teechah, we staart now?"

For the next fifteen months, Souleymane subjected himself to a routine even more brutal than the one he had placed Kano under during the time of captivity. Daily running was the worst part. In the desert, scorching heat and dust seared his lungs, but he had never felt the need to stop. The sprawling capital of Bamako, with heavy pollution lingering in the streets, regularly sidelined him with vicious fits of coughing. Cars, bikers, and motorcycles constantly swerved into his path, occasionally knocking him off balance.

He had fallen into an open sewer twice to avoid a collision which would have resulted in even greater damage. Fortunately, the resulting gashes did not become infected as Caleb insisted they would. They argued that he should go back to the hospital to have them treated, but Souleymane stubbornly maintained he had been through worse. He was unwilling to sacrifice even an hour of his savage routine to attend to a simple wound.

Most human bodies would have rebelled in one way or another, but the strength of Souleymane's determination simply overrode the natural inclinations to slow down, or give up entirely. Neither option entered his consciousness.

Caleb was awestruck at the progress being made. He had been the one to convince The Scholar to delay admission for a year, in spite of the opening that had, in fact, been available. It was clearly the right choice. Caleb watched as his student pushed himself beyond all reasonable limits. More could not be accomplished. Crushing nearly twenty years of schooling into fifteen months was a minor miracle, although The Scholar had indeed laid solid groundwork. Three months would have been impossible.

Caleb knew Souleymane would continue to hit, and exceed, every target set for him. Academically, he would be ready to perform at one of the highest levels of education. His growing concern was about how the vastly different environment would take its toll. *Could Souleymane cope with the winters? The abundance? The culture? The freedom?*

Caleb thought freedom was likely the most dangerous element of Souleymane's future. The boy had never experienced it. *What would he do with it? How would it corrupt his choices? Could it be limited in some way?* He resolved to share his own experiences with American culture shock. In the meantime, the almighty routine dominated and brought purpose to both of their lives.

At the end of it all, Caleb presented his student with a gift, its heaviness resounding like a cannonball as he gently placed it on the desk. The splattered egg had been removed long ago, and it was polished to shine like a precious gem.

Caleb spoke. "You are curious. You are determined. You are stubbornly unwavering in your path. This rhinoceros reminds me of you. It was given to me by a good friend. I now have a large collection of Malian artwork, but this was my first piece. Just as you are my first student. Take it with you. Whenever you feel lost, alone, and ready to quit, pick up this treasure and remember that you have the spirit of the rhino within you."

Phase Six: Vaporization

Vaporization   *noun*   / veɪpərəˈzeɪʃən /
The dissipation of something that was once cohesive.
Transforming from a liquid into a gas.

May 2014

Wine glasses clinked together. That penetrating sound which usually dominates the table for a brief snapshot of a moment when indoors, evaporated into the light breeze and through fresh leaves fluttering above them. Ryan studied the two faces across the table with a look of suspicion before saying, "We shouldn't be here, you know."

Kano laughed a little. "Oh, and who is spying on us this time? The government? Her competitor?" He nodded at Eremita, who responded with an amused smile.

Ryan replied, "No, I mean, yes, someone is definitely spying on us, even if they call it collecting data, but that is not what I am trying to say. We made a deal to come back to this spot a year ago. These silly agreements never really happen because the probability of an alternate outcome is immense! There are four of us. Something should have gotten in the way. Eighty-five percent of couples would have broken up. Someone should have made definite plans so there would be nothing to discuss. Flights get delayed. I mean, really, honestly, what are the chances that the *exact* table we sat at a year ago was open today!?"

Johanna couldn't help herself. She put a hand in front of her mouth, making it even more obvious she was trying not to laugh. She responded, "Kano told me to call ahead to make sure this specific table was held for us. He wanted to enjoy your reaction."

Ryan rolled his eyes and then directed them toward Kano. "Sometimes I think you know me better than she does," he nodded to Eremita.

Kano smiled with satisfaction. "I know people. You are not so complicated, my friend. Tell us, how was the snow this season? Was Tahoe all you dreamed it would be?"

Ryan beamed. "And more! Maybe not the greatest career move, but I have never felt so alive! I don't know if I will be able to go back to a real job."

Eremita poked him with her elbow. "That isn't what you told me."

Ryan looked sheepish. "I won't go back to working for a giant corporation anyway." He gazed at her with longing in his eyes and continued, "Even though we came here to decide our future, we already have some pretty big plans."

Johanna raised an eyebrow. "So things are becoming rather serious with you two?"

Eremita mirrored her expression and responded, "I suppose you could say so. Ryan won't stop complaining about the distance between us. What I need is more space—from my company anyway. And the Bay Area. Too many people. I want to have a real impact on the future of a community. To do this effectively, it needs to be smaller."

Ryan jumped in, clearly excited, "I hated the distance partly because I had to be away from her, but partly because I hate driving. It is such a waste of time. Traffic jams, road conditions, pushy people, all of it got me so *agro!* During the long trips back and forth this winter, I decided there was nothing I would rather do, apart from skiing of course, than create autonomous vehicles. Mainly because I want one, but it seems like a pretty cool challenge to work on."

Kano caught a whiff of pizza drifting out from the kitchen and felt his stomach rumble. He tried in vain to catch the attention of an unmotivated waitress.

Eremita pulled a face at his lack of success and took a big gulp of wine before diving in. "Well, here it is, the perfect match. I can do a lot of programming for the cars. In addition, my app keeps growing. Having a fleet of autonomous vehicles to meet demand is a logical next step. Why pay someone else for the technology when we can develop it ourselves? Ann Arbor is the perfect place to get started. In fact, they *have* already started. We want to jump on board and steer things in our direction by piloting ways to expand our reach into hot food while implementing self-driving cars and drones as delivery options."

"Yeah! Ann Arbor is the perfect spot." Ryan raised his glass to Kano and continued, "Enough demand to sustain the system, but city congestion won't block our efforts like it would in the Bay Area. People are forward-thinking and open to new ideas."

"Well, sounds like you have it all figured out," Kano glanced at Johanna, "what do you need us for? I mean, you could have just told us your plans over the phone."

Ryan's eyes brightened for an instant. "Hah! But we had a deal. And besides, with Eremita and I busy with the technical side of creating a viable system, we need someone to see to the mundane details. Getting permits in order, managing employees, collaborating with the University and the car companies. Like you said, you know people, and I told Eremita that you have an uncanny tendency to get whatever it is that you want."

Eremita frowned as she narrowed her vision at Kano. "You know what I think of you. My younger self would probably push me straight into that canal if she caught me here. There have been countless arguments between the two of us about you, but ultimately, Ryan convinced me to make the offer. He is right to say we can create the ideal system, but without someone to see to its proper implementation, it will never get off the ground. We do need someone like you." She turned a withering gaze in Ryan's direction. "And he has made it abundantly clear that he will be sticking to the slopes unless you join us."

Kano smiled and his eyes twinkled a little. "You two get the prize for throwing the worst pitch ever. Not so sure I want to be involved as a forced partner...and besides, it isn't just up to me." He grabbed Johanna's hand, and her face lit up with alarm at his touch, sensing that she needed to take this seriously.

Eremita glared at him, admonishing his reluctance. "Nobody is forcing you. We understand if you have other plans."

Kano laughed. "I know that. It sounds to me like you are the one being forced. The obligatory technical genius who happens to be sitting next to you would rather be a ski bum than make a real impact, and you know that your persuasive capabilities do not extend beyond convincing someone of the power you hold over them by default. That won't be enough to get your plan off the ground, which is the only reason you came here."

Eremita's eyes sparked with fire, but she lowered and restrained her voice. "Don't assume you know why I am here. You may be a great poker player, and you might even have a pretty good idea of the cards I am holding, but don't ever question my motivations. Is that understood?"

Kano stood up abruptly, squared up his stance, and held an exaggerated salute while staring above her head. He spoke with an overdone Southern accent. "Yes, ma'am. It would be a great pleasure working with you. Should we choose to move forward, I require full partnership along with Lieutenant Ryan in any future gains made by our collaboration. I will allow you a moment to consider this while I speak privately with the missus. Please order us each a *Pizze Greca* if you ever get someone's attention." He dropped the salute sharply and stepped behind Johanna's chair, pulling it back as she delicately rose to her feet.

They climbed the worn brick steps in silence. Johanna's heart pounded and she felt rather dizzy. Not from exertion or wine, but from the suddenness and the magnitude of the prospect. *Had he just accepted the offer?* She knew something like this was inevitable, although she hadn't expected it to come so quickly.

They continued to walk along the canals without speaking; rumbling hunger made silence difficult to maintain. Kano had learned the hard way that patience was an effective way to prevent a shouting match. Generally, he was able to reach conclusions much faster than those around him, and he knew Johanna always felt attacked and manipulated when she couldn't keep up.

Johanna knew he had made up his mind, but felt grateful nonetheless for the space to put her thoughts, emotions and objections in order.

After ten minutes of wandering without a word, Kano was ready to burst. He had a massive amount of self-control, but this was testing his boundaries. He stopped, released her hand, and grabbed onto a worn metal railing overlooking the sluggish water. Johanna slid her arm around his waist and rested her head on his shoulder.

She smiled at the obvious restraint that seemed to make his eyeballs bulge, and spoke with a perfectly calm voice. "Looks like we have a lot to arrange. I am not ready to give up my country, but I am also not prepared to be apart from you again. This puts a lot of pressure on us both. I want the flexibility to come back for visits easily, together, and I also want your sincere efforts in helping me to adjust. Not only culturally and emotionally, but bureaucratically as well." She paused and then spoke with a tone of warning, "You must understand that I will make your life extremely difficult if you get too distracted to provide the support I need."

Kano turned to her and flashed a smile which made her knees wobble; he kissed her with an intensity that had almost been forgotten, and said, "Another adventure. But we will do it together. The first thing we have to find for you is a car. Can't be trying to live in America without the right one."

She crossed her arms. "I don't need a car. Never have. Not even sure why I got my driving license. If there is somewhere I can't get to on a bike then I can just borrow whatever you have."

He rolled his eyes. "And what if I am using it? Visiting America is not the same as living there. Trust me, you need a car to get by. Consider it a moving present from me."

"Well, if you're buying, maybe we can pick something out before we go and have it shipped over," she joked with a sarcastic tone, knowing it would be completely impractical.

He thought this over for a moment and realized the idea made perfect sense. "Of course! People import cars all the time. I can't see you in anything typically American. What do you think you would like to drive?"

She laughed at his enthusiasm. "I was only joking, you know." Dutch pragmatism tended to dominate her decision making process. "We can pick something out when we get there if you really think I need a car. Doesn't matter what it looks like as long as it gets me where I need to go."

"*Pah, pah, pah.*" Kano slowly shook his head as he made the Malian sounds indicating that a grave misconception needed correction. "You have a lot to learn about cars. They can define who you are in America. Just like clothes, but more important. Cars become physical manifestations of a piece of our soul. What about a Mini-Cooper? Those are really European, and we wouldn't even have to import…"

She cut him off with a dirty look. "I am not British, and those things are ugly and overpriced. They aren't even British. BMW makes them. I like French cars. They don't have many of those in America!"

He groaned. "Okay, maybe you do know something about cars, but French cars are the worst! Designed for people who don't like cars. I am sure you can do better!"

She thought for a moment and then smiled. "It's the new ones that you don't like. What about a classic? Don't you remember that episode of *Top Gear* we watched the other night? About the Peugeot that conquered Africa? I want one of those. Big luggage rack and all. Station wagon, not sedan. Bike needs to fit in the back, and you should be able to put a mattress on top and sleep out under the stars."

Kano contemplated this and then fished out his phone. After a few minutes of searching, his face lit up and he showed her a picture. "This is it! The perfect car for you! I never would have thought of it, but now that you say it, I can see it fits you like a glove."

She stared at the ocean blue 1977 Peugeot 504 with its bulky, hand-made roof rack which could carry anything from a bundle of skis to a herd of goats. Chunky wheels and a determined nose made it appear the car could go anywhere. No wonder it used to be so popular in Africa. As she swiped through pictures of the clean and simple, no-nonsense interior and imagined the exotic places this car must have seen, she knew it was the one.

A sinking feeling fell into her stomach and the canal blurred slightly. She would really go. They were doing this. She gave the phone back and nodded with tears forming in her eyes. "You found it. Go ahead and make it happen," she said in a barely audible voice.

He responded with a huge grin and failed to hold his thoughts back in spite of her obviously fragile state. "Things would probably be easiest if you joined our company, at least in the beginning."

Johanna snapped back to reality. "Are you serious? Join your unholy trinity? That is a nightmare. I would rather make sandwiches all day."

"Yeah," he said with caution, "but a sandwich shop can't arrange a work visa and…"

"There are other ways," she interrupted confidently. "I know my studies here are wrapping up, but perhaps I could do some kind of master's program there."

Kano nodded in agreement. "Or if that doesn't pan out, we could always get married," he said with a mischievous grin.

He got an angry stare back in return. "Too much, too soon."

"I know," he laughed. "It is a lot. One day you will be ready."

"We will be ready, you mean."

He kissed her again, and they wrapped their arms around each other, leaning against the railing, allowing time to drift away into the soft spring breeze.

September 2014

Johanna's eyes were bright with excitement. "Can I say it one more time? So glad I didn't try to become a doctor. I talked *again* to someone today who grew up in Argentina, did training and residency there, top of his class. Decided to practice in the USA. He started last month, but he moved here *ten years ago!* Can you believe it? He had to work as a cab driver in the beginning, then in a restaurant. It took *ten years* to get his paperwork in order. What a nightmare. He said he almost went back home three separate times, but couldn't face his family. PA's fly under the radar. We do pretty much the same work, but skip a lot of red tape."

Kano grinned at her from across the table and took another huge bite of his number twelve, the Beach Club sandwich. He reached over to squeeze her hand in acknowledgment. With a full mouth he replied, "Ou ave no idea ow uch I missed this… you know, some Jimmy John's don't even put sprouts on the Beach Club? South U is …best."

She strained to understand his obstructed speech but he took the next bite before completely swallowing and continued, "Ryan, ooh else," he rolled his eyes, "once exlained at ere was only one ay to eat…andwich. You ave to bite rom top to bottom," he swallowed. "Not from the sides, like everyone else does. If you attack from the sides, it all slides out the top. He said something else about coefficients of friction and principles of sandwich construction but I stopped paying attention." He took another enormous bite.

Kano would have continued picking on Ryan, but he saw something entirely unexpected over Johanna's shoulder. An involuntary gasp forced a half-chewed chunk of Beach Club into his airway. Johanna's heart rate increased rapidly with concern as he dropped his sandwich. The plummeting pile of overstuffed bread clipped a plastic cup filled with water a fraction of a second before the edge of the table dislodged half of its contents. Johanna's pants were quickly soaked and Kano was covered in the remains of his beloved Beach Club.

His eyes no longer bulged from the initial shock of what he had seen, but from the inability to breathe. Although it felt like an eternity to Kano, it didn't take long for Johanna's medical training to kick in. She efficiently slid him out of the booth, held him from behind, and forced the obstruction out with several well-positioned jolts to his midsection, just below the ribcage.

The angry red glow receded quickly from his face as if a hole had been pricked in a party balloon. It shriveled and was replaced by a pale, empty pallor. He stumbled to the bathroom and was unable to get the door closed behind him before the retching started. Oddly, the only thought surfacing in Kano's mind was that his love for the Beach Club had been forever tainted.

Before going to him, Johanna whirled around to see what had given Kano such a shock. She was met with an odd sight. A bewildered young man stood frozen, blocking the busy entrance, staring in surprise. Even though it was a beautifully warm fall day, he wore a heavy sweatshirt with the hood up. She knew she had never seen him before, and yet, she felt a strange familiarity.

Johanna turned again to help Kano back onto his feet, but by the time he was finished, the dark man had vanished into the sunlight.

She hurriedly cleaned things up and led Kano outside toward the nearby Diag, the eye of the University storm. It was always a relatively quiet place to sit. No cars, only muffled footsteps and the occasional biker.

Brilliant yellow leaves above their bench made the crisp, blue sky feel even brighter. The tree on the other side of the path was beginning to turn from green to red.

She was used to a fall dominated by browns, darker yellows, and gray skies. The colors appearing before her eyes made her feel as though she had arrived in a truly exotic location.

Kano stopped shaking and his breathing returned to a fairly normal rate. She squeezed his hand and said, "So, are you going to tell me what that was all about? Have you seen a ghost?"

Kano raised an eyebrow slightly. "Did you notice someone come through the door? Rather oddly dressed?"

She nodded and replied, "Yeah, a black guy who seemed to think it's winter."

Kano shuddered. "Then he really is here. That was Souleymane."

Johanna experienced her own sharp gasp. Fortunately, her mouth was empty. "How is that possible? How can he be here?"

"I have been asking myself the same. He doesn't believe in coincidences, and I guess I don't either, but how could he have known we would come here? We didn't even know ourselves until a few months ago. Even if he did know, why would he take the risk? I could turn him in to the police."

She adopted a firm tone. "That is exactly what you need to do. That man held you captive for two years! He tortured you!"

He sighed. "You are right, but as you know that really isn't the whole story, and he didn't torture me. I was clearly shocked to see him here, and some memories of that dark pit did come flooding back, but they were followed up with something quite different after I finished up in the bathroom. In Timbuktu, he was just following orders. He took care of me. Being locked up and apart from you was torture, but that wasn't his doing. He actually taught me a lot. We formed an odd sort of friendship."

Anger seeped into her voice. "I still don't see how you can call yourself friends with a terrorist! Don't you realize what he has done? Stole two years from our lives? Ruined your parents?"

Kano stared up at the sky for a moment before looking her in the eyes. "And yet, our relationship is strong and we are together. My parents got set back financially, but they seem happier now. When The Scholar told me I was there for a purpose, I nearly spit in his face. Now I see he may have been right. I am a much better person. It is like a dark shadow has left me. We are now in a position to have a real impact on the future."

She rolled her eyes. "Really, a *real impact*? By changing the way food gets delivered? If it works, you will make lots of money and people will lose their jobs. I can't see how that is a good thing."

Kano smiled cautiously. "You make another good point, but this is just the beginning. There is more to come. I know you want Souleymane punished for his role in my kidnapping, and at one point I felt the same way, more strongly than you can imagine, but now I don't. How else could I have become the person I am today?"

Johanna's face grew dark and stormy. The sunlight cut it into knifelike shards after passing through angular gaps between maple leaves. "So you won't go to the police?"

Kano looked down at the worn pavement dotted with old pieces of chewing gum. "I won't go to the police. He would never harm me, so it would be unjust to do such a thing."

Fury spread like rolling thunder and she struggled to contain it. Standing to face him, she delivered the ultimatum: "You will have to choose. Him or me. You can't have both." Unable to keep herself together, she crossed her arms and leveled a vitriolic glare at him before storming away.

Jittery, electrified energy filled the streets of Ann Arbor every fall, but this time it had no impact on Kano. Although his path was relentlessly obstructed by large groups of students noisily in search of a late lunch before they started drinking again, he continued to wander, allowing thoughts to drift in and out meditatively while his subconscious mind tackled the dilemma placed before him.

He found himself walking down a hill on Oxford street; stately houses blended in with massive trees on either side. Music and shouts emanated from fraternities that were using their daytime hours to set up another party for that night. He realized this was the edge of campus, and imagined the wealthy elite of Ann Arbor getting annoyed with the chaos and noise. Thoughts of permanent residents had never crossed his mind before.

Life and energy quickly faded as he entered a different world. Manicured lawns, accent lighting, and cars hidden by stylish garage doors imposed a veneer of beauty and order upon the world. Occasionally, a passing vehicle would disturb the peace. Kano felt an odd feeling of relief that his mother was Japanese. He had the distinct impression a black person in this neighborhood would be out of place.

Other thoughts drifted in and out, thoughts of where Johanna would like to live one day, thoughts about how his parents would feel at home here, and yet, he couldn't shake the image of Souleymane from his mind, and the thought of what it would be like for him to live in America. No friends. No family. All alone.

He passed a front porch protecting a red door with a sign next to it: *Welcome to the Nelson's*. It rolled about in his mind like a pinball, bouncing from one side to the other, eventually disappearing down a secret hole in the machine. After a moment, the lights lit up with a solution as three new balls popped out!

Nelson Mandela helped to get the concept of restorative justice into the spotlight nearly twenty years before, in 1996, with the Truth and Reconciliation Commission. Many black South Africans were able to face those who had abused them, and in some cases, the offenders were given amnesty. Kano realized this tactic gave hope for moving forward to both sides. Exactly the sort of thing they needed at the moment.

He would persuade Johanna. Surely she would be able to see the value in sitting down to confront Souleymane. His stomach twisted at the thought as dizziness overwhelmed him. The curb provided a perfect place to sit for a while before making his way back to the chaos of campus.

The only thing keeping Johanna from calling the police immediately after Kano walked away were the television shows she had seen growing up. They did not present a positive image of American law enforcement. She couldn't trust them to do the job properly, or to take her seriously as a foreigner.

It became the first real moment she got homesick, wishing desperately this had occurred in her own country where it all would be sorted out appropriately. After calculating the time change to make sure it wasn't too late in the Netherlands, she called Olivia to vent for an hour, careful not to mention anything specific about finding Kano's captor. Afterward, she couldn't bear the thought of returning to their oversized apartment. She still had not gotten used to the idea she was no longer a student, let alone how big everything was.

Johanna began to question the dilemma. *How will Kano respond to my ultimatum? Was there a different solution?* She couldn't imagine one as she wandered through the tumultuous streets of downtown Ann Arbor, feeling more alone than ever before. She passed the hospital where she worked and continued on toward the Huron River into a parking lot which divided the city from a forest.

A sign indicated she had reached the edge of Nichols Arboretum. She felt tension and turmoil loosen their grip as sounds of traffic faded into the background, replaced by a gentle breeze rustling colored leaves. Flowing water reminded her of a family vacation to Austria many years before.

The path climbed steeply among shaded rhododendrons until she reached a secluded spot on a ridge. A bench beckoned her, surrounded by beer cans poking out among fallen leaves. She sat in silence, allowing an inordinate amount of time to flow with sounds of the forest. A feeling of gratitude welled up from a hidden spring inside. It was a flower opening right before a hailstorm. Quickly it shattered under a barrage of uncertainty regarding her future.

She needed to speak with Kano. Imagining life without him once again was devastating. Beginning to regret her ultimatum, she wandered along, searching for a different exit. It was farther away than expected. She stopped to pick an apple while climbing up and out of the massive park, finding it once again hard to believe how big everything was.

Souleymane was in a state of shock. He sat on a quiet bench in the middle of the Law Quad rocking back and forth, mumbling words from the Koran. The few people who passed by took him for a homeless man going through severe withdrawal, not the graduate student he had so recently become.

Peaceful trees and gracefully ornate stone architecture had often soothed his mind, acting as a refuge from the pulsing chaos lurking beyond the arches. Now it felt like it was closing in, taking him captive. Formerly elegant spires became menacing teeth of a giant, ready to crush him into oblivion.

There was nothing Caleb could have said to prepare him for the cultural onslaught he received upon his arrival in Ann Arbor. Souleymane felt as though he had been dropped into a teeming pit of demons; the wealth and opulence these people took for granted went far beyond what he had ever imagined could exist.

Caleb tried, but his stories had seemed to be pure fiction, embellishments crafted to prepare him for a different sort of society. A single sandwich cost as much as a family from his village spent on food for an entire week. He saw students his age driving vehicles which, in Bamako, were only available to government ministers. Some of the homes these students lived in made The Scholar's elite residence seem like a shack.

What could they possibly do with so many valuable possessions? Souleymane's room was nearly empty. The only possession he valued was the ebony rhinoceros Caleb had given him. He wouldn't trade it for anything, not even one of those outrageous cars. The desire to hold it, as Caleb had told him to do, overwhelmed him. He wanted to get up, but, unexpectedly, couldn't remember how to get back to his apartment.

He stayed on the quiet bench as his thoughts continued to spiral, reflecting on the life surrounding him. Alcohol was everywhere. The liquid poison corroded their minds and souls to the point of debauchery, where women wandered the streets with more skin visible than he had ever seen, their loud cackling voices filling him with revulsion and shame. *Was it even possible they were here to study? To build their futures? Or was this merely a showcase for the Evil One?*

Souleymane had already been driven to the edges of his capabilities academically. Dealing with the bombardment of American culture pushed him well beyond his limits. Seeing Kano, a ghost from a different world, caused his tightly strung consciousness to snap. Like a delayed chemical reaction, something inside disintegrated, and as he sat in the Law Quad rocking back and forth, he could no longer remember who he was.

A man walking on the wide, stone pathway stopped abruptly and stared at the deranged figure on the bench. He did not know what to do. *Ask for help? Call the police?* Clearly the dark form hiding under a hoodie rocking back and forth while muttering out loud was disturbed. Mentally. Could be a threat to himself and others.

The man stared for endless minutes, contemplating what to do. Eventually, his mind could no longer suppress the giant weather balloon of an impulse which rose from within. It lifted him over and lightly set him down next to the shadowy, muttering creature.

He could not make out the incoherent words, but they had a repetitive tone. As if an endless string of different syllables somehow wove together into a circular pattern. The rocking continued, interrupted by a masochistic display of a fist pounding against a temple.

The unexpected violence that broke through the apparent trance shocked the observer to his core. Losing all regard for his own safety, when the fist rose again to strike as though stinging wasps covered the cranium, he grabbed the arm.

The dark face looked up in shock, ready to direct his violence to the one who had broken into his hypnotic state, but froze when the face before him somehow registered. Recognition dawned in his eyes, starting to pull him back to the reality his life had become. Like a blast of arctic wind felt late at night, his thoughts involuntarily snapped to attention.

Words in his native tongue, Bambara, stammered forth upon their own volition. The observer heard and understood them. "How...how...how are you here?"

Kano answered back in Bambara, "I ask you the same, my friend."

Those last two words, the lilting syllables, *n terikay,* melted Souleymane's heart and crystallized parts of his shattered consciousness. It was the first time their implausible friendship had been acknowledged aloud.

Souleymane had never admitted to himself or to anyone else the guilt he carried from forcibly holding someone captive, justifying the action as being the will of Allah. All at once, his concealed emotions flowed out, released by the simple sounds, *n terikay.* The fact Kano had come to him and called him friend after all that had happened released a muddy torrent of tears.

Souleymane now knew his name and could remember his past. Kano had restored him to the realm of mankind.

October 2014

Three weeks after the shocking reunion, they clinked their glasses of club soda together and devoured beer battered steak fries and burgers. "I can't believe I am hanging out at Ashley's without a beer. Don't you know they have over *seventy* on tap? That is insane, but not as crazy as failing to order one."

Souleymane slowly looked over his left shoulder, then his right. He leaned forward and replied in Bambara, "Do you know what I think is crazy? You brought me to this place. I told you how much alcohol and the waste of time and money bother me. You didn't listen at all."

Kano laughed, and spoke back in English. They easily slipped into this comfortable mode of communication. "My friend, you are mistaken. I listened to your every word. Do you not know what country you have come to? Do you think you can continue to live the life you did with The Scholar? Sheltered from alcohol, women, and every other sort of indulgence? You have come to the land of indulgence. You cannot hide from it. Could I hide from the desert during those walks we took every day? You must learn to adapt to this environment, or you will simply go from one breakdown to the next until they send you back to the Sahara."

Souleymane pondered these words inside the chaos. They could barely hear one another speak. *Music. Laughter. Shoes sticking to the floor where beer was spilled. A line of people crammed together out the door waiting for a table; pungent cigarette smoke wafting in through the opening. Chairs scraping across wooden planks. Beads of condensation dripping down every frothy glass in sight.*

Suddenly a smile spread across his face, and out came the musically lilting syllables of Bambara overpowering the background noise. "Do you know, I have never eaten something so delicious in my entire life? When I focus on the taste of this food," he held his burger in the air for emphasis, "everything around me disappears. I would never in one thousand years have set foot inside this den of sin, but now that I am here my mouth rises up in praise. How could I deny that even in such a horrific place, the greatest of joys can exist?"

"So that means you are ready to order a beer now?"

Souleymane narrowed his eyes and then broke into hearty laughter. "Never, my friend. Alcohol is not something for me. But you are correct when you say that I need to learn how to live in any sort of environment. I suppose that is what you did during your unexpected stay in The Scholar's house. It must not have been easy for you." His eyes lowered with lingering shame.

Kano nodded thoughtfully. "It wasn't easy. I didn't say this during our Truth and Reconciliation Ceremony with Johanna because it would have caused more fighting, but if I had the choice to go back to that hotel before the sun set and avoid the whole mess of being held hostage I wouldn't do it. I mean, of course I would if it could bring Jerry back. That hurt the most. But the experience purified me. Strengthened me. Brought balance and meaning to my life. Established essential perspectives I never could have found in any other way. I now know that I can do anything in life, so every choice I make is a fearless one because I have already gone through one of the most terrifying experiences imaginable."

Souleymane carefully dipped a fry into his ketchup, savoring every bite as he collected his thoughts. Slowly he met the gaze of his friend. "As terrifying as it is for me to sit here in this bar?" He offered up a half-joking grin before continuing, "I understand how you can forgive me. After some time, you found a way to use my oppression to your benefit. I became your teacher instead of your captor. I can also understand how Johanna will take more time. I am simply grateful she has not yet contacted the authorities."

After downing the last swig of club soda, Kano responded gravely, "I wasn't sure that I could stop her. You couldn't imagine the look on her face after I explained it was seeing you that made me choke on that sandwich. I thought she would grab a knife and go hunt you down."

"I hadn't even thought of that," he said with wide eyes, "good thing it was you that found me instead of her. I never would have been able to defend myself."

"Not such a big boy without your AK-47?" Kano taunted, trying in vain to lighten the conversation.

Souleymane shook his head sadly. "It is not the gun that I miss. Not at all. Having that sort of power over another person is not for me."

"Okay, so no guns, and no alcohol. Good thing we don't live in Northern Michigan—you would never survive!"

Sighing while popping the last bite of burger into his mouth and closing his eyes to absorb the flavors, he spoke with resignation. "I do not know if I will survive here, but I cannot go home. The Scholar would turn his back on me and I would not find work with only one hand."

Kano replied with a twinkle in his eye. "It would seem that now it is you who is in need of a teacher. You said Caleb prepared you academically, but someone needs to guide you through this deviant American culture. Perhaps we should reinstate our desert walks. This time we will not walk through a place devoid of water, but a college campus—devoid of the morality you crave."

December 2014

"You were right when you told me I should not be afraid. It is magical. A gift from above. I had no idea." Souleymane stopped in his tracks, put his arms out, and stared up at huge, wet snowflakes falling into the yellow glow of lights emanating from stately buildings. "Do you hear that? Nothing! Silence! Allah himself has pressed the mute button!"

Kano stopped alongside his friend and laughed. He responded to the familiar sounds of Bambara in English. "Don't worry, once February is here you will be sick and tired of this stuff. The magic will be long gone. You will forget that green things can grow outside."

Souleymane stuck his tongue out to catch a snowflake, but jerked his head back with surprise when one fell into his eye instead. "That may be," he said warily, "but the silence that surrounds us soothes my soul. I cannot believe all that has come to pass in only four months. It would seem years have gone by since I first set foot upon this strange and hostile land."

"It becomes less hostile every time we talk. Perhaps that indicates the hostility is mostly in your mind. Adapting to a foreign environment is not an easy thing to do." He gathered up a handful of snow from a bush and packed it together. "This is called a snowball. The kids that grow up in this hostile environment throw them at each other like the barbarians they are. Where I come from, it never snows, and we go surfing instead." He barely missed the top of the lamppost.

Souleymane smiled and tried to do the same with one hand, his poorly packed snowball breaking up in midair. "You see, this is not the sort of place people should live in. It may be magical, but my hand screams out in pain! My feet ache as well."

"You need better clothes. It isn't even that cold outside yet."

Eyebrows shot up with fear. "Are you saying it can get *colder* than this? Impossible. Also, you know all The Scholar has done for me. He spends more money on my small room and the food I eat than he does on his entire household. I could never ask for more."

They walked again, shoes compressing the inch of snow beneath their feet with satisfying squelches. "Tell you what. Remember how I got that old phone for you from Ryan? He is not much bigger than you, and he grew up in this awful climate. I bet he has some old winter clothes that would fit."

"Yes, I am ever so grateful to this friend of yours. Perhaps one day I can meet him so I can thank him properly."

"Well," Kano started uncertainly, "I suppose that would make sense if you want to try on his old clothes. We will need to invent a cover story though. Nobody other than Johanna and I should know how we really met. I suppose we can pretend the first time we crossed paths was on the bench in the Law Quad when you were in the middle of your breakdown."

"You know I am not to lie."

"I know that. You won't have to. Everything that has happened since then we can talk about. You will just need to leave out a few things here and there. That isn't lying. Besides, I will introduce you to Ryan and Eremita, so I will tell any necessary lies. I don't mind."

Souleymane nodded with acceptance. "Very well, otherwise I will certainly freeze to death. Or at least they will need to cut off my other hand once my fingers no longer work," he said with a laugh.

January 2018

"My teet...are...witerally chattewing...when I...tawking...I can't...contwol it." Johanna kicked the snow off her boots as she slammed the garage door. Ice crystals turned her blond eyebrows white, helping her light blue eyes shine with an uncommon intensity.

Ryan looked up from the kitchen table and laughed. "I would say, *Welcome to Michigan,* but isn't this your third winter already?"

Johanna glared at him as she slowly extracted frozen toes from her stylishly uninsulated footwear. "Dis is my...fouwth...winter hewe."

"Well, by now, you should have realized why people drive cars instead of riding bikes." Ryan took a sip of coffee and raised an eyebrow with amusement.

"Yes, but, dey wouldn't...have nowticed the way...the air spawkles above the snow. When I try to tawk my...wips don't move wight."

Ryan laughed again. "You sound like you have a speech impediment. To be fair, I think this is probably the coldest it has been since you got here. You probably wouldn't complain so much if you gave up your European fashion and dressed like us natives."

She glared at him again. "And you should know by now I am about as wikely to...adopt your stupid wooking, oversized, American clothes as I am to...stop widing my bike."

"Then quit complaining about the cold!" He shook his head slightly with annoyance. "Do you want a cup of tea?"

Johanna spoke through the shivers. "Could you even...imagine...me saying no to that question?" She moved toward the couch to cover herself in blankets.

Ryan set the steaming cup of tea down next to her and sank into an overstuffed La-Z-Boy recliner.

She looked out at him from her trembling cocoon. "Where is everyone?"

"Kano and Eremita are on the track. They wanted to make sure all the hardware functions in the cold."

"Hah! You mean you sent them out there because you wanted to make sure!"

Ryan grinned sheepishly. "They still have fun with these temperatures. I just get kind of annoyed. And besides, I think Eremita is trying to break something so she can blame it on me."

Johanna rolled her eyes. "That sounds healthy."

Ryan, as always, came to Eremita's defense. "My hardware has generally been the limiting factor. In the last few months it has finally started to perform as it should. Now her software needs to catch up. You know how much she likes to be ahead."

"Yeah," she frowned, "enough to build her own track so the competition couldn't see what you are up to."

"There were a lot of scheduling issues…"

"Lame excuse. You all think you are better than everyone else. Now that sharing resources and collaboration are no longer *problems* for you, Kano is effectively out of a job. Or was that your plan all along? To push him away?"

Ryan felt a chill quite different from the winter air, and automatically took up a defensive tone. "Nobody is pushing anyone. Actually, we are the ones keeping you from pushing Souleymane out."

"A lot of good he has done. He sits in his room with those heaters on full blast, working endlessly on his thesis. Useless waste of energy. We should send him back to where he came from. Along with that stupid truck your girlfriend bought for him." She was referring to the deep yellow 1982 Toyota Land Cruiser FJ40. The stubby vehicle was like a WWII Jeep on steroids, trimmed out in matte black with a heavy-duty winch mounted between round headlights.

After a deep breath he responded. "Wow. She bought it for the facilities here—Souleymane can't perform his duties as caretaker without it and…"

She cut him off sharply. "He sure could do his job with something less expensive and not so much…how can I say it…representing the personality that Eremita wants him to be. He doesn't belong here. Have you ever seen the way he holds onto that stupid black rhino of his like a scared little boy? Clearly he has a few loose screws."

He shook his head in disgust. "You do know this is America, right? When will you stop being such a racist? I know you still parade your little black slaves around for Christmas, or whatever you call it, but here in Ann Arbor anyway, we try to show some respect. Souleymane does a great job and you know his role in our progress goes way beyond looking after this property. That ebony rhinoceros is beautiful, and it is probably the only thing he has to remind him of home."

She buried her face under the blankets, wishing that she could be instantly transported back to the Netherlands, racist traditions and all. She had solemnly promised Kano never to reveal their connection with Souleymane. Forgiving him was one thing, but accepting him into their daily lives was quite another. Perhaps she never truly meant the words of pardon she had spoken more than four years ago. *Better to be thought of as a racist than to reveal the truth.*

After an uncomfortable silence, Ryan walked back toward the table to continue what he had been doing. He was unable to focus. Eventually, his exasperation bubbled up and steamed out. "Do you even know what he has been working on in that sauna of his? Did you bother to ask?"

All of Johanna's energy went toward controlling her temper. She seethed, "What a ridiculous question. I have suffered through so many of your stupid discussions. Of course I know what he is researching. He even tried to interview me. I have no interest in resolving conflicts. I don't care how other cultures do it. I leave my conflicts in the past where they belong so they don't bother me anymore."

Ryan took a long sigh and dug in. "Look, I know you don't like him for whatever reason, but I think his research is pretty clear in showing that your method is one of the most unhealthy ways to deal with conflict."

As the stinging in her toes diminished, Johanna was able to collect herself. "I know what the research shows. Everyone has their own situation though, and broad generalizations don't always apply. What I prefer to focus on is avoiding future conflicts. I am worried about Kano's position. He seems to be drifting now that you have built this private test track."

Ryan smiled at the unintended word choice, imagining Kano drifting: burning the rubber off the tires of his expensive sports car while sliding it sideways through the corners, Japanese style. He took a sip of lukewarm coffee before responding. "Well, it is one thing to worry about a problem, and quite another to find solutions. What do you think we should do?"

Johanna sat up and reached for her steaming cup of tea. It was still too hot to drink; too hot to warm up her hands. Her ears were bright red and burning, overcompensating from their recent, semi-frozen state. Her mind also seemed to be overcompensating for something. Everything was bothering her. Everything was different here, even though she should have adjusted by now. *What if I never adjust?* The thought sunk into her. A brick thrown into thawing mud. Her heart rate soared as panic stampeded throughout. Just then, the stairs creaked and a dark form slowly descended.

The revulsion she normally felt at Souleymane's presence gave way to startling thoughts. *He must feel the same sort of culture shock. He can't adjust to the cold either. No wonder he spends so much time secluded in his room. Take his pride out of the picture, and he would hop on the next flight back to that godforsaken country he came from!* She smiled to herself at the realization, but avoided eye contact out of habit.

Souleymane started talking amiably with Ryan but she didn't register anything that was being said. Her mind had found an opening that needed to be explored. This city was full of people from all over the globe. *How many of them felt this way? How many were unhappy with the way things were in Ann Arbor? In America?*

Every day she had conversations about politics, healthcare, culture, and so many people complained about the same entirely fixable things. Ryan's question resonated throughout her as though she sat in a Buddhist temple feeling a gong's reverberations in every cell of her body. *What do you think we should do?*

She had never considered the question, but the mud began to flow. She thought out loud, interrupting the irrelevant conversation taking place. "What do you think we should do?"

The two stared oddly at her for a moment before she continued. "As it turns out, I do have a few ideas. Why haven't I thought of it before? Everyone I talk to complains. They all have problems with the system. Where I come from, the government is in place to take care of the masses, not to enable the rich to get richer."

She paused for a moment and Souleymane jumped in with a joke. "And where I come from, dere is no seestem at all!"

Johanna's eyes narrowed. "That isn't true and you know it. Stop playing the poor African card. Your social structures are much richer than ours. People live in real community in Mali, knowing everything about each other and sharing with more generosity than I have ever seen."

After putting Souleymane in his place, she paused again for a sip of tea to collect her thoughts. "My point is this, American society is crumbling before our eyes. The people aren't happy about it, but they don't know any better because most of them don't even have a passport. They can't experience examples of how things can be improved."

Her eyes darted from one face to the other as she plowed ahead. "Why don't we show them? Why not create an example for them? A pilot program? The city of the future. Ann Arbor is the perfect place. Progressive, international, academic. You are all thinking too small, and I wasn't thinking at all, until now. I mean, all you want to do is set up an autonomous delivery system. Why not create a city where all the cars can be autonomous? And free from fossil fuels…"

A blast of frigid air invaded the room as Kano and Eremita came in from the garage. Faint wisps of exhaust from her brand new, two door, burnt orange, BMW 4-Series tried to follow the cold inside. They were in the middle of their own heated discussion about the disappointing results they had just witnessed, but it quickly fizzled as they felt the sparkling energy in the room. Clearly they had interrupted something important.

Johanna tried to include them. "I was explaining how I can't even deal with an American cup of tea. It is so big. A cup of tea should be cooled off by now, but I can still barely even take a sip from this one!"

Kano laughed. "Oh, and here I thought you were talking about something new!"

She flashed him a heated look of warning and continued, "I was also talking about how I can't cope because Ann Arbor needs fundamental changes, and you need a job. Look around this room. We have an expert in community and social interaction, a person who knows how to read people and can almost always steer things in his direction, an engineer, a programmer, a healthcare professional, and plenty of capital. Like I said, everyone here is thinking too small and doing their own thing. If I am going to survive in this place, a lot needs to change. I don't think I am the only one here with this outlook."

Souleymane waved his arms to interrupt her monologue once again. "Look, look," he stammered, "I am but monts away from feenishing my tesis. Perhaps when I am all don den I can help, but now I must focus entirely on what it is dat I do."

It didn't take Eremita long to process the implications of what Johanna was working toward. "It sounds like you want to build a prototype." Eremita's tempo grew with excitement as she continued, "We can change the way our world works with autonomous deliveries, but I have been so caught up in making this specific system function I haven't given much attention to the next phase. We had always planned to implement in Ann Arbor first, but why not take things a step further? All sorts of resistance will get in the way, so we need a close friend in power." She leveled her gaze at Kano. "Time for you to get serious. How about a bid for mayor?"

Kano smiled and raised an eyebrow at the thought. "The whole prisoner-of-a-terrorist thing would get some traction…but maybe too many people have seen *Homeland*." He shrugged nonchalantly. "I bet we could spin things effectively."

Ryan's thoughts flowed out as well, oddly uncensored. "Think of what we could do! Not only autonomous cars, but put a ban on fossil fuels entirely, like Johanna said. We can set up garages to convert to electric, produce biodiesel, install district energy plants to provide heat and power, supplement with a bit of wind and solar, build more greenhouses, and this entire city could be self-contained in no time!"

"En wat ehbout die justice seestem? Eremeta ere likes to play wit her apps. How ehbout using dis technologia to create someting where da people are enformed en da people decide." Everyone looked over to Souleymane, surprised by the quality of his idea.

In the pause which followed, a strange sensation descended upon Johanna. The layers of hatred she carried dissolved within her, one after the next, like an Everlasting Gobstopper. Suddenly she felt a lightness in her soul as though a dark web which had held it in a tight grip blew away with a spring breeze. She realized that Souleymane had just become an essential part of their future. This wouldn't work without bringing increasingly polarized viewpoints together, and he was the expert who could figure out how to do that.

Kano stepped into his leadership role without hesitation and began delegating tasks. Fiery excitement burned in his eyes as he naturally assumed command. "I know we have a few bugs to work out, but like Eremita said, our systems are basically up and running. Why don't we put together a solid plan while we finish things up with the cars."

He shifted his tone slightly. "Johanna, I want you to figure out how to revamp the way healthcare works for this city. Make sure none of the money is flowing up to make someone disproportionately rich. Those profits should be used to get the best professionals available by offering significantly higher salaries—exactly like the Ann Arbor schools already do for their teachers. We also need to eliminate the possibility of lawsuits by setting up a reliable way to handle complaints internally with bonuses and penalties. This can drive expenses way down."

Johanna jumped in with a smile. "And we need to focus on preventative treatment by making sure insurers and providers are one in the same. Let's legitimize alternative practices that have proven efficacy!"

Kano agreed and then turned to Ryan. "Ann Arbor already has some of the best schools in the state. I think students should be a part of our infrastructure adaptations. There is plenty of work to be done, and they should have a role. I can see those city planning gears turning in your head. Getting to 100% renewable energy should be straightforward enough, but we need everyone on board, and students may be the best tool for driving public opinion. They can convince their parents and do some of the actual work, making their education much more valuable."

"We could get the kids to help install rainwater collection systems!" Ryan was talking so fast Souleymane could barely follow. "We could install a tram network. And heat the sidewalks in the winter…"

"Slow down, tiger," Kano interrupted, "money is still an issue. Eremita isn't a billionaire yet."

Kano felt a surge of hope as the potential opened up his mind. He turned to his former captor. "Souleymane is right. Democracy is dead. Only dollars have an impact in today's society. Let's find a way to bring it back to life. His direct democracy approach needs a lot of thinking, because we need informed choices, not just everyone having a say. I want you and Eremita working together on this."

Souleymane smiled and opened his mouth to speak, only to be cut off as Eremita started thinking out loud. "Yeah, and we can use a similar platform to my app. Every citizen is a part of it, and they can have a say in decisions being made. The jobs of lawyers, judges, and politicians can all shift from making decisions to succinctly presenting their case, and allowing the people to decide. This is a perfect place to test the artificial intelligence I have been developing. I can sign up a few bots as citizens to see how they do. Eventually, some of the decision making can be handled by computers and then…"

"Ummmm, I don't know about that," interrupted Johanna, "I mean, I thought we were trying to give the power back to the people, not take it away from them."

"Right," continued Eremita, "but that is the whole point. If the AI could predict with perfect accuracy what the people will choose in some cases, there would be no point in bothering them. When the numbers are uncertain, we can bring the case to the people. Otherwise they will be bogged down in frivolous decision making, and too much of that will make them lose interest."

"You both make a good point," said Kano. "We can't give people the idea that parts of their lives will be determined by a computer, even though that is already happening to some degree. On the other hand, we need to keep them participating once the novelty wears off. Perhaps we can use a jury concept as well, where a few random people are chosen to decide each case. For the bigger ones, we can have bigger samples of the city."

"This seems like a slippery slope to me," said Johanna, "I mean, how do we stop people from abusing the system, invading privacy, manipulating things to get their way?"

Eremita responded, "That will always happen. People are people. We will safeguard as much as possible and adjust as we go, but could it really get much worse? Our society…"

"…is spiraling out of control." Ryan finished her sentence and continued, "we know the story. You talk about it a lot. The problem is that this is your perspective. A lot of people like things the way they are and change is scary to them. I think Kano should run for mayor, and I like the improvements we could bring about, but let's be realistic. Even if he makes it, he isn't a dictator. He can't just wave a wand to get everyone on board."

He shifted uncomfortably under the irritated looks directed at his typically negative outlook on change before continuing. "Too many people in power benefit from the status quo and they will strangle any proposed adjustments. This will take a lot of time, and we can't tackle everything at once. We need to think of these ideas as long-term goals, and prioritize what comes first. If word gets out about what we actually want to do, any progress we try to make will be squashed."

Eremita rolled her eyes. "That is your conservative Western Michigan background speaking. The people are ready for this. Some of them might not know it yet, but they are. I know it won't be easy, but this is Ann Arbor, not Grand Rapids."

"Look at Kano," said Souleymane thoughtfully, "he es yung. He es fresh. He must ave ideas dat reflect our generayshun. Ef anyone es to notice im he must stand out not just en appearance but also in ideas. How else weel da people become interested? Is dit America or not? We must be careful a dose in powah, but it is da people who ave a true voice ere. It is not so everywhere. Anyting is possible ere in dis laand."

"You might think anything is possible," said Kano with a slightly patronizing tone, "but that is all relative. I know I don't talk about it much, but there were times in Mali I felt much more freedom than I did here, before I got captured anyway. It makes me angry to hear people say America is the land of the free. Most of them haven't been outside the country. Whatever system we create, I want it to bring about a feeling of increased freedom."

November 2020

"Figured I would find you here." Frozen gravel crunched under Ryan's cautious approach. He reached into his pocket to lock the beloved Acura he had bought with his signing bonus all those years ago. Cancerous rust was beginning to bubble out of the wheel wells. He crouched and then sat next to his unresponsive friend. They stared out over the lake together. Low sun pierced through leafless trees.

Ryan tossed a pebble toward the open water and it skittered noisily across thin ice before disappearing into calm, black depths without a sound. Kano mirrored the action, but his rock cleared the icy perimeter of the lake altogether and splashed into frigid water.

After throwing a few more rocks, Kano spoke up quietly. "So why did you think I would come to *your* favorite place? You are the one who disappears up here, not me."

Ryan smiled. "Pinckney would probably be your thinking spot too if you make time for it. Now you have time." They threw more rocks in silence.

"We should have listened to you," Kano admitted with his head down. "From the very start, you saw this coming. Why didn't you stop me?"

"I knew I couldn't. You know what they say...if you can't beat 'em, join 'em." Ryan sent a rock sailing high up into the air. It broke through the fringe of ice with a satisfyingly muffled bloop.

"Why would you put almost two years and so much energy into something you knew was going to fail from the start?" Kano tried for the same trajectory, but his spinning chunk of gravel merely cracked the surface and bounced back toward him.

"I didn't know for sure. The four of you were so captivated by the ideas that I was sucked in with your enthusiasm, and I really hoped it would work. Besides, we did better than I initially thought. We learned a lot too. Next time even more people will go for it."

A bit of color drained from Kano's face before he replied. "Next time? This was it. This was our chance. We tried to make the world a better place and we couldn't. I don't have the stomach to put myself out there again."

"Well," said Ryan as he broke another stone through the ice, "then I guess you aren't cut out for politics after all. That's what politics is. Putting yourself out there again and again. Resilience. Come to think of it, that's what life is."

After a long pause, Ryan continued with amusement. "You haven't experienced this feeling before, have you?" He laughed a little. "You must be the only thirty-five year old on the planet who is discovering what failure feels like for the first time!"

Ryan turned toward his best friend, energized with the realization. "Everything you have ever tried you have been good at! Even being a hostage! Now you finally come to the point where you put it all on the line and perceive failure, although I see it as a temporary setback, and you have no clue what to do because you have never been in this position before!"

Ryan shook his head back and forth and tapped his foot as if the motions would help process his latest deduction. Kano flopped down onto his back, staring up at a perfectly blue sky, ignoring the uncomfortably cold and sharp gravel.

"Well, there is a first time for everything," proclaimed Ryan effusively with his hands. "Do you know how many times my designs have failed? I can't even count or remember. After a while it became normal and expected."

He knew Kano might have tuned out already, but he continued anyway. "What about school? You saw how hard I worked. You saw me after some of those bad grades. I was devastated! Did I quit? Did I drop out? No! I kept going! And that is exactly what you have to do. This city needs us. Our ideas can improve the lives of so many people. We can make it happen! The election was so close. All we have to…"

Kano interrupted with quiet bitterness. "Johanna hates it here. Now I do too. It is time for us to go. She literally begged me to go back to the Netherlands with her before all this election nonsense began. That is exactly what we are going to do. Life actually makes sense there, even if the sun doesn't. We wouldn't have to pour energy into making big changes because they have already been made. What is the point in fighting to make a better society when clearly the people don't want it? American institutions have grown sick beyond repair. Greed and corruption rule. Let their world fall apart. We don't need to be here to watch it happen."

"Beyond repair? Are you nuts?" He paused and took a breath to eliminate the anger from his tone. "Just because you lost doesn't give you the right to make such a claim. Things have been much worse in the past. Granted, some things have also been better, but we are gaining momentum. I told you, this is only a temporary setback. One could even call it a victory, getting as many votes as we did. Why would you want to go to a place where you can't make a difference? What is the point of life then?"

Kano stiffly rose to his feet. "To live it. I don't want to look back in thirty years realizing that I dedicated my life to a lost cause. The point is to create a family. To thrive in a stable and balanced existence. And it is exactly what we are going to do. There is nothing stable or balanced about running a city and trying to shape the future. You will just have to make a difference without us. I am sure you can."

"That's it?!" Ryan stood up, towering above Kano. "You are giving up? Don't you realize what you are going to miss? This place is amazing. Perhaps it could use some changes to its social structure, but look around you. Trees. Lakes. Wildlife. Hills. It is a land of opportunity! You can create your own life here. You don't need to run a city to find purpose, but think of what we have already accomplished together. Do you really think you will find this raw potential in the New Jersey of Europe? It wasn't just the weather that caused you trouble."

He shrugged. "You are from Michigan. Not me. At this point, I am not really from anywhere. I will probably miss some things, but now it is time to focus on building a family without the stress and pressure of trying to do so in a society that doesn't support the process. Perhaps that is the real reason why we worked so hard to create that very thing here. We wanted the best of both worlds. Maybe when our kids are older and Europe's problems get too big for us we will want to come back. Who knows. I made my decision. Now all we need to do is pack up our stuff and say goodbye."

Kano Griffin turned his back to the lake and his friend, walking toward his car with an unfamiliar lightness in his step. He felt as though he had been released from captivity for a second time, unshackled from the weight of the world. Thoughts of a peaceful life, away from the inevitable pressures and stresses of power beckoned him.

He was ready to be done fighting. Done convincing everyone in his path his way was the right way. Time to focus his energy on creating something closer to himself. Something more manageable.

As he slid into the seat of his beloved car, he decided it couldn't be left behind. Fuel would cost a fortune, but it would be worth every penny. He smiled as the roar of the 3.8 liter turbocharged engine under the dark red hood of his 2017 Nissan GT-R catapulted him out of defeat and up to sixty in about three seconds.

The distant rumble resonated in Ryan's consciousness, traveling down through his bones long after the actual sound faded away. He stood, treelike and numb, as the thought of losing his best friend once again, along with the enormous potential they dreamed up during the past two years sank in. He tried and simply failed to imagine Ann Arbor without Kano.

Phase Seven: Crystallization

Crystallization   *noun*   / ˈkrɪstəˌlaɪzeɪʃən /

*The process of bringing order and clarity to chaotic thoughts,
feelings and ideas.*
Transforming a gas or a liquid into a structured solid.

November 2020

Johanna sat in a chair twirling her hair with a pinky finger, something she tended to do when she felt uncomfortable. In front of her, Kano feverishly packed one bag after another. He had just finished telling her about his conversation with Ryan.

She wasn't ready to hop on a plane and never look back, so she needed to buy time to talk things out. Johanna asked innocently, "If we can find a plane that actually flies, how many bags can we check?"

Kano paused and stood up straight for a moment, clutching a pair of socks in confusion. "I know it costs extra after the first one, but I am not sure how many you can pay for. That could complicate things. We will probably have to pick the airline that allows for the most."

Now she was getting somewhere. "Well, you have four bags sitting over there ready to go. Don't you think we should look into that?"

He flashed her a look of annoyance. "You haven't even started. You were the one that hated this place and wanted to move back. Why don't you check instead of sitting there doing nothing."

She sighed a steely warning. Kano knew it meant that the task would be completed, but if he didn't fix his tone soon, they were in for a fight. She pretended to research intently on her phone. After his fifth bag was packed, she broke the silence. "We don't have many options. Looks like we can each check three bags. Maybe one of yours can be a carry-on?"

He sat down on the bed angrily. "How did we get so much stuff? All I had was a carry-on when we came here. Maybe we should leave it all behind and go back the same way."

"Or maybe we shouldn't go at all," she replied. Her words left him shocked, mouth hanging open, unsure of what he just heard. Eventually she continued, "I know it made you mad, but I think what Ryan said is right. You have never learned to deal with failure. Any time you put yourself out there, unsure of the outcome, you might not succeed. Do that enough and you are sure to fail on occasion. Don't do it at all and you aren't really alive."

She set down her phone and looked at him intently. "You have never gambled before, Kano. All those poker games weren't gambling. You knew the likelihood of each outcome. If you lost, it didn't matter because you could reduce the situation to an abstract math problem. When you won it was further affirmation of your dominance and superiority over others. This truth became so much a part of your identity that losing the election shattered the ego that has never let you down. You got caught up in our bubble, assuming you knew what was best for the people of Ann Arbor, thinking logic and reason would determine their votes, when, in reality, logic and reason don't play much of a role in American elections."

He sat there without blinking. "Let me get you a cup of tea," she said, and promptly left the room. Kano's breathing slowed as he allowed his mind to race, realizing Ryan may have had a point. He had failed, and didn't know how to deal with it. But there was more. Suddenly the reality of the situation landed, and he understood moving to Europe wouldn't provide a way out.

Johanna gracefully walked back in with two steaming mugs, noticing the look of a gathering epiphany on his face. She knew it was best to keep quiet and let him speak once it had all been worked out. After pulling her feet up into the chair, angling her knees together onto the armrest, and holding the deep blue mug against her shoulder, she could have been a picture in a magazine.

Eventually, he broke the silence. "I think I figured it out. Maybe all of it. I don't know. What is wrong with the world I mean. We think of giving ourselves to others, selflessness I mean, as a good thing, right? How can we have a relationship or a community without doing that?" He paused for a moment to set down his mug.

"But what if it goes too far? What happens when our lives become all about doing the things others expect us to do. We have been trained for this. School is not optional. Go to a good school, get a good job. Make money. Start a family. A mortgage. Now a minimum income is required. The bank says we have to pay." He paused to grab his tea with a furrowed brow.

"Why do most people buy the clothes they buy? Is it because they are comfortable? Or maybe they have an interesting story? They like the way they look? Or is it because of the way others will view them in those particular clothes? Most people have cut their souls up into pieces and given them away. They base their decisions and lives upon what others think and expect of them. Doesn't this result in an unthinking mass consciousness? Society has become a network of second degree individuals—consumers who derive their value from others, many of whom they have never met. Reflected light."

"How many first degree individuals are left? People who are creators, who have the will to make decisions based on what they want and value, not based on what is expected of them?"

She took a sip of tea and waited for him to continue. "Without first degree initiative, those prepared to live contrary to the pervasive culture when the need arises, how can we not be a bunch of lemmings heading straight for the cliff? Logic only appeals to people who can think for themselves. Most of us have stopped doing that. Or maybe we never really started. Ironically, our individualistic society thinks collectively and so many decisions are based on emotion. Mostly fear, I suppose. Can we distance ourselves from that? Can we find a way to live in first degree initiative?"

She sat and absorbed not only the words, but the atmosphere of a terrifying clarity that was quickly building. It was as if they had been living on top of a skyscraper surrounded by pervasive fog. After some time, the truth of how high they really were was lost. They casually lounged near the edge. There was no railing. Suddenly the fog lifted, and their stomachs turned as they watched tiny humans and tiny cars crawling below them like specks from another planet. One unpredictable gust of wind could knock them off. The relentless push to shape the city of the future had jeopardized their very existence. It had simply become too big.

As she stared through the steam rising from her cup of tea, he finally broke the silence. His words brought her back to the bedroom. "Wait a minute, didn't you say, *maybe we shouldn't go at all,* a few minutes ago?"

"Yeah, I had to jolt your mind out of the rut it was in." She took another sip of tea, allowing the strong flavors of ginger and turmeric to fill out the dimensions of warmth and security which had become associated with their bedroom.

"But you are the one who has been complaining about being here the whole time. I thought you would jump at the chance to leave."

"You never asked. You assumed. Complaining doesn't necessarily mean I want to take off, it means there are things here worth fixing. Some things are better in my country, others aren't. If we find a way to capitalize on the advantages your country has to offer, there won't be so much to complain about. I think we took on more than we could handle with this whole mayor thing. Even if you got elected, you could never have survived the inevitable onslaught of the…what did you call them? Second degree egos or something? The non-thinkers?"

He flopped himself back on the bed, fingers linked together under his head, staring at the textured ceiling before starting to think out loud. "I suppose you are right. One necessary compromise would have led to another until the whole vision became murky and useless. What if we started smaller? What if *that* is the key to cities of the future? Reducing the size of our communities to create less efficient, but more robust systems? Like Ryan says, *broken supply chains cause chaos*…maybe if we stop focusing on what is broken, and simply work to create what we love in more of a self-sufficient way we can all find our freedom." He let the thought linger and began pacing like a caged leopard, following the slight trough he had worn into the carpet alongside their bed over the past two years.

"I am reminded of the junior high school I went to. It was in rough shape. Built during the depression, but a lot of people liked the way it looked. School board decided it was time for a new building. The community flipped out at the thought of demolition, so the school board put it to a vote. Twenty-four million to build from scratch; twenty-eight to restore the place. They voted to restore. I never would have. That place sucked. Ugly, drafty, either too hot or too cold, no space for creativity—all the rooms felt cramped and small. My point is, trying to fix up something that already exists is often more work with less potential than starting from scratch." She nodded with understanding.

He continued, "What if we stop trying to fix this city and start from nothing? Ryan had the time of his life figuring out how to bring Ann Arbor's infrastructure into the future. What if he had a blank canvas? Think about our test track. We already have twenty acres, a house, and there is not much more than fields and forests to the north. What if we buy some of it up? Find a way to start from scratch. Maybe we can't build a city, but at least a tiny village? I bet Ryan would go nuts."

Johanna stayed quiet as she felt her opportunity for a life in the Netherlands crumble like an ancient fortress finally giving way to a long-lasting siege. Somehow, butterflies floated out of the shifting ruin. They brought splashes of color and light to the dusty air. She truly let go of the country she loved as the excitement of creating a new home flitted up from her core and danced about within her mind.

Involuntarily, a smile crept across her face as Kano's pacing grew heavier, like a polar bear, deep in thought. She broke into his trance with the slightest of giggles.

He straightened up and looked over at her with a look of consternation. "What is so funny?"

She laughed in a carefree way he hadn't seen for a long time. "I can imagine Ryan's reaction to this idea. You said it, he will go nuts. Can't you see the light bulbs burning above his head? The gears turning inside it? The week after we break the news to him, I bet he will only get five hours of sleep every night and drink two liters of coffee per day."

Kano stopped and smiled at the thought. "Should we make a bet? I am guessing three hours of sleep per night, and a total of thirty liters of coffee for the week. Maybe we should get him a new, bigger mug so it is easier to keep track."

"What does the winner get?"

Kano didn't have to think for long. "How about a plane ticket to anywhere for two weeks?"

"Make it a month. We go together. Just the two of us. Winner picks the destination."

"Deal. At least I am already packed," he said with a grin. "How should we tell him?"

She furrowed her eyebrows with thought, one of his favorite expressions. "Well, we can't make this happen without Eremita. It will be the greatest present she could give him. The chance to design and build his own village."

"Yeah, but how do we convince her?"

Johanna smiled knowingly. "This is her dream too. Don't you remember? She made that app to bring people closer together. The scale was all wrong though. Just like trying to create the city of the future here in Ann Arbor. She needs the chance to build the community she has always longed for."

She took her last sip of tea before continuing. "Besides, her design capabilities are huge. She knows how to make logos, apps, and campaign videos all look great. It goes beyond marketing though. This village needs to look incredible. Ryan can work out the technical stuff. He will make sure we produce more than enough food and power, but if we leave it up to him, it will be like a giant…what did we see in that stupid old movie about the kids playing baseball with the scary dog you made me watch…oh yeah, erector set. She will make sure it looks good, a place people now and in the future would actually want to live."

Kano nodded. "All right. You have a point. What about us? You can provide medical care, but where do I fit?"

She gave him a condescending look. "Don't you see? You are the one who gets things done. You wanted to be mayor. Now you can be project manager. As for me, I am not ready to give up my job. I enjoy the work and my colleagues. I like routine and security. Eremita has paid your salary for a while, but I still want to earn my own without anyone's help."

"Okay, but what about Souleymane? Is he a part of this? Can you finally learn to deal with him?"

Her eyes turned a steely gray color, but the tone of her voice lacked the acidic hatred that once underpinned any thoughts that surfaced about Souleymane. "I don't think I will be able to keep him out, and honestly, the past two years have shown me his added value. Eremita made him her pet project. Whatever she does he will do too. He seems to have one of those second-degree personalities. Always depending on other people. He is curious, but the only creative idea I have heard come out of his mouth was two years ago, when he figured out how to improve the criminal justice system."

"Think of how far he has come since then," replied Kano with a hint of pride, "his English is almost perfect, and he didn't just come up with the idea, he gave structure to the entire principle. Some form of it should be a part of whatever village we build."

She sighed with deep acceptance and stood up. "I suppose you are right. So this will be our lives?" Their eyes met, sparks flaming into something bigger. Joy and excitement flowed between them as they embraced, barely able to contain their shared energy.

October 2021

Ryan had never felt so alive. On a fundamental level, this somehow surpassed the sensation of carving down a mountainside full of fresh powder. Crisp, autumn scents sharpened the air; yellow and red leaves blazed for one final moment against the sapphire sky as they floated toward the forest floor. The delicate swish and rustle of his steps mingled with voices of birds. His spirit pulled him ahead toward the structure which delicately revealed itself.

Approached from three of the cardinal directions, it looked like an oddly symmetrical hill. The surrounding landscape being far from flat, a casual hiker would fail to notice anything man-made about Ryan's destination. He rounded his way down the path, making his final approach from the south. A concave wall of windows shaped like an eye gently opened toward him, reflecting the surrounding forest.

He smiled as he observed rays of sunshine reaching beyond the generously curved eyebrow, finally penetrating into cave-like depths. Only eight months before, the gentle protrusion had been nothing more than an idea. It would keep the sun away from triple-paned glass during warm summer months, working together with deciduous trees and deep layers of insulation to ensure a cool interior. When leaves fell to the forest floor, rendering the green roof invisible, precisely calculated angles allowed oblique solar radiation to bring warmth and light into the cavernous space during colder months. Being mostly underground, very little additional energy was required to regulate the temperature within the structure.

As the door sealed shut behind him, all forest sounds fell away. The space was designed to keep loud noises from escaping. Silence was overwhelmed by a strong smell, sharpening Ryan's awareness. Kilns were busy drying freshly cut boards to a precise moisture content of twelve percent; the scents of various species mingled together to form an intoxicating aroma.

Ryan spoke and music played. Rich sound came from all around, gently swirling among machines to fill the cavern with smooth, honey-like tones. He took a deep breath and felt grateful he wasn't stuck in an office reworking Ann Arbor's infrastructure. Kano losing the bid for mayor was the best thing that could have happened to them. Ryan now knew he didn't want to simply design systems; he also wanted to build them with his own hands.

An enormous wall on wheels stood before him. It was quite long, thirty-two feet to be exact. Plywood came in eight foot sheets, so the wall was eight feet tall, plus the base—a chunky block of 2x8's on giant casters. The plywood looked rather thin in comparison to the other dimensions, but its three inch depth helped to make the whole structure rigid in spite of its mobility.

There were thick, waxed chunks of oak stacked neatly on a nearby shelf. They ranged in size, but all of them had a square cross section with rounded corners. The smallest were only a few inches wide and a foot long. The largest were a foot wide and at least two feet long. Clear buckets of long, thick screws and a jug of glue sat next to the chunks.

Ryan calculated the precise curve of a gentle arc, plotting it out on the plywood, and attached chunks of oak securely to the curve so they stuck out of the wall like the pegs of a giant's coat rack.

He then found a stack of recently dried twelve-foot boards, powered up the minimalistic 4-post planer, and smoothly brought multiple lengths of aromatic cedar down to a thickness of precisely five-eighths of an inch. He placed the first board on top of the arced chunks of oak. It sagged so its ends were hovering above the last giant pegs. He smeared the cedar surface with glue and placed a second board on top. After repeating this process several times, he got out the clamps, aligned the ends of the boards, and tightly secured the curved layers to the oak.

Much of the glue dripped out, spattering against 2x8's like a viscous thunderstorm. He took a step back to observe the result and felt it was good. Time for lunch.

Afterward, he repeated this process several times until both sides of the wall were full and its base was covered in little puddles of glue. Then he went online to order more clamps and the materials to build a second wall. Efficiency could always be improved.

The heavy door sucked itself closed behind him. As he began the commute back home through the forest, a robot entered the work floor in search of the few stray bits that somehow avoided getting sucked into the ravenous dust collector.

The curved beams Ryan had made were too heavy to carry alone, so he brought in his old weightlifting buddy to lend a hand.

"I still can't believe you spent this much money on a workshop," Kano said as he crossed the threshold of the eye, shaking his head at the obvious waste of time and resources.

Ryan grew tired of defending his space after all the fights with Eremita about the cost, so he spoke with a deflated tone. "You know it is much more than a workshop, and it will pay for itself eventually. Think of everything we can do ourselves now instead of hiring someone else. This is where our energy and materials are stored. Where the whole community will be made and maintained. It is the heart and soul of the infrastructure we are creating, even if it isn't the most visible piece of the puzzle. How can you expect great things to come from an ugly garage?"

Kano laughed. "That happens all the time. Look at Apple."

Ryan smiled. "You got me there. But they ditched that garage as soon as possible. Speaking of Apple, just look at these machines." He gestured at the varied shapes and sizes of matte black, polished metal, and surgically sharp blades. "This is the Apple of the woodworking industry. Nothing would look better in this space."

"I suppose Eremita's net worth can cover your costs after the sale of all that technology you developed, but these choices still seem rather extreme to me. I think she is right in insisting we maintain a healthy cushion to fall back on. You seem bent on spending everything at once."

"It's you who likes to say, *go big or go home*. I just happen to be the one who actually does it." Kano chuckled in response as they started removing clamps. Ryan made sure each one was left completely open and systematically hung in its designated location. Kano interrupted the meditative process. "You know, you could probably buy a more efficient setup for this."

Ryan smiled, knowing his friend was trying to get under his skin. "Probably. But I wanted to design my own. And build it myself. Would we truly feel at home here if someone else designed and built everything? Maybe you would, but I wouldn't. Perhaps that is what is tearing this country apart. A simple lack of ownership."

Kano sighed with resignation. "Let's try to focus. Can we get this job done quickly? There is a lot that still needs to be done with the township. Turns out those permits are not easy to get."

They worked in silence for some time. Even though Ryan hadn't explained the task beforehand, Kano seemed to know precisely what to do. Sometimes Ryan would pause for a moment to let Kano figure out what was required of him. Their teamwork was effortless and intuitive.

Ryan handed Kano a scraper; hardened drops of glue fell from one side of the curved shape, clicking and scattering across the polished ferrock floor like misshapen candy sprinkles. Together, they hefted the ungainly beam onto their shoulders and carried it toward the table saw. The scraped face nestled against the saw's appropriately positioned fence. After adjusting earplugs and safety glasses, a fresh blade whirred into motion.

A giant vacuum system sucked up nearly all the tiny bits of dried glue and sawdust, the absence of which formed a beautifully clean edge. They spun it around, brought the fence in slightly, and repeated the process. The beam then found its way over to a telescoping miter saw to have its ends trimmed, ready for finishing touches.

The sanding table was a large surface covered in a thick rubber mat filled with holes. Air was sucked down through the holes by the vacuum system, so whoever was sanding did not need to wear a mask. Ryan grabbed two small but powerful sanders to round off the edges, giving the beam a streamlined look. Once satisfied, they took it to the dust-free finishing room where it would be oiled as soon as enough beams were ready.

Upon entering the relative stillness inside the finishing room, Kano broke the silence. "So, what is tung oil anyway?" He gestured toward the small bottles filled with yellowish liquid perfectly spaced and aligned on a shelf.

Ryan felt relieved Kano was trying to fix the tension. They had fought the night before about monkeys. Kano couldn't see the point in creating a tropical environment without monkeys. Ryan was worried about the chaos they would bring. He raised an eyebrow and said, "You really want to know?"

Kano chuckled. "Just figured you would like to talk about it, but I suppose I am slightly curious."

Ryan handed him a bottle from the shelf for closer inspection. "You figured right. Tung oil is amazing stuff. The Chinese have used it for thousands of years to waterproof their boats. It is simply oil pressed out of the nuts of a tung tree. Takes a long time to dry, or more precisely, to cure—it is classified as one of two penetrating oils, the second being linseed oil which is like its weaker, cheaper cousin that requires the addition of heavy metals. I mix tung oil with citrus solvent to help it soak into the wood, where it forms chemical bonds..."

Kano had tuned out, but knew it was wise to let his friend talk. "Okay, enough about the oil. Tell me, why do you have to curve the beams in the first place? Seems like a lot of extra work, and all the domes I have seen have straight beams."

"Well, since when have you wanted what everyone else has?"

Kano laughed as he continued to play with the small bottle, shaking and turning it to watch the bubbles slowly drift up and down through the syrupy substance. Ryan wiped the beam and continued, "The whole point is to depixelate the dome while making the hub connectors flat..."

Kano placed the bottle back on the shelf with a sharp crack, interrupting Ryan's explanation again. "Alright, let's finish this job!"

They repeated the process with the second beam, blowing all the leftover dust off with compressed air and then lifting it onto their shoulders, carrying it toward the finishing room. As they walked in tandem, Ryan's thoughts turned to Souleymane. "You know," he started, "these struts were meant to be a lot longer. How is it that a guy who grew up in a mud hut taught me something about design?"

Kano smiled knowingly. "I am sure all he did was help you to realize what you already knew."

Ryan laughed out loud and said with surprise, "Did you hear the end of our conversation? He said the very same thing!"

Kano explained, "His name derives from King Solomon, supposedly the wisest of all kings. Perhaps it comes with the name, but it seems like the very act of talking with him about something helps me figure out what I need to know. What did he help you with this time?"

Ryan shook his head in amazement as they approached the dust-free zone. "Well, I was looking through potential dome configurations, and the main differences have to do with the number of struts and therefore the size you can build. These are known as the *frequency* of the dome, but the word frequency is denoted by a lowercase v. He was asking me what it all meant, and why they chose a v to represent the word frequency. I had no idea and got annoyed by his questions."

They carefully placed the curved beam next to the first one. "I tried to get rid of him by explaining I would make the biggest dome that I could, so that meant a frequency six configuration. He must have sensed the doubt in my voice as I was nervous about doing this for the first time. *But there are only five of us,* he told me, *shouldn't you make a frequency five dome?* I wasn't sure if he was joking as this seemed like the logic of a child, but for some reason it struck me as he continued on. *Perhaps it would be better to start smaller and work your way up to frequency five, connecting the domes as you go?*' Ryan shook his head with the recollection.

"I had been designing nonstop all day, this guy comes in for two minutes, asks a few questions, and suddenly I am back at square one. Of course, he was right. I need to test my ideas on smaller structures first. Once we have all that connected space, there is no need to go bigger than a frequency five dome."

Kano nodded as they lifted another beam onto their shoulders. "He does have a way of cutting to the core of what is important. This project wouldn't be the same without him. Shouldn't we come up with a real name for what we are doing here? Your big dome sounds cool. Frequency Five. What do you think?"

Ryan smiled and paused to consider. "You had fun in Timbuktu. Souleymane is from Mali. How about *Timbuktu* Frequency Five? Sounds much cooler."

Kano solemnly agreed with more depth of feeling than Ryan could place.

August 2023

The domes arched gracefully over her bent figure, accentuating the curve of her back. She noticed someone approaching as she straightened up, clutching a handful of tiny weeds in the process. They never made it more than an inch or two past the mulch.

Souleymane followed a path which meandered along the bending stream. He walked up the gentle arc of a wooden bridge to cross over rippling water until he stopped in front of her.

With a grin, he said, "The others would never be working in this heat. They think we are crazy."

Eremita laughed. "Maybe we are, but it reminds me of where I grew up. And look at how happy everything is." She waved a hand with pride. "Tomatoes, herbs, beans, pineapples, papayas, avocados, and even the mango trees are taking off!"

He nodded thoughtfully. "Can you imagine how this will look in ten years? The plants will make you forget we are actually inside. Maybe if we build mud huts I will feel completely at home. Then I could sleep in one and forget about the winters." He was still working hard on the remaining bits of his accent, which had become nearly undetectable.

She tossed another handful of green into the wheelbarrow. "Good idea. Ask Ryan if you can build some. It's hot enough to dry mud bricks."

He bent over to help her with the weeds. Filled with genuine curiosity, he asked, "Why are you growing so much? We will never be able to eat it all."

She smiled. "The gardens do most of the work themselves. Plants and animals take care of each other and fight pests as a team, like our chickens that turn slugs into fertilizer and eggs. For now, we can sell extras at the farmers market to get our name out there, then maybe open up a little cafe and make meals from what we grow. Our guests could even pick part of their lunch themselves if they want to. This is so much better than that stupid app I made! Now I can really build a community around food."

He gave her a knowing look. "Yeah, but your app made all this possible. We sure won't make much money at the farmers market, or by having people come to pick their own dinners, but at least it is something."

A few years ago, she would have responded sharply, but plants and heat conspired to mellow her temper. "We can do a lot more than that. People will pay for experiences, especially when it is cold outside." Souleymane opened his mouth to comment but she cut him off.

"We can have workshops, retreats, and even summer camps here. Those beautiful sugar maple trees can share some sap with us so we can make maple syrup." She responded to his puzzled look, "You know, the ones that turn bright yellow in the fall on the other side of Ryan's workshop? Maple syrup? You put it on pancakes." Understanding registered in his eyes.

Souleymane was caught for a moment in admiration. Eremita was successful by any measure of the word, could have retired comfortably a few years ago, and yet here she was, working harder than ever before. Creative energy flowed from her without end. It wasn't simply used as a means to get what she wanted. Creating was what she wanted.

He pondered this as they gathered up scattered weeds in silence. He wondered what it was that he truly wanted. By the time the wheelbarrow was overflowing, he found the answer. It had to do with his curiosity. Even if he tried, preventing himself from figuring out how things work was an impossible task.

People and relationships tended to be his area of interest. He had spent many long nights with Ryan learning about engineering methods and structural integrity. Prying answers from her wasn't easy, but Johanna taught him about medicine. Kano seemed to know something about everything.

Just as Eremita grabbed the wheelbarrow to push it toward the compost bins, he made up his mind. "Eremita, wait a moment. May I ask you something?" She turned to look at him expectantly, resting one gloved hand on a worn handle. "I am tired of writing academically. My research and papers only reach a small audience. I would like to share what I have learned with many people. I think the best way to do that is by writing a biography. I would like to write about you."

Eremita raised an eyebrow with surprise. The fresh smell of earth and young plants filled the space between them. Eventually she answered, "I would be honored, but shouldn't you write your own story? Yours is much more interesting than mine. It would sell more books."

Souleymane nodded thoughtfully to himself. "Perhaps at a later time. I have nothing to learn from my own story."

She casually shrugged with acceptance and effortlessly lifted the handles of the wheelbarrow. "Why not? Just so long as you let me read it before anyone else."

"There are too many weeds! The latest batch of compost must not have gotten hot enough before I spread it out. Now I need to bring in more wood chips to put over the top," Eremita grumbled as she plopped another basket of vegetables down on the curving butcher block countertop Ryan had painstakingly built for her. "You should quit your job and help me."

Johanna sat with a cup of tea at the kitchen island, thinking about this while enjoying the cool breeze Ryan had engineered into the space. Sitting under a thatched roof at the edge of one of the domes, looking out over a flowing stream and exotic plants, she felt like she was in the tropics, minus all the malaria, bugs, and sweat.

Eremita insisted on having a kitchen that felt like it was outside. It was the only part of the project she designed entirely on her own. It tended to be the spot where everyone gathered.

While washing vegetables, Johanna answered. "Maybe it is time to quit my job. Now that Kano and I gave up our apartment to live here, commuting into the city seems like a waste of time and energy. Not sure if I really want to be your sous-chef though, and I still haven't gotten used to the idea of cooking with poop."

Eremita laughed in a carefree manner which had only recently become commonplace. "You never thought about where the gas came from before. Why does it matter now? Biogas is a lot cheaper than running a natural gas line and installing a septic tank." The knife was incredibly sharp. Gravity did most of the work as the blade slid effortlessly through dark red tomatoes that were clinging to a vine only minutes before.

Johanna unplugged the drain to let gray water flow into the frog pond. "Ryan did come up with some pretty cool systems to cut costs. Helping him use leftover grease from restaurants to power the backup generator and the truck is actually kind of fun, and that fancy boiler from Belgium turns free wood chips from the city into more heat than we need. It no longer feels decadent to lie by the pool in January!"

Eremita smiled in agreement while chopping pointed peppers into tiny bits like a machine. "That pool is amazing. The streams and waterfalls flowing out of it help moderate temperatures, and they take care of the watering for me."

Johanna snitched an uncut chunk of pepper. "I am surprised we can make enough energy to pump so much water."

"Ryan designed everything with efficiency in mind, and nothing is wasted." Eremita paused to think for a moment. "Oh, I forgot the cucumbers. Will you grab a few?"

"Sure, but do you know what I just realized?"

"Tell me."

"I think we did it. Five years ago, we set out to transform Ann Arbor into the city of the future, right?"

"Mmmm, hmmm," Eremita replied while sampling a juicy wedge of tomato.

"Well, what if this is it? What if the way to move forward as a society is to...what is the word Ryan likes to use...oh yeah, *decouple* ourselves from urban environments and build small communities that produce more than they consume. Support more life than they take. Use technology to boost our personal health and the health of the planet. If enough people start doing this, most of our problems would be solved."

Eremita nodded knowingly. "You may be onto something. Now about those cucumbers..."

Johanna took her time wandering through carefully selected plants which weren't in orderly rows or confined to sections. The thoughtful blend was an artist's caricature of abundance. She opened her palms and felt different textures of leaves brush past. She grabbed some mint, crumpled it up, and inhaled the fresh, living scent. Something about it set off fireworks in her mind.

Although she managed to get herself lost on the way to the cucumbers, she found a certain type of peace which had always eluded her. Plants provided a feeling of home. She sat down, hidden by leaves, closed her eyes, and took in a calculated series of deep breaths.

As her mind expanded, she fully realized, as she once suspected, that this place had great healing potential. She could cultivate and process medicinal plants into a variety of products, create meditative spaces, and maybe Ryan could even build a floating chamber.

Western medicine was incredible when it came to surgeries and the healing of traumatic injuries. What doctors and engineers could do together was nothing short of miraculous. In spite of these accomplishments, they were failing terribly when it came to preventative medicine, some chronic disorders and mental health issues.

Perhaps she could create a way to bridge the gap. Give individuals the experiential education needed to tackle issues that hospitals can't seem to address. Eremita could help out with the food part.

Her eyes opened with excitement. These domes could become so much more than just their own home. People could use this place to heal. In her mind, she had already quit her job and was designing programs to address various mental and physical disorders with techniques ranging from simple soap making to complex forms of spiritual healing.

By the time she got back to the kitchen, she was out of breath. Eremita said with frustration, "You really would make a terrible sous-chef." Holding up a prickly cucumber she continued, "I had to get them myself. Did you seriously forget where they were? Maybe having people pick their own lunches in this jungle is a bad idea after all."

Johanna laughed. "Perhaps, but do you know what is a great idea? Quitting my job! In fact, I think we can use this place to not only give people more ownership of their lunches, but of their general health as well. They are too dependent on a doctor to solve their problems. All they need is the right environment and someone to teach them a few things. By the way, this tea is terrible. We should grow our own."

October 2027

Kano felt like a kid again. Hide-and-seek was his favorite. Now that all the permits were issued, work crews managed, and businesses structured, Kano was done with the adult world. He wanted to play all day.

Eremita and Johanna had both given birth to twins. Eremita first and Johanna three months later, exactly one year after the day she decided to quit her job. They made a solemn vow never to get pregnant again upon the conclusion of that miserable experience.

The little ones were becoming old enough that saving their lives a few times each day stopped being completely necessary, so the two mothers didn't worry as much when they heard peals of laughter followed by screams. The occasional child flying through the air became a normal thing. No broken bones yet.

Kano commandeered one of the domes. After the kids were asleep, Ryan helped him to design and build an environment which had the potential to make a lot of money. If they ever did choose to open it up to the public, lawyers would need to get involved from the start to make sure liability was well-managed. Injuries seemed inevitable.

Banks of angled trampolines rimmed a huge standing wave pool where Kano surfed during nap time. A waterfall connected it to a second, deeper, more natural looking body of water with a climbing wall angling out of one side. Giant water slides twisted around and through the cliff face which was topped off with a high dive.

In the neighboring skate park, one side of the half-pipe had a foam pit while the other led to a multi-story jungle gym which would make a monkey's head spin. Unfortunately, there were no monkeys to test it out. Ryan successfully blocked that initiative over and over again.

A zip line angled from the top of the jungle gym over the skate park and into the pool. Palm trees filled any leftover space, effectively completing the task of bringing a piece of California to Michigan.

The mothers had insisted on a safer, more manageable play space. Kano wouldn't budge. He believed toddlers should learn to walk, talk, swim, skate, surf, climb, bike, and anything else their little hearts desired all at the same time. All day long.

The sheer joy the quadruplets experienced when the first trampoline went in was enough to wear down overprotective maternal instincts. After all, Kano was the one who wanted to look after the little ones, enabling the other parents to focus on their projects. He never said it out loud, but he believed his job was the most important of all. His efforts shaped the future. Someone would need to take over when his generation got too old.

Twigs snapped under Souleymane's feet as he climbed the narrow trail up the hill with a prayer mat tucked under the handless arm. A few months ago, Ryan started building a lookout tower. The first platform was finished. An ideal place to greet the sun. Crisp air turned his exhalations into small clouds drifting straight up into the stillness of dawn. He thought back to the terror coursing through him the first time he had witnessed this phenomenon. It was as though pieces of his spirit relentlessly escaped the confines of his body.

Souleymane paused at the steps of the tower to pick up a deep red maple leaf with ice crystals delicately extending around its edge. He held the stem between his thumb and forefinger, spinning it faster and faster until glittering crystals broke away into a miniature snowstorm.

It felt like a different lifetime, but he laughed to himself at the memory of first hearing about a land encased in ice and snow. He had easily placed this notion together with the ghost stories and myths of his childhood. Perhaps his life had become a myth.

Anemic fingers of yellow and orange sharpened the horizon. Smooth domes below remained in shadow. Their dark forms rose from the forest floor, mimicking the cluster of mushrooms growing near the tower's base.

Birds interrupted the silence to greet the dawn with their song. Fresh air carrying the scent of fall, the kind which can only come after a hard frost, mingled with avian notes. A squirrel jumped from the branch of one tree to another, scattering a shower of yellow leaves finally ready to float down to join those who had gone before.

With a delicate push, the prayer mat settled comfortably into place revealing several sheets of paper and the mechanical pencil Souleymane had once taken apart and put back together over and over again just to understand the magic of its inner workings. He set these items aside to focus his entire being upon the task of prayer.

Eventually, a peaceful certainty filled the dark form perched upon a tower illuminated by the rising sun. He pulled a thermos filled with tea from the generous pocket of his oversized parka and allowed its warmth to mingle with rays of light.

Gathering his writing supplies, he knew the time had come. He could not move forward with his life without reconciling the alternate worlds of his past and his present. He whispered one final prayer that the words he was about to commit to writing would never find their way into the hands of the authorities.

He began each of the three letters in the same fashion, although they were all written in different languages. To the village Chief of Sakoro, in lieu of his biological father, who taught him to survive, he wrote in Bambara. To Mister Traore, who showed him how to work, he wrote in French. To The Professor, who gave him purpose, he wrote in Arabic.

Dear Father of Mine,

It is with a heart filled with love and gratitude that I write to you. If it weren't for what you have done, I would never have become the person I am today. You have given me the opportunity to live a life that has become more than anyone from my humble beginnings could have dreamed of.

Although there have been times of peril and times of destruction, your influence has led me through them to times of strength and grace. Peace has found a way to follow in my footsteps. I wish to give you an account of these events so that you might know the outcome of your guiding hand...

By the time Souleymane had signed his name at the end of the final letter, the blessed sun warmed his cramped hand. His toes still ached with cold. He straightened his stiff back with pride as a smile spread widely across his face.

The sensation of freedom gathered like the tingling flow of blood restoring life to limbs. Now the words existed on paper, so the events no longer chained his spirit to darkness. He thought this may have been the same feeling Kano had when his parents finally came for him.

His head tilted slightly as he realized this was not the case. Kano must have had this same experience, but it had come long before his release. Something had changed within him during captivity, not after it. Questions formed in Souleymane's mind. *What, exactly, freed Kano? What had it felt like for him? Will the unshackling I just went through have the same lasting effect?*

Quickly collecting his things, Souleymane wanted to find the answers to these questions. He rushed down the hill, but then slowed his pace, remembering that he would have to wait until the precious little ones were taking their afternoon nap before he could have Kano's full attention.

Waves of gratitude washed over him as he thought of the lives which had become so deeply entwined with his own. Thoughts and emotions spread through his entire body and into the surrounding forest, uniting him to this place and these people in a way he had never experienced before. For the first time in his life, as he considered the future, freedom took the place of fear.

A NOTE FROM THE AUTHOR

Naturally, this story is a work of fiction, but many of the events are based on reality. For example, my friend, who happened to be a pilot, would let me ride along on occasion when I was in the Peace Corps. During one flight up to Timbuktu in 2009, we ran into a thunderstorm and experienced weightlessness for a few seconds when we hit a downdraft. After we arrived in Timbuktu, we walked out to the dunes at dusk and heard the gunshots of Al Qaeda executing a Malian informant. We thought it was just fireworks. I was the last Peace Corps volunteer allowed to travel there, for good reason. Several Europeans were taken hostage soon after.

Historical events and figures were portrayed as accurately as possible, with the exception of the moldy manuscripts. In reality, the smuggling operation was a great success, and although mold did pose a huge threat, I exaggerated the destruction to make the storyline work.